It wasn't so easy to shut away the memory of the afternoon before.

If she closed her eyes, Laurel could still feel Alec's arms around her, feel the disturbing moment when she had pressed against the hard warmth of his body. It had been like standing at the center of a lightning strike, caught in the flare of white-hot heat, blinding light and searing power. Nothing had prepared her for the conflagration, or for the rush of need that poured through her in response. She had been stunned, held immobile by feelings so long repressed, she had forgotten they existed. If she had ever known them.

She wasn't sure she had. Even in the days when she was first married, when loving was so strange and new, she had not felt so fervid or so uncertain of her own responses, her own will.

No. She wouldn't think about it. She would forget she had ever touched Alec Stanton. And she would pray to high heaven that he did the same.

Jennifer Blake

GARDEN *of* SCANDAL

MIRA BOOKS

ISBN 1-55166-281-7

GARDEN OF SCANDAL

Copyright © 1997 by Patricia Maxwell.

Printed in U.S.A.

For my husband, Jerry,
with loving appreciation for the man who, at our
home known as Sweet Briar, constructed the
real garden of antique roses which provided the
inspiration for this book.

1

She tore out of the lighted house like a banshee. Screaming in a shatteringly clear soprano above the growling of the great black German shepherd, she skimmed across the front porch. She was halfway down the high steps before the ancient wooden screen door slammed shut after her.

Part harridan, part avenging Valkyrie, she raced toward him wearing a nightgown with light streaming through it from behind. Her long hair shifted and whipped around her, shimmering silver-gold in the moonlight. Her feet barely touched the ground. Fleet, slender, with the pure lines of her face twisted in concern, she was the most fascinating thing Alec Stanton had ever laid eyes on.

"Sticks! Here, boy!" she called out as she ducked under the low-hanging limb of a magnolia, dodged the rambling branches of a spirea. Her gaze was riveted on the dog standing ferocious guard on the mossy brick walk.

The German shepherd growled, a ragged warning that resonated deep in his massive chest. His eyes never left Alec. He lifted his ruff, baring his teeth in challenge. As the woman came nearer, the animal moved protectively to block her path with his body.

"What is it, boy? What have you got cornered?"

Her voice was anxious but not fearful as she slowed her pace. Then she saw Alec.

She stopped so quickly that her hair swirled forward, covering her arms like a cape of captured moonbeams. Her hands clenched into fists. Her eyes widened. She squared her shoulders, then stood so motionless she might have been turned into pale, warm marble.

The dog ceased to exist for Alec. And he forgot why he was there amid the tangled briers, vines and overgrown shrubbery that were the front garden of the Steamboat Gothic mansion known as Ivywild. Moving like a man in a daze, he stepped forward out of the night.

The German shepherd launched off his haunches in attack. Eighty pounds of hard muscle and death, he sprang straight for Alec's throat.

"Down! Down, Sticks!" The woman's shout mingled with the dog's snarl. Yet there was no hope the animal would, or could, obey.

Alec's instinct and training kicked in. He spun away as the dog hit him, moving with the force of the assault, flowing with it to lessen the impact even as he snatched the dog's huge black head in an iron grip. Finding the pressure points, Alec drove his thumbs against them. He sank to his knees, still turning, flexing hard muscles as he came about in a full circle.

It was over in a moment. When Alec rose, the animal was stretched out, limp and barely breathing, on the walk between him and the woman.

She moaned and dropped to the ground, gathering the lolling head of her guard dog into her lap. Holding tight, she rocked back and forth.

"He'll be all right," Alec said with stringent softness.

She made no reply. Then he heard the catch in her breathing as the dog stirred, whimpered.

Abruptly, she looked up with the wetness of tears glittering in her eyes. "You might have killed him!"

"If I'd wanted to kill him he'd be dead. I just put him out for a few minutes while we get things cleared up here." Alec could have pointed out that her precious Sticks might have crushed his throat, but it didn't seem worth the effort.

Her fingers sank into the dog's coat, holding him closer. "You're on private property. I want you off in the next two seconds or I call the police. Is that clear enough for you?"

This was not the way things were supposed to go. He had meant to knock politely, then stand outside on the porch while he spoke his piece. He hadn't expected to feel his heart squeezed in a breath-catching vise at the sight of a woman's form in a whisper-thin nightgown. He had never dreamed it could happen—not to him, and especially not here with this woman. It was too unexpected for comfort, much less acceptance.

Putting her pet out cold was not a good start, no matter what he had in mind. "I'm sorry if I hurt your dog," he said.

"Oh, yes, I can tell!" The look she gave him was scathing.

"He shouldn't have attacked."

"He was just— He thought I needed protecting."

It was entirely possible the dog had been right. Wary and off-balance, Alec tried again, looking for some kind of stable ground. "You're Mrs. Bancroft, Laurel Bancroft?"

"What of it?"

"I...wanted to talk to you." That had been his original purpose. Things had changed. For what good it would do him.

She didn't give an inch. "I can't imagine we have anything to discuss."

"The lady who keeps house for you, Maisie Warfield, is a good friend of my grandmother's. She said you need help clearing this jungle of a garden, that it had more or less gotten away from you since your husband died." His grandmother had said a great deal more. He should have paid attention, he thought, as he added, "I have a little experience with that kind of work."

She watched him for several seconds, her expression intently appraising. Then she said in disbelief, "You're Miss Callie's grandson?"

Stung by the amazement in her tone, he made his agreement short.

"You're no gardener!"

He shook his head. "Engineer. But I worked as a yardman to put myself through school." He gave the words a hint of an edge to let her know he didn't care to be prejudged.

"I can't afford an engineer," she said baldly.

He considered telling her she could have his services for free—any service she wanted, any time. But that wouldn't work, and he still had sense enough, just, to know it. "Manual labor at the going rate is what I'm offering."

"Why?"

The single word hung between them for a moment

as Sticks lifted his head and shook himself before turning to lie on his belly. The dog looked up at Alec, then away again, as if embarrassed. Whining, he crawled forward a few inches to lick his mistress's hand in apology.

Watching the animal with a hot sensation very like envy, or even jealousy, pervading his skull, Alec said, "A lot of reasons, but let's just say I need the money."

"You can get a better job anywhere else."

"I need to hang loose, not be too tied down."

Her gaze was concentrated as she smoothed her hand over the dog's head in a gesture of comfort, then got to her feet. "Because you don't like wearing a suit? Or is it your brother?"

"Both."

She knew all about him and Gregory; he might have guessed. That was one of the glories of small towns. Also their major pain in the backside.

He allowed his eyes to glide over her, then away. But he could still see the slim moon-silvered shape of her burning in his mind like a candle flame. He swallowed hard.

"If you expect me to be sympathetic—" she began.

"No." He made an abrupt, slicing gesture. "Sympathy is something we don't need. Either of us."

She stiffened. "My situation has nothing to do with you!"

He looked back at her, speaking gently as he tilted his head. "I meant my brother and myself. Though I guess it would be safe to include you in it, too."

She didn't answer; only stood staring up at him. The moonlight washed across her features, highlighting the scrubbed freshness of her skin that was so translucent it responded to every shift of emotion beneath its surface. He could see the blue of her eyes, wine-dark as the Aegean Sea, yet clear, as if she knew more than she wanted to about people. Particularly men and their baser urges.

His were the basest of the base.

She had just come from a shower, he thought; he could smell the fresh soap and clean-woman scent of her. It was as potent an aphrodisiac as any he had ever imagined. He ached with it, hardening beyond comprehension from no more than sharing the same warm night air.

She seemed fragile, yet there was inner strength in the way she stood up to him, a stranger in the dark. She was real—a little shy, but self-possessed to the point of being regal. She wasn't perfect; there were fine lines at the corners of her eyes, and her upper lip was not quite as full as the lower. She was almost perfect, though, so close to beautiful that it was nearly impossible to look away from her.

It wouldn't do. She'd never have anything to do with Callie Stanton's California-hippie grandson. To her, he must look like a kid with more brawn than brains. It was downright funny, if you thought about it. Only he wasn't laughing.

Laurel shivered a little under the impact of Alec Stanton's gaze. His eyes were so black, the pupils expanding, driving out all color, leaving still, dark pools of consideration. He was tall and broad, a solid presence holding back the night that crowded around them. She knew instinctively he would be more than able to protect her from whatever might be lurking in the darkness. Yet she did not feel safe.

He was too big, too strong, too fast. The defense he had made against poor Sticks was some dangerously competent form of martial arts; she knew enough to recognize that much even if she didn't know what to call it. Beyond these things, he was far too exotic with his long black hair tied back in a ponytail with a leather thong, the dark ambush of his thick brows and lashes in the strong square of his face, and the silver slash of an earring shaped like a lightning bolt that was fastened in his left ear.

He was dressed entirely in black: boots, jeans, and a sleeveless T-shirt that emphasized the sculpted muscles of his torso. The skimpy shirt also exposed the multicolored stain of an intricate tattoo on his left shoulder, dimly recognizable as a dragon winding across his pectoral and around his upper arm.

As she avoided his black gaze, her eyes flickered over the tattoo, then back again. Her fingers tingled, and she curled them tighter into her palm against the sudden impulse to touch the dragon, stroke the warmth and smoothness of its—his—skin and feel the power of the muscles that glided beneath the painted design. If she tried, she might be able to span the beast with her spread hand, feeling its heartbeat under her palm where the pumping heart of the man lay beneath the wall of his chest.

She drew a sharp breath, snatching her mind from that image as if backing away from a hot stove. She must be crazy. At just over forty-one, she was at least ten years older than he was, maybe a little more.

She had been alone too long, that much was plain. She had grown so used to her solitude and isolation here at Ivywild that she had come flying out of the house in nothing more than her nightgown. Worse than that, she was having wild fantasies simply because she was alone with an attractive man. Definitely, she was losing it.

The warm spring night pressed against her, as if driving her toward the man in front of her. She could smell the wafting fragrance of magnolia blossoms from the tree that loomed above them. The chorus of night insects was a quiet and endless appassionato, an echo of the feelings that sang through her.

At her feet, Sticks struggled upright, then stepped forward to press against her knee. The movement was a welcome release from the curious constraint that held her.

"Look," she said abruptly, her voice more husky than she intended. "All I had in mind was hiring some older man to cut down a few trees, hack back the brush, maybe dig a rose bed or two—"

He cut across her words in incisive tones. "I can do twice as much in half the time."

"I'm sure you could, but the point is—"

"The point is you're afraid of me. I don't suit the notions of backward, provincial Hillsboro, Louisiana, about how a man should look. I'm not your average redneck—crew-cut and squeaky clean, with nothing on his mind except fishing, hunting and drinking beer. Or at least, nothing he can share with a woman. I don't fit." His voice softened. "But then neither do you, Laurel Bancroft."

Her lips tightened before she opened them to speak. "I don't know what you're talking about."

"Don't you?"

The smile that accompanied his inquiry lasted only

an instant. Yet the brief movement of his mouth altered the hard planes and angles of his face, giving him the devastating attraction of a dark angel. There was piercing sweetness in it, and limitless understanding. It saluted her independence even as it deplored it, applauded her courage in spite of her intransigence. It plumbed her loneliness, offered comfort, promised surcease.

Then it was gone. She fought the chill depression that moved over her in its wake. And lost.

On a deep breath, she said, "That isn't it—or at least I'd like to think I'm not so petty. But I don't need any more problems right now."

"You need help and I need money. We're a natural." His words were even, an explanation rather than an appeal.

She flung out a hand in exasperation. "It isn't that simple!"

"Not quite. My brother has cancer in the final stages. Did you know that? I took unpaid leave from the firm where I work in L.A. to come visit Grannie Callie with him. Now he wants to stay. Good home-cooked food and quiet living may help or may not, but at least it's worth the chance. Still, I'll be damned if I'll live off my grandmother's charity. I could get a more permanent—not to mention better paying— job, yes. But I'd have to be away all day, and that's not what I need. Your place is close, the work shouldn't be too confining. I'm a fast worker, I get the job done and I'm not too proud to follow orders. I know a rose from a rutabaga, and I can lay brick, pipe water, whatever it takes. What more do you want?"

What more, indeed? Nothing, except to listen, endlessly, to the deep, steady timbre of his voice. Which was reason enough to be wary.

"It's just a small project," she said. "I might install a little fountain in the middle of the roses after things are cleared away, but it's not really worth your time, much less your skill."

His smile came again, warming her, enticing her against her will. "Neither are worth all that much just now. They'll be worth even less if you turn me down."

"I don't think..."

"Tell you what," he said, easing forward. "I'll work the first day for free. If you decide I'm no use to you, that's the end of it. If you like what I've done, we'll take it from there."

"I can't let you do that," she said in protest.

"A fair trial, that's all I ask. Starting at eight in the morning. What do you say?"

She was definitely crazy, because the whole thing was beginning to sound almost reasonable. What was the difference between hiring him or old man Pender down the road, or even young Randy Nott who did odd jobs for her mother-in-law? This man would be hired help, a strong back and pair of able arms. Probably more than able, but she wouldn't think about that. A couple of days, maybe a week, and then he would be gone.

In sudden decision, she said, "Make it seven, to get as much done as possible before it gets too hot."

"You're the boss."

Somehow, she didn't feel like it.

He nodded once, then moved away, melting into the darkness along the overgrown path toward the drive. After a moment, Laurel heard the low rumble of a motorcycle being kicked into life. Then he zoomed off in a blast of power. The noise faded and the night was still again.

A shiver moved over her in spite of the warmth of the evening. She clasped her arms around her, holding tight. Sticks looked up, whining, as he picked up on her disturbance.

"What do you think, boy?" she asked, the words barely above a whisper. "Did I make a mistake?"

The dog gave a halfhearted wag of his tail as he stared in the direction Alec Stanton had gone.

She sighed and closed her eyes. "I thought so."

Her new hired hand was on time the next morning—Laurel had to give him that much. She had barely pulled on her old jeans and faded yellow T-shirt when she heard his bike turn in at the drive.

Maisie Warfield, her housekeeper, hadn't arrived yet, since she always had to get her "old man"—as she called her husband who was nearing retirement age—off to work before she could show up. Rather than waiting for Alec Stanton to come to the door and twist the old-fashioned doorbell, Laurel picked up her sneakers and moved in her sock feet toward the side entrance. At least she didn't have to worry about Sticks. He had spent the night on the screened back veranda and was still shut up out there.

Alec Stanton was not on the drive where his bright red Harley-Davidson leaned, looking as out of place in front of the old, late-Victorian house as a ladybug on the hem of an ancient lace dress. Nor was he in the tangled front garden. However, a ripping, shredding sound led her to the side of the house. He was already at work there, tearing a clinging green curtain of smilax and Virginia creeper away from the overlap siding.

He looked around at her approach. His nod of greeting was brief before he spoke. "The whole place needs painting, though I can see at least a dozen boards that should be replaced first. You'll lose more if you don't protect them soon."

"I know," she said shortly.

"I could—"

"I can take care of it," she said, cutting off the offer he was about to make. "You're here for the garden."

He yanked down a long streamer of smilax and let it fall, leaving it to be dug up by the roots later. Stripping off his gloves, he tucked them into the waistband of his jeans. He ran a critical eye over the house, which loomed above them, with its balustraded verandas that were rounded on each end in the style of a steamboat, its gingerbread work attached to the slender columns like ice-covered spiderwebs, and the conical tower set into the roofline. "It's a grand old place," he said. "It would be a shame to let it fall into ruin."

"I don't intend to," she answered tartly. "Now, if you'll…"

"Your husband's old family home, I think Grannie said. How did you wind up with it?"

"Nobody else wanted it."

That was the exact truth, she thought. The place had been the next thing to abandoned when she first saw it. Her husband's mother, Sadie Bancroft, had moved out not long after her husband left her back in the sixties. His sister Zelda had no interest in it; she'd had more than enough of the big barn of a place as a child and couldn't comprehend why Laurel had begged to buy it from the family after she and Howard were married. Even Howard had grumbled about the upkeep and often talked of trading it in for a small, neat ranch-style house during the fifteen years they were married. But that was all it had been—talk.

"It's mighty big for one person."

"I like big," Laurel said and felt a sudden flush sweep over her face for no reason that made any sense. Or she hoped that it didn't, although that seemed doubtful, considering the ghost of a smile hovering at one corner of Alec Stanton's mouth.

"Where shall I start?"

"What?"

He tilted his head. "You were going to tell me where to start to work."

"Yes. Yes, of course," she said and spun around, leading the way toward the front garden.

She had meant to help him, in part to be on hand to point out what she wanted to keep and what needed to go. She soon saw that it was unnecessary. He knew his plants and shrubs; his time as a yardman had been put to good use. He was also efficient. He didn't start work until he had checked out the tools in the shed behind the detached garage, then oiled and sharpened them.

"You could use a new pair of hedge shears," he suggested as he ran a callused thumb along the edge of a wide blade. "It would make your job around here a lot easier."

He was right, and she knew it. "I'll tell Maisie to pick them up next time she goes into town."

"You're also out of gas for the lawn mower."

"She can get that, too."

He studied her for a moment, his eyes as dark and fathomless as obsidian. "You know you have a flat on your car? And the rest of the tires are so dry-rotted you'd be lucky to get out of the driveway on them."

"I don't go out much," she said, avoiding his gaze.

"You don't go at all, to hear Grannie tell it—haven't left this place in ages. All you do is read and make clay pots in the shed out behind the garage. Why is that?"

"No reason. I just prefer my own company." She gave him a cool look before she turned away. "I'll be in the house if you need anything."

To retreat was instinctive self-protection, that was all. She didn't have to explain herself. Certainly it was none of this man's business whether she went out or stayed home, worked with her pottery or flew to the moon on a broomstick. Nor did she need someone watching her, giving unasked-for advice, prying into her life. She would pay him for what he did today, regardless of what he had said, then send him on his way. She had gotten along without Alec Stanton before he came, and she could get along without him when he was gone.

As the day advanced, however, it could not be denied that he was making progress. He cut away dozens of pine and sassafras saplings from the old fence enclosure, exposing the unpainted pickets almost all the way across the front of the garden. He rescued and pruned the Russell's Cottage Rose in the corner, tearing out a head-high pile of honeysuckle vines in the process. An arbor and garden bench of weathered cypress were unearthed from a covering of wild grapevines. And the debris from his efforts was thrown into a pile that made a slow-burning green bonfire. The gray pall of smoke rose high enough to cross the face of the noonday sun.

Laurel tried not to watch him. Yet against her best intentions it seemed everything she did took her near the front windows of the house. It was only natural to look out. A perfectly ordinary impulse. That was all.

He had removed his shirt in the middle of the morning. A sheen of perspiration gilded the sun-bronzed expanse of his back, shimmering with his movements, while dust and bits of dried leaves stuck to the corded muscles of his arms. The soft hair on his chest glinted like damp velvet, making a conduit for the trickling sweat that crept down the washboard-like ridges of his abdomen to dampen the waist of his jeans. He was hot and sweaty and dirty and magnificent. And she disliked him intensely for making her aware of it.

The last thing she wanted was to think about a man—any man. She had gotten along fine without being reminded of the male race; had hardly thought of love or sex since her husband had died. To be forced to return to all that now would not be helpful. She wouldn't do it, she wouldn't.

"I've got cold roast chicken and fruit salad for lunch," Maisie said from behind her. "You want I should serve it for you and Alec out on the veranda?"

Laurel swung to face the housekeeper with guilty color flooding her face. Maisie Warfield, rotund and white-haired, stood in the doorway that led from the dining room to the parlor. She wiped her wet hands on a dish towel as she studied Laurel. There was a shrewd look in the snapping blue of her eyes, and faint amusement crinkled the tanned skin around them into shallow wrinkles.

"No. No, I don't think so," Laurel replied. "You—can take him a sandwich and a cold drink."

Maisie's smile faded and she set her hamlike fist that held the dishcloth on a padded hip. "Why? You got something against Alec?"

"Of course not. I just prefer my privacy." Laurel turned back to the window, ignoring the other woman's stern gaze.

"He's not going to bite."

A wry smile curled Laurel's lips. "How do you know?"

"What?"

She turned to give her housekeeper a straight glance. "I said, yes, I know. But I still don't intend to eat with him. Or anything else."

"You'd rather stay shut up in this house instead of keeping him company."

"That's about it."

The housekeeper shrugged. "You don't know what you're missing."

Laurel made no reply. She was too afraid Maisie might be right.

2

Alec worked like a man possessed, slashing and hacking and piling brush without letting up. The sun burned down on his head. Sweat poured off him in streams. He tied a bandana around his forehead and kept working. His shirt grew soaked, clinging to him, confining his movements. He stripped it off and kept working. He could feel the sting of long scratches on his arms from his bout with forty-foot runners from an ancient dog rose. He ignored them and kept working.

He didn't care about any of it. It was good to use his muscles, to feel them heat up until they glided and contracted in endless rhythm, responding effortlessly to his need. He liked the heat of the sun on his back, enjoyed the smells of cut stems, disturbed earth and smoke. It gave him a sense of accomplishment to rescue antique shrubs and perennials, to watch some semblance of order emerge from what had been a confused mess.

He had to prove himself to make sure he got this job, but there was more to it than that. He needed to show Laurel Bancroft that he was as good as any redneck at achieving what she needed done.

He had thought from the way she was dressed this morning that she might work with him. He had been looking forward to the prospect. But she had gone inside the house and shut the door. He hadn't caught so much as a glimpse of her since.

She was good at closing herself off, from all accounts. Grannie Callie had said she'd hardly left this old place since her husband had died. People seemed to think she had gone a little peculiar. Not crazy, exactly, but not your average grocery-shopping, soaps-watching, club-and-tennis young matron, either.

The kind of work he was doing didn't take a great deal of concentration, and his mind had a tendency to wander. If he let himself, he could see Laurel Bancroft as some kind of enchanted princess under a spell; she had that fragile look about her. She was trapped in her castle of an old house, drugged and sleeping while life passed her by. And he was a knight-of-old come to hack his way through the thorns and briers to save her.

Jeez, he must be losing it.

Some knight. No armor, for one thing. A pair of hedge clippers in his hands instead of a sword. Hardly perfect, either. And he was definitely not pure.

A screen door slammed at the side of the house. Maisie rounded the corner and leaned over the railing.

"Lunchtime, boy," she called. "Sandwiches up here on the veranda. You want water or tea?"

He stopped, wiping sweat from his eyes with his forearm before he frowned up at her. "'Boy'?"

She gave him a grin that put a thousand wrinkles in her face and made him feel good inside. "You don't like that? I could have called you dummy for being out in this sun without a hat. Water or tea?"

"Water." He should have known better than to try intimidating a woman who claimed she had changed his diaper when he was a kid. "Where's Mrs. Bancroft?"

The elderly housekeeper's gaze slid away from his. "She don't eat lunch. You want to wash up, there's a bathroom off the kitchen."

It looked as if Laurel Bancroft was avoiding him. He didn't know whether that was good, because it was a sign that he disturbed her, or bad, because it meant she couldn't stand him. Either way, he was going to have to do something about it.

At least Maisie didn't desert him. She brought her chicken salad and tea out to the table on the shady front veranda. While he ate, he teased her about her diet fare and how much her old man was going to miss her curves when they were gone. After a while, he got around to what he really wanted to say.

"So what is it with the lady of the house? Is she a recluse or just stuck-up?" He leaned back in his chair, rubbing the condensation from the sides of his water glass with his thumb while he tried to look bored and a little disgusted.

Maisie gave him a narrow look. "She doesn't have too much for people, is all."

"How's that?"

"Her husband died, you know that?"

He nodded as he massaged the biceps in his right arm that had begun to tighten on him.

"Did you know she killed him?" she asked.

Shock brought him upright. "You're bullsh— I mean, there's no way!"

"She did it, God's truth," Maisie said with a shake of her head. "Not that she meant to. He stepped behind her car as she was backing out of the garage.

But there were folks who claimed it was on purpose. The mother-in-law, for one.''

"Nobody else believed it, though, right? I mean, just look at her. How could they?''

"Some people will believe anything. Anyway, seems Laurel and Howard had been having problems. Then there was a big life-insurance policy.''

"But nothing came of it?''

"Nothing official, no investigation. Sadie Bancroft, the husband's mother, said it was on account of Sheriff Tanning being Laurel's old boyfriend. Maybe, maybe not. I don't know. Anyway, it blew over.''

"Except for the gossip?''

"Yeah, well, there's always that part.''

He tilted his head. "So she's hiding out. But why, if she really didn't mean to do it?''

"You want to know that, you'll have to ask her.''

Maisie was avoiding his gaze. Alec wondered why. "Think she'll tell me?''

"Might.'' The older woman stood and began stacking dishes. "Depends maybe on how you go about it and why you want to know.'' She walked off with her load, leaving him to himself.

Alec sat on for a few minutes, drinking water as the ice melted in his glass, and gazing out over the garden at what he had done and what he still needed to do. From up here, he could see the outlines, barely, of what had been a typical front yard in the old days. It had been fenced with white pickets to keep out the cows that ranged freely back then, with a gate accessing the driveway, which passed in front of the house, then made a sharp right turn into the garage that was separate from the house. A straight brick sidewalk cut from the front gate to the steps, and curving walkways followed the oval ends of the house around toward the back.

Planting had apparently been haphazard, except for the great treelike camellias and Cape jasmine at the fence corners and the roses along the pickets and over the arbors above the gates. He had found evidence of bulbs of all kinds everywhere, from daffodils and iris to licoris. Originally, the soil between the plantings would have been swept clean of every blade of grass and raked in patterns. Sometime in the forties or fifties, probably, Saint Augustine grass had been planted in the open spots. There were still patches of the thick sod here and there, although the rest was choked with weeds and briers and enough saplings to stock a small forest.

And he had to get after it. He drained his glass, picked up his sweat-damp gloves and went back to work.

Maisie left in the middle of the afternoon, flipping him a quick wave as she drove off in her old boat of a car. He dug up the tough tubers of a mass of saw briers that were trying to climb a column while he allowed a little time to pass. When he thought it might not look too much like he had waited for the house-keeper to leave before storming the house, he pulled his discarded shirt back on, then went and gave the antique brass doorbell a quick twist.

The harsh, discordant sound rang through the house, and from around back, Laurel's German shepherd, smart dog that he was, started barking immediately. Earlier, Alec had seen Sticks shut up on the porch. The two of them had eyed each other through the screen. Leaning against the doorjamb now, Alec wondered whether Laurel Bancroft was protecting him from the dog or the dog from him.

Laurel didn't want to answer the door. She felt threatened, almost beleaguered inside her own house. She wished she had never mentioned the garden to Maisie, then this Alec Stanton would never have shown up. She could have gone on as she had been for nearly five years, in comfortable solitude with little contact with the outside world beyond her housekeeper, her grown children, and the man who drove the brown truck that brought her mail-order purchases.

Catalogs had become her lifelines to the world. It was a catalog of antique roses from a place in Texas that had started her thinking about the garden again after all this time. Now look where it had gotten her.

It was a strange blend of fear and irritation that made her snatch open the front door after the third ring. Her voice sounding distinctly tight and unwelcoming, she said, "Yes?"

"Sorry to disturb you, ma'am," the dark-haired man who leaned on the doorjamb said, "but I needed to ask a couple of questions."

He wasn't sorry at all; she could see that. What she couldn't see was why he couldn't have come to the door before Maisie left. The urge to slam it in his face was so strong, a tremor ran down her arm. The main thing stopping her was the suspicion that he might prevent it if she tried.

Through compressed lips, she asked, "What is it?"

"I wondered if you could show me where you want your fountain? And it would help if I had some idea how you'd like to lay out the rose beds you mentioned. Plus, I'm not exactly sure what to save and what to get rid of.''

She glanced at the yard beyond him with a doubtful frown. ''Surely you haven't got as far as all that? I thought you were just clearing and cleaning.''

He smiled, a lazy movement of sensuously molded lips that made her breath catch in her throat. ''It always helps to have a plan. Would you mind stepping out here just a minute to tell me a couple of things?''

How could she refuse such a polite and reasonable request? It was obviously impossible. In any case, she was intrigued by the clear line of sight he had created by fighting back the growth along the sidewalk from the steps to the gate. It had seemed a great distance between the two points before, when trees and brush had choked the passage and obscured the view. Now it appeared to be only a few yards.

Before she knew it, she had moved across the porch and down onto the brick path. Alec was talking, pointing out dying jonquil foliage along the walk, asking if she wanted to leave the yellow jasmine vine that had woven its way through a huge spirea near the side gate, and a dozen other questions.

She answered, yet she was painfully aware of being outside in the afternoon sun, exposed and vulnerable to another human being. At the same time, she felt a rising excitement. She could almost see the garden she had envisioned emerging from the shambles around her. In a single day, this man had laid bare the form of the front yard so she could tell how things used to be and how she wanted them again.

Roses. She wanted roses. Not the stiff, formal, near-perfect hybrid blooms everyone thought of when they heard the word, but rather the old Chinas, teas,

Bourbons and Gallicas of years gone by. They were survivors, those roses. They had been rescued from cemeteries and around the foundations of deserted houses where they'd been growing, neglected, for countless years. Tough, hardy, they clung to life. Then in early spring, and even through the searing heat of summer and into fall, they unfurled blooms of intricate, fragile beauty, pouring their sweet perfume into the air as if sharing their souls.

Standing in the center of the front garden, Laurel said, "I'd like the fountain here, with the path running around it on either side, then on to the steps. I thought maybe an edging of low boxwood of the kind they have in French gardens would be good, with a few perennials like Bath's pinks, blue *Salvia* and Shasta daisies. Beyond that, just roses and more roses."

She glanced at Alec, half afraid she might have spoken too extravagantly. He was watching her with consideration in the midnight darkness of his eyes and a faint smile hovering at one corner of his mouth. For long moments, he made no answer. Then, as if suddenly becoming aware of her gaze, he gave a quick nod. "I can do that."

"You think it will work?"

"I think it will be perfect."

He sounded sincere, but she could hardly take it on trust. "You're only saying that because you can see it will take weeks of work."

His smile faded. "I wouldn't do that. Actually, what I am is relieved. I was afraid you were going to want big maintenance-free beds of junipers all neatened up with chunky bark mulch."

She made a quick face. "Too West Coast subdivision."

"Exactly," he agreed, his eyes warm and steady.

For a fleeting instant, she felt such a strong rapport with the man beside her that she was amazed. They were nothing alike, had little in common as far as background, yet they seemed in that moment to be operating on the same wavelength.

Perhaps this would work, after all. Just so long, of course, as they kept it simple and businesslike. She not only wanted this garden, she needed it. She had come to think, lately, that without it she might go into her house one day and never come out again.

"Let me show you something around here," Alec said, intruding on her thoughts. Turning, he led the way toward the back of the house where the old outdoor kitchen had been before it was moved inside just before World War II. Her footsteps slowed as she saw where he was headed.

He kicked aside a tangle of brier and weeds, which he had apparently hacked down earlier at the house corner. Underneath was a low brick curbing covered by a large concrete cap. Moving with quick efficiency and lithe strength, he bent and lifted the heavy concrete cover. It made a harsh grating noise as he shoved it from the curbing.

"Don't!" she cried, stepping back.

He straightened, putting his fists on his hips. "You know what this is?"

"A cistern, of course," she answered, incensed. "But my husband never— That is, he always said it was extremely dangerous. No one ever goes near it."

Alec frowned. "It's just a brick-lined hole in the ground. There's not even any water in it anymore."

"Howard was always afraid somebody, one of the kids, would fall in."

"Then he should have filled it in. But it could be used now as a reflecting pool, if you wanted. It wouldn't take much to seal the brick lining, make it watertight."

"It would be so deep," she protested.

"So's a swimming pool," he offered with a shrug, "but that doesn't stop people from having them. Anyway, it's not as if there are any kids toddling around to fall in."

She shook her head, suppressing a shiver. "I'd rather not."

"Suit yourself. It was just an idea."

He was disappointed, she thought. The enthusiasm had died out of his face and his movements were stiff as he replaced the heavy concrete cap. Abruptly, she asked, "Did you see the creek?"

"I saw where one crosses the road below here. That it?"

Nodding, she led him toward the winding waterway that ran behind Ivywild, gliding among tall beeches, sweet bay trees and glades of ferns. She was halfway there before it came home to her what she was doing. She had actually left the fenced-in yard. She was moving farther away from the safety and comfort it represented with every step. How long had it been since she had done that so easily?

A shiver moved over her and the skin on the back of her neck prickled. She felt naked, as if she had deliberately abandoned her protective covering. Panic rose inside her, but she choked it down, breathing slowly in and out.

She would be all right—she would. The wide shoulders and hard body of the man at her side spelled protection. He was solid, like a wall or fence that stood between her and whatever danger might lie around her. She had felt it the night before, felt it even more strongly now.

Not that there was really anything out here, of course. Any jeopardy was all in her head, and she needed to get rid of it. She knew that and was determined to keep telling herself so until she believed it. Anyway, she would not be away from her house for long—only for the time it took to show Alec Stanton the small stream.

As she pushed on, moving ahead of him down the tree- and brush-covered slope, following a winding animal trail, she was hyperaware of the warmth and solidity of him beside her. He moved so quietly, with the natural grace of an Indian. In the dusky tree shadows, she thought she could see a copper tint in the deep bronze of his skin.

The awkwardness between them lingered, but it had a different quality from before. She couldn't remember the last time she had been quite so aware of another human being. Nor could she recall the last time she had cared how any male felt other than her teenage son.

Alec was impressed with the creek. Standing knee-deep in the ferns that edged it, with his hair trailing in its damp ponytail down his back and leaf shadows making a tracery of gray dimness and golden light on his brown skin, he turned to her with a heart-stopping smile. Voice deep and reflective, he said, "This has possibilities."

"I know," she said and caught her breath, suddenly more afraid of those possibilities than she had been of anything in five long years.

He tilted his head, the darkness of his eyes as meltingly warm and sweet as chocolate. "Does this mean I get the job?"

He had done so much in so short a time. He could clear all the choking debris from Ivywild. He could make her rose garden for her. If she had not ventured out to see what he had done—what he could do—if she had not seen the promise, she might have answered differently. Now there was only one reply possible.

"Yes, I...suppose it must."

Pleasure flared across his face in sudden brightness. "Good," he said softly. "In fact, that's great."

Laurel wasn't so sure.

She was even less certain when night closed in and Alec finally roared away down the drive on his Harley. She had grown used to being alone, and yet tonight she really felt it for the first time in ages. It was a warm evening, but she was chilled. Wrapping her arms around herself, she wondered what it would be like to have a man's warm arms to hold her, or a firm chest to support her as she pressed close against it. It had been so long.

Of course, Howard had never been particularly good at simple affection. Whenever she'd tried to cuddle in his arms, she had usually gotten sex. That part of their marriage had been all right; not especially inspiring but no disaster, either. They had talked—mostly practical conversations of the kind necessary between husband and wife, about plumbing repairs, the children's progress in school, what was for dinner. Sometimes they had gone out to eat or visited friends, driving home in companionable silence. Now and then, Howard had taken her hand. But no, he'd had no gift for gentle caresses, no interest in the passionless need to hold and absorb the essence of another person. It was foolish, perhaps, to miss what you had never had.

She was lonely, that was it. The night stretched empty and still and dreary ahead of her. There was nothing on television she wanted to watch, and she had read everything of interest on her bookshelves. She wasn't sleepy, wasn't even tired.

She couldn't stop thinking of Alec Stanton. The way he looked at her, the way his smile started at one corner of his mouth and spread across his lips in slow glory. The deep set of his eyes under his brows, and the planes of his face that swept down from the high ridges of his cheekbones, giving him the predatory look of some ancient warrior. The easy way he moved, his deceptive strength. The gleam of his skin with its gilding of perspiration, the rippling glide of the dragon on his upper chest as his pectoral muscles contracted and relaxed.

How stupid, to indulge in sophomoric mooning over a hired hand, a young hired hand. It was even more stupid to allow herself the twinges of such a ridiculous attraction. If she could just be objective about it, she might laugh at the trick her mind had played on her, getting her worked up over such an unsuitable partner, like a canary eyeing the iridescent magnificence of a pheasant.

It was only hormones run amok, that was all. Nothing would come of it. Alec Stanton would do his job, then he would be gone and everything would be the same again. Everything, except she would have a new rose garden.

She would have to be satisfied with that.

It had been a mistake to leave her house, perhaps.

There was more than one kind of safety, more than one kind of danger. Still, if she stayed inside now until after Alec had finished her garden, then she couldn't get hurt.

Could she?

3

Laurel Bancroft was keeping an eye on him from the windows; Alec knew this because he had caught her at it.

He didn't like it, didn't appreciate being made to feel like a criminal she needed to stay away from at all costs. Or worse, that maybe he wasn't good enough to associate with her. It had been going on for three days. He'd about had a bellyful of it.

He didn't care if she was a widow, didn't give a rat's behind if she'd actually killed her husband and had good reason to shut herself away. It didn't even matter that she didn't see another soul beside Maisie. He wanted her out of that house. He wanted her to talk to him.

The anger that simmered inside him while he dug and chopped and ripped weeds from the ground was strange, in a way. What people thought and how they acted toward him had ceased to bother him years ago. But Laurel Bancroft had opened old wounds. She'd made him as self-conscious as a teenager again. She'd made him care, which was something else he held against her.

What it was about her, he didn't know. It wasn't just that she was an attractive woman, because there were jillions of those in California, and he had known his share. Nor was it, as his brother sometimes claimed, that he had a weakness for problem females. He might feel the need to lend a hand to those who seemed to be struggling, but that had nothing to do with the woman who owned Ivywild.

There she was again, behind the draperies that covered the window on the end of the house. She was standing well back and barely shifting the drape, but he had learned to watch for the shadowy movement.

That did it.

He dropped the shovel he was wielding, then stripped off his gloves and crammed them into his back pocket. He was not going to be spied on any longer. Either she was coming out or he was going in.

Maisie answered his knock. Her gray brows climbed toward her hairline as she saw the grim look on his face. Wiping her damp hands on her apron, she asked, "Something the matter?"

Alec gave a short nod. "I'd like to talk to Mrs. Bancroft a minute."

"She's busy," the older woman answered, not budging an inch. "What do you need?"

"Answers," he said. "Could you get her for me?"

Maisie considered him, her faded gaze holding a hint of acknowledgment of the human capacity for dealing misery. Finally, she nodded. "Wait here a minute."

Alec put his hands on his hipbones as he watched the housekeeper move off into the house. Wait here, she'd said. Like a good boy. Or the hired help. His lips tightened.

After a few seconds, he heard the murmur of voices, then a silence followed by the returning shuffle of the house slippers Maisie wore. She spoke while still some distance down the hall.

"She says find out what you want."

"I want," he replied with stringent softness, "to talk to her."

"Well, she don't want to talk to you, so don't push it."

"What if I do? You going to stop me? Or will you just tell Grannie Callie on me?" He stepped forward into the long hallway.

"You'll get yourself fired," Maisie warned, even as she backed up a few steps.

"Fine. I'll be fired."

"I thought you wanted this job."

"Where is she?" He strode deeper into the house while Maisie turned and trotted along behind him.

"In her bedroom," the older woman answered a bit breathlessly. "You can't go in there."

"I think maybe I can," he said, heading for the door Maisie had glanced at as she spoke.

"It's on your own head, then."

The warning in the housekeeper's voice as she came to a halt was fretted with something that might have been grudging approval. He didn't stay to analyze it, but turned the knob of the bedroom door and pushed inside.

The widow Bancroft was sitting on a chaise longue with pillows propped behind her back, her feet curled to one side and a book in her hands. Her gaze widened and a tint of soft rose crept into her face as she stared at him. Her lips parted as if she had drawn a quick breath and forgotten to release it.

The bedroom was like her, Alec thought—a medley of cream, blue and coral-pink; of substantial Victorian furniture and fragile, sensuous fabrics. It was a retreat and he had breached it. More than that, he had caught her unawares, before she could raise her defenses. She was barefoot and almost certainly braless under an oversize and much-washed T-shirt worn with a pair of white shorts. Her hair spilled over her left shoulder, shimmering with the beat of her heart, and she wore not the first smidgen of makeup to obscure her clear skin or the soft coral of her lips. She was the most enticing sight he had ever come across in his life.

In the flicker of an eyelid, she recovered her outward aplomb. Setting her book aside, she uncurled from the chaise and got to her feet. As she spoke, her voice was edgy. "What is it? Do you have a problem?"

"You might say so. I want to know why you're afraid of me." He hadn't meant it to come out just like that, but he let it stand anyway.

"I'm not," she said in immediate denial.

"You could have fooled me. Unless you have some other reason for hiding in here?"

She stared at him an instant too long before she spoke. "Who said I was hiding? Just because I don't feel the need to oversee everything you do—"

"You're letting me make this garden on my own, and you know it. When I get through, it won't be yours but mine."

She shrugged briefly. "So I'll make it mine when you're gone."

"There's no need. I can make sure that it reflects what you want right now. You won't have to lift a finger except to point. You can tell me what you want moved and what stays as is, what you want pruned to size and what you prefer to be left natural. I've gotten rid of the briers and vines and everything else that obviously doesn't belong, but now it's decision time.''

"You decide, then," she said through compressed lips. "You seem to know more about it than I do, anyway."

"I don't know what you like or what you want." The words were simple and he meant them, but the emphasis he put on them in his own mind turned his ears hot.

"Do whatever you like!"

He stared at her, then gave himself a mental shake. She was talking about flowers and shrubs, that was all. "Suppose I clear off everything," he said, "take it down to the bare...ground."

"You can't!"

"I could," he growled with absolute conviction. "Nothing easier."

"But there are camellias out there over eighty years old, and one big sweet olive that—" She stopped, her eyes narrowing. "But you know that."

"I know what's there," he said. "I just don't know what you care about."

"I can tell you—"

"Show me." He cut across what she had intended to say without compunction.

Her lips firmed. "I don't think—"

"Unless it's me," he said softly. "Since you're not afraid, then you must not like the company."

Surprise and dismay flashed in the rich blue of her eyes. "That isn't it at all."

"Then what's the problem?"

"Nothing!"

"I don't think so."

Her lashes flickered. "At least it's nothing to do with you, nothing to you. I can't imagine why you're so concerned."

"Call me perverse. I like to know where I stand."

"Where you don't belong, actually. In my bedroom." She flashed him a look of irritation before she turned away again.

"Level with me and I'm gone," he stated with precision.

Her lips tightened, and she crossed her arms over her chest as she sighed. "It's not you, all right? If you must know, it's me. I don't deal well with people."

"That right?" he said with a raised brow. "You don't have to deal with me, just talk to me. I'm not complicated and I don't bite, but I hate being ignored."

"I'm not ignoring you!"

"Maybe you just have no use for me, then."

"That isn't it at all. I don't know what to say!"

His smile was slow but sure as he turned to the door and stood holding it open, waiting for her. "Then there's no excuse left, since I can talk for both of us, and I don't mind your company."

The look she gave him was fulminating yet resigned. He had her and she knew it. She was not the kind of woman who could be cruel just to protect herself, no matter the provocation. He had suspected it, even counted on it. Which didn't say much for him as a person, but it said even less for all the other idiots stupid enough to think she could commit murder. He watched her closely as she pushed her feet into her sandals, which sat beside the chaise, then moved ahead of him down the dim hallway.

Yeah, he had her number. He had Laurel Bancroft out of her bedroom, out of her house again. Now where was he going from here?

It was a good question—one he pondered often during the next week. He might be guilty of arrogance, thinking he knew what was best for her, but he didn't intend to let that stop him. He was nothing if not high-handed.

At least he'd managed to coax her into the garden every morning. It had taken a lot of thought and energy, not to mention dozens of asinine questions that he could have answered himself without half trying. But on the sixth day, just yesterday, he'd kept her outside long enough to get her straight little nose pink from the sun, and dirt under the nails of her long, aristocratic fingers. As his reward, she had come out of the house this morning with her gloves in her hands and a straw hat on her head.

Working beside her was both a pleasure and a royal pain. She wanted to save everything recognizable, which was going to make her garden one unholy jumble. Not that he cared. Or had any right to complain.

She also had a reverence for living things that caused her to jump in and save every turtle, frog, lizard or even snake that came anywhere near the ax or shovel he might be wielding. This morning, she had spent an hour chasing a half-grown rabbit up and down the garden to be sure it found its way outside the fence.

As compensation for his tried patience, he could stand downwind from her while she worked and catch the incredible scent of roses and jasmine and warm female that drifted from her skin. He got to take his orders directly from her, which she always couched as courteous requests. He was permitted to admire the view when she bent over in close-fitting cutoff jeans to plait dying bulb foliage or to turn over a few shovelfuls of soil. He got to talk to her whenever he pleased. And sometimes, when he least expected it, he was rewarded for some quip or comment by her rare smile.

She was the kind of woman he might have laid down his life for in another place and time. As it was, he meant to drag her out of her self-imposed exile and see to it that she began to live again. He wasn't quite sure why he was so bent on it except that he maybe needed something to distract himself, occupy his mind. Or maybe he just hated waste.

Yes, and maybe he was an idiot to think it was that simple. Denial had never been one of his problems before.

They were eating their lunch on the veranda. He was having trouble choking down Maisie's homemade hamburger, although it was fine eating. His throat kept closing when he turned his head to look at Laurel sitting so naturally beside him. She was hot and tired, and her T-shirt was damp with perspiration so it clung in all the right places. Her hair was coming loose from the long braid down her back, and a piece of trash was caught on her gold-tipped lashes. He thought he had never seen anything so gorgeous in his life.

"Hold still," he said, reaching out to touch her cheek, gently closing her eyelid with his thumb before sliding the offending bit of dried leaf from her lashes with two fingers.

She blinked experimentally as he took it away, then grinned at him. "Thanks."

Incredible, how a single word could make him feel ten feet tall. Ready to leap tall buildings. Save the world. Or do lascivious-type things on the table between them that would get him booted off the property before he could turn around.

She was watching him, her gaze faintly inquiring. He suspected his face might be flushed, considering how cool the breeze felt that wandered down the long length of the veranda. Blowing the piece of trash from his fingers, he picked up his water glass and drank deeply.

"You don't eat much, do you?" she said in tones of mild censure. "At least, not compared to how hard you work."

"I eat enough." The words were short. The last thing he wanted from her was motherly concern.

She frowned a little. "I only wondered if it was on purpose, some kind of California health-food thing."

"I guess you could call it that," he allowed finally. "The old man I used to work with thought overeating caused all sorts of problems. Fat rats die young, he used to say. He was Chinese, laughed at the American diet while he stirred up ungodly mixtures of rice and vegetables. But he was eighty-six and going strong last time I saw him."

"You did yard work with him?"

Alec gave a quick nod, pleased that she had remembered something of what he'd told her that first night. "Mr. Wu was a gardener. He taught me what I know about plants, and a great deal more, besides."

Her smile was whimsical. "The wisdom of the venerable ancients?"

"You've been watching too many old Charlie Chan movies," he answered with a grin. "Mr. Wu was big on Zen meditation and martial arts, but I never heard him quote Confucius.''

"Martial arts? Did he teach you that, too?"

He shrugged. "Only as a form of exercise—something else Mr. Wu was big on."

"I'd have thought gardening would give you more than enough of that." The words were dry as she flexed her neck muscles.

"That was my idea, too," he replied with a faint laugh of remembrance. His gaze skimmed the softness of her breasts that were lifted into prominence as she turned her head and arched her back to relieve strain. "Mr. Wu had a way of changing a person's mind."

"You miss California, I expect. I mean, it must seem so different here."

"I did miss it," he replied with a slow shake of his head as he watched her. "But not anymore."

She avoided eye contact. Relaxing, she used a fingertip to pick up a sesame seed that had fallen from her hamburger bun. "You'll be going back, though, I guess?"

Would he? He had certainly thought so, once. Now he wasn't so sure. With his brain feeling tight in his skull as he watched her place the sesame seed on the pink surface of her tongue, he said, "Not anytime soon."

"Because your brother isn't well enough? Or is it that he just doesn't want to go?"

She was avoiding the issue of what he himself wanted, which seemed to indicate that she understood him a little better than he had figured. Although that might be wishful thinking on his part. After a moment, he said, "Gregory's happy here, or happy enough. I'm not sure he'll ever...leave."

"That's good, then. There must be something about it he likes."

He gave her a straight look. "Yes, but that's not what I was getting at."

"Oh." Her head came up. "You don't mean..."

He gave a slow nod as he turned his head to squint at a blue jay just landing on a fence picket. Voice low, he said, "He isn't going to make it."

In the sudden quiet, the sound of a jay's call was loud. After a moment, she said softly, "He knows?"

Alec nodded, since he didn't quite trust himself to speak.

"How old..."

"Thirty-five in October, four years older than I am." He was laying the age thing on the line between them. The way she had hesitated over the question made him think it might be what she wanted.

"Does he— That is, is he...all right about it?"

"No," Alec said deliberately, "I don't think you can say that." Far from it, in fact. Gregory wasn't taking it well at all, and who could blame him?

"He's lucky to have you with him."

It was the last thing he expected her to say—so unexpected that he laughed. "I'm not sure he would agree."

"Maisie says your grandmother told her that you're up with him all hours of the night."

"Somebody has to check on him, give him his medication. Grannie fusses over him during the day, but she needs her rest." He was surprised Laurel had spoken to Maisie about him. His brow quirked into an arch as he wondered why.

She colored slightly under his regard. "I saw you taking a nap after lunch that first day. Maisie told me you probably needed it, and why. You haven't done it again, so I just wanted to say that I don't mind, if you...feel the need."

The need he felt had little to do with sleeping, though a great deal to do with lying down. Or not. "I appreciate the thought," he said carefully, "but I've been managing a catnap in the evening while Grannie Callie cooks supper. I'll get by."

"It's up to you." She lifted one shoulder.

"You suggesting I'm too out of shape to do without it?" he asked in a weak effort to lighten the mood, change the subject.

Her gaze skated over his chest where he had left his shirt unbuttoned for coolness. Her mouth twisted in a wry smile. "Hardly."

He held his lips clamped shut—it was the only way he could keep from grinning. He hadn't been fishing for compliments, but he wasn't immune to them, either.

He pushed his plate aside and leaned back in his chair. His wandering attention was caught by the scaling paint along the edge of the porch, and he grasped at the subject like a lifeline.

"When was the last time this house was painted?"

She shrugged. "Six years, seven maybe. I know it needs it, but..."

"As I said before, it would be a shame to let it go too far. It's such a grand old place."

"I know," she said unhappily. "It's just that it's such a hassle."

"I also told you I could do it."

"You'd be here forever."

Exactly, he thought. Instead he said, "Not quite. It's amazing how fast you can cover ground with a few cans of paint and an air compressor."

"Spray it, you mean?"

He lifted a brow. "It's not a new concept."

"No, but Howard always did it the hard way, with a brush."

"Your husband, right?"

She nodded, her gaze on her plate. She put what was left of her hamburger down as if she were no longer hungry. Alec thought she looked a little pale. Remembering what Maisie had told him, he couldn't blame her too much. "It isn't your fault he died," he said, his voice gravelly. "Don't let it get to you."

"You don't know anything about it." Her eyes flashed blue fire as she looked at him.

"Nothing except what I've been told. But even I have sense enough to know a woman who won't hurt a turtle would never kill a man." There it was, out in the open. He waited for her to tell him to get lost.

She looked away, swallowed hard. "One thing doesn't necessarily cancel out the other."

"You saying you really did run him down?"

"I might have." Her face was flushed and a groove appeared between her brows.

"Sure. Pull the other one." He caught himself waiting for the blowup, the show of temper in defense of her innocence. Where was it?

"Maybe I saw him coming up behind me before I backed out of the garage. Maybe I could have slammed on the brakes—but I didn't."

She was dead serious. Incredible as it seemed, she really believed she might have killed her husband on purpose. "Right, and maybe you figured he was bright enough not to walk behind a moving vehicle. Hell, anybody would.''

"But not everybody."

"Forget them. Get on with your life."

"That's easy to say, but I can't—" She stopped, took a deep breath as she lifted both hands to her face, wiping them down it as if she were smoothing away the remnants of horror. "Never mind. I don't know how we got onto this, anyway. I— We were talking about painting. If you really want to fool with it, you can get what you need at the hardware store in town and charge it to me."

"I could, or we might run into town now and you can pick out the paint colors." The words were deliberate. He waited for the answer with more than casual interest.

"Oh, I don't think that's necessary. White will do."

"With green shutters, I guess." His tone was sarcastic, a measure of his disappointment.

"What's wrong with that? It's traditional, the way it's always been."

"It's boring."

"I guess you would like to fancy it up like some San Francisco Painted Lady?"

Her annoyance was more like it—it made her sound feisty and full of life. She was right about his taste, too. In self-defense, he said, "The Victorians liked things colorful."

"Not around here, they didn't. Whitewash was all anybody could afford after the Civil War, you know. Later on, everyone figured that if it was good enough for their grandparents, it was good enough for them. And it's also good enough for me."

"Well, heaven forbid we should go against tradition. Do you want antique white or bright white?"

"Antique."

"I should have known."

She was silent for a moment, staring at him. Then she got to her feet. "Fine. If that's settled, I think it's time we got back to work."

It served him right.

The afternoon went quickly, at least for Laurel. One moment the sun was high; the next time she looked up it was spreading long blue shadows along the ground. She was fighting with a honeysuckle vine that had snaked its way through a baby's-breath spirea. She had decided the only way to get rid of it was to cut both plants down to the ground when she heard a faint noise directly behind her. She swung with the hedge clippers wide open in her hands.

Alec sidestepped, lashed out with one hand. The next instant, the clippers were on the ground and her wrists were numb inside her gloves. She caught her left hand in her right, holding it as she stared at him.

He cursed softly as he stepped closer to take her wrists, then stripped off her gloves, which he dropped to the ground. Turning her hands with the palms up, he moved the bones, watching her face for signs of pain. Some of the tightness went out of his features as he saw no evidence of injury. Voice low, he said, "I didn't mean to hurt you. It was just a reflex action."

"I know," she replied, controlling a shiver at the feel of his warm, suntanned hands on hers. "You didn't hurt me. I was only surprised."

He flicked her a quick, assessing look. "Yeah,

well, so was I. I didn't know you were armed and dangerous."

She could make something out of that, or leave it alone. She chose to bypass it. "You wanted something?"

His grasp on her arms tightened before he let her go with an abrupt, openhanded gesture. "As a matter of fact, yes. I was going to ask if you'll show me where the headwaters of your creek are located. I'd like to know what kind of floodplain drains into it from north of here."

"You have a reason, I suppose?" Realizing she was still rubbing her wrist where the feeling was returning, she made an effort to stop.

His eyes were jet-black and his smile a little forced as he inclined his head. "I was thinking of diverting water from the creek for your fountain."

"But why?" She gave him a quick frown. "They have those kits that recirculate the water. Wouldn't that work?"

"You have to keep adding more water, plus the fountain goes stagnant after a while." He summoned a grin. "Besides, I have a passion for water projects, and what's the point in being an engineer if you're going to take the easy way out?"

"I don't think you want to go tromping through the woods to follow the creek. It's nothing but a thicket back in there, and the snakes are already crawling."

"You mean you don't want to do it, I think," he said. "Doesn't matter. You point me down the right roads, and I can get enough of an idea from the back of my bike."

"If you mean you want me to lead you in my car—"

The quick shake of his head cut her off. "What I had in mind was you riding with me."

"I don't think so!" She hovered between amazement, doubt and anger, and was uncertain which was uppermost in her mind.

"Why? Afraid I'll overturn you?"

"No, but—"

"There're no buts about it. Either you trust me or you don't. What's the big deal?"

"You don't understand," she said a little desperately.

He didn't budge an inch. "So make me."

"I don't like motorcycles." She glanced away, past his shoulder, as she spoke.

"You don't have to like them. Just ride on one."

Her lips tightened. "This is ridiculous. I don't have to give you a reason. I'm just not going."

"You're chicken," he said softly.

She snapped her gaze back to his. "You have no right to say such a thing. You don't know what it's like when I leave here. You just don't know!"

"What makes you so sure? You're not the only one with problems," he said with a swift gesture of one hand. "At least I know one thing, which is that you have some kind of phobia about your Ivywild. If you don't get out of it, you're going to wind up locked inside with no way to leave. Ever."

She bit the side of her lip. In a voice almost too low to hear, she asked, "Would that be so bad?"

"It would be criminal," he answered without hesitation. "You have too much living left in you. Will you let it all slip away? Will you let fear dictate what you can and can't do?''

It was a novel thought. She wasn't sure she had any life—or courage—left, not that it made any difference. ''Look,'' she began.

''No, you look,'' he countered, setting his fists on his hipbones. ''It's just a little bike ride. All you have to do is hold on. I won't go fast, I won't overturn you, and you can choose the route. What more do you want?''

''To be left alone?'' she said sweetly.

''Not a chance,'' he replied with a grim smile. ''Not if you want that fountain.''

She stared at him, wondering if she had imagined the threat behind his words. Could he really mean that he wouldn't tackle the fountain project if she didn't help him with this part of it? It was just possible he could be that stubborn, that determined to have his way.

She didn't want to put it to the test, and that was both irritating and depressing. ''Oh, all right,'' she told him, bending to snatch up her gloves he had dropped. ''When do you want to go?''

''Now?'' he said promptly.

He obviously thought she would back out if they waited. It was possible he was right, although the last thing she would do was admit it. ''Let me tell Maisie, then.''

''I already told her,'' he said and had the nerve to grin. Turning, he walked away toward where his Harley stood in the driveway.

She watched him go; watched the easy, confident swing of his long legs, the way his jeans clung to the tight, lean lines of his backside, the natural way he moved his arms as if he were comfortable with his body, comfortable in it. He expected her to follow, was supremely certain she would.

Of all the conceited, know-it-all, macho schemers she had ever seen, he took the prize. She would be damned if she would trot along behind him like some blushing Indian maiden, all hot and bothered because he wanted her company.

He turned, his smile warm, almost caressing, a little challenging as he held out his hand. "Coming?"

She went. She didn't know why, but she did. It was better than being called chicken.

Alec didn't give Laurel a chance to balk, but led her straight to the bike. He swung his leg over it, then held it steady with his feet on the ground either side while he helped her climb on behind. As she settled in place, he put her hand at his waist as a suggestion. She took it away the minute he released it, and he had to duck his head to hide his disappointment.

"It's bigger than I thought," she said, her voice a little breathless.

"You've never done this before?" he asked, grinning a little to himself at the private double entendre.

"Never."

"First time for everything. Ready to get it on—the road?"

"Just do it and stop talking about it," she said through her teeth.

He flung her a quick glance over his shoulder, wondering if she could possibly tell what was going on in his head. But no, her face was tight and she certainly wasn't laughing. He turned the key, let the bike roar, then put it in gear.

She was holding on to the seat, but it wasn't enough to keep her steady for his fast takeoff. With a small yelp, she grabbed for his waist, wrapping her arms around him and meshing her fingers over his solar plexus. He could feel her breasts pressed to his backbone—a lovely, warm softness. Her cheek fit between his shoulder blades. Perfect, he thought, a grin tugging at the corner of his mouth. Just perfect.

He settled back a little and decreased his speed. His passenger would like it better, no doubt. Besides, it would make for a longer ride. After a moment, he turned his head to yell, "Am I going too fast for you?"

"No, it's fine," she replied above the engine noise, but she didn't sound too sure.

Still, he was good, the soul of restraint. He spun along the blacktop roads, took the turn onto the dirt-and-gravel track she indicated without a murmur or hesitation. He didn't show off, held the bike dead straight. The only time he stopped was to look at the creek where it passed through culverts or under bridges in its winding passage toward Ivywild.

It was a decent-size stream, fed along its route by a number of springs, which kept the water fresh and clean. Several dry washes fed into it, which, he guessed, must run fairly high during spring and winter rains. It also carried the runoff from a series of low ridges that twisted and turned for quite a few miles. Dams had been built along its course for a pond or two, but they hadn't slowed it down a great deal.

The creek would be fine for his purpose; he saw that much in short order. Tapping it for a fountain should not cause a problem with either landowners or environmentalists. And it certainly wasn't as if Louisiana had any shortage of water. If the state could only find some way to pump it out west, it would be rich.

"I've seen enough," he said as they idled beside a rusting iron culvert. "What shall we do now?"

"Go home," she replied, the words definite.

He gave a slow nod. "Right. But first, I'd like to see where this road comes out."

She said something in protest, he thought, but just then he gunned the bike into motion so he didn't quite catch it.

It was a dirt road, a hard-beaten, sandy track that meandered through the woods. There were a few big old trees standing on nearly every rise, as if it had once been lined with houses. All this land had been farms back before the turn of the century, with pastures and fields stretching over the rolling hills as far as the eye could see. That was according to Grannie Callie, anyway. She could still remember a lot of the family names, could tell him who gave up and moved to town to work in the mill, who took off to Texas, who went away to the big war, World War II, and never came back. It was strange to think about all those people living and working, having children and dying here, and leaving nothing behind except the trees that had sheltered their lives.

"Turn around!" Laurel yelled into his ear. "We've got to go back!"

He nodded his understanding, but didn't do it. Zipping around the tight curves of the unimproved road, passing from bright sun to dark tree shadow and into the sun again, he felt free and happy and lucky to be alive. He wouldn't mind riding on forever. He couldn't think when was the last time he had enjoyed anything so much as roaring along this back road with Laurel Bancroft clinging to him, bouncing against him as they hit the ruts, tethered together now and then by a long strand of her hair that wrapped around his arm like a fine, silken rope.

"Stop!" she shouted, shaking him so hard with her locked arms that the bike swerved. "This road cuts through to the main highway. We're getting too close to town!"

She was right. There was an intersection ahead of them as they rounded the bend—one with a red octagonal stop sign. He could hit the brake right here and throw them into a skidding stop, or he could coast to a halt within spitting distance of the road where cars whizzed past. It wasn't much of a choice with Laurel behind him. He coasted.

She was trembling; he could feel the tremors running through her and into his own body as he pulled up beside the stop sign. This fear of hers must have been coming on since they'd left her house. It was not a reasonable thing—not something she could control at will—or she would be doing just that instead of letting him know it. He grimaced, mouthing a soundless curse for his misjudgment.

"Which shall it be?" he asked over his shoulder in quiet concern. "A fast trip back to the house on the main road, or a slower one the way we came?"

There were cars passing in both directions in front of them. The occupants turned their heads to stare as they sat there. Laurel hid her face against his back. "The way we came," she answered, her voice uneven. "Please. Right now."

"You got it." Swinging in a wide circle, he headed back.

She was okay by the time they pulled up in front of the house. At least she had stopped shaking. Regardless, she didn't say a word, only jumped off the bike and stalked away. Cutting through the garden, she ran up the steps. The door slammed behind her.

Alec cursed softly as he struck the handlebar of his bike with a knotted fist. He was such an idiot. Why couldn't he have paid attention? Why did he have to keep on when she'd said turn back? Things had been going so well.

He hadn't realized. Even when he'd accused her of having a phobia, he hadn't really believed it ran that deep. He had drawn her outside easily enough; somehow he had thought getting her to go the rest of the way would be the same.

But he recognized, as he sat staring at the garden in front of Ivywild, that the yard was fenced in, a small enclosed space almost like an extension of the house. She could only take that much, or so it seemed.

Seen in that light, the fact that she had gone with him on his bike at all was a near miracle. She'd trusted him more than he knew, had depended on him to take care of her, keep her hidden, secure.

He had let her down.

After today, he would be lucky if he ever got her out of that house again. Hell, he would be lucky if he still had a job.

Dear God, but he couldn't stand it. He had been so close. Now he would have to start all over.

But he would do it. He would. His heart and mind left him no other choice.

4

Laurel stood grasping the handle of the front door, staring out the sidelight panes that surrounded it. Her husband's mother was coming up the walk. Overweight and shaped like a pear, the older woman was graying to a color best described as "dirty mouse." Her dress was a polyester tent, her shoes were too small for her wide feet, and she carried her mock alligator purse from the crook of her arm. She was searching the garden with darting glances. Her pale, formless lips were drawn into a tight line and mottled color lay across the grooved skin of her face.

Laurel's heart throbbed at a suffocating tempo. Why, she wasn't sure; it wasn't as if the visit was unexpected. She was only surprised that her mother-in-law had waited until Maisie and Alec had gone for the day. It wasn't like Sadie Bancroft to waste breath when there was no audience.

At that moment, Sticks came hurtling around from the back of the house, barking and growling as if at a sworn enemy. He very nearly was, since he had taken a dislike to Mother Bancroft as a puppy, after she'd kicked him for trying to chew the toes of her new shoes. There was little danger he would actually attack her, of course, but the older woman never saw it that way. She always squealed and ran from him as she was doing now, which naturally brought out the worst in the dog.

Laurel pulled the front door open and called off Sticks, then waited while her portly mother-in-law scurried up the steps and inside. As Sticks came loping up onto the veranda behind her, Laurel blocked his entrance, but gave him a reassuring scratch behind the ears to show she was not upset with him.

"Vicious animal," Sadie Bancroft snapped from the safety of the long hallway. "I can't imagine why you don't have him put down!"

Laurel ignored the suggestion. Closing the door, she said as agreeably as she was able, "How are you, Mother Bancroft? It's been a while since you were here."

"Too long, from the looks of things. What on God's green earth have you been doing to the place?"

"Just a little clearing. You'll have to admit things had gotten out of hand."

"That's no excuse for butchering everything," the older woman said. "And don't tell me you've been doing it yourself, either. I know very well that's not so."

She knew about Alec, then; Laurel had thought as much. At the same time, her mother-in-law couldn't resist getting in a barb to suggest that Laurel was lazy, though it was one so old and often repeated, it no longer had the power to sting. Sadie had always resented the fact that Laurel had kept Maisie on after her two children were out of diapers. The older woman didn't have household help, and saw no earthly reason Laurel should need any. Of course, she conveniently forgot that she herself had moved away from Ivywild, her husband's old family home—with its huge rooms, hardwood floors that needed constant waxing and polishing, and antiques that collected dust—the minute it was clear he had deserted her and was never coming back.

The place had stood empty for years, until Laurel and Howard married. Mother Bancroft had been ecstatic that Laurel actually wanted to take on responsibility for the old barn of a building, though she naturally maintained a proprietary interest. Since this took the form of inspecting the premises and pointing out any laxity in upkeep with more accuracy than tact, she had never been a particularly welcome guest, even before Howard's death.

"I wouldn't dream of telling you anything," Laurel muttered under her breath as she closed the door.

The other woman swung around. "What was that?"

"I said, would you like anything to drink? Coffee? Juice? Iced tea?"

"I never drink coffee or tea this late in the day, you know that. I don't suppose you have any Perrier?"

"I don't believe so," Laurel said dryly.

"Forget it, then." Mother Bancroft turned and marched into the parlor. She seated herself in an upright chair, crossed her thick ankles, then set her purse in her lap and closed her hands on it as if she thought someone might take it. "I can't stay long," she went on as if Laurel was pressing hospitality on her. "I only came because I feel it's my duty to talk to you about this young man you have doing all this yard work."

"You mean Alec Stanton?"

"Who else would I mean? You don't have other young men hanging around, I hope?"

"No," Laurel said simply. She had thought they'd slide easily into the inevitable discussion, but now she dropped down onto the overstuffed couch and waited to see how Howard's mother meant to handle the subject.

"He's got to go."

That was certainly short and sweet. "I suppose you have a reason?"

"Several of them," the other woman replied in tones of grim condemnation. "To begin with, it can't be good for your reputation to have someone like him making free of the place."

"I don't think you can call it 'making free' when all he does is work."

"He comes and goes as he pleases, riding that outlandish motorcycle like some kind of Hell's Angel. Which is another thing. He's not our kind at all."

"And just what kind is he?" Laurel crossed her arms over her chest as she leaned back against the couch.

"You have to ask, when it's as plain as day? Just look at all that long hair and earrings."

"One earring. A lot of men wear them these days."

Her mother-in-law dismissed that without a pause. "If that's not bad enough, there's that disgusting tattoo he flashes for everybody to see!"

"Yes, and he's from California, too," Laurel said in dulcet and entirely false agreement.

"Exactly! Full of weird ideas of all kinds, I don't doubt. Politics, religion—"

"Sex?" Laurel supplied helpfully. The word, she

knew, was one her mother-in-law always had trouble saying.

Mother Bancroft's indrawn breath was perfectly audible. "What do you know about that? What have the two of you been up to out here? I can just imagine it's nothing good, with you being a widow and him a—I don't know what!"

It had been so long since Laurel had felt the almost-painful anger that threaded through her veins. Voice taut, she said, "A nice-looking young man?"

Disgust squirmed across the other woman's wrinkled features. "He *has* been up to something! I knew it."

"Don't be ridiculous," Laurel said sharply. "Nothing whatever is going on except that I'm reclaiming the front garden and planting it with roses, and Alec is giving me a hand with the heavy work. Well, he's also going to paint the house, but—"

"There! You see?" the other woman exclaimed in triumph. "He's moving in on you. He'll find more and more to do around here until you won't be able to get rid of him. The man's a hustler, Laurel."

"Oh, come on, that's crazy."

"Can't you see it? Are you so naive you can't tell from the way he acts and talks to you?"

"Apparently not. How is it that you know when you haven't even met him?"

Sadie Bancroft breathed heavily through her bulbous nose, kneading her purse with fat, white fingers. "He's got you under his spell, I can tell. This is awful. He'll be climbing into your bed, if he hasn't already. Then he'll start asking for money. He'll take every penny you've got."

"Oh, for crying out loud," Laurel snapped as the heat of indignation rose in her face.

"He will! He's a gigolo, can't you see it? He preys on lonely older women. You may not be as old as some he's taken, but you keep to yourself out here, don't have any friends, so you're fair game. He'll smile and pay you all sorts of compliments, but then he'll screw you unless you get rid of him first."

Laurel was startled her husband's mother would use such a word, though not especially surprised she would think it. She was the kind of woman who kept the tabloid press in business; it was her favorite entertainment next to listening to television preachers and joining right-wing conservative letter-writing campaigns. For all her discomfort with talking about normal sex, she reveled in the salacious and bizarre, loved knowing people's secrets, and positively enjoyed believing the worst about the best of people.

Her voice tight, Laurel retorted, "There's not a word of truth to anything you've said. You just want to be sure I don't change anything here at Ivywild, including myself. You would like to keep me from ever looking at another man."

"Laurel!"

"It's true. I'm supposed to bury myself here because Howard is dead."

"Oh!" Mother Bancroft fell back with a hand to her chest. "How can you say such a thing to me?"

"Because it's the way it is. You think I don't know how you feel? You think I don't realize that you want me shut up here as a punishment for causing Howard's death? I've always known!"

"You're getting hysterical, saying things you don't mean—"

Was she? If so, it felt good. "I'm saying what should have been said a long time ago. You think I killed Howard on purpose and have been telling people so for years. You feel I should have gone to jail, that maybe I still should. Ivywild is a substitute, and you don't care who you hurt so long as you keep me shut up here where I belong."

The older woman came slowly erect. Eyes narrowing, she said, "All right, then, since you brought it up yourself. I know you murdered my Howard. You never were the right wife for him, not from the first. You thought you were better than my son—smarter, sharper—and you even made him believe it. You were always idle, always dreamy-eyed and artistic, reading or playing with that disgusting pottery mud out in the shed. What's more, you were no proper mother to his children. I dread to think what Marcia and Evan will say when they hear what you're up to now."

"And you'll make certain they do." The pain in Laurel's chest was sharp as she thought of her son and daughter hearing the ugly things coming from her mother-in-law's mouth.

"They have a right to know," the woman said, compressing her lips. "But you were never smarter than my Howard. And you're sure not so smart now if you can't see this Alec person for what he is."

"You don't know what you're talking about. You don't know Alec or anything about him."

"Any fool can figure it out. All you have to do is listen to the things his brother is saying all over town."

Alec's brother. Dread for what might be coming

moved along Laurel's nerves, though she refused to let Mother Bancroft see it. "And what is that?"

"Gregory Stanton told Zelda herself, down at the beauty shop, that this Alec of yours lived with an older woman out in San Francisco. Seems he started as her gardener, but wound up a lot more than that before it was over. She even married him, the silly fool. And when she died, she left him all her money."

"No," Laurel whispered. The protest lacked conviction. Howard's sister, Zelda, was always the first to hear everything.

"Yes, indeed. Ask him if you don't believe it. Just you ask him!"

There was gloating triumph in the other woman's face. Laurel turned away from it since she couldn't deny the rumors. How could she, when they had come from Alec's brother, his brother who was dying?

When her mother-in-law had gone, Laurel wandered around the house, too disturbed to think of dinner, unable to settle anywhere. She didn't want to believe what had been said about Alec, yet it made a terrible kind of sense. Why else would he appear out of nowhere to help her? What other reason could he have for slaving so hard? People didn't do something for nothing—that had been one of Howard's maxims. More often than not, it had turned out to be depressingly true.

She thought of Alec's concern for her, and the appreciation she had seen in his eyes. Fake. Why should he feel such things for someone her age? No reason unless it was because he wanted something from her.

Laurel crossed her arms over her chest as she paced. She had almost believed him, almost let him get to her. She felt like such a stupid, sentimental fool.

He was gone, then. History. She would pay him for what he had done so far and send him on his way.

Yet that didn't seem enough somehow. She wanted to pay him back for the ache of betrayal inside her, for making her feel things she didn't want to feel, had never wanted to feel again.

Not that she was in love with him, or anything like that. How could she be? She hardly knew him.

But he had gotten to her. For him, she had taken a small step out of her protective isolation. She had almost been willing to risk a bigger one.

She was so angry. She could feel the rage simmering, circulating through her like a poison in her blood. How long had it been since she had felt that strongly about anything? She had almost forgotten what it was like. In a strange way, it felt good, as if she were really alive.

So much life inside her. Alec had said that. But he had been an old woman's darling, a gigolo.

A gigolo. Was it really possible?

It must be, had to be. There was no other explanation.

She reached up to remove the elasticized cloth band that held her hair, dragging it free of the length and stuffing the band into her jeans pockets. She ran her fingers through the heavy strands as if that would help cool her temper. No, she wasn't going to fire Alec Stanton. That wasn't good enough. It wouldn't help her feelings one iota.

It would be much better if she let him work like a dog, doing all the things Ivywild required, then gave him nothing in return except his hard-earned wages. Let him charm and cajole; it would get him nowhere. Let him waste his time, thinking he had another gasping, panting older woman ready to fall into his arms. Then, when he was done, she would smile politely and send him on his way.

Fall into his arms. God, but what a thought. Was that really what he wanted of her? Maybe she could lead him on, just a little, just enough to…

No. How stupid could she get?

Still, it would make him think he had won, wouldn't it? When she got rid of him later, he might feel as used and as enraged as she felt now.

Could she do it? Did she dare?

Probably not, but it was a fascinating thought. Entirely too fascinating. That should tell her something, but she wasn't sure just what.

As she passed through the dining room, she caught sight of her reflection in the tall windows beyond the heavy mahogany table and chairs. It had grown dark outside without her noticing, turning the window into a mirror. In it, she looked pale and wild with her hair flying around her. Maybe it was a good thing her mother-in-law had come while Alec was not there, after all. If he saw her like this, he would think she was crazy.

Yes, and maybe he would be right. Moving to the window, she put her hand on her reflection, staring into her own glittering eyes. Then she lowered her lashes and bent her neck to let her forehead rest against the cool glass.

She didn't want to feel like this, caught once more in pain and guilt and, yes, despair. She had gotten over all that, had been comfortable, almost, in her numbness.

Of course, she had not felt a great deal before Howard died, either. Hers had been a jailbreak marriage right out of high school; she had needed to get away from home, where her mother drank and screamed at her and her father. The irony was that her parents had died in a car wreck just seven weeks after the wedding.

Howard. Her heart felt heavy as she thought of him. He had loved her with silent, dogged devotion, and she had been grateful. Affection and compassion had kept her with him. Sometimes she had wondered about the grand, death-defying passion she read about in books but didn't think she was capable of feeling.

If she closed her eyes, she could remember the last quarrel with her husband. It had been no great thing, though it had seemed important at the time. Howard had wanted to buy his son a pickup truck, since his own father had bought him one when he was fifteen. He didn't see anything wrong with letting Evan drive up and down the back roads before he had his license. But Laurel had known Evan wouldn't be satisfied with that. He was immature, spoiled by his grandmother who always gave him anything he wanted. Evan would be speeding up and down the main highway before the truck was a week old. He would kill himself, or maybe someone else.

Instead it was Howard who had died. Laurel had killed him, then withdrawn into guilty solitude. The reason, she knew, was not because she had cared so much, but because she hadn't cared enough.

She was so tired. Tears rose, burning like acid as they squeezed from her eyes. She didn't try to stop them.

What the hell was going on?
Alec slammed the lid on a paint can and hammered

it down as he asked himself that question for at least the thousandth time.

He had expected to start over with Laurel, using all sorts of strategies to get her back out of the house. It hadn't been necessary. She had greeted him with a bright smile when he showed up again, given him a list of about a million things to do, and disappeared into a shed at the back of the house. Emerging now and then, she pointed out any errors he had made or problems he needed to solve, then went away again.

She didn't eat her lunch with him on the veranda, but showed up there to check on his progress as if he might not get anything done if she didn't keep after him. She was polite but firm—the lady of the house— but any special courtesy or consideration was gone. She gave orders and expected him to obey. She didn't look at him at all.

Alec had never worked so hard in his life, but he couldn't seem to please her, no matter how he tried. He was tired of it, so tired.

At least the house was nearly painted. He had one more wall to do, then he could clean the sprayer and take down the paper covering the windows. After that, he was going to have a talk with Mrs. Bancroft.

He found her in the shed. The building, standing back behind the garage, dated from the same time period, as it was built from identical lumber. Construction was probably in the late twenties or early thirties, when whichever set of Bancrofts that owned Ivywild at the time had bought their first Model T. Lined with small-paned windows on three sides, floored with unpainted pine boards, it was fairly large.

The front wall supported a woodworking bench that was cluttered with carpenter's tools, which must have belonged to her husband. The back wall was lined with floor-to-ceiling shelves crowded with bags and boxes of supplies. A big black ovenlike kiln occupied one corner. In the center was a potter's wheel, over which Laurel was hovering with her hands deep in swirling clay.

As he appeared in the doorway, Sticks, lying beside her, lifted his massive head from his front legs and began to growl low in his throat. Alec stopped. It was the first time he had seen the dog in several days. Laurel must have been keeping him close again.

She looked up, staring at him as he lounged in the open doorway. Ordinarily, she called the dog off when he arrived. Sticks had learned to tolerate him as long as he was given an early-morning assurance that Alec was acceptable. This time Laurel didn't open her mouth.

Sticks rose to his feet. With his ruff raised, he looked twice his normal size. He padded forward with his neck outstretched, snarling like a crosscut saw.

Alec held his ground. He had no particular fear of the dog, though he didn't want to hurt him again while Laurel watched. Neither did he intend letting himself be mauled to protect her tender sensibilities.

Sticks came on, showing his canines, but easing lower. He stopped a few feet away, half crouching as his growl slowed. Alec held the dog's gaze without moving. The dog growled once more, then looked away. He whimpered and dropped to the ground.

Alec hunkered down and put out his hand, letting the dog lick it. "Good boy," he murmured, leaning to dig his fingers into the thick ruff and shake it before smoothing the fur down. "Good dog."

The clay Laurel was forming collapsed abruptly.

She squashed it onto the wheel with both hands, squeezing the slick, malleable mass with unnecessary force. In a chill voice she asked, "You wanted something?"

There were a lot of answers he could make, but he didn't trust himself to keep them civil. He settled for neutrality. "I didn't know you were a potter."

"There are a lot of things you don't know about me."

"I'm learning." That was too true. "What are you making?"

"A pot."

That told him exactly nothing. He watched her for a long moment, his eyes on the expressive clarity of her face. What he saw there, he was fairly sure, was contempt.

"Okay," he said on a tight breath as he rose to his feet and braced a hand on the doorjamb. "What did I do wrong?"

Her rich blue gaze was steady. "Nothing that I know of. Can you think of anything?"

"I'm sorry I didn't turn the bike around when you asked me. I didn't understand. Now I do, all right?"

Her smile was cool and brief, a meaningless movement of the lips. "Certainly. Don't think of it again."

Fat chance. "I didn't mean to upset you or make you do anything you didn't want."

"You didn't make me do a thing, Alec. I know my own mind."

He should be happy that she had used his name. Instead, it made him feel like the hired help. Which was exactly what he was, he supposed. Voice grim, he said, "If everything is all right, then why did you stop working with me?"

"I had other things I would rather do."

He had no right to complain; that was what galled him. He wanted the right. But if this was the way she preferred it, he could do that, too.

"I've finished the painting. Unless you have other ideas, I'd like to get started on the fountain."

Without looking at him, she said, "I think the big pine next to the fence shades the garden too much for roses. You could cut it. That's if you know how to do it without letting it fall on the house."

She expected him to refuse. He wouldn't give her that satisfaction. "No problem. I'll need to take out the big limbs, then top it, so will have to have climbing gear."

"My husband's belt and spikes are around somewhere."

"He worked in the woods?"

Her hands stilled, buried in the clay she was molding with quick, hard movements. "He was a lineman for the utility company—a good one."

He'd had to ask, he thought with resignation. Changing the subject slightly, he inquired, "If he had the equipment, why didn't he take the tree down?"

"He liked it there." The look she gave him was brief. "You'll have to ask Maisie about a saw. I think her husband keeps one for cutting firewood."

Maisie's old man was a mechanic, kept tools of all kinds, if he remembered right. "I'll check it out. In the meantime, I can start gathering supplies for the fountain. I've run up quite a bill at the hardware already, but I'll need plastic pipe, fittings, and so on. And I should lease a ditchdigger, or contract somebody to do the work."

She squashed the clay flat again. "You're asking if I have the money?"

Her tone set his teeth on edge. In taut control, he replied, "I'm asking if I have the authority to spend it."

"So long as I see a copy of the bills. Otherwise, you needn't concern yourself with my finances."

"What's that supposed to mean?" he demanded, his brows meshing in a frown at her scathing tone.

She looked at him, her gaze steady. "Did I say something that struck a nerve?"

She knew. He didn't know how she knew, but he would bet on it. Jesus. He thought he'd left all that behind him; but no, he was dragging it along like a piece of toilet paper stuck to his shoe. Not that it made any difference. He had beaten the odds before. He could do it again.

"For the record," he said deliberately as he pushed off the door frame and started walking away, "it isn't your money that interests me."

It was the next morning that the opportunity came for Alec to talk to Maisie. Laurel had just gone back into the house after instructing him to prune the paint-spotted leaves on the shrubs around the base of the house. As if he couldn't see for himself that it needed doing. She hadn't said a word about the paint job, either. He didn't expect compliments, exactly, and it annoyed him that he still wanted her approval, but she could have made some comment. For two cents, he would tell her to find herself another man to cut down her pine tree.

"What is it with her?" he asked the white-haired housekeeper in frustration when she brought him a glass of water. "Why is it I can't get the time of day from her?"

A shrewd look came into Maisie's fine old eyes. "She gets like this sometimes, usually when her mama-in-law has been around, or Zelda—that's the sister-in-law, you know."

"They get on her nerves?"

"You could say so. Mostly, they pick at her. Pickiest, most negative people I ever saw. Never a good thing to say about anything or anybody."

Alec turned his water glass in a circle. "You think they've been talking? About me?"

"Wouldn't be surprised. Not that they got a lot of room for it. Zelda Bancroft is no better than she has to be. Never was. But she likes making trouble. The mama-in-law, now, she just has it in for Laurel."

"Because of how Howard died?"

Maisie nodded. "Did her best to have Laurel arrested, called everybody she knew, pulled every string she could get hold of. Didn't do her any good, mainly because of the sheriff. Tanning's always been sweet on Laurel. Said any fool could see she couldn't bring herself to hurt a flea if it was having her for supper."

"She thinks she may have. You know that?"

Maisie nodded. "Have to say I'm amazed she told you, though. She didn't say anything about her kids, did she?"

"Not much."

"Something else she don't talk about—guess it hurts too much. They think she did it, too. Got the idea from that mama-in-law of hers." The housekeeper paused with distant consideration in her eyes. "Well, and maybe from the way Laurel acted at the time. She never said she didn't mean it, you know. Never could say exactly how it came about."

"Rough." The comment didn't seem adequate but was all he could manage.

"You got that right," the older woman said and heaved a gusting sigh. "Strange, but she couldn't make herself leave him while he was alive, still can't leave him now since he's dead."

"You think she wanted to? Leave him, I mean?" He was much too eager for the answer, but he couldn't help it.

"Lot of women would have left. Howard was a moody sort, not what you might call a barrel of laughs. Sort of tormented like, you know? What matters, though, is that he thought she might. That's why he ran out after her that day."

"She tell you that?"

"Lord, boy, she didn't have to. I was there."

He gave her a hard look. "You saw what happened?"

"Saw him take off after her, saw the look on his face. The rest I just heard." She shook her white head. "They'd been arguing, something about their boy Evan and what Howard wanted to do for him, though it ran into all sorts of other things as fights will between husbands and wives, like what Laurel could and couldn't do in the yard. Howard was hollering like a crazy man when he stepped behind that car, telling her he'd do anything if she'd stay. Pitiful, really."

Alec was quiet as he tried to imagine how he would feel if he thought he was losing Laurel. Of course, he had to imagine having her first. Neither one was easy.

He drew a deep breath and let it out. Deliberately, he said, "Laurel wants that big pine over next to the fence, there, taken down. She says you might have a saw."

5

It was Grannie Callie's idea for Alec to take Gregory to Ivywild. Gregory should get out of the house, she said. He needed something else to think about besides himself and the symptoms and progress of his illness. Alec thought his grandmother probably needed to get out for a while, as well, but didn't want to leave Gregory alone.

She had been more than generous about letting his brother and him stay, but she had her own life and routine, which they had interrupted, her own friends she was neglecting while she looked after them. Alec had done everything he could think of to make it easier for her. They couldn't expect her to devote all her waking hours to the invalid.

Not that Gregory was bedridden. He got around well enough, though his energy level was low. He could handle dressing and undressing himself and was able to take his pain medication when it was set out for him. The main problem was seeing that he didn't take too much of it, and that he ate regular meals and got some fresh air and sunshine to keep his spirits up. Another good reason for taking him out on the job.

Gregory seemed to appreciate being out and about. He walked slowly around Laurel's garden, stopping now and then to smell a flower or finger a leaf. He even tried to help a little, picking up a hoe to tackle a patch of nut grass.

Alec watched his brother for a moment to be sure he was all right, then turned back to the ditch he was working on with a shovel. It was for the water line to feed the fountain. The garden space inside the fence was too confined, too filled with plants, for him to bring in the ditchdigger he had rented. Once he had the piping finished to the other side of the fence, he would climb on the digger, but for now he was it, since he had to be sure nothing was torn up that Laurel wanted saved.

In the midst of his concentration, he heard the screen door slam and Laurel scream his name. He whipped around, saw Gregory starting to fall, crumpling like a scarecrow with the stuffing spilling out. Dropping his shovel, he lunged for him in a full, desperate stretch. He barely caught him.

"Up here," Laurel called from the steps. "In the shade on the veranda."

Alec was grateful beyond words for the offer. He should have known better than to let Gregory do anything strenuous, should have watched him more closely. The trouble was, Gregory didn't like being watched over like a kid; definitely didn't like being told what he should and shouldn't do. He was proud and touchy, which was a fine and necessary thing, but still made it hard to decide when it was best to let things ride and when to knock him flat for his own good.

Gregory's moment of weakness lasted only a second. He roused himself in plenty of time to curse Alec for refusing to let him make his own way to the big wicker swing that hung at the rounded oval end of the veranda. Laurel, recognizing correctly that his brother didn't like her seeing him being carried, moved back into the house. She returned with a glass of ice water when Gregory was settled.

For a second, Alec was aware of a flash of jealousy; Laurel had never brought him a glass of water, never looked so concerned for his health. Of course, he had never collapsed in her front yard, either.

Watching Gregory drink the water, studying the haggard paleness of his thin face with its straggly beard, Alec said to him in abrupt decision, "I should have known this was too much. Rest a minute, then I'll take you back home."

"Don't worry about me, little brother," Gregory answered irritably. "I'll be fine right here. You just get on with your job."

"It's my job to worry. It's what I'm here for." Alec kept the words patient, but implacable. "It will only take a few minutes to run you back."

"I said I'm fine. I'll just sit here and watch you flex your muscles. Maybe the nice lady will keep me company."

Alec was afraid she might at that, which was one reason he was determined to get Gregory away. Without looking at Laurel, he said, "Mrs. Bancroft is busy. Come on, now."

"I'm not that busy," she corrected him in clear tones. "I'll be glad to sit down for a little while."

"You don't have to," he said, the words stark as he finally allowed his gaze to move over the cool, lovely planes of her face, the sunbeam sheen of her hair, the long, flowing skirt of lavender cotton she wore with a cool sleeveless blouse.

She gave a brief smile without quite meeting his gaze as she answered, "I know that."

Gregory glanced from one to the other, as if becoming aware of the undercurrents between them. "See?" he said with satisfaction as he waved a hand vaguely toward Alec. "Run along. We don't need you."

Alec felt his stomach muscles tighten as if in anticipation of a blow, but there was nothing he could do. He turned on his heel and went back out into the hot sun.

Laurel, watching Alec go, thought he was upset. He was concerned about his brother, and who could blame him? He was also mad at her for going against him. That was too bad. As Maisie would put it, he could get glad in the same britches. Laurel wanted to talk to Gregory.

Looking around, she caught the arm of a rocking chair and dragged it closer to the swing. As she sat down, she said easily, "It's been so hot and humid these last few days, it could get to anyone who isn't used to it. I really don't know how Alec stands it out there all day."

Gregory glanced at his brother with a brooding look in his eyes. "He's strong as a bull elephant, can stand anything."

"Most of the time he doesn't even wear a shirt."

He looked at her, the expression in his brandy-colored eyes bland. "Sun doesn't affect him quite the same as you and me. He has Native American blood."

When it appeared he was not going to elaborate,

she said, "You mean your father was a Native American?"

"Not mine, just Alec's." His smile was thin, as if he had expected some reaction from her that he had not received. "Actually, I think the guy was a half-breed, though who knows? He didn't stay around long enough for anybody to find out too much about him."

"I see," Laurel said. The main thing she understood was that Gregory was trying to shock her, though she didn't intend to provide amusement for him by allowing it. Features composed, she glanced from him to his brother. She had thought Gregory's illness accounted for his slighter frame and lighter skin coloring, but it appeared she was wrong, at least in part. At the same time, she didn't believe Alec was immune to the sun's effects.

Gregory's gaze was tinged with black humor as he studied her face. "No, we're not much alike, are we, Alec and I? My dad was your typical WASP, some kind of traveling salesman from the West Coast who took our dear mother away from all this." He waved his hand in a vague gesture that took in Hillsboro and the state of Louisiana as well as the woods around them. "Our younger sister Mita, now, was fathered by an Asian. Being your typical sixties and seventies woman, Mom was determined to prove her lack of prejudice. Besides, she liked having her own variety pack of kids, or so she said. She bought into the whole earth-mother, single-parent bit. Didn't care whether the fathers stayed around or not."

"She must be an unusual woman."

His lip curled. "She was in her way. She died trying to have a Latino baby. At least we think that was the nationality, but only she knew for sure. Anyway, something went wrong and neither she nor the baby made it. I guess she was getting a little old for it since I was eighteen at the time.''

"I'm...sorry," Laurel said, not sure whether she meant for his loss or for her urge to pry that had led her into so private a history.

He looked away. "I don't suppose it matters. It was a long time ago."

She thought it did matter—possibly always had, always would—to him and Alec both, but she couldn't say so. Instead she said, "You were young to take on so much responsibility."

"Me? Responsible?" He laughed, a harsh yet hollow sound. "You've got the wrong guy."

"But, well, I assumed there was no other man around to take over."

"There wasn't, except for Alec."

She leaned her head against the high seat-back, rocking a little as she frowned in thought. "But he must have been, what? Only thirteen? Fourteen?"

"Something like that. Our little man, though, he was always big and tough for his age."

"I don't know what you're trying to say." She stopped rocking.

"You wouldn't," he answered with an edge of rudeness as he looked around at Ivywild. "You've always been respectable, I would imagine. I bet you've never been hungry, really hungry, a day in your life. You've always known exactly who you are, where you came from, and where you belong. No doubts, no wild guesses, no looking for yourself in the bottom of a bottle or in the white dust of some drug with a name you can't pronounce...."

He trailed off, but she did finally understand. Gregory had been a drug user at eighteen, and so Alec had taken over, fending for himself and his little sister.

"Surely some government agency could have helped out?" she asked.

"Oh, right. Helped Alec and Mita right into separate foster homes, is what they would have done. No way, not on your life. Alec fooled them when they came around. He may be a bastard, but he's a smart one. Of course, he had old lady Chadwick by then."

A chill moved over Laurel. In her compassion for Alec—for them all, really—she had almost forgotten the point of her questions. Lips stiff, she said, "Old lady Chadwick? Who was she?"

"Our landlady, after Alec moved us all out of the slum apartment where we'd been staying." Gregory grimaced. "She owned this big estate—swimming pool, tennis courts, golfing green, guesthouse, groundskeeper's cottage, the whole nine yards, complete with a chauffeur and even a Chinese gardener."

"Mr. Wu," she said in quiet discovery.

"Alec mentioned him, huh? Figures. The old guy was his idol, lived down the street from our apartment on the edge of Chinatown before we moved—preferred it to living on the estate. I think he admired Alec's gumption. Anyway, Mr. Wu used to pay him a little something for helping out at the old lady's house after school, whenever Alec could thumb a ride to get there."

Laurel, watching Alec's stiff movements as he wielded his shovel, thought he knew they were talking about him even if he couldn't make out the words. She couldn't help that. Sunlight moved back and forth along the filaments of his hair that were as dark and gleaming as the feathers on a raven's wing. Indian black and shiny. It made sense.

Aware, suddenly, that Gregory was looking at her with a malicious grin for her preoccupation with his brother, she collected her scattered thoughts. As if the question had her entire concentration, she asked, "Mr. Wu wasn't, by any chance, related to Mita?"

"Her father, you mean? Lord, no. I mean he was ancient, white hair and beard down to here." He leveled a hand near his navel. "He did have a soft spot for her, though, and I wondered once or twice about his eldest son. Anyway, after Mom died Alec had the nerve to ask old lady Chadwick if we could stay in the groundskeeper's cottage at the back of the property since Mr. Wu wasn't using it."

"You moved to avoid the child welfare authorities," she said, clarifying the situation in her own mind.

He gave a nod. "Alec said nobody would think to bother us there. Turned out he was right. Of course, he only told the old lady that Mom was sick in the hospital. She believed him for three months or more—time enough."

Laurel didn't even try to disguise her sharpened curiosity. "Time enough for what?"

"To win her over. Our Alec has a way about him, or haven't you noticed?" He watched her, a faint smile playing over his thin features and a suggestive look in his eyes.

"I thought you said he was thirteen?"

"He was."

"This woman, then..."

"She seemed old at the time," he said whimsically,

"though I don't imagine she was more than, oh, about your age now."

Old enough to be Alec's mother, almost thirty years older than he had been then. Laurel scowled. The Chadwick woman couldn't be the one he had married. Could she?

"You've heard the story already, haven't you?" Gregory guessed. "That's not like Alec. He's usually too embarrassed to talk about it."

She gave him a straight look. "But you aren't?"

He shook his head. "No, but I've got no manners and no shame, you know. Mrs. Chadwick never had much time for me even when I was around, which wasn't often. Mita, now, she treated her like a doll, dressing her up, showing her off. But Alec was her darling."

"You make it sound as if there was something wrong with that." She couldn't quite put the thought in plain words.

"I do, don't I? And there was, in a way. He isn't perfect any more than I am. He makes mistakes. And like me, he pays for them. With interest."

She heard the bitterness lining his words. Still, her preoccupation with Alec's life story was too intense to spare his feelings more than a glancing thought. "What exactly was his mistake?"

"He said yes when our landlady asked him to marry her."

So it was true. More than that, it was worse than she had thought. A woman old enough to be his mother. Dear heaven.

She hadn't believed it; she recognized that, as she felt the sick acceptance move over her. Somehow, she had thought talking to Gregory Stanton would prove

Mother Bancroft had lied, or else that she had embellished some less damaging story to suit herself.

Wrong. All wrong.

"I suppose," Laurel said quietly, "that we all make our mistakes."

"Some more than others," Gregory said on a huffing sigh.

She wanted to be absolutely fair. With great care, she said, "Alec doesn't seem to have benefited a great deal from this odd marriage."

"Depends on how you look at it. He became an engineer thanks to Chadwick money. Mita was able to zip through eight years of training for her Ph.D., and is interning now in pediatrics. Me, well, I didn't have to worry about eating or a place to sleep for ages, only about supporting my habit."

"You lived on him." She spoke before she thought, then wished immediately she hadn't.

"Yeah," he answered, looking away. "I lived on him."

That explained a lot—not that it was any of her business. "But I have to say it doesn't sound like very much return in exchange for his freedom, especially considering the size of the estate you mentioned."

He shrugged. "There were a few problems with the old lady's heirs after she died, though Alec still took care of everybody. Now—" Gregory stopped.

Now Alec was still taking care of him, she finished silently for him, because Gregory was dying in slow stages. "You resent him for it," Laurel said in sudden comprehension. "You would rather he had taken the money and used it for himself. You'd rather he wasn't here with you."

"Nobody asked him to be so almighty noble,"

Gregory said with a tight snarl. "I don't need him to look after me. I don't need him for anything."

Oh, but he did, Laurel saw, and his bitterness was in direct proportion to his need. Did Alec realize that? Yes, he must, since Gregory made no effort to hide it. Regardless, Alec stayed with him. He was lending his brother his strength because he had more than enough to spare. He was helping him live because he was so alive himself.

She didn't want to think like that, didn't want to feel any sympathy or admiration for Alec. It wouldn't make it any easier for her to do what she must.

But do it she would. She was no gullible older woman ready to fall for hard brown muscles and practiced charm. Already, she could see how it could happen. To become dependent on him, to look to him for strength and comfort, to learn to watch for his smile and teasing comments, would be fatally easy. Because he was so vital, yes, and she longed for some of that living warmth to ease the coldness inside her. In some strange way she didn't quite understand, she needed desperately to touch the passionate enjoyment of being on this earth that she could sense burning inside him.

Impossible. She didn't know how much longer she could stay aloof from him and still have him around. Such a short time, so few days, they had worked together on the garden, yet she missed talking to him, missed the stimulation of his constant nearness. There was no pleasure in setting him at a distance, giving him orders and watching him work until his jeans were so wet with sweat that they dripped as he walked. In fact, it made her feel vindictive and ashamed.

In the silence that had fallen, Gregory said wearily, "I think maybe it's time I went home, after all. I'm so...tired. I guess you should tell Alec."

"Home being your grandmother's, not California?" Laurel asked, unwilling to summon the man in the garden again so soon after sending him away.

Gregory's glance was bleak. "The three or four visits to Grannie Callie's house were the best times I ever had as a kid. Mom used to come back home to Louisiana when she was down on her luck, usually when she had a new baby. One time she left all of us with Grannie Callie for a whole long summer. Too bad she ever found her way back again."

"You don't mean that."

"You don't think so?" The corner of his mouth curled. "I'd have been a redneck Southerner, driving around in a pickup truck and pitching beer cans into the back, instead of a washed-out druggie on his last legs. And Alec would be—" He stopped, dragged air deep into his lungs. "Call him for me, will you, if you don't mind?"

He wanted her to do this little chore for him. Why? So he need not look as if he were backing down, so it would seem like her idea? Or did he think that Alec might not like having to answer to her in front of him? Was it one more snide dig at his brother?

Rising, she walked to the railing. Lifting her voice in clear appeal, she called, "Alec?"

At the first sound of her voice, he looked up from the ditch he was digging, his dark eyes flashing like obsidian caught by the sun. He lifted a brow in inquiry.

"I believe your brother would appreciate it if you could take him home now."

He met her gaze for a long moment before he gave a slow nod. It might have been no more than an acknowledgment, but it felt like an instant of intense communication. The two of them, she thought, understood each other very well. Possibly too well.

She heard Gregory's curse from behind her, but she didn't care.

It was later, after Alec had returned from seeing his brother home, when she noticed the low rumble of thunder. She looked up from the catalog in front of her where she was reading about Monsieur Tillier, an old-fashioned red tea rose she thought she might like to order for her garden. The rumble came again— closer now, and louder, as if it meant business. From the corner of her eye, she caught the flicker of lightning through the lace curtains over the windows. She counted only to five before thunder rolled again. The lightning strike was close, at least according to country wisdom.

Was Alec still working in the front garden? Maybe he should take shelter on the veranda. Or he could step into the safety of the garage if he was in the side yard.

She might have to let him in the house if the wind got too high. He would get wet on the veranda since the rain sometimes swept in under the overhanging roof, wetting the floor all the way to the inner wall. The garage, of course, was tight enough and perfectly safe, if he only had the sense to head in that direction.

On the other hand, being brought up in California he might not realize what a late-spring storm could be like in Louisiana. It was possible he didn't know how quickly it could blow up, or how strong it could become. She hesitated, flipping her pen between her fingers in a nervous gesture, as she considered checking on him.

He was a grown man, for pity's sake; surely he could take care of himself! He didn't need her to baby him. Or did he?

Wasn't that what some younger men were supposed to want when they sought out an older woman? He could be a classic case since he had lost his mother while still young, and had been forced to nurture others instead of being nurtured himself.

Yes. And just maybe she was attracted to him as a substitute for the son and daughter Mother Bancroft had virtually taken away—or some such psychological claptrap. It made about as much sense, didn't it?

She could hear the first drops of rain rattling in the hard glossy leaves of the magnolia outside her window. Pushing back her chair in sudden decision, she walked quickly toward the front door.

Alec wasn't in the front garden. She stood for an instant, absorbing the moist coolness of the rain, listening to its patter on the roof and breathing in the wet-earth smell of it. The wind lifted her hair and swirled under her skirt, cooling her in places she hadn't even known were warm. Then, in the distance, she heard the hissing advance of a stronger downpour as it marched over the woods toward the house. Glancing toward the sound, she saw the heavy, dragging curtain of dense rain.

She swung toward the steps, hastening down them, ducking her head against the rain splattering from the roof. Turning right at the bottom, she followed the curving steps around to the side yard. At the gate, she leaned to stare into the garage.

It was empty. Alec wasn't there.

She swung back the way she had come, taking the path to the other side of the house. There was no gate here to block the brick walkway that rounded the curving end of the veranda and continued to the back. As the rain increased, she started to run.

Then she saw him. She stopped dead still.

He was sitting on top of the cistern, balanced on its concrete cap with his feet folded and hands resting on his bent knees in what she recognized vaguely as the lotus position. His fingers were lightly cupped, his eyes closed, his face perfectly still and upturned to the rain.

It beat down on him, wetting his hair, beading on his shoulders, then running in rivulets over his bare chest and the flat surface of his abdomen. It glistened, sheeting his muscles and the corded veins of his body, washing over him as naturally as if he were no more than a fence post or a tree. It was cool now, especially with the wind, but he seemed not to feel the chill. His skin shone, smooth and golden brown, without the goose bumps that beaded her own flesh.

Peace. Pleasure. Passionate joy. These radiated from him in waves, reaching out to her as if to draw her nearer. She took a step. Another.

Abruptly, he opened his eyes. And the emotions she felt coming from him increased a hundredfold. They were frightening in their intensity as he held her gaze. But most frightening of all was how much she wanted to respond, how deep her need was to go to him and join him in his rain bath. In his warmth and peace. In his burning passion for life.

She forgot to breathe as she hovered there. Then she remembered with a soft gasp. Sanity returned along with the air in her lungs. She whirled with her wet skirt swinging around her calves, spraying water. Ducking her head against the rain, she ran for the safety of the house.

6

Laurel studied the bowl she had taken from the kiln. It was as large as she could make it, yet fairly shallow like a birdbath. She had bisque-fired it on the outside first, then glazed it with ripple shadings of a pellucid blue-green on the inside. She was proud of the way it had turned out. It was actually one of the best things she had done since she had begun to concentrate on her pottery in the years after Howard died.

He had never liked her "messing around with pots," as he called it. He seemed jealous of the time she spent at it, though she tried to stay out of the shed except when he was at work. He also claimed the clay dried her hands, making them rough and forcing her to keep her fingernails too short. Mainly, he was embarrassed by her artistic leanings. It wasn't the kind of thing women around Hillsboro did in their spare time. Gardening was all right so long as it was something practical like growing vegetables; at least he could understand such a traditional female pastime. He could have accepted her taking up embroidery or crochet or even painting. But what, he asked, did she get out of pots?

She could never provide an answer that satisfied him. She just liked forming things from the smooth, sensuous clay, enjoyed watching them come to life under her hands, loved the moment when she opened the kiln and could see how the colors and designs she had applied with metallic oxides were transformed by the firing. Making pots left her feeling confident and creative, and somehow well-formed within herself.

The shed was also her retreat, though she hadn't been able to explain that need, either. Howard would have considered it a silly affectation; yet he'd been one of the most withdrawn people she had ever seen. He had seldom gone anywhere except to work during their marriage; had had no use for leisure-time activities or socializing. He'd been such a stay-at-home that Laurel sometimes thought he had used Ivywild as his sanctuary. As she did, now.

This week, she was using the shed mainly to stay away from Alec. From its windows, she could sometimes catch a glimpse of him as he rode the ditchdigger or laid pipe. She could monitor his progress with the fountain as she moved back and forth between the shed and the house. In a way, she could be a part of what he was doing while remaining hidden.

At least she was working again with her pottery after several days away from it. Smiling a little, she ran her fingers along the inside of her bowl, which was still warm from the kiln, delighting in the silky-smooth slide of the glazing. She had intended to plant the piece with succulents and put it beside the back door, but it would really be a shame to hide the gorgeous color with potting soil. She would leave it on the cooling table while she considered what other use she might find for it. Something would come to her; it always did.

Turning back to her workbench, she looked at the three-foot oval of clay she had prepared earlier. Next to it was propped a page from an artifact catalog showing a plaque inspired by the *Bocca della Verità,* or "mouth of truth." Taken from the original in the Santa Maria in Cosmedin church in Rome, it showed the gargoyle-like face of a man with his mouth open and tongue exposed, and with hair and a beard formed of stylized leaves. According to legend, the mouth of the Italian original would snap closed on the hand of anyone who told a lie while touching the tongue. The illustration also resembled the traditional Green Man of Europe, the sculpted face signifying the more lusty aspects of Beltane, or Midsummer's Eve, the night of the summer solstice when the ancients celebrated the fecundity of nature.

The face and the idea behind it intrigued Laurel—had from the moment she'd first seen it. Just as fascinating, however, was the notion of sculpting one in clay. Rather than send off for a Green Man from the catalog, she was in the process of making her own.

Placing her hands on the clay, she began to pinch and form it. She wasn't copying the catalog picture, but rather using it as a guide for general size and proportion. It was such a pleasure, watching the face form under the strong push of her thumbs. She dipped her fingers in water, stroking, pulling, forming the nose and brows in relief. Reaching for a trimming tool and scalpel in turn, she carved the curves and grooves of graceful leaves.

Time lost its meaning as she worked to refine and perfect her clay man's features, adding texture, creating contrast. She was oblivious to Sticks lying at her feet, the hungry growl of her stomach, or the increasing heat inside the shed as the day advanced. She was content, as happy as she had been in years, perhaps in her whole life, with the exception of when her children were small.

Maisie brought her a snack in the middle of the afternoon, grumbling with every step because Laurel had missed lunch. Laurel thanked her absently and ate a piece of cheese, then followed it with a couple of bites of apple while she studied her plaque. After a moment, she put her apple down to adjust a curve. When she glanced up again, Maisie was gone and the apple was covered with sugar ants.

It was some time later when a shadow moved at the doorway. Sticks looked up, but only thumped his tail and put his head back on his paws. Alec. It could be no one else.

She looked at him over her shoulder as he stepped inside. A faint smile touched his mouth as he saw her, saw what she was doing. The gladness of it held a vivid reminder of the afternoon of the rainstorm— one that made her uneasy.

She returned her gaze to the slab of sculpted clay in front of her. Shock moved over her. Her fingers curled around the trimming tool she still held, gripping it tightly.

The face of the Green Man she had rendered so painstakingly in soft, malleable clay bore a striking resemblance to Alec. It was his wide forehead, his thick brows and high cheekbones that she had depicted there, his hair that flowed in loose curves to mingle with vines and leaves. His pleasure and glowing yet quiescent life was carved into the clay just as she had seen them when he looked at her through the falling rain. But there was also something of him that she had taken from that first night, when he had appeared from out of the tangled growth of her front garden. It was an impression of latent danger along with a warm satyr's smile on the slightly parted lips, a promise of rare and forbidden delights.

Laurel put down the tool she held and dipped her hands in water before reaching for a towel. With elaborate unconcern, she dried her hands, then dropped the towel over the sculpture. Only then did she turn toward him.

"You're through for the day?" she said, lightly. "I hadn't realized it was so late."

He inclined his head. "I had something I wanted to show you. If you can find a stopping place."

"Yes, of course." Relief at having an excuse to get him away from the shed and her sculpture made her more cordial than she had been in several days.

Instead of swinging to leave as she moved toward him, he stepped farther into the open building. "What's this?"

She stiffened for an instant, then saw that he was talking about the bowl she had taken from the kiln earlier. Moving to block his view of the workbench, she picked up the bowl and handed it to him as she explained.

"You really made this?" he asked, tilting the bowl to the light, then slanting her a look of surprised appreciation.

"With my very own two hands." The words were stiff.

"Fantastic," he murmured with a shake of his head.

Gratification as foolish as it was impossible to resist spread through her. "It was just an experiment with color."

"Reminds me of the bottom of the sea," he said.

"Ripples in the sand with the sun sparkling through the water."

That was exactly what it looked like, she saw, though the most amazing thing about the description was his total lack of self-consciousness as he gave it. In any case, she refused to take credit. "An accident. I just liked the design."

"Some of the best things happen that way."

"You have an interest in pottery?" The astonishment in her voice, she realized, might not be as flattering as that he had shown her.

He shrugged. "I've tried my hand at a few pieces. Mostly big things—urns, basins, columns."

"Mr. Wu taught you, I suppose."

"You got it." His wry grin tipped one corner of his mouth. "The old guy liked arbors and small pools and so on. He called them a garden's bones. Not much he found in garden centers or supply houses suited him, or else the prices were off-the-wall—you should have heard what he had to say about that, most of it in Chinese. He imported a piece or two from Europe or Asia, but mostly he built his own."

"An amazing man."

"Yeah," he said, his lashes coming down over his expression like defense shields. After an instant, he said, "I have an idea for your bowl."

"What?"

"I'd rather show you when it's done. If you don't like it, all you have to do is say so."

She gave him a dubious look, but his features revealed nothing. "You won't put a hole in it?"

"Wouldn't think of it."

The firmness of his voice was reassuring. His instincts had been excellent so far. Besides, she was curious to see what he would do. "Fine," she answered, then added briskly, "Now, about whatever it was you wanted to show me?"

His face changed at her tone, and he set the bowl down. "Yes, ma'am," he said in a credible Southern drawl as he swept a hand toward the door. "This way, ma'am."

Moving ahead of him, she discovered she didn't mind his mockery. In a peculiar way, she even appreciated it. Yet she could also see that it might be only a step from mockery to familiarity, and that could well be a step too close.

She heard it before she saw it—the thing he wanted her to see. She flashed him a look and saw the corroboration in his eyes. She increased her pace, almost running toward the gate in the side fence. She skimmed through, rounded the oval end of the house.

There it was. Her fountain, glittering in the slanting light of late afternoon as it sprang from its graceful fountainhead. It arched, leaping in liquid grace, dancing with the sunbeams and catching rainbow fire before splattering back down into the square brick pool Alec had built to catch it. Its water music warbled on the air, a sweet and natural sound. Clean, pure, endlessly flowing, captured yet free, the fountain held the spirit of the creek in its heart. It was everything she had wanted, yet so much more than she'd expected that fullness strained her chest. She could not stop smiling, smiling.

Alec, coming to stand at Laurel's side, watched the blaze of joy rising in her face. The backbreaking labor of the last few days fell away from him as if it had never been. He had his reward. If she never spoke a word of gratitude, he would still recall this moment and feel it was all worthwhile.

Then she turned to him, her smile so brilliant, her face so clear and candid that he felt his heart jar in his chest. No conscious decision moved him, no rational cause and effect. It was instinct alone that made him step forward with his arms open.

She stepped into them—he would always remember that—swaying against him as he pulled her close. Holding his breath, he fitted the slender and resilient softness of her body to the hardness of his own, matching curves and concaves as if they were a paired set meant to be brought together. He closed his eyes as he absorbed the feel of her, took the essence of her into the core of his being, savored the sense of completion. Then he inhaled slow and deep, letting the sweet yet sensuous scents of roses and jasmine and warm woman rise to his brain until he felt lightheaded.

Yes, and feverish. Desperate for more.

He had only thought her smile was reward enough.

Patience, patience. He mustn't push it. He had to release her, should do it now. Ought to step back if he could only make himself move. Hide the pounding of the blood in his veins. Say something, anything, to release the tension that was bound to spring between them the minute she realized what he had done, and how she had reacted.

God, but he wanted her. Wanted her smiling, always. Willing. Trusting. In his arms.

Was it so much to ask?

A small, inarticulate cry of protest sounded in her throat. He was released from the tight grip of the spell she had cast over him. His face smooth, he set her away from him. He lifted a brow, grinning as he said, "Got any more waterworks projects you want done?"

The blue of her eyes was almost indigo. The soft denim of the work shirt she wore vibrated minutely with the throbbing of her heart. She was shatteringly close to tears. Or maybe it was rage; he couldn't tell. And he didn't really want to know because he wasn't sure he could handle either one.

Her indrawn breath was perfectly audible in the late-afternoon stillness. Voice husky, she said, "This one is more than enough. It's glorious. Exactly as I saw it in my mind, though I don't know how you knew."

He thought of all the things she knew about him, the things Gregory had taken such pains to let him know he had told her. He couldn't explain them because she hadn't asked, and volunteering would mean he thought she cared. Or that he had any right to expect her to believe him.

Yet with so much against him, she had been generous and forgiving, and honest enough not to blame him for her own impulses. Or condemn him for taking unfair advantage of her moment of gratitude.

She was grateful. That was all.

Standing there, then, he accepted what he had known all along—Laurel Bancroft was a class act. She was also something more. She was beautiful and self-contained and special beyond anything he had ever imagined. And not for him. Never for him.

He swallowed the knowledge, accepting its bitterness. Then he nodded, a stiff-necked gesture. In quiet tones, he said exactly what he meant, regardless of its inanity. "I'm glad you like it."

"I love it," she said with the same soft certainty.

He began to back away. He had to, before he did something, said something incredibly stupid. His chest hurt. The muscles in his body seemed leaden in their weight.

"I'll see you in the morning, then."

"Monday," she corrected, the word offhand, as if her thoughts were elsewhere. "Today's Friday."

"Right. Monday, then."

Turning quickly, he made the bike in a few long strides and climbed on board. He was out of there as if he had a stick of dynamite tied to his tail.

The following morning, Laurel set the Green Man plaque in the kiln to be fired. That evening, she turned off the heat and let it cool overnight. She had intended to destroy it, obliterating her folly by compacting the clay into a nice, formless ball again. She couldn't do it. It might be ridiculous and superstitious, but it had seemed too much like destroying Alec.

The plaque came through the firing amazingly well, considering how long it had been since she had worked with clay sculpture and her inexperience at it. There were no cracks, no fallen edges. Looking at it with a critical eye the next day, she saw a few places that could have been rendered more perfectly, but she was satisfied with it.

Actually, it had the quality considered by most potters and sculptors as an indication of good work, she thought as she smoothed the strong jawline of the face with her fingertips. It made her want to touch it. She had caught the slashing indentation of Alec's cheek, which appeared when he smiled, and the fanlike crinkling of the skin at the corners of his eyes. Yes, and the sensuous curves of his mouth were not only well molded, but felt almost real, as if they might warm to life, move against her own if she...

She jerked her hand away, curling her fingers into a fist. After a moment, she forced herself to reach for the large, flat box that she had set aside. Placing the plaque inside, she carried the box over to the rough shelving that ran along one end of the shed and pushed it onto the highest plank. She shoved it as far back as it would go, well out of sight. Turning away, she left the shed and closed the door behind her.

It wasn't so easy to shut away the memory of Friday afternoon. If she closed her eyes, she could still feel Alec's arms around her, feel the disturbing moment when she had pressed against the hard warmth of his body. It had been like standing at the center of a lightning strike, caught in the flare of white-hot heat, blinding light, and searing power. Nothing had prepared her for that conflagration, or for the rush of need that poured through her in response. She had been stunned, held immobile by feelings so long repressed she had forgotten they existed. If she had ever known them.

She wasn't sure she had. Even in the days when she was first married, when loving was so strange and new, she had not felt so fervid or so uncertain of her own responses, her own will.

If a hug carried so much force, what would a kiss be like? And if a kiss was even more intense, how would it be possible to survive the overwhelming power of...

No. She wouldn't think about it. She would forget she had ever touched Alec Stanton. And she would pray to high heaven that he did the same.

It was later that afternoon when Marcia and Evan

came to see her. Sticks bounded out to meet them, dancing and wriggling in his joy. He had been a Christmas gift for them as a puppy when Marcia was ten and Evan only eight, so he had shared their childhood and adolescence. It was Laurel, however, who had fed him, brushed him, taken him for long walks in the woods behind the house, so he had become her dog.

She was as delighted to see her children as Sticks was, maybe even more so. Meeting them on the steps, she enveloped them in warm hugs. They looked more like Howard than they did her, with the same sandy hair and hazel eyes he had inherited from his mother. Evan had Howard's stocky build, though Marcia's body shape was like Laurel's. Her daughter was too slender, too pale and fragile, Laurel thought, but then she herself had little room to find fault.

Marcia didn't look happy. Laurel would have liked to ask her what was wrong, and would have if she had not been well aware of how useless it would be.

As she led the way toward the kitchen, the natural place to relax and talk, it occurred to her that there had been something even more awkward than usual in their greetings. She tried to dismiss it as normal. It had been, what, at least three weeks since she had seen either of them?

They were so busy these days—Evan with spring courses at college and his fraternity friends, Marcia working in a lawyer's office and taking care of her house and husband. Laurel called when she thought she could catch them, which wasn't often. It wasn't unusual for there to be less-than-perfect ease between them; they hadn't been really close or free with each other since their father died.

Excuses. She was making excuses for them. She knew, but didn't want to face it.

Marcia's first words when they were seated around the table made the situation unblinkingly clear. "I see Meemaw was right," her daughter said in accusation. "You've been tearing the place apart."

"I thought I was taking care of it, doing some of the things that have been needed for a long time." The painful awareness that Marcia and Evan were there only because their grandmother had been talking to them made her voice low and compressed.

"It was necessary to have a fountain?"

She watched them for a long moment, her gaze level. Evan looked away, but Marcia returned the scrutiny with set features. Laurel answered quietly, "No, the fountain was just something I wanted."

"But why in the world would you—"

"Call it a whim," Laurel said shortly. The carping tone of her daughter's voice was beginning to wear on her nerves.

"I'd call it expensive," Marcia stated, her pale face pinched with disapproval. "Where is all the money coming from to pay for housepainting and brick and pipe, not to mention the labor?"

Laurel tilted her head. "Which of it bothers you the most, honey? The expense or the man I'm paying to do the work?"

"Meemaw said you wouldn't be reasonable about it, and I didn't believe her!" Splotchy color spread over her daughter's face and neck, making her look almost ill.

"Tell me why I should be reasonable. I can't believe you're complaining because I decided to clear the front garden—which never should have been allowed to grow up in the first place. Or that you can have any possible objection to the fact that I had the house painted to keep it from rotting down around my ears."

Evan cleared his throat, giving his sister a quelling look. "Nobody is objecting to a little clearing and painting, Mother."

The too-reasonable tone of his voice, so close to patronization, too much like the one Howard had used when he thought she was getting angry, set Laurel's teeth on edge. Because of it, she refused to give them any help with this absurd discussion. "Then what is the problem?"

Evan hunched his shoulders, not quite meeting her eyes as he sat forward at the kitchen table. "Mee-maw's a little upset about the whole thing. She hates to see anything changed here, you know. She's saying that if you can afford all this renovation, then you can afford to pay my college expenses."

"Yes, of course," Laurel said promptly. "You know I would have been glad to do it if she hadn't insisted on taking over."

"I know, but it's not just the tuition. There're dorm fees and car expenses and walking-around money. She was going to buy me a new Mazda before all this came up. Now, well…" He shrugged.

Howard's mother was leaning on Evan, using the generous allowance she gave him and the promise of a new car to persuade him to intervene with Laurel. The sickening part of it was that her son had given in to the pressure.

No, she mustn't think like that. Evan was torn between the two of them, as he and Marcia had been since their father died. On the day of the funeral,

Mother Bancroft had taken Marcia and Evan home with her. She had said it was for Laurel's sake, to give her time to adjust without the loud comings and goings of a pair of teenagers. Laurel had been too confused and upset to argue; she had only just managed to endure the interment. Still, she had wanted her children near, to be able to hold them and have them hold her, to take away the pain and horror they were all keeping inside. But they had been hustled away, and it was weeks before she saw them again. When she did, they had looked at her with accusing eyes. Never again had they acted or felt like the son and daughter she had borne, the children she had loved before the accident.

"I had a little money from my parents," she said, "and it's cost me very little to live these past few years. The insurance money from—that came to me after your father's death is still in the bank. I can take up your expenses where Mother Bancroft leaves off, then, Evan. I might even be able to buy you that car. But just tell me one thing. Do you really think your grandmother will penalize you for what she considers to be my faults?"

"I don't know," he muttered.

"Neither do I," she said, "but I wouldn't like to think so."

Marcia said, "There's something else going on here that we need to talk about, Mother. It's downright shameful for you to keep that Stanton boy hanging around."

The prissiness of her daughter's tone was almost funny, but Laurel easily refrained from laughing. "That Stanton *boy*, as you call him, is quite a few years older than you are."

"Well—well, he's younger than you are, by a long shot!"

"So? He's not just hanging around, you know. He's working for me, and extremely hard, I might add. Which you would notice if you took your mind out of the gutter long enough to look around you."

"Yes, I can see he must be handy to have around. In more ways than one, I'll just bet."

"Marcia!"

"What, Mother? Don't you know how it looks? Do you have any idea what people are saying? I'm so embarrassed, and Jimmy is absolutely mortified. He has prayed on his knees every night this week that you will give up this wicked connection and find redemption in the Lord. He even got up in church on Wednesday and asked the congregation to join him in beseeching God on your behalf—"

"He what!" Laurel's head came up in shocked anger.

Marcia blinked rapidly. "Well, what did you expect? Did you imagine we would just ignore what's been going on? That you could do as you please and no one would say a word?"

"I thought," Laurel said distinctly, "that my children would have some consideration for me. At the very least, I think someone should have asked whether I'm sleeping with a man before you start praying in public that I'll stop!"

A defensive light appeared in her daughter's eyes. "It was Jimmy, not me. You know how he is."

She did know. Her daughter's husband, the eldest son of a family that belonged to one of the more conservative nondenominational churches, considered himself a deeply religious man. He didn't approve of his wife's mother because she didn't attend church anymore. To Laurel, he seemed an outright fanatic. But then, no one had asked her opinion before Marcia had married him two years ago.

"Jimmy could hardly have known about the situation here unless you told him," Laurel said. "He has no reason to think Alec is doing anything more than maintenance work, and wouldn't if you—or someone—hadn't suggested otherwise."

Marcia gave a sharp laugh. "Then he *is* doing something more!"

"I didn't say that."

"But he is, isn't he? You might as well admit it."

Laurel stared at her daughter, sick to the heart that it had come to this, yet unable to see how it could have been avoided. Her voice even, she said, "If you have to ask, then you don't deserve an answer."

"That's convenient, isn't it? Especially if you'd rather not lie about it. And you never lie, do you, Mother? Never, ever."

"Marcia, don't." It was Evan who spoke, cutting across his sister's sarcastic remark. But he wouldn't look Laurel in the face.

The suggestion in Marcia's words was that Laurel had lied on the afternoon their father had died. Laurel had known they thought she had, but it had never been made quite so plain before.

Crossing her arms over her chest in a protective gesture, she lifted her chin. Staring from Evan to Marcia, she said, "Think what you please, it makes no difference to me. But you might remember this. I am a widow and responsible to no one. Whatever I do is really none of your business."

As Marcia opened her mouth, Evan made a quick

sign to prevent her from answering. His hazel eyes earnest, he said, "Give us credit for a little consideration, Mom, can't you? We care about you, we really do. But you can't expect us to sit back and do nothing when your safety's at stake."

"My safety." The words were flat.

"We know what this guy is, what he's after. Besides, I made a point of checking him out, and he doesn't look like the kind of man you want to mess around with, even if it wasn't for the rest of it."

Distaste for his choice of words colored Laurel's tone as she said, "The rest of what?"

"I don't mean to sound ugly, Mom, but let's face it. His kind preys on lonely older women like you."

She didn't know whether to be outraged or amused. "Really, Evan, I don't have one foot in the grave, and I think I just might have sense enough to recognize when someone is trying to use me. Believe me when I say that Alec Stanton has never by word or deed tried to get money from me, nor has he said or done anything that would lead me to think he might try." It was, she discovered, the exact truth. Which was amazing when she thought about it.

"No, I expect not. He's too smart for that."

"And what is that supposed to mean?"

"He'll wait on that until after you're married," Evan answered in hard tones.

Laurel flung up her hands. "Now you've got me married to him! Well, that ought to make Jimmy happy, at least. He can stop bending God's ear about me living in sin!"

"Or maybe," Evan went on with grim persistence, "this Stanton guy will wait until you're dead."

Laurel's irritation became cold anger. "That's it,"

she retorted. "I've had it up to here with this slander about someone who has never done anything to either of you, someone you don't know from Adam."

"Mom," Evan said, "if you'll just listen…"

"I've heard all I want to hear, thank you very much. What makes you think you can come here and meddle—"

"Meddle?" Marcia laughed. "Well, you can be sure we won't do it again. Come on, Evan."

"Shut up, Marcia," Evan said without looking at his sister. "Mom, Alec Stanton's first wife, an older woman just like you, died out in California."

"I know that, and for your information, she was much older, nearly—"

"Did you know he was arrested for her murder?"

Laurel felt the blood drain from her face. She was suddenly cold, chilled to the heart. A shudder rippled over her, leaving goose bumps in its wake. "No," she whispered.

"I thought not," Evan said in satisfaction.

"No," Laurel said again, but not in response to his smug comment. It was denial, pure and simple. She didn't want Alec to be a murderer. She couldn't stand for it to be true.

7

Alec didn't make it to work on Monday morning, after all. Gregory took a bad turn Sunday night and had to go to the emergency room of the local hospital. They admitted him for observation. When Grannie Callie left Gregory's room in the early-morning hours to go home and get a little rest, Alec asked her to call Laurel and explain. Then he spent the rest of the day with Gregory while they ran him through every exhausting test in the book.

The basic diagnosis was never in doubt, but then the cause of this most recent collapse was no great surprise, either. Undereating combined with overmedication was the verdict. The doctors changed the prescription of Gregory's pain reliever and sent him home again.

On Tuesday, when Alec pulled up in front of Ivy-wild, things seemed quiet, too quiet. Everything looked fairly normal on the outside. Maisie's car was in its usual place behind Laurel's ten-year-old Buick in the garage, and the smell of browning onions and garlic indicated Maisie was doing something interesting about lunch. He caught a glimpse of Laurel through the window of the pottery shed where she was busy with her pots. The fountain was working fine, the stream jumping and splattering with a noise like rain trickling from the roof.

No matter, a greeting of some kind would have been nice. Such as, "Hi, how are you?" maybe. "How's your brother? Are you all right? We missed you."

Yeah. Right. At least Sticks could have come out and barked. Something, anything.

Sticks, that was what was missing. The big German shepherd hadn't appeared on the veranda to warn his mistress about a vehicle pulling into the drive, hadn't come barreling out for a tussle and ear-scratching as was his habit lately. He must be with Laurel, on guard like a good dog. Either that or she had him shut up somewhere again, for some reason. Of course, old Sticks could be off chasing rabbits or visiting a girl-friend.

Thoughts of the dog faded as he noticed where Laurel had started tying up a running rose, a rich pink Zéphrine Drouhin, to the arbor over the side gate that he had repaired last week. He picked up the green plastic tape she had been using, then reached for a long runner to finish the job for her.

The rose was wet with early-morning dew, but the tape was dry. He frowned at the roll of green plastic as he realized it had not been lying there near the rose for long. Had Laurel been interrupted in using it, maybe by Maisie's arrival or a ringing phone? Or had she, just maybe, heard him coming and escaped to the pottery shed because she couldn't face him after what had happened Friday afternoon?

No, surely not. She probably hadn't given him or their quick hug a second thought. Just because he had let his imagination run away with him about it all weekend didn't mean she cared two cents, one way or the other. He certainly had no reason to think she would go to the trouble of purposefully avoiding him.

Finished with the rose, he walked over to the huge pine Laurel wanted cut, staring up at its big limbs outlined against the sky. He still hadn't checked out the climbing equipment, wherever it was located, nor had Maisie remembered about the saw. On the other hand, the roses Laurel had ordered for the new beds hadn't come in, either. The tree could wait.

Heading to the garage, he circled Laurel's broken-down car inside, then opened the hood. It wasn't as bad as he had thought. A good cleaning and lube, a few new belts and so on, plus a wash and wax might work wonders. Within minutes, he was up to his elbows in dry-rotted hoses, grease and dirty filters, wondering what Laurel would say when she discovered how he was using his time.

First, he was going to make the car run, then he was going to get Laurel into it. She might never belong to him, but he couldn't stand seeing her shut up here. It was a grand old place, and he knew she loved it; still, there was more to life than its high walls. Having a garden wasn't enough; he would make her see that, no matter what it took. He was going to get her out of Ivywild if he died trying.

He was down on his haunches wrenching off a flat tire when he heard the noise. He paused to listen.

It came again, a low whining. He recognized distress when he heard it. Dropping the tire tool, he rose to his feet and walked out of the garage. He scanned the yard, turning his head in a slow half circle as he listened.

Nothing. Yet he had been almost certain it was Laurel's dog he heard.

"Sticks?" Hard on the call, he whistled in piercing command.

The dog whined in answer. The sound came from the high grass near the woods that grew along the creek at the back of the house. Alec jolted into a quick trot in that direction.

Sticks was trying to crawl, scrabbling with his big paws in the weeds and dirt. He moved his tail as he saw Alec, but it was a weak effort. There was pain in the fathomless darkness of his eyes and he couldn't hold his head up. A stench hovered about him that, with the spittle rimming his muzzle, told its own tale.

"What happened, boy?" Alec said softly as he went down beside him. "Who did this to you?"

The dog made a low sound, lolling out his tongue. He was thirsty. Alec reached toward his head, meaning to gather him up in his arms, make a run for the vet. Then, as he turned the lax neck, he saw the glazing at the edges of the big, soft eyes.

"Aw, Sticks," he whispered in pained acceptance. Gently, he rubbed the massive brow. "What's Laurel going to say? How is she going to take it? And what in the world is she going to do without you?"

Just then, he heard Laurel give a thin cry. He swiveled on his haunches to see her running toward him from the direction of the shed. His first impulse was to keep her back, to not let her see, but it was too late. Her face was pale, her eyes huge in her face. Her gaze was fastened on the long, dark form of the dog at his feet.

Then she was there, falling to her knees beside him. Alec eased out of the way. She reached out to the dog as he had done, though her hands were shaking. She saw the dullness of his eyes, the gathering of buzzing bluebottle flies. A moan of helpless agony caught in her throat.

Sticks curled his tongue around her slim fingers once. His sides heaved in a last, labored breath. Then he was gone.

Laurel turned on Alec with her eyes blazing with rage and grief. "What did you do to him?" she demanded. "Why in God's name did you have to kill him!"

Alec sat for long seconds as if he had turned to stone. Then he rose to his feet.

Laurel felt her breath catch in her throat as Alec moved in a slow uncoiling of muscles to tower above her. His face was set in grim lines, his mouth tight. His body was rigid with leashed temper, the muscles standing out in hard, sun-burnished relief.

"Your dog was poisoned," he said with lethal quietness. "It happened hours ago. I wasn't here." Swinging from her in taut control, he began to walk away.

Poisoned. She glanced back at Sticks's body in sudden uncertainty. Yes. Oh, God, yes. The evidence was there: the foam around the muzzle, the rictus that exposed the gnashed teeth, the dreadful stench. She was country-bred, familiar enough with the signs when not blinded by suspicion. She felt winded, as if the knowledge and the brief words Alec had spoken in his defense had been blows to her solar plexus.

"Alec!"

He didn't stop, didn't turn, gave no sign that he heard.

"Alec, wait. I heard you call him. When I looked out, I saw you bending over him. I thought—"

Her halting explanation made no impression. He kept walking.

Why should he listen? She had prejudged him and found him guilty in mere seconds, with no proof, no effort to consider that things might not be the way they looked. It had happened because she had once seen him put Sticks out, just that quickly.

That wasn't all, of course. The terrible things that had been said about him added to her suspicion.

Gigolo.

Preys on older women.

Arrested for murder.

She couldn't get them out of her head. If he could kill a woman, why not a dog?

Yes, but what if they were wrong—Mother Bancroft and Evan, and even Gregory Stanton? That thought had haunted her, too. She had been tried and found guilty in absentia herself by the gossip of her peers and her relatives. Why shouldn't it have been that way with Alec? And if it was, if he was innocent, then what she had done was so wrong.

She knew how it felt to be falsely accused. She knew the pain and futile anger carried like a weight on her shoulders. She knew the humiliation of not being believed, was intimately acquainted with the withdrawal that was the only defense against it, and against everyone who looked at her in judgment.

She sprang to her feet and ran after Alec with quick, pounding steps. Catching up with him, she snatched his arm and swung him around. "Alec, I'm sorry," she said, searching the dark, bitter-chocolate brown of his eyes. "I didn't mean it. Please, I—"

Her voice failed her, choked off by the sudden rise of tears. Suddenly she was crying for Alec, for herself, and finally, for Sticks and all that he had meant to her.

Alec's face changed as compassion rippled across it. "Don't," he whispered. Reaching out, he caught a teardrop on his knuckle.

"I can't help it," she said, scrubbing at her cheek with the heel of her hand. "Everything is so—so terrible."

"Yeah." He dragged air into his lungs, then let it out in a rush. Looking away from her, he squared his shoulders. "Go on into the house. I'll get a shovel."

She didn't have to ask what he meant. "I can't let you do that, not alone. Sticks was mine, my responsibility. I wish— I knew he didn't come back when I let him out in the middle of the night, but sometimes he doesn't."

"You let him out? Why?"

"He heard something, I think. He was barking and trying to scratch under the screen door."

"You shouldn't—" He stopped, folding his lips together as if to keep back the words he wanted to say.

"I know," she cried, running a hand through her hair in distraction. "I should have kept him inside with me, but how was I to guess this would happen?"

"You shouldn't have opened the door at all, I meant to say. What if whoever was out there had been waiting until Sticks was out of the house?"

She stared at him. "I hadn't thought."

"Then think about it now." His words were rough.

"But Sticks is gone."

"Exactly," he said, his voice grim. "Sticks is

gone. Now." He looked away. "Will you get the blanket, or shall I?"

They wrapped the big German shepherd in an old piece of quilt and buried him under a huge and ancient oak not far from the creek. It was a pleasant spot, a small clearing where honeysuckle grew and a breeze drifted, sighing, among the dark green branches overhead. Though Laurel was no longer particularly devout, she said a silent prayer. Alec marked the grave with a flat ironstone rock turned up on end and set in the ground. Afterward, they walked back to the house in the quiet warmth of the spring day.

Alec had not said a great deal, but he had been kind and efficient and had shielded her from the more horrifying aspects of the burial. Walking beside him now, she could feel wordless sympathy and comfort coming from him in waves. They surrounded her with a sense of endless support.

She could not help wondering what would have happened to her if Alec had been there when Howard died, if she had been able to depend on his understanding and strength when everyone else took theirs away. It was, she had to admit, a strange thing to wonder about a man who might be a murderer.

Oh, but surely he wasn't. If he had been convicted of his wife's death, he would be in prison, wouldn't he? Unless, of course, he had received one of those light sentences for which the liberal California legal system was famous. In that case, there certainly must have been extenuating circumstances. That only stood to reason.

Rationalizing, that was what she was doing. She was good at it; maybe too good. Yet, even if what everyone said was true, all she had to do to be safe was refuse to surrender to his charm. Wasn't it?

She should also abandon her half-baked impulse to lead him on then send him away unsatisfied. It was far too dangerous to her peace of mind, for one thing, but mostly it was unwarranted. Alec had given her no cause to think he had ulterior motives where she was concerned, and it was ridiculous to accept Sadie Bancroft's word for it when her mother-in-law had been wrong about so much else. He deserved a chance. It was the one thing she could do to show her appreciation for his help. And she would stop thinking that the situation might have been contrived with just that end in mind.

As they reached the side gate, she turned to face him. He glanced down at her, his features blank; carefully so, she thought. She wondered what he was thinking, what he saw when he looked at her so intently.

The question that rose to her lips was graceless, abrupt, and not quite even. "Will you stay?"

He watched her with swift consideration in his eyes. "Why would I go?"

Her heartbeat accelerated, thudding with feather strokes in her ears. It was sheer terror that drove it. She must be crazy for what she was saying, for what she meant to do, something that was far beyond anything she had ever done in her narrow, restricted life. But she didn't feel crazy. She felt stubborn and defiant. She felt a deep empathy that was like nothing she had ever known, a positive compassion for another human being whom everyone wanted to turn into an outcast. As they had her.

"Because of what I said earlier," she answered when she could.

He gazed past her shoulder, squinting a little as if looking at something he didn't much care to see. "You had reason enough."

"I should have asked what happened, listened to whatever you had to tell me."

"Will you next time?" he asked, the words compressed.

"Yes, of course." It was a lie, and she never lied. But there were times when the truth was too dangerous to make known.

"Then," he said softly, "I'll be here as long as you need me."

It was what she wanted. Some things were worth a little risk.

Laurel left Alec at the gate and continued into the house. He had a project he had been working on, she thought; probably getting the lawn mower running again, considering the grease she had noticed on his hands.

Maisie was in the kitchen; Laurel could hear the low mutter of the radio her housekeeper liked to keep going, as well as the splash of water in the sink. Feeling unsettled and morose, she wandered in that direction.

Maisie turned from the sink to give her a shrewd look. "You and Alec got the job over with?"

Laurel gave a disconsolate nod.

"And you're all right?"

Laurel shrugged a little as she sighed. "I feel as if I've lost a member of the family."

"Guess you have, in a way. Sticks was about all you had these last few years."

Laurel made no answer as she moved to the cabinet and took down a cup, poured coffee from the pot that was always ready, then turned with it toward the table.

"You should have asked Alec if he wanted a cup."

"He doesn't drink the stuff, haven't you noticed?" Laurel grimaced. "Sometimes I wish I could break the habit."

Maisie dried her hands on a dish towel, then stepped to check on the gumbo she had simmering in a black iron pot. "Reckon if that's the worst vice you ever have, you'll be fine."

"You could sit down and keep me company," Laurel suggested.

"Might at that," the older woman replied, her voice a little grim.

Laurel studied the housekeeper as she went through the motions of getting her own coffee. Laurel could feel her nerves growing taut as Maisie finally sat down across from her, stirring sugar into her cup with a steady movement that made the spoon clink musically against the sides. Finally, Laurel said, "Something's on your mind, isn't it? Something I should know."

"You got so much on your plate," Maisie said with a shake of her head, "I hate to go adding to it."

Voice taut, Laurel asked, "Is it about Alec?"

"Sort of. Leastwise, it's talk about you and Alec, and also about Gregory. There's so much stuff going around, really, that it's hard to say exactly who it's about."

Laurel put her fingers to her eyes where a headache was beginning to throb. "Maybe you'd better just tell me."

"You noticed we've been having more traffic out this way lately?"

"Have we? Oh, I guess you mean the two or three who have turned around in front of the house."

"More than two or three, and that's not counting the ones who slow down to look. Gawkers, that's what they are, wanting to see if Alec's motorcycle is sitting out front, though what they think that can tell them, I can't figure." Maisie shook her head without quite meeting Laurel's eyes. "Then it seems that idiot son-in-law of yours thought to ask God to watch over the fornicating going on—"

"I know about that," Laurel interrupted.

"Good, that's good. I expect you can imagine, then, that it was the most exciting thing to happen in his church since the song leader was caught in the choir loft with the deacon's wife. The old biddies have their panties in a major twist over it."

Laurel couldn't help smiling over Maisie's acid drollery, which was probably what her housekeeper intended. With a faint shake of her head, she said, "I suppose it will all blow over."

"I doubt it." The woman's words were dour.

Laurel tilted her head in inquiry.

"Seems somebody is making sure it doesn't. I had two people stop me in the grocery store yesterday evening, wanting to know if I'd seen a copy of some letter that's going around."

Laurel was silent for a long moment. Finally she asked, "What kind of letter?"

"I'd call it poison-pen, though I don't know what the sheriff would make of it. The thing names the names and tells the nitty-gritty, or pretends to. And it doesn't stop there."

"What do you mean?" Laurel's headache was a steady throb now, pulsing with the hard beat of her heart.

"The letter claims Gregory has AIDS. That he's here to die."

Laurel breathed a soft imprecation. Ugly, so ugly. How could anybody do such a thing? They had to be insane. There was no other explanation. Was there? "I don't suppose there's any way to keep it from Alec?"

"Doubt it. Anyway, he should know what he's up against, don't you think?"

"I suppose. But it's just so—" She stopped, at a loss for words to express her depression and disgust.

"Embarrassing?" Maisie supplied. "Sure it is. There wouldn't be any point, otherwise."

"I meant that the talk is bad enough, but putting it all in writing, then making Gregory a part of it, is adding insult to injury. Gregory is so sick. How will this make him feel? And then there's Sticks being poisoned." Laurel ran the fingers of her right hand through her hair, clutching at the silky strands. "What's going on, Maisie? I just don't understand."

The older woman shook her head. "Neither do I, not really." She paused. "Who do you think would write a letter like that?"

The question, Laurel knew, was rhetorical. As she met the expectant blue gaze of the woman across the table, she was sure they both had the same person in mind. Slowly, she said, "She certainly thinks there's something going on between me and Alec."

Maisie nodded. "Yes, and she didn't much like you standing up to her."

"I have to admit she always did like stirring things

up using the mail. According to Howard, she was big on complaints to the newspaper, recall petitions for crooked politicians, write-in campaigns against all sorts of evildoings.''

"Nobody so sanctimonious as a reformed sinner," Maisie mused with a twist of her wrinkled lips.

"What?"

The other woman looked self-conscious. "Well, what else would you call her?"

"We are talking about Mother Bancroft?" Laurel asked in sudden doubt.

"Don't know about you, but I sure am."

"But she has always had such contempt for anybody who strayed from the straight and narrow, always talked about them as if they were the lowest form of life."

"Camouflage," Maisie said with a snort. "I could tell you a few things that would make your hair stand on end."

Ordinarily, Laurel had little use for gossip. Being so private herself, she disliked prying into the lives of the people around her. Still, it was also true that she didn't have a lot of interest in other people's lives. Books, ideas, and preoccupations of that nature had always been more important. Now it was different. Now she was personally involved, whether she wanted to be or not.

Her gaze level, she asked in answer to Maisie's hint, "Such as?"

"Well," the older woman began as she reached up to pat her white curls, then smoothed her apron over her rotund stomach, "you might not think it to look at me, but I used to be a rounder, back in the fifties. That wasn't so long after the war, you know, and all us girls were crazy about anything in uniform. We used to get a bunch together and go down to Leesville. We'd meet up with soldiers from Fort Polk, then take off to find a honky-tonk with a band. Dance? You should've seen us! Real dancing, too, not this jumping and wiggling they call dancing today.''

Smiling a little at the picture Maisie painted, Laurel asked, ''Was Mother Bancroft one of the bunch?''

''Not her, no way. She was married and had two little babies. She and her husband were having all sorts of troubles, fighting like cats and dogs. He was a secret drinker, they said, and she was high-tempered. He liked the ladies, and she was mean jealous. I remember one time they had the police over. Story was, they got into an argument over his drinking. He wouldn't fight, just fell into bed in the middle of the argument. So she heated up the grease she had been using to fry potatoes for supper and poured it in his ear.''

''Ouch,'' Laurel said, wincing.

''Yeah, she was something, all right,'' Maisie replied, shaking her head. ''But what I was thinking about was the other way she had of getting back at him. He used to do shift work, worked nights from time to time. Then we'd see her in the honky-tonks around Leesville with soldiers. Don't know whether she was passing it out free or making extra money on the side, but she sure wasn't at home tending to little Howard and Zelda.''

Laurel put her elbow on the table and propped her chin on her palm, staring at Maisie. After a moment, she said, ''I can't believe it. I just—can't believe it.''

''I know, but that's the way with a lot of people—not exactly how they look on the surface. Anyway, wasn't too long after that her husband left her, just took off one night and never came back. Somebody said he wrote once, on Howard's birthday, but, after that, nothing. After a while, Sadie settled down, moved out of the house here and bought a place in town, got religion and everything.''

Laurel shook her head in silent amazement. Then a frown drew her brows together.

"What?" Maisie asked, her gaze measuring.

Laurel removed her elbow from the table and took a sip of her coffee that had grown lukewarm. With a grimace, she said, "I was only thinking. It seems a woman who would pour hot grease in a man's ear might do most anything.''

"Crossed my mind, too," Maisie said.

Laurel hesitated. "Even kill Sticks?"

"She never liked the dog, did she?"

That was true, yet Mother Bancroft had also been deathly afraid of Laurel's pet. She had trouble picturing her mother-in-law walking up to him and handing him a poisoned hamburger patty, or whatever it was he had eaten. That didn't mean, of course, that she hadn't put it out while he was shut up in the house, leaving it for him to find later.

A shiver ran over her, and she shook her head to banish the image. That was one more thing she didn't want to think about. In a tight voice she asked, "What am I going to do?"

"Guess you could start by getting your hands on one of those letters.''

"I doubt anybody is going to hand one over to me.''

"No," Maisie agreed. "But they might let me take a look, have a photocopy made.''

"Then what?" Laurel asked. "If it turns out to be Mother Bancroft, what can I do about it? Have her arrested for improper use of the mail, or whatever the charge might be? Maybe sue her for slander?"

"She'd stop pretty quick, I'll bet, if she thought everybody knew she was behind it."

Laurel rubbed her temples, feeling a little sick to her stomach with the pain. "So I go and talk to her, then? I suppose that's a possibility."

"Better than nothing."

That was too true to be denied.

Maisie drank the last of her coffee, then pushed back her chair and got up to carry her cup to the sink. Over her shoulder, she said, "I finally remembered that chain saw Alec wanted, though he didn't ask about it this morning. Guess you can tell him to get it out of the trunk of my car before I leave."

"Yes, all right."

"And you might ought to take something for that headache," Maisie added in stringent tones.

"I'll do that," Laurel said, recognizing the caring behind the abruptness. Still, it was some time before she could force herself to move.

8

Laurel couldn't stand to watch.

Alec was near the very top of the big pine. Perched at least fifty feet off the ground, he was anchored by nothing more than the climbing spikes on his boots and the wide belt that circled both his taut waist and the great tree trunk. His confidence in the equipment was sublime as he reached to maneuver the whirling chain-saw blade against the thick limb next to him. His shirt strained across his shoulders with the contractions of the muscles of his back. He looked powerful and magnificent. And in heart-stopping danger.

Laurel had been routed out of bed this morning by the earsplitting rasp of the saw. When she came out to see what was happening, Alec had already sawed through one limb, letting it fall with a heavy crash, and was reaching for the next.

He had explained the evening before that he would have to cut the limbs first, then top the tree and take down the trunk, section by section, from the top to be sure it didn't fall on the house, garage, fence, or shrubs in the garden below it. She had known he would have to climb to the top of the huge pine to do it. She just hadn't realized quite what that meant, or how tall the tree was in actuality.

The impulse to yell up at him now, tell him to come

down, hovered in her mind. However, he couldn't hear her for the buzz of the chain saw, and she wasn't sure he would pay any attention if he did.

Brown bark and yellow sawdust spewed from the saw once more, showering down. The resinous scent of pine sap was strong in the air. The cut limb creaked and the noise of the chain saw changed. As Alec drew back the spinning blade, the limb fell in heavy, whistling descent. It struck the ground with a thunderous boom. Laurel felt the vibration all the way to where she stood at the bottom of the steps.

If Alec fell, he would come down just that way. Or if he slipped, hit something besides the tree with the saw, that powerful cutting chain would rip through his warm flesh in milliseconds.

No, she couldn't bear to watch; her nerves wouldn't take it. Swinging around, she stalked back into the house.

That retreat lasted maybe five minutes, because she couldn't stay inside, either, not knowing what was happening. Dragging a pair of black jeans from the closet, she slid into them, then pulled on a cream-and-black striped scoop-neck T-shirt. It was early yet. Maisie hadn't made it to work, wouldn't for another hour. Taking a peach from the fruit bowl in the kitchen, Laurel headed out to the pottery shed.

She had started on another Green Man plaque the evening before, after Maisie and Alec left; it had seemed better than wandering around the house by herself. She worked fairly late on it, trying to tire herself out so she wouldn't lie awake thinking about Sticks and listening to every creak and rattle in the night. It had been the big dog that made her feel safe in the rambling old place, it seemed, and now he was gone.

This new plaque was much closer to the spirit of the *Bocca della Verità*, reflecting the face of an open-mouthed old man. But she had taken away the fierceness of the original, substituting an expression of benign benediction. The man in her plaque assumed the truth would be told instead of threatening dire consequences for the telling of lies.

There was not much left to be done to it—not really. In any case, she couldn't concentrate for listening to the long silences between the buzzing of Alec's saw and the hard thuds of falling limbs. She could switch on the kiln, however, and get it ready to fire the plaque.

It was as she turned away from the big oven that she noticed her sea-ripple bowl was missing. Alec must have done something with it—whatever it was he had been so secretive about when he saw it. But where had he put it? Leaving the shed, she went in search of the bowl.

She almost didn't recognize it when she found it, for it had become a small pool. Or perhaps that was the wrong word, she mused, since it was really more like a water mirror.

Alec had set the bowl on top of an old tree stump where ferns and moss grew and an ancient wisteria climbed an iron post to arch overhead. Filled to the very brim with water, from one angle it reflected the twisted and gnarled stems of the wisteria, while from another it gave back only the clear blue basin of the sky. With the bowl dead level and balanced on the stump, the surface of the water mirrored perfect stillness. Occasionally, a breeze might shiver across it or a cloud shadow pass over, but for now it radiated calm and infinite peace. Not even the shattering roar of the chain saw and raw smell of fresh-cut wood could detract from that impression.

It was so simple—a bowl filled with water. Yet the placement and purpose turned it into something approaching a work of art. Slowly, Laurel turned, searching the top of the big pine that she could just see above the roofline of the house, looking for Alec.

He was topping the tree now, bracing with one foot against the stump of a limb cut minutes before. His muscles were corded with strain as he leaned against his safety belt, bending away from the trunk to make the horizontal cut into the wedge he had already carved out. His arms shuddered with the whining force of the saw. Wood chips kicked out from the saw blade, spewing up as they hit his body to dust his hair, coat his chest and arms and the legs of his jeans, then falling like sharply aromatic confetti.

She heard a harsh, rending sound. The top was swaying. It groaned as it slowly began to list. It was toppling, ready to fall. Alec snatched the saw free and it rumbled into silence. He leaned back and to the side, letting the safety belt take his full weight as he strained as far away from the trunk as possible to avoid the butt of the treetop beginning its downward turn.

The top broke free. The butt twisted, kicking against the severed stump as it heaved over and hurtled downward. The huge trunk shuddered and rocked, flinging Alec back and forth like a rodeo rider on a wild bull.

Suddenly the thick belt holding him sprang loose, became a curling brown snake against the blue sky.

The saw that was chained to it dangled an instant, then plummeted, dragging the belt with it.

Laurel caught a breath so hard and deep that she felt its rasp far down in her throat. Through burning eyes, she saw Alec twist in midair with a wrenching of hard muscles. He snatched the severed stump of a limb. Clinging one-handed, he whipped around to hug the trunk, trying to dig in with his spiked boots.

The climbing spikes scaled bark, ripped free again. Alec's grip broke. He fell, plunging feetfirst. He disappeared behind the roof of the house, following close behind the great treetop.

Laurel screamed—a thin, shrill sound lost in the crash of the treetop hitting the ground. Then she broke into a run for the front of the house.

Red horror burned in her mind. Her breath rasped in her aching throat. A stitch like a knife wound pierced her side, though she ignored it as she flung around the end of the house. Skimming between the garage and the house wall, she fought off terrible images of Alec lying broken and impaled on the picket fence, or crushed by the treetop if it had rolled, or maimed by the saw as he fell on it.

Then she saw him. He was lying on a bed of dark green pine limbs. Scraped and skinned and half buried in loose pine straw, wood chips and bark, he was sprawled bonelessly with his arms outflung and his thick lashes deathly still upon his cheeks.

A sob caught in her throat as she dropped to her knees. What should she do? Call 911? Phone the hospital for an ambulance? Or would it be faster to drag him to his bike and try to— No, she could never manage that. Shouldn't move him. An ambulance, then, as fast as possible.

Even as the thoughts streaked through her mind, she reached with shaking fingers to brush bark from his eyelids, his nose, the hollow of his cheek. Her gaze moved over his arms and legs. They seemed all right—nothing obviously broken. The pile of cut branches had cushioned his fall somewhat, but there was a limb under him that might have broken his back if he hadn't fallen just right.

Quickly, fingers desperately unsteady, she unbuttoned his bloodstained shirt and spread the edges wide. She pressed her hand to the scraped and raw surface of his chest, pushing her fingers through the soft matting of hair to center her palm over his heart.

It was beating. Thank God, thank God.

His chest was also quivering, vibrating under her hand with a movement suspiciously like laughter.

His voice came low and not quite even, yet fretted with humor. "If you'd like to try a little mouth-to-mouth about now, I think I could bear up under it."

She squeezed her eyes shut, feeling tears rim her lashes. Then she snapped them open. Closing her hand into a fist, she slammed it down on his chest with a hard thud. "Damn you," she said through set teeth. "Damn you to hell for scaring me half to death!"

"Hey, I was scared, too." He made a snatch for her wrist, grabbing it as she raised her fist to hit him again. "Go easy on the cuts and bruises, will you? Can I help it if I got a kick out of waking up to a hovering angel?"

She stilled, her gaze wide as she skimmed it over him again. "Are you sure you're not hurt?"

He gave her a look of mock wariness. "Are you going to wham me again if I'm not?"

"I might."

"Then I've got a twisted knee, a wrenched shoulder, and a knot on the back of my head the size of a basketball. I need a strong drink and some TLC, not necessarily in that order. If you can't manage either one, could you at least spare a little first aid?"

Her face tight, she said, "Possibly, if you really need it."

"Good, because I think I do." He grimaced as he raised himself on one elbow, then changed his grasp on her wrist to a fireman's grip. "You can start by helping me up."

He was going to be sore. Alec knew that much without a doubt, as every bone in his body protested at being hauled upright. He didn't remember the last time he had been so shaken up, unless maybe it was after his first street fight. That time, he'd been mauled by three guys twice his size, four years older and ten times as mean. The big pine was a close second.

It had been a near thing. He'd had only a snatched glance to choose a landing spot. When he hit the ground, he'd been out of it for real for a few ticks of the clock. But, hell, he thought groggily, as Laurel stepped against his side and put a slim arm around his waist, it just might be worth it.

"What happened up there?" she asked as he tested his knee before putting weight on it.

"Belt broke." It was the most he could manage through set teeth. The shoulder was all right, he thought, but the knee was going to take a couple of days before it was up to par again.

The look she slanted upward was sharp. "I thought you checked it?"

"Did. A day or two ago." He hadn't this morning, though. Why should he? The thing had been fine before.

She was quiet for a few minutes while they made slow progress through the gate and along the sidewalk toward the front steps. Then she said with irritation, "I shouldn't have asked you to cut the stupid tree in the first place."

"Wasn't your fault," he said with appreciation for her concern in spite of his rather breathless negotiation of the steps. "I should have been more careful."

"Yes, you should," she said in acerbic answer.

He grinned, he just couldn't help it. She sounded tough, but it was all an act. He had her number now.

Her hand was spread on the bare skin under his open shirt as if it belonged there, while the soft curves of her breast brushed his ribs with every limping step he made. More than that, he had heard the panic in her voice as she knelt beside him back there, had seen her wet lashes. Yeah, she was a softie. His favorite kind of female.

Man, yes, and look at this. He was finally going to get invited inside the house, even if he did have to get himself half killed to do it.

She took him to the bathroom and set him on the best seat in the house, the toilet with the lid down. It was a big room, the way they used to make them—foursquare with a high opaque-glass window, claw-footed tub, pedestal basin, space heater, and even a rocking chair with a wicker magazine rack and fern stand beside it. Alec took in his surroundings with a comprehensive glance, then sat unmoving, watching Laurel as she ran hot water into the basin and took a few things from a shallow closet in one wall. She wet a bath cloth, rubbed soap on it and turned toward him.

"It's been a while since anybody washed me like a baby," he said, enjoying the look of trepidation on her face.

"It'll be a while longer if you don't keep quiet," she informed him.

"Yes, ma'am."

"Don't do that," she said, her lips tightening.

"What, ma'am?" His gaze was as innocent as he could make it.

"Act all subservient when you know good and well you're nothing of the kind."

"No, ma'am, I won't."

Her jaw clenched, but she didn't rise to the provocation. It was just barely possible she had his number, too.

Putting two fingers under his chin, she tilted it up while she ran the warm cloth over his face, taking care around the gouges on his cheek where he'd attempted a brief love affair with the tree trunk. He could get used to this, he really could, he thought, as he let his pent breath out on a soundless sigh.

Of course, she was standing entirely too far away from him. Her arms were going to get tired if she kept having to reach across the long lengths of his thighs. He opened his knees and put his hands on her narrow waist to draw her between them. She hardly seemed to notice as she concentrated on cleaning his face. He allowed his grasp to linger.

She was so soft yet resilient under her thin cotton shirt. She smelled of jasmine soap and sunshine with an acidic hint of pottery clay. His fingers tightened an instant, then he released her with an effort. Distraction was needed here. Big-time.

His voice a tad husky, he said, "You're pretty good at this first-aid business. Or is this the TLC part?"

"Neither one. Could you please be quiet while I wash your face?"

"Yes, ma'am."

"I told you not to call me ma'am." Her glance was jaundiced.

"Why? It make you feel like my mother or something?"

"Hardly." The word was tart.

"Good. You can't be that much older, anyway."

"Oh, can't I?" she snapped. "I must have at least a decade on you."

"Yeah? Well, it's not the years but the miles, so they say, and I've got a few thousand on you, maybe more." He could hear the satisfaction in his voice at finding an opening to slip in that particular theory. "Besides, you look like a kid, like maybe time forgot about you while you've been shut up here. I figure that makes us about even."

She paused, a startled look in her sea blue eyes. "That's a weird point of view."

"But my very own," he said, holding her gaze. "One I've been thinking about for a while."

She made no reply as she turned back to her job, though an intriguing shade of wild rose mounted from the scoop neck of her shirt to shade her cheekbones. The color was so bright it looked as if she had been heavy-handed with the blush. Not that she was wearing a trace of makeup. Her skin was fresh and clear and so fine-grained he could see the faint shadows of the veins at her temples and along the curve of her neck. The sweetly comforting scent of her went to his head like a shot of fine bourbon. He didn't need a drink after all.

He was beginning to smell like jasmine, beneath the pine resin and sweat, since she was using her own scented soap on him. He loved it. Actually, he was enjoying the whole thing far too much, he thought, as she leaned over him to strip off his shirt, then began to wipe wood chips and grit and blood from his chest. If he didn't watch out she was going to look down and see exactly how much he loved it.

Her hands stilled in the neighborhood of his right collarbone. He could feel her tracing the shape of his tattoo, although he was too busy watching the fascination in her face to look at what she was doing.

Voice subdued, she said, "Your dragon nearly lost his tail."

"It'll grow back." He hoped it would. He could remember pressing his shoulder against the tree fairly hard while he looked for a good place to fall.

"Is there something behind it? I mean, why a dragon?"

"Several reasons, but mainly good luck," he said. "The dragon is the Oriental symbol for regeneration, the ever-returning possibility of new life and happiness. Sort of like our diapered baby who turns into an old man by the end of the year, he can always be reborn, and so stands for eternal hope."

"And what else?"

"Well, there's the tradition of Oriental-style combat, which says the dragon fights with patience and intelligence—compared to the tiger, for instance, which uses bravery and brawn. Also, dragons were considered guardians in the old days, guardians of

sacred places, special treasures. They fought to protect what they guarded, even sacrificing themselves
for it.''

"Did it hurt—to have it done, I mean?'' Her question was intent and somber as well as curious.

He shifted a shoulder. "A little.''

"Then why do it?''

"Because some things matter more than the pain.''

The look she gave him held greater understanding
than was comfortable. Turning away, she stretched
one-handed to rinse her cloth, then turned back, bending over him to give closer attention to the bloody
gouges on his abdomen. He clasped her waist with
both hands to move her back a bit.

"Here, let me stand,'' he said. "You're having to
work way too hard.''

She stepped away, indicating the pedestal wash-
basin at the same time. "It would help if you'd move
closer over here, too.''

He was willing. Anything to oblige. Or to prolong
the operation.

He leaned his backside against the cool porcelain
of the pedestal. Realizing his chest was a little too
high for her comfort, he spread his feet and slid down
a couple of inches. Guiding her between his thighs
again, he asked, "Better?''

"I suppose,'' she answered, though she kept her
lashes lowered so he couldn't see her eyes. Her
cheekbones, however, still carried a flush.

She set to work on his chest again. The gentle
sweep of the warm cloth over his skin did incredible
things to his libido. His heartbeat throbbed in his ears,
and he was nearly as dizzy as he had been the moment he came to after the fall. The fight to control

his reaction sent an involuntary shiver over his skin that left goose bumps in its wake.

She flicked him a brief glance. When she returned to her job, she caught her bottom lip between her teeth. The need to soothe the small dents she was making was so strong he felt his insides twist.

The sweep of her cloth caught one of his paps, which instantly hardened until it looked like a brown-red pencil eraser. As she glanced up at him again, he shook his head with a wry smile. Dredging up his best imitation of Bogart in *The African Queen*, he drawled, "There's not a thing I can do about it, ma'am."

She put down her cloth and picked up a bottle of alcohol and a gauze square. Wetting the square liberally, she slapped it against his chest.

"Ouch!" he exclaimed, caught unprepared in his preoccupation with the taut yet sweet curves of her lips.

"Serves you right," she muttered, rubbing his scrapes and cuts without mercy.

"Think so, do you? You wouldn't be trying to cool me down?"

Her glance was sour. "I'm trying to keep you from dying of infection."

"Thanks a bunch, but I think— Ouch!" he ended in indignation as she wet her gauze again and smacked it over a particularly raw spot.

"Don't be such a baby!" she said with a challenging look.

"Right," he replied as he reached to close his hands on her upper arms. "You want me to act like a big boy, huh? Maybe even like a man?"

Alarm flared in her eyes, probably in response to

what she saw in his face. Her lips parted as she said, "No, I don't—"

But it was too late. He pulled her against him. Tangling his long fingers in the silk of her hair, he lowered his mouth to hers.

God, she was delicious—a blend of apple lip-gloss, spring day and sweet, sweet woman. She was as right as he had known she would be, her mouth as warm and soft. And he was a fool. But even fools had to get lucky sometimes.

Laurel wanted to be outraged, wanted to be cool and strong. But she knew she had provoked him, had maybe even meant to do it. So there was remorse in her mind along with the warm, rich feelings that flooded through her while she spread her palms against the satin of his skin. He was so solid, so strong there in the close bathroom, so overpowering among the feminine array of pink towels, bottles of bath salts and dishes of perfumed soap. How was she to resist such potent magic, especially when his hold was so firm and commanding yet gentle, his intent so plain? And her need so great.

His kiss was hot and consuming magic, like tasting the fire of the dragon. It burned away doubts, ignited long-buried desire. With a low murmur, she moved against him, into him, absorbing the smooth wonder of his lips, accepting the tender probe of his tongue.

As he gathered her closer into the hard circle of his arms, she slid her fingers into his hair and stripped away the leather thong that held it. Clutching a handful of the coarse black silk that retained the warmth of his body, she pressed deeper into the cradle of his thighs, wanting, needing to feel his hard strength against her. The heat of him was like a balm, his firmness at the apex of her legs a wanton incitement.

He touched the delicate inner surfaces of her mouth with his tongue, twined around hers, abrading the slick underside with sure friction. He tended the sweet, magic fire inside her with courtesy and careful, plundering strokes, until her heartbeat shuddered into the same rhythm that throbbed beneath her breasts and her mind swam with perilous inclinations. They breathed the same air, blended their scents and body heats. And he was her match, her mate in experience and need, the lost twin of her soul, the other half of her whole.

Yes, and she was a silly, deprived widow who had not only succumbed to Alec Stanton's charm without a struggle, but who had not even been able to recognize it in time to guard against it.

With a soft sound of distress, she put her hands on his shoulders and shoved backward. Eyes wide, lips trembling, she searched his face, looking for triumph in the smoky darkness of his gaze, or at least for the complacent assurance that he had her where he wanted her.

There was nothing. Nothing, except, possibly, valiant patience and regret.

He recovered first, to her chagrin.

"Oh, Mrs. Bancroft," he said with a faint smile as he slowly shook his head, "I've heard of kiss and make it better, but I had no idea. If that won't fix me up, then nothing will."

9

"So how are you making out with the beautiful widow?"

The question came out of the evening dimness where Gregory sat at the other end of Grannie Callie's screened front porch. Alec turned his head in that direction, but all he could see was his brother's slight form. If anyone else asked him such a thing, he wouldn't bother to answer. As it was, he made it as brief as possible. "I'm not."

"What's the problem, bro? Losing your touch?"

Alec didn't need the reminder of what had happened in the bathroom at Ivywild, didn't want it. He had been searching for peace and quiet here in the gathering dusk, with the smell of frying pork chops perfuming the air from the kitchen and the call of a whippoorwill echoing from back in the woods. The dumb bird sounded as mournful as he felt, and about as hopeful of finding his mate.

"Maybe," he answered finally, his tone moody.

"Don't take it so hard. She'd have to be a brave woman to take you on after hearing about your sins."

"And you made sure she heard," Alec said softly, "didn't you?"

"I did my best for you."

"Yeah, sure."

"Hey, women love an outlaw. Didn't anybody ever tell you that?" Mockery was plain in Gregory's voice.

Alec sent a hard stare in his direction. "Yeah, but the idea of some guy being out for what he can get from them doesn't strike women as quite so romantic."

Gregory gave a mirthless chuckle as he said, "So you have to try a little harder. That should keep it more interesting."

"Supposing that keeping it interesting was the idea," Alec said with suppressed savagery.

"My, aren't we touchy. What happened? She object to your manly attention? Is that where you got all the scratches?"

"That isn't funny." Alec glared down the porch.

His brother shifted in his seat, then sighed. "Guess maybe it wasn't, at that. Forget it, will you?"

Alec leaned back in his old-fashioned metal lawn chair without answering. He could feel the layers of paint that crusted the arm under his tight grip. He had put a couple of those layers on himself during different summer visits. By counting the layers and colors of paint you could get a pretty good idea of how old the porch chairs were, since giving them a new coat to fight off rust caused by the damp climate was a yearly job.

Gregory spoke again into the growing dusk. "So what did happen?"

Alec told him, knowing his brother needed something to take him out of himself, as well as requiring the sound of a human voice to remind him he was not alone. That was one reason they were here at Grannie Callie's place. Gregory couldn't take the silence in his California apartment.

"God, Alec," his brother said when he had finished, "you don't have to kill yourself trying to impress this woman."

Beneath the rough disparagement in his brother's tone was concern, or so Alec thought; it was hard to tell with Gregory. There were a lot of things he couldn't tell about him, in fact. They hadn't been close in years. Gregory had been on his own since Alec and Mita moved into the cottage at the Chadwick mansion. Until he got sick.

"There'd have been no special danger if everything had been equal," Alec said.

"It wasn't?"

"Not exactly." The words were without expression. "The safety belt was cut."

Gregory stared at him through the dimness. Finally he said in a biting tone, "The widow?"

"Don't be an idiot." Alec let his annoyance show.

"You think somebody wants you out of the way, then?"

"Looks like it."

"Fine, then why the hell don't you go? Tell the lady to get herself another boy."

"I would," Alec drawled, "except she might."

A crack of laughter greeted that comment. "That's rich! Who's she going to get?"

"I don't know. You, maybe?"

"I wish." Gregory was silent for a long moment. Then he said, "Come on, she'd never give me a second look and you know it."

Implacable in his annoyance, Alec said, "Maybe, maybe not. But that's what made you pass along the sordid details of my past, wasn't it? That's what it was all about. You wish she would, wish some woman could see you the way you used to be.''

"God, Alec.'' The pain lacing his brother's tone was real. Too real.

Alec drew a sharp breath and let it out slowly. He rubbed the side of his face where the scraped skin was beginning to scab over. "Forget I said that, too, will you?''

"No, you're right,'' Gregory said, the words abrupt from his end of the porch. "I get like that, sometimes, I guess. I start thinking that if I can't have the light, then I'd as soon the whole world was dark. I'm jealous because you're still healthy and hearty, always fine, no matter what you come up against. So, yeah, I let the widow lady know what's what with you. You got a problem with it?''

"Oh, hell, no,'' Alec said, surging to his feet, turning toward the door into the house. "Nothing I can't handle.''

Gregory, watching him go, said under his breath, "That's exactly what I thought.''

Grannie Callie turned from where she was stirring the ingredients for corn bread in a blue earthenware bowl. She was as small and feisty as a bantam hen, and kept her silver-streaked brown hair cut short in a style that framed her face like soft feathers. She watched Alec, her bright, intelligent eyes holding his a long instant, before she went back to what she was doing.

Over her shoulder, she asked, "You and Gregory at it again?''

"I guess,'' Alec answered with morose resignation. "I don't know what gets into him, sometimes.''

"He's fighting as best he can, lashing out at everybody as well as his problem,'' she said. ''It takes some that way.''

She was right, Alec knew, but knowing didn't necessarily make it easier. In a deliberate change of subject, he asked, ''Something I can do to help with dinner?''

''I've got it under control. Supper, that is,'' she replied as she scraped corn-bread batter into sizzling hot oil in a heavy iron skillet and shoved it into the oven. ''Just sit down and talk to me. I heard what you were saying out there about your fall.''

''I should have known.'' The words held humorous resignation. Instead of doing as she said, he moved to the cabinet and took out plates and glasses to set the table for the meal. With his back still turned, he asked, ''So, you have any idea who might want me out of the way? Or why?''

She stepped to the sink beside him to rinse the bowl she had been using before she answered. ''Not really. I talked to Maisie, though, this evening.''

''Yeah? What did she have to say?''

''She wanted to be sure I was up to speed on all the latest goings-on in town.''

He sent her a quick look, alerted by a hint of purpose in her voice. ''And?''

She told him about the poison-pen letter and the stir in the church attended by Laurel's son-in-law. As he started to swear under his breath, she went on. ''Maisie didn't say so, but I also heard a couple of women at the beauty shop dredging up all that business from when Laurel's husband died. They were hinting there might be more to it than meets the eye.''

''Trial by gossip,'' he said in disdain.

''It's the American way,'' she quipped.

Turning to the table, he carefully placed forks on the left side of the three plates he had set so he wouldn't have to meet her gaze. "You think I ought to back off, leave the lady alone?"

She clicked her tongue in a soft sound of consideration. "I don't know. Sounds to me like something is coming down."

The phrase seemed so strange on her lips that he flashed her a grin. "Doing what?"

"You know, smarty," she returned with acerbic affection. "Anyway, it's hard to say whether you're the problem here or the cure. But I can't see how you can quit until you find out."

"Not my style, anyway," he said with a shake of his head. "A trait I picked up from you, I guess." His grandmother wasn't a quitter, either. She had never given up on her daughter or her grandchildren. No matter how far away they were, she had always been there for them.

She came up behind him, putting her arms around his waist to give him a quick squeeze. "You're a good man, Alec," she said. "I've always been proud of you."

"Thanks, Gran." He leaned into the hug, grateful for her affection and acceptance, as he put one hand over her wrists that were clasped above his belt buckle. He was warmed by it, even if he did have to breathe lightly against the pressure of her clasp on his sore ribs.

"I just wonder—" She stopped.

He felt his stomach muscles tighten at something he heard in her tone. "What?"

"Do you know what you're doing? I mean, just what's really keeping you at the Bancroft place? Is it the job, the money? The woman? Or is it, as they say, déjà vu all over again?''

He went still. "You think I've got something to prove?"

"I think you've got a bad case of needing to make things come out right for a change."

"Could be," he said, staring straight ahead at nothing. "Or maybe it's all of the above."

"Whatever it is, you'll be careful, won't you? I—wouldn't like it much if anything happened to you."

"I'll be careful," he repeated.

"See that you do," she ordered, then cleared her throat with a sharp rasp. Stepping back, she caught the long length of his hair that hung between his shoulder blades and gave it a tug. "Now, how about a haircut after supper?"

It wasn't the first time she had made the suggestion, and it wouldn't be the last. He gave her a bland glance over his shoulder. "No way."

"Don't tell me, let me guess. The girls like it."

"Some of them," he said, feeling again the shuddering pleasure of Laurel's fingers threading through the long strands, her nails raking delicately along his scalp.

"You'd be a handsome devil with about six inches less," she said in coaxing tones.

His grin was lopsided. "What am I now?"

"A conceited jackass?" she suggested.

"But you love me anyway, right?"

She sighed. "Don't we all."

"Not quite all." He laughed, a soft, short sound.

"Not to worry," she said, giving him a comforting rub across the back before moving away to check the progress of her corn bread, which was beginning to perfume the air with its homey smell. "It's just a matter of time."

He stared after her, wondering if he was that easy to read. Or if it was possible she thought there was something to the gossip that he and the widow Bancroft were seriously involved with each other.

If she could even begin to think so, then there was no telling what everybody else in Hillsboro thought, or what they could bring themselves to believe. No telling at all.

At Ivywild the next morning, the first thing he heard when he got off his bike was the sound of hammering. It was coming from the rear of the house. He followed it around to the backyard.

Laurel was there. She was pounding with more energy than effect at a nail stuck in a fence post, though that wasn't what stopped him in his tracks. It was the way she looked.

She had on turquoise knit shorts, a matching shirt with no bra, and strappy sandals so light she might as well be barefoot. Her hair was braided and hanging down her back nearly to her waist. Her skin was damp from her efforts, making her T-shirt cling so that every movement of her round, firm breasts could be plainly seen. She looked about sixteen and good enough to eat. And he felt as if he had been starving all his life.

He walked up behind her, moving in close with an easy stride. As he reached around toward the hammer, he said, "Here, let me do that."

She screamed and whirled. He caught the hammerhead in time to keep from being decked with it, but it was a close call. He was going to have to be more careful around her for his own protection.

She wilted visibly as a sigh of relief hissed through her lips. Then she straightened. Eyes flashing blue fire, she demanded, "What do you think you're doing, sneaking up on me like that!"

"Offering a hand?" he suggested. The words were bland, but he couldn't help the smile that went with them, or the warmth in his eyes.

For a long moment, the memory of the kiss they had shared the day before hovered between them. It was there in the strained silence, in the way his fingers and lips tingled, the way her lips parted. He looked away at last. So did she. He thought that she must have decided, as he had, that it was a subject best ignored. That maybe it would go away if they didn't make too much of it.

As he averted his gaze, however, it brushed over the front of her shirt. That wasn't good. It was all he could do to keep his hands to himself as he noticed what her deep breathing was doing to the tender curves under their draping of knitted cotton. He put one hand in his back pocket while he took a death grip on the hammer with the other.

"I didn't expect you for another hour at least," she said with a trace of accusation. "Why are you so early?"

He had wanted to catch her, of course. He had figured out that she got up at daybreak to work in the garden, then retreated into the house when it was time for him to show up. However, confessing didn't seem like a good idea at the moment. He said, instead, "I didn't give you a full day yesterday."

Her brows drew together and she looked him up

and down. ''Are you sure you should be working at all?''

''Positive. I'm a fast healer.''

''You don't have to do this. The job will wait. It'll still be here when you're ready.''

''I'm ready now,'' he answered with a silent groan for his private double entendre. ''I'm good—I mean, I'm fine, just fine.''

He looked away again, less than comfortable under her assessing gaze. He caught sight of the box on the ground beside her. It held what appeared to be a piece of sculpted terra-cotta. ''What's this?''

She told him, though she seemed self-conscious and even wary about it, as if she expected some snide comment.

''Mouth of Truth, neat,'' he said as he knelt to study the piece. ''I've seen Green Men based on Bacchus or the four seasons, but not this. Yours suits you. It's softer, not quite so fierce.'' Afraid he might have said too much, he nodded at the nail she had been driving into the post. ''That where it goes?''

At her nod, he came erect, then stepped up to the post and drove the nail in to the right depth with a couple of hard taps.

''Show-off,'' she said.

He gave her a sidelong smile, knowing full well she was right. Though between her and his gran, he would be lucky if he had any ego left.

He lifted the heavy plaque and hung it on the nail, adjusting it to her instructions as she squinted from a distance. Then he stepped back beside her to admire it. Except being too clean and new, it looked as if it belonged there. And it gave him an idea.

In thoughtful tones, he said, "You know what you need?"

"No, but I expect you're going to tell me."

He let that pass as he replied. "Columns."

"Columns?" she repeated blankly.

"Tall posts, you know? Greek, Roman, maybe Mayan?" As her features cleared with comprehension, he went on. "They make great bases for hanging plants, or I could use one for a trickle fountain that would cover itself with moss before you know it. Add a lintel to a couple, and you've got a gate, an entrance for any kind of garden room you might want—maybe something with an Italian or Spanish flavor."

"Or English, if you did a Stonehenge look?"

"Exactly," he said, gratified by how easily she followed him.

"Where would we get these columns?"

He liked the sound of that; the "we" business. "Make them out of cast stone, with reinforcement from concrete and steel for the taller ones. The longer they stand the harder they get, once they're out of the molds, until they actually become like stone. It wouldn't cost that much if the two of us did the work."

She gave him a long look, as if she knew what he was up to, or suspected it. He wondered if it was good psychology, trying to expand her surroundings, pull her more outside the house. The way he saw it, it couldn't hurt.

"You know where to find the makings for this cast stone?" she asked finally.

He nodded, hiding his smile. "No problem. Leave it to me."

She didn't go back into the house. Pulling on a pair

of work gloves, she helped him stack and burn the limbs from the cut pine, along with the brush and debris from the garden. He wasn't too sure whether she did it because she knew how stiff and sore he was and felt sorry for him, or if it was guilt. Not that he objected. He was too glad of the company, even if it was pure torture.

Watching her gather armloads of trash made him feel light-headed. Every time she stooped from the waist, her shorts rode high on the backs of her legs, testing his sanity. They never hiked quite as far as the curves of her trim backside, but that didn't keep him from hoping.

He thought about climbing the trunk of the big tree that still stood, finishing the job as well as taking himself away from temptation. He wasn't sure his knee could stand it, however, even if his resolution would. He abandoned the idea while he gathered the strength to look in some other direction besides at his helper.

The temptation disappeared, anyway, when Maisie drove up. Laurel went inside with her to discuss the lunch menu and didn't come back. It galled Alec more than a little, mainly because he had thought they were making progress. It seemed Laurel had been looking for an escape from his company.

He finished piling the last of the pine tops on the fire. Then, since he could watch the blaze from the garage, he went back to the job of working on her car, which he had abandoned the week before. He didn't like much being finished. He would bring the tires tomorrow; his finances would stretch that far.

It was after lunch when he found the footprint. Pressed into the soft dirt under Laurel's bedroom window where he had dug up a sassafras sapling by the roots, it appeared to be a track made by a running shoe. He fitted his work boot into it without disturbing the pattern, just to be certain it wasn't his print. The answer was no. No, indeed. The footprint was a shade shorter than his ten and a half and the markings were entirely different. On the other hand, it was way too large for Laurel to have made it, and Maisie wore the smooth-soled leather shoes favored by nurses and waitresses.

Laurel had a prowler.

Should he keep the news to himself, or let her know? Alec hated to scare her, but there was no choice.

She answered his knock with one eyebrow raised. As soon as she opened the door, he asked, "Do you have a minute to look at something?"

"What are you up to now?" she replied, putting a hand on her hip.

He had already turned away as she spoke. Now he swung back. "Nothing," he said, his voice curt. "Just come take a look, will you?"

"You handle it. I'm busy." She started to shut the door.

He flung out a hand to hold it open. Maybe she had a right to be suspicious, and maybe she didn't, but he was in no mood to play games. His voice hard, he said, "This isn't a joke and it's not a trick to get you outside. I have something I want you to see. You can come willingly, or I can carry you. Whichever."

To Laurel, it almost seemed Alec Stanton had two distinct personalities and could switch back and forth between them at will. Sometimes he was a boy grinning with a mischievous light in his eyes, and sometimes he was hard and predatory and a thousand years old. Either way, he disturbed her more than she cared to admit.

Narrowing her eyes, she said, "I'm not going anywhere until you tell me what's so important you can't be civil about— Hey!"

Her breath left her as he scooped her up as if she weighed no more than an armload of pine boughs. Swinging around, he strode with her down the steps and around the side of the house. There was a slight halt in his stride from his injured knee, but a night's rest seemed to have helped it immensely. She held on with an arm around his neck and a handful of his shirt clutched in her hand. At the same time, she fought to control the erratic thud of her heart and the slow seep of something in her veins that should have been terror, but definitely was not.

She had made a mistake, that much was clear. But she wasn't going to add to it by fighting him. Dignity, that was what was needed here. Dignity, composure, and a firm grasp on just who had the upper hand.

Her voice sweet and soft, lips a fraction of an inch from his ear, she said, "You're fired."

He flinched, though she couldn't tell whether it was from what she had said or the feel of her warm breath. Still, he answered without a beat. "You can't fire me because I quit."

"Fine."

"Fine. Only the next time you hire somebody, you might at least try not to hide from him."

She stiffened. "I have not been hiding from you!"

"Could have fooled me. Why else do you shut yourself up?"

''I can choose not to see people without it being called hiding.''

''Oh, yeah? I think you're afraid.''

''Don't be ridiculous!''

''You're scared people will stare at you. You're terrified of what they'll say—never mind that the only reason they talk about you is because their own piddling little lives are too boring for words.''

''You don't know the first thing about it!''

''Don't I just?'' he retorted with a scathing look from the corners of his eyes. ''But if that isn't it, then you're afraid of me.''

''Now that is really stupid. You're the only person besides Maisie who doesn't make me feel...''

''What?'' he demanded as she trailed off. ''As if you don't have the right to live because your husband died? That you should shut yourself away like a criminal because you don't deserve to be running around free?''

''I don't feel that way.'' The words were ragged.

''I think you do. But who is it who causes it, if it isn't Maisie or me? Your mother-in-law? She shouldn't have the power. Your kids? Why should you care when they have so little time for you?''

She was shaking as if the words he spoke were blows. ''I like my privacy,'' she said, tilting her chin, ''and I like my house. Everything I want or need is here. Why in the world would I want to leave it?''

''It makes you feel safe,'' he replied.

''Exactly,'' she cried in triumph.

''Well, don't get to feeling too safe,'' he said as he stopped at the rear of the house where her bedroom lay and set her on her feet. ''Any place can be invaded.''

For an instant, she couldn't imagine what he was talking about. Then, with a brusque gesture, he indicated the footprint under her window.

She drew a deep, hard breath while she stared at the indentation in the soft earth. Fear brushed her with cold fingers. Releasing the air from her lungs with a shudder, she said, "A Peeping Tom?"

"Maybe. Or maybe," he added softly, "just somebody mighty interested in what you do when you're shut up inside. Have you ever had anything like this before?"

She shook her head. "Not with Sticks around."

"But he isn't here anymore." His words were freighted with meaning.

"You don't think somebody got rid of him just so they could..."

"It wouldn't be the first time."

"Who?" she asked in despair. "Who would do such a thing?"

"Anybody," he answered, his voice hard. "You're a beautiful woman who lives alone out here away from everybody. The amazing thing is that the problem hasn't cropped up before."

Clenching her hands into fists, she whirled from him as she cried, "Why is all this happening now—Sticks, the horrible talk, somebody sneaking around spying on me? What have I done?"

He caught her arm, swinging her to face him. His voice rough, he said, "You haven't done anything! Get it out of your head that any of this is your fault."

"Then whose is it?" she demanded, trying without success to free herself from his grip.

"Maybe it's mine. Maybe it's nobody's. Who knows? But it isn't yours!"

"How do you know? You don't have the slightest idea what I'm like, or what I did or didn't do. You can't even begin to guess what I'm capable of when I have the right reason!"

A faint smile curved his lips and he shook his head. "Oh, I know you," he said in a low tone. "And I'd be willing to bet everything I own that you would never willingly hurt anything or anybody. But you're right about one thing—I don't know you well enough to guess all the things you are capable of doing. This much I'll promise you, though. One day I will."

The words he spoke sank into her like a benediction. She wanted to believe them, needed it more than she had ever dreamed possible.

But she didn't dare. There was too much against them, even if she could trust him to mean what he seemed to be saying. The knowledge left her defensive and testy.

With emphasis, she said, "Don't press your luck."

His smiled widened, hardened. He released her, propping his fists on his hips. "What are you going to do?" he asked in quiet derision. "You already fired me."

"I can call the police." Where that threat had come from she wasn't sure. She only knew she couldn't let him under her guard.

"Do it," he said, dark shadows swirling in the depths of his eyes. "It won't be anything new."

She hadn't meant it. Or had she? And what was he saying? That the rumors were right, that he was well acquainted with the police because he had been jailed for the murder of his wife, his much older wife?

"Of course, if you did," he continued after the briefest of pauses, "you might have to deal with your good friend Sheriff Tanning. Are you sure that's what you want?''

She stared at him with wide eyes. She didn't want to contend with Dan Tanning or anyone else, but how had he known? "Just go away," she whispered. "Go away and leave me alone."

"I might do that if I thought it would help," he answered in sober consideration. "But I don't think it will. Not now. So you're stuck with me."

"That's what you think," she snapped. "You can't work for me if I don't pay you."

He gave a low laugh. "Oh, Laurel, this isn't about the job. But then, you know that, don't you?"

"No. No, I don't." It was the best she could manage in the way of self-protection.

"I think you do," he said, his gaze level. "And you know you can't hide from it or anything else—not anymore."

10

Laurel was planting roses when Alec showed up the following morning. The brown delivery truck had brought them the afternoon before, twelve of them in gallon pots. She had watered them well and ruthlessly clipped off the blooms and new buds to save their strength. This morning, she was setting them in the ground before the sun got too hot.

She straightened from her task as she watched Alec swing off his bike and stride toward her, his movements free and easy. His various scratches and scrapes were beginning to heal, his limp had disappeared. He looked so good, so confident, that she felt a welling of despair.

She thought of reminding him he had been fired, of telling him to go away and never come back. It wasn't what she wanted, but it would be best. What was the point, though? He had paid no attention the day before.

When he reached for the shovel in her hand, she held on to it. He watched her, his gaze dark and penetrating, his pressure on the handle insistent. She felt her heartbeat accelerate. Abruptly, she released the shovel, let him take it. Triumph flared across the dark surface of his eyes, but at least he didn't crow about it.

Together they planted roses, formed soil around them, watered them. Moving in tandem and with scant comment, they recognized each other's barest gestures, anticipated each other's needs, as if they had been working side by side for years. It was curiously satisfying, even with the sun beating down on them and perspiration trickling between their shoulder blades. Afterward, they had coffee and croissants on the veranda, or rather, she had coffee and he had herb tea.

They stared out at the molten sunlight gathering beyond the overhang of the roof and hardly talked at all. It seemed best that way. Once he yawned, deep and heartfelt, covering his mouth with his fist. Immediately, she did the same.

He laughed a little, then the amusement faded from his face. His voice was quiet as he said, "Too scared to sleep last night?"

"A little nervous," she admitted.

He hesitated, as if he meant to make a suggestion, then turned away without speaking.

After a moment, Laurel asked, "So what's your excuse?"

"Too much on my mind," he answered.

She opened her mouth to ask what he meant, but something about the set, closed-in look on his face as he stared out over the railing made her think better of it. Working together, they were fine. Shared plans and tasks made for a decent impersonal relationship, at least on the surface. However, something more than that hovered unacknowledged between them. They both knew it, even as they ignored it. The trouble was, it was hard to overlook when they were at rest, when they were able to stop and look each other in the face.

After a while, they got up and went back to work.

That morning set the pattern for the next several days. The only thing that varied was the tasks they undertook and where they ate their impromptu meals. It was amazing, the things they accomplished—the shrubs that got pruned, the perennials that were moved, the fertilizing and watering, raking and burning that occupied their days.

Alec finished taking down the pine, cutting it in four-foot lengths, then rolling the logs to the edge of the woods where he arranged them into squares to hold compost. The next morning, he appeared with bags of material for cast stone stacked in the back of Grannie Callie's old truck. With Laurel's help, he spent three days making an Italianate portal and a collection of columns in several sizes.

By the end of the week, the yard around the house was beginning to take on its final character. The entire area was so well designed and organized that it felt right to call it a garden. The rose beds in the front, around the fountain, had taken shape with the companion planting of Bath's pinks, blue *Salvia* and Shasta daisies, and were outlined by a low hedge of boxwood. Balance and background had been added by the big camellias and other shrubs in the fence corners. The low-hanging branches of the magnolia tree had been trimmed high to reveal its stately proportions, while the old roses on the arbors added neat and lovely harmony.

The right side of the house had become a special section. The lid of the old cistern held a collection of Laurel's hand-thrown pots planted with trailing European geraniums. Opposite it, along the fence, was a pergola arching over a matching bench, while the shrubbery border farther down was inset with a rectangular pool featuring a fountain bubbling from the top of a tall column and cascading down into a lily pool.

The new Italian portal marked the entrance to a Roman garden at the right rear corner, where aromatic basil, oregano and thyme grew along a flagged path. The flagstoned center was walled on two sides by columns topped with pots of ivy or spiky, upright forms of yucca. Across the back was a free-form stone wall onto which her *Bocca della Verità* had been transferred as a focal point.

On the other side of the house, the freestanding garage wall supported a large Bacchus Green Man that Laurel had sculpted. Alec had turned the drolly leering Bacchus into a fountain, though, unlike the original from which it was taken, it did not pour wine. Instead, the water that fell from it filled a catch basin set with water plants, while grapevines had been planted on either side with the idea of eventually training them to frame it.

Near the back porch, other water mirrors complemented Laurel's sea bowl, creating what Alec liked to call a Zen garden. One deeper basin was placed to catch a carefully metered drip, producing a recurring ripple that spread to the edges and returned again to the center with the constant rhythm of a slow-beating heart.

Day by day, the garden came to magic life. Birds, frogs and dragonflies were attracted to the water. Toads and chameleons and blue-tailed lizards appeared among the greenery. Butterflies drifted in graceful loops, and bees hummed drowsily as they explored the blooms. Laurel watched and smiled, feeling her spirit relaxing, expanding into the unique space she and Alec had created with sweat and aching muscles and, yes, with love.

The peace was short-lived. It was Alec himself who broke it.

They were having a late picnic lunch on an old quilt spread over the flagstones of the Italian garden where a tall cedar cast its shade. She had finished and was sitting with her knees drawn up, watching Alec down the last of a canned drink. The lean brown line of his throat, the way it moved as he swallowed, gave her an odd feeling low in her abdomen. In her concentration, she hardly noticed when he lowered the empty can, crumpled it in one hand, then spoke without looking in her direction.

"Would you mind backing your car out of the garage for me?"

Her first impulse was to refuse outright, but she swallowed it down. Instead, she asked, "What for?"

There was trenchant appraisal in his dark eyes as he turned to her. "I've about got the yard beyond the fence clear enough to cut the grass and weeds. There's a riding mower in the back of the garage, but I can't get to it unless you move the car."

The request was reasonable. Still, one of the major reasons Ivywild had been in such bad shape was because she couldn't stand to get into her car, and so couldn't use the mower. "I doubt the thing will start," she said, her voice carefully casual.

"The car or the mower?"

"Either one." The words were clipped, a direct result of the knowing look on his face.

"The mower doesn't have to start since I can roll it outside to take a look at it. The car will, I think, because I've already been working on it—gave it new points and plugs, a new battery. I hot-wired it to test it, but didn't want to move it without telling you." He waited, his expression impassive.

"You had no right!"

He lifted a firm shoulder. "It was one more thing that needed doing."

"I didn't ask you to work on it."

"You didn't say not to, either. Come on, Laurel. This is no big deal. Just back out the car."

"You know—" she began, then stopped.

"Yes, I do know," he said with a hard nod. "I also know that you don't get rid of fear by giving in to it. You've done great so far, leaving the house to come outside, staying out longer and longer to work with me. Now it's time for another step."

"Oh, please," she said in derision, "don't go all Zen on me. I'm not an idiot or a child you can tease into doing something because you think you know what's best. I don't want to drive the car. I don't know how I can make that any clearer."

"What you're making clear is that you're terrified."

She clasped her arms more tightly around her knees. "So what? Everybody is afraid of something. Even you."

An arrested look came into his eyes. "What am I afraid of?"

"Failing," she said without hesitation. "Letting people down, especially the ones who depend on you or you care about. You work so darn hard because you think that will fix it. What you don't see is that not everything can be fixed."

"Don't you go existentialist on me," he said, flinging some of her own back at her. "At least I try."

It was all she could do to sustain his gaze. Searching for more stable ground, she said, "It doesn't matter, anyway, because the tires on the car are flat."

"Not anymore."

Her eyes narrowed. "You put new tires on my car?"

"What if I did?"

"What makes you think I'll pay for tires I don't want!"

"You won't have to. They're on me."

"You can't afford—" she began, then stopped, warned by the sudden tightening of his face. She drew a breath, then let it out. "You can just take them back where you got them."

"No," he replied, the word stark in its quietness.

"Then I'll find the keys and you can back the Buick out yourself, because I'm not getting in it."

He studied her for a moment, then said, "You must have enjoyed being picked up and carried the other day."

"You might be able to put me in it," she challenged, tilting her chin, "but you can't make me drive the thing."

"Wanna bet?"

There wasn't a trace of a smile on his face. In bitter irony, she said, "Oh, of course. A threat will get it every time. What kind of attitude is that?"

"Mine."

She was shaking, not sure whether it was from terror for what he wanted her to do or rage that he would try to force her to do it. Her fingers were turning white where she gripped them, but she couldn't make herself release them. Through tight lips, she said, "I can't."

"Yes, you can."

"I can't! I promise you, I can't!"

"Show me," he demanded. "Prove what a bastard I am by letting me see what it does to you. What's so hard about that?"

"I don't want you to see!" Tears were burning their way into her eyes. She blinked hard, trying desperately to hold them back.

"Why? What does it matter? You don't care what I think."

"But it does. I do." The words, not entirely coherent, were wrung from somewhere deep inside.

"Then do it for me," he said in soft entreaty. "Because I ask it."

How could she? Dear Lord, how? But if she didn't try, he was going to pick her up in his arms and put her in the driver's seat. She didn't want that, didn't need it. No, not again. Yet he wasn't going to let it go, wasn't going to give up until she'd made a fool of herself. Well, then, she might as well get it over. The sooner, the better.

Scrambling to her feet, she stalked away from him toward the back porch that led into the house. The keys to the car hung on the Victorian brass hook by the door, exactly where they had been hanging for five solid years. She reached for them, felt their cold, metallic chill against the palm of her hand in spite of the heat of the day.

Maisie, turning from the sink where she was washing dishes, asked in concern, "What's the matter? What was all the shouting between you and Alec out there?"

"Nothing," Laurel said. She didn't want to talk about it, didn't want to think about it. If she made her mind a blank, maybe she could manage. Yes, that was it. Blank, she needed to keep her mind absolutely blank. Then she might be able to show him. Swinging from Maisie, she jerked open the back door.

She would show him. Yes, she would. Men, they were all alike. This was the way she had left the house that day, the day Howard died, slamming out the back door and marching along the concrete path to the garage. Down the side wall and around to the open doors, too hurt and angry to think or pay attention to where she was going, what she was doing.

Howard had said she worked in the yard too much, that she was neglecting her house and children while she yearned after rosebushes that cost too much, anyway. But if they could afford a truck for Evan, then they could afford a few roses, and she was buying them this very day. Howard could like that or lump it!

The garage, as always, smelled of fertilizer overlaid with old oil and ancient dust. Snatch open the car door and slide behind the wheel. Put the key in the ignition. Turn it and listen to the motor. Reach back for the seat belt to fasten.

Automatic. Don't think. Glance in the rearview mirror. Nothing behind her. Put the car in gear and ease down on the gas. Don't think, don't remember. Moving. Turn and look back over her right shoulder, just to be sure. That was the way she had seen Howard that day, coming after her from the front garden. Howard, running after her, yelling as he—

Alec!

Alec was behind the Buick.

Laurel jammed her foot on the brake pedal so hard, she felt the pressure in the top of her head. Too late! The back bumper struck with a sickening thud. She whipped forward against the belt, stopped. She sat perfectly still for a bare moment. Then, with a gasping sob, she folded her arms on the wheel and crumpled forward against them as she dissolved into tears.

The door jerked open beside her. Alec reached in to ram the car into Park and turn off the motor. Then he caught her arm and pulled her out, dragging her against him while he held her, rocking her, murmuring against her ear. "It's all right, I'm all right. You didn't hit me, you didn't. The back wheels just bumped a pine log, that's all."

She heard him but the words hardly penetrated. In the agony of remembered horror and new fear, she pressed closer.

Alec cradled the back of her head with his hand, nestling her face in the turn of his neck. "It's all right. You slammed on the brakes the second you saw me, as fast as was humanly possible. Understand, Laurel? You tried to stop, you really did. You used the brakes, but you hit the log, anyway, just like you hit your husband that day. You couldn't have stopped then. There was no way, don't you see? Move the car, and you'll see the skid marks to prove it. You hear me, Laurel? You tried to stop but couldn't. It was an accident. All this time it was just an accident."

Alec hurt inside with a jagged, tearing ache. He recognized Laurel's pain, her terror and shuddering grief, as if it were his own. He felt the hot tears that wet his shirt and kept coming, endlessly falling.

He hadn't known it would be like this. He had expected her to be enraged with him, but so relieved to know she was really innocent that it wouldn't matter. Oh, he had been prepared for a few minutes of nerves and recriminations, maybe, but nothing like this. And he had never dreamed it would be so hard for him to take, that every tear would burn him with acid pain.

He should have known.

He had wanted to set Laurel free from her fears, not cause her more grief. The way she trembled in his arms was enough to make his chest hurt and his own throat close in sympathy. All he could think of to do was to rock her slowly and wait to learn his punishment for what he had done.

Still, it was so sweet to hold her, so sweet that she permitted it. He could go on like this forever, talking nonsense, stroking the thick braid down her back, imprinting the feel of her warm curves and soft femininity on his mind. He was even enjoying her dependence, her acceptance, in a peculiar sort of way— enjoying it far too much. As she was going to find out in short order if he didn't do something.

"Don't cry, Laurel," he said, his voice not quite steady as he spoke against her hair. "Please, don't. You were right about me. I am afraid of not being there for the people I care about, afraid of doing the wrong thing, of hindering instead of making things better. I messed up big-time here, but meant it for the best. It may still work out all right if you'll just get back in the car right now and try again...."

She stiffened against him, partly in shock, he thought, but also in anger. Lifting her head from his shoulder, she said in watery disbelief, "You want me to get back in that car?"

"It's no monster, just a vehicle made out of metal and plastic. It only does what you tell it."

"I nearly ran over you!" Her face changed. "I thought— Did you say I hit a pine log?"

He nodded, deliberately letting his trepidation show to encourage her anger.

"You let me think... You threw it down behind the car for me to hit, didn't you? You jerk!"

She grabbed handfuls of his shirt and gave him a shake, though Alec barely swayed. "Well, I wanted to prove a point," he said reasonably, "and it was better than letting you run over me."

"That's a matter of opinion." The set of her mouth was mutinous. "Anyway, I don't care! You are the most arrogant, unprincipled, impossible man I've ever met. I'd be willing to bet you don't even want to fix the lawn mower!"

"Wrong. I'd like to get at it right now. If you'd be so kind as to get your cute little fanny back in that car, I'd appreciate it." It was sheer provocation, as arrogant and unprincipled as all get-out. But he didn't care what she called him, what she did to him, so long as she stopped crying.

"Would you, indeed?" she retorted, her eyes narrowing to blue slits. "Why don't you go stand behind it again, and we'll see how fast you can jump this—" She stopped on a sharp intake of breath and clapped her hand over her mouth.

He gave her a wry smile. "I do make you mad, don't I?"

"I didn't mean it," she said, her face changing as she lowered her hand. "Oh, Alec."

"I know you didn't. Don't worry about it. Besides, I have thick skin and a hard head. You couldn't hurt me if you tried.'' He caught her arm, led her toward the open car door again. ''But I'm going to move the log, and get in the Buick with you. This time, you'll back out nice and easy. Then we're going to look for tread marks.''

She resisted every step of the way. Her hands trembled so badly he thought he was going to have to put the thing in gear for her. It took several more outrageous gibes, but she finally set her teeth and reversed the car. Once the Buick was sitting in the drive, he pointed out the two sets of tread marks—one black and new, the other faded and filled in with blown dirt and leaves. Watching the tension drain out of her face as awareness and acceptance moved over her, he couldn't help wondering why no one had shown her before.

Yet it wasn't hard to guess—not really. No one had listened to her, no one had cared how she felt about her husband who'd died, or about the guilty thoughts that spun in cycles through her head. And because they didn't know, couldn't begin to imagine, they had no answers for her.

He knew because he had been there. There and back again.

Laurel Bancroft was quite a lady, though. When it was all over, she turned to him. Relief and a new ease showed in her face as she smiled at him. Her voice quiet and clear, she said, ''Thank you, Alec.''

Thank you. After what he had done to her. He felt as if she had given him a medal. And stabbed him through the heart when she pinned it on.

The afternoon turned oppressively hot and sultry. Alec tinkered with the lawn mower, changing the spark plug, cleaning the carburetor, clearing the gummy residue of old gas from the tank, and sharpening the blades. He didn't try to start it, however, because Laurel was resting. After watching over his shoulder for a few minutes, she had wandered away and settled on the front-porch swing. She had been still so long she was almost certainly asleep. He smiled at the thought, because it meant she felt safe as long as he was close by. He also thought it was an indication that she had let go of some of the old guilt and pain and could be easy in her mind. He hoped so.

She was up and about a half hour or so before quitting time. By then there was a blustery wind whipping around the house that threatened rain. He knocked off early and headed for home. He even managed to catch a quick nap himself before Grannie Callie called him for supper.

By midnight, Alec was back at Ivywild in what had become his regular place, the bench seat under the pergola. He had brought a rain slicker that he'd found in Gran's closet. The rain that threatened earlier had faded away, but a black patch of cloud had heaved up again out of the northwest in the past hour. It hovered over the house now, flickering along its flat underbelly as if it held giant lightning bugs captive inside instead of rain.

He hadn't ridden all the way up to the house on his Harley, but had left it pushed into the woods a couple of miles down the road. Laurel didn't need to know what he was doing, what he had been doing every night since he'd found the footprint. Everybody had their weak spots, and one of his was a dislike for having his more foolish impulses pointed out by a woman. He knew it was a bit melodramatic, playing the bodyguard, but he was the one losing sleep because of it. If he didn't mind, he couldn't think why anyone else should.

Laurel would, of course. She would worry and try to make him leave until he was ready to do something desperate to keep her quiet. Most of the methods he contemplated to accomplish that feat did little to make his vigil more comfortable—especially when he thought about her actually cooperating with them. They did, however, go a long way toward helping the hours pass more quickly.

Seeing her shadow move across the window curtains now and then helped, too. That, and watching her on the rare occasions when she stepped out on the veranda to walk up and down in the cool night air. It was something for his fantasies, all right, the way her hair and the flowing caftan thing she wore over her nightgown shimmered and swayed in the moonlight.

There was no moon tonight because of the clouds, though it would be full in a few days. That would signal Beltane, Midsummer's Eve night. He wondered if Laurel realized it, if she was aware of all the lecherous legends associated with the night coming up and the Green Man plaques she kept making.

Beltane, Mr. Wu had once said, was the night the pagan worshipers of the old Earth Goddess wove flowers and ribbons in their hair and danced naked among the grain crops to celebrate life and love and fecundity. Afterward, they made love in the moonlight to seal the bond between mother earth and her children. Sounded like a fine custom to Alec.

The Green Man, on the other hand, was the symbol of the lust that lay hidden in the moonlit midsummer darkness—or so the Christian fathers had believed. Actually, the concept was a metaphor for the latent sensuality in all of nature, and for the perfectly normal response of lovers to a full moon on a warm night.

If Laurel had no idea of the implications of her sculptures, far be it from him to enlighten her. If she did, then it put an entirely different spin on the whole thing.

Alec shifted uncomfortably on the hard bench. He had better turn his thoughts to something else, anything else. Not that his state of helpless arousal was anything unusual lately. He couldn't remember a time when nothing—not even unrelenting hard work—prevented him from reacting to the thought of holding a woman. Only not just any woman, but the widow Bancroft. Mrs. Bancroft. Laurel. He groaned silently as he realized even her name could do it to him.

There was a light on in the parlor tonight, and another in her bedroom. It must be almost midnight and she was still up, probably because of that afternoon nap. Or maybe she just couldn't sleep for thinking of what was going on around her. Or possibly of this afternoon when he had held her.

Jeez, but he needed another direction for his thoughts.

He was neglecting Gregory for this vigil. He felt bad about leaving Gran with the responsibility, but she understood. In any case, his brother was doing better with the new pain medication. He was sleeping for longer periods, seemed less on edge. He even appeared to be getting around better.

Anyway, it wasn't as if it was a permanent job,

watching over Laurel. It shouldn't take long to find out what was going on at Ivywild.

The storm was coming on. The rising wind swayed the trees in the woods behind him, sending bits of new green leaves flying. The low rumble of thunder jarred the air. Lightning walked high in the night sky, giving off a blue-white light that drained the world of color for the seconds it took to streak from cloud to cloud.

Alec heard the car just seconds before he caught sight of it in the glow of lightning. It crept down the road as if sneaking up on something.

He slid off the bench in a smooth movement, then leaped the picket fence and ghosted toward the encroaching line of trees. He had barely slipped into their cover when the vehicle rounded the curve near the house and came even with the driveway of Ivywild.

It slowed still more, barely moving. A late-model Lincoln, its powerful engine made little sound above the noise of the wind and thunder. The color was light, but its exact shade was impossible to tell in the darkness. One thing was certain, however. Whoever was at the wheel was up to no good. He was driving without headlights.

Cursing softly, Alec jolted into pursuit, skimming along the edge of the woods for cover as he tried to get close enough to catch sight of the license plate. That had to be close, indeed, since there was no illumination over it with the car's lights off.

It was no good. Either the driver had seen whatever he wanted to see, or didn't fancy his chances for mischief as long as lights were on in the house. He stepped on the gas and sped off down the road.

Alec said a few more choice words as he stood staring after the receding vehicle. What in hell was going on here? There had to be something more than what he had been told, but he would be damned if he could figure it out.

The first drops of rain began as he turned toward the house once more. They were chilly, but too scattered for him to get in any hurry. Shoving his hands deep into his pockets, he slouched morosely back along the drive, then swung beside the fence and skirted along it toward the pergola. He vaulted the pickets again, landing in part of the flower bed that he had left conveniently unplanted.

Thunder grumbled, rolling into a roar like a cannon barrage. Hard on it, lightning crackled in a white explosion. He was startled into stillness by its sudden power and sulfurous smell, was caught flat-footed in its bright glare before it zipped the world up into darkness again.

It was as the last of the light faded that he saw the pale shape moving from the shadows of the veranda. It came forward, and leaned at the curved end of the railing.

Laurel's voice, perfectly even and without expression, floated toward him in the darkness. "You'd better come inside," she said. "It's a great temptation to let you get scorched, but I don't think the residue would help the roses."

"I'll take my chances," he said in stark denial.

She crossed her arms. After a moment, she said, "What if I offer to put you back on the payroll?"

"What if?" He kept his tone laconic, unimpressed.

"I seem to need a night watchman. You could sleep on the job."

She couldn't possibly intend that the way it sounded—or the way his one-track brain chose to interpret it. His voice taut with suspicion, he prompted, "Meaning?"

"The idea of you out here in the storm is keeping me awake. This house has six bedrooms. Surely one of them would suit you?"

"No doubt, but what will the neighbors say?" He was fighting hard, but he was afraid it was a losing battle.

"Who will know?"

"Gran and Gregory, for starters."

"Where do they think you're sleeping now?" she asked irritably. "Come inside, you're getting wet."

He was. And he hadn't even noticed. If that wasn't enough to convince him that even thinking about what she was suggesting was a mistake, then nothing would.

Nothing whatever.

He hesitated, he really did, hovering where he stood long enough to discover he wasn't half as noble as he should be. Then he gave it up.

11

"**W**hy?"

The question seemed natural enough, yet Laurel felt as if she were pushing her luck to ask it. Alec was different again tonight; there was something strange and sure about the way he moved, the way he spoke. In an odd way, it made her different, too. She didn't care at all if what she asked was dangerous.

She had shown him to the middle bedroom and given him a towel to dry himself. She had almost left him to it, but she'd turned back at the door. Now she let the question stand, knowing very well that he understood. He paused for a moment, considering her from where he stood in the middle of the floor with the towel clutched in his strong, brown hands.

"Because I don't like sneaks," he said at last, "and I hate seeing anybody take advantage of you being alone out here."

"I'm not your worry."

"Aren't you?" he asked and smiled.

Charm. As Gregory had said, it was so easy for him. The light that came into his eyes was what got to her, she decided. It was calm and serious, yet it also laughed at her and himself and the world, inviting her to share the joke. And she wanted to share it, so badly.

Fighting that weakness, she said, "I don't want to be. I need to look out for myself."

His smile widened, as if that was the biggest joke of all. "Can't help it. You're the kind of woman a man just naturally wants to take care of."

The tremor that ran along her nerves had as much to do with the velvet texture of his voice, and the construction she put on what he said, as the words themselves. "I have a gun," she informed him with a tilt of her chin, "and I know how to use it."

"Good for you. But have you ever shot anything more lethal than a tin can?"

"No. Have you?"

"I have a few other methods of self-defense," he said evenly as he began to towel the raindrops from his shoulders. He went on without a pause. "Who do you know that drives a Lincoln?"

That was easy. "Mother Bancroft. Zelda, Howard's sister. Half the doctors and lawyers in town. Your grandmother. It's a popular make, not to mention the only car dealership still open around here."

He frowned as he rubbed the towel over his hair, then slung it across a chair arm before he began to unbutton his shirt. It was time she left him alone, she thought; she had made her point. "Well, if you have everything you need, I'll say good-night."

His glance skimmed from her head to her heels. "Sure," he said abruptly. "Good night."

In her bedroom, she turned out the light and climbed into the high four-poster bed. Pulling the covers to her chin, she lay listening to the rain. It was still coming down in a steady pounding. Lightning blinked beyond the windows, the kind of constant, low-level flickering that she associated with the threat of tornados. She hoped there was nothing like that in store. It would make such a mess of the garden, even if it didn't touch the house.

She felt safe from the weather, however. She always had at Ivywild. The big old house had withstood the storms of more than a hundred years. There was no reason it couldn't take a few more.

She also felt safe from any other threat, at least for now. She shouldn't, she knew—not given the things people had said about Alec. Yet she did.

She thought of him as she had seen him earlier, standing in the garden with lightning outlining him in its silver fire, glinting in his hair, flashing off his earring. It had given him an unearthly appearance, like something out of a myth or a dream. She had wanted to go to him then, to touch him, as she had never wanted anything in her life. Instead, she had invited him inside.

She must be crazy.

Invite the murderer in, the man who preyed on older women? Sure. And she felt safe? Yes, as insane as it seemed.

He wasn't sleeping. She recognized the familiar creak of certain floorboards as he prowled the hall, moved from window to window in the parlor, passed by her door to check the other bedrooms. She thought he stepped out onto the screened back porch, stayed a moment, then came inside again.

What would happen if she got up and followed him, approached him in the dark? If she slid her arms around him and pressed against him, would he hold her? Would he carry her to bed and love her while the rain fell and the lightning glowed in his eyes?

She didn't dare, of course; wouldn't really dream

of such a thing. Yet the thought made her shift uncomfortably on the mattress and fling back the covers to cool the sudden flush of warmth that engulfed her.

It had been a long time since she had been troubled by such feelings. That she was aware of them now was disturbing. It was possible that any attractive and personable man might have brought them on, but she didn't think so. In fact, she was certain of it.

She felt so alive, so exhilarated at having Alec in her house. It might simply be the clandestine thrill of it all, the secret delight of doing something she knew everyone would consider scandalous. It could also be that she was enjoying the sharp edge of danger after so many dreary, uneventful years.

She had been reasonably content with the endless, secure monotony of her life before Alec arrived on her doorstep. Now that had changed. There were many things that could be said about him, but no one could call him dull.

He was coming back down the hall; she recognized the groan of the board next to the marble-topped petticoat table, though she could not hear his quiet treads. Outside her door, he paused, listening. She lay perfectly still while her heart thudded against her ribs.

What would she do if he opened the door and came in, if he slid into bed beside her? Reached to hold her. Touch her. Cover her with his warm, hard weight. She didn't know, couldn't think.

He moved on. Laurel let her breath out in a long, silent sigh. The noise of the rain on the roof drummed in her veins, in her mind. It was a long time before it faded into stillness, longer still before she drifted into sleep.

In the morning, Alec was gone. His bed was neat,

unused. It almost seemed she had dreamed he had been there—except for the fresh, rain-wet rose that sat in a bud vase on her kitchen table. And when he showed up for work at the usual time, he smiled but did not wish her a good-morning.

The day passed, somehow. Alec spent the early hours of coolness mowing and trimming outside the picket fence and did not come near the house. They ate lunch but said nothing of the night before or the night to come. He went back to his mowing afterward. When he left for the day, the air was sweet with the scent of cut grass drying in the sun.

Laurel took her bath early and sat trying to read. He would come; she knew he would. Still, she jerked and dropped her book when the knock fell on the back door.

The light spilling from the house reflected in his eyes when she opened the screen door. It also illuminated the rolled sleeping bag he carried under his arm.

"Hi," she said and immediately thought the greeting sounded silly and breathless coming from a grown woman. He had showered before he came—she caught the wafting scent of clean male, soap and some subtle grass-and-wood aftershave.

His smile was grave. "I thought I'd sleep out here on the porch, if you don't mind."

"Why should I mind?" she asked, though somehow she did. It seemed like a rejection of her hospitality, or as if he considered himself nothing more than a watchdog like Sticks, who had also slept on the screened porch. As she held the door open for him, she added, "Though I don't know why you would want to."

"It just seems for the best," he said, shielding his gaze with his lashes. "I can keep an eye on things just as well, maybe better. You can pretend I'm not even here."

Yes, indeed. She could do that; nothing easier. Sure. "Whatever you prefer," she said, the words formal.

"What I prefer—" he began in compressed tones. He stopped, folding his lips over the words an instant before he started again. "I'll be able to hear if somebody comes up, and I can get out to make an occasional security check around the house without disturbing you."

"If anybody does come, they can also get to you easier," she said.

Alec, hearing the concern in her voice, was overwhelmed. That she might be afraid he would be hurt had never crossed his mind. He couldn't remember the last time anybody had cared what happened to him, except for Grannie Callie. It made him feel humble. It also gave him a startling sense of invincibility.

"Don't worry about me," he said softly. "I'll be fine."

Her denial was instant. "I wasn't worried. But what if someone comes up and you don't hear them?"

"I'll hear them."

"Well, if you're sure." She bit the inside of her lip, then released it before she went on. "You...really don't have to do this at all, you know."

"I know," he said, watching her with a slow smile. "I'll stay anyway, if it's all the same to you."

"It isn't that I mind, only..."

"What?"

"I'm still not sure why you should be involved with my problems."

"If I said because I'm madly, passionately in love with you, would you believe me?" he asked, tipping his head to one side.

The humor that rose in her eyes had a wry edge to it. "I don't think so."

That was too bad. He tried again. "Suppose I told you I had extremely improper designs on your body?"

"Highly unlikely."

Her flush was apparent even in the dim light, and her voice was fretted with uneasiness. Time to back off. "You think so? How about that I have an exaggerated sense of responsibility to my elders?"

"Thank you very much!"

"I guess you don't like that, either," he said, his tone mournful. She was so much fun to tease since she rose so well to the bait. "There's nothing left except the truth, then, which is that I'm getting gray hairs from worrying about you here by yourself. I mean, if something happened to you, there would go my job, and then where would I be?"

"Gray hair, huh?"

"Sure. See?" He bent his head, pointing to where he knew several should show up.

She rose on tiptoe to look. Her surprise was plain as she said, "You really do have gray hair."

"I'll match mine against yours any day," he answered promptly as he straightened. "Not to mention my wrinkles."

"Smile lines," she corrected him, her gaze touching on the crinkles at the corners of his eyes.

"Exactly so. Years versus miles, as I said before."
He watched closely to be certain she got the message.
As her lashes flickered, he allowed himself a moment
of satisfaction before he went on. "Now that you see
I'm just protecting my own, is everything okay?"

She was silent so long he began to be alarmed, then
she gave a shake of her head. "What am I going to
do with you?"

It was too good an opening to pass up. Besides, his
relief was so great he felt light-headed and not quite
responsible. With grinning audacity, he drawled,
"Whatever you want, ma'am. Anything at all."

"Right," she said, swinging smartly from him back
into the kitchen. "Now that we've had this little talk,
I think maybe the porch is the best place for you,
after all."

Alec watched the door close behind her, shutting
off the light. He dragged air deep into his lungs, then
let it out on a gusting breath that ended in a shiver.
She didn't believe a word he said. She thought it was
all a big joke, or else that was what she wanted to
pretend. He didn't know whether to be glad or sorry.

Dropping his sleeping bag on the floor, he knelt to
unroll it. He lowered himself to it and turned onto his
back, clasping his hands behind his head. It was cool
here in spite of the warm night. The screened space
had been designed as a hot-weather sleeping porch
back in the days before air-conditioning, so was ori-
ented to catch the prevailing winds. He could smell
honeysuckle on the breeze that drifted down its long
length, as well as the hedge scent of the photinia
planted around the Italian garden. The melodious
sounds of the different fountains came to him as a
soothing three-part harmony. It would be very easy

to sleep, he thought, if that was really why he was here.

It wasn't—not by a long shot. Something he would do well to remember.

Laurel made herself walk all the way to her bedroom before she stopped. Just inside the darkened room, she put her back to the wall and slumped there, closing her eyes. *Whatever you want...*

No, she wouldn't think about it. She wouldn't. He didn't mean it, anyway, but was only teasing her.

It was curious, but she didn't feel older anymore. It had something to do with his assurance, plus the knowledge that he had so much more experience than she had. Not to mention more gray hair.

Madly, passionately in love...

Her lips tilted in a reminiscent smile. Whether he meant it or not, he had managed to make her feel better. Charm? Lord, yes, he had it by the gallon.

Still, just suppose, for the sake of argument, that he did mean it? Or at least that he wanted her to think he did so that he could move in on her? Well, it had worked, hadn't it? In a way? He was sleeping on her porch.

Yes, but he could have been just down the hall. Why would he refuse that advantage if what he wanted was to seduce her? Take her to bed? Get into her pants? Whatever the current phrase might be.

Actually, the word *seduction* was much more meaningful since it implied mental persuasion, not to mention a certain finesse when it came to the physical part. Yes, and it was just like her to be distracted by the semantics of the whole thing.

Wasn't that exactly what Alec was doing, though—

seducing her with his teasing and his smiles, his attention to her comfort and security and the things that gave her pleasure? He might not be the suave, sophisticated type, full of compliments and grand gestures and expensive gifts, but that didn't make his methods any less effective.

She had no intention of succumbing. It would be stupid after she had been warned.

Why would he come on to her? She wasn't wealthy or well-known. All she had was a decent bank account and a half interest in a house she had inherited with her children under Louisiana heirship laws. Neither was worth the time of a real confidence man. Still, why else would he move in on her except for money?

It would serve him right if she took him up on his offer, if she used him as he meant to use her. If she accepted the fleeting pleasure he offered and gave nothing in return, he would have no one except himself to blame.

But could she do that? Did she dare? Would she be able to make love to him and not become emotionally involved? Could she treat sex like food—something to reach for in answer to an appetite? Would she be able to keep her heart under control if she let him take her in his arms?

Why not? Men did it all the time, didn't they?

Oh, but the very idea seemed so cold and mechanical and unloving. Bodies grappling in the dark. Flesh against flesh with each person trying desperately to take pleasure from the other while giving nothing of themselves. A mere—what was the pseudosophisticated phrase?—*exchange of bodily fluids*. What was the point when both of them would be as alone when it was over as when they had begun?

Besides, what on earth would she say to him when he came to work in the morning? *Don't work too hard, honey, because you'll need your strength tonight.*

Good grief, no.

So why, then, was she rummaging among her principles and less admirable inclinations for answers to fit a situation that might never arise? There was nothing to show that Alec wanted her in any way whatsoever. The man had been joking; that was what men his age did. It was a joke, ma'am, just a joke. Don't you get it?

She got it, and why not? It was on her.

Pushing away from the wall, she moved across to her bed and climbed in. Lying flat on her back in her usual position, she pulled up the sheet and closed her eyes tight against the ache of tears. And when the night was over, all she had to show for it was another rosebud from her own garden.

She didn't expect him the next evening until after ten, and she wasn't disappointed. She had finally figured out that he waited for darkness to cover his approach. With it being Beltane—May Day in the old style, on the night of the full moon—he would have plenty of light to guide him when he returned for the evening. The secrecy seemed a little cloak-and-daggerish to her, but she didn't mind. She was beginning to look forward to pretending to be nothing more than his employer all day, then letting him in at night like a secret lover.

She had lemonade ready, as well as some soft, but-

tery sugar cookies that Maisie had made that afternoon. They ate them sitting on the back steps, talking
in a desultory fashion. He wanted to know if her
housekeeper had said anything about his night vigil.
Maisie hadn't, as he was being so discreet, leaving
no unmade bed, no extra plate and cup in the sink,
nothing. Apparently no one had spotted his bike or
seen him coming and going, either. At least, no whisper of gossip had yet placed him there at night. War-
ranted or not, Laurel had the comfortable feeling they
were getting away with something.

She knew they shouldn't press their luck, however,
and so they didn't linger where they might be seen.
Laurel read for a time after she went back into the
house—a fascinating medieval romance Maisie had
recommended. But it wasn't long before she turned
out her light. She lay for a while, wondering if the
porch floor under Alec's sleeping bag was too hard,
if he needed a pillow, or if he was too hot and could
use the small electric fan in her closet. She could get
up and check, and as a concerned hostess probably
should.

Excuses. Ordering herself to stop and go to sleep,
she flounced over onto her back and did deep-breath-
ing exercises until she drifted off.

She was jarred awake perhaps an hour later. She
was groggy with sleep, but alert enough to know
something wasn't right. Some sound lingered at the
edge of her consciousness. She couldn't quite grasp
it, but knew full well she should not have heard it.

Heaving up on one elbow, she flung back the sheet
that covered her and slid from the bed. Her caftan lay
across the foot of the mattress, and she reached out
to drag it on. Barefoot, sure of her way, she crossed

the dark room, listened a moment at the door, then pulled it open and stepped into the hall.

At that instant, the knob of the front door turned with a discreet, stealthy rattle. She stiffened, going completely still as she recognized the same sound that had awakened her. Whipping around, she sped down the hall in the opposite direction. She put both hands on the back door as she eased it open, trying to keep the old-fashioned hinges from shrieking. As she slid out onto the porch, she could see Alec's sleeping bag. It was empty.

Where was he? Could it have been him at the front door? It was unlikely. He had stood beside her while she turned the old-fashioned key, making certain the lock was secure.

Had he heard the prowler, then, and gone to investigate? Was he around in the front garden as before, watching whoever was trying to get in? Or could he be lying hurt somewhere out there after tangling with the intruder?

She clasped her arms around her, trying to control the tremors that shook her. Think. She had to think. What should she do?

Going back into the house was out of the question. Whoever had been at the door might be inside by now. Nor could she stay where she was—not when Alec might need help. But if she went stumbling in the dark to find him, she might get in the way of whatever he was doing to protect her.

The night beyond the screen was not truly dark. The rich, silver light of a full moon shone down, beckoning in its brilliance. It shimmered on the grass, reflected, glittering, in the water mirrors grouped near the corner of the lawn, and turned the leaves of trees and shrubs to shapes cut from black glass. In its bright glory there were few places to hide.

Where was Alec?

She couldn't just stand there, waiting for him to come back, waiting for the prowler to find her. She had to do something even if it was wrong.

Swinging around, she slipped from the back porch, closing its screen door behind her with exquisite care. She scurried down the steps and along the path to the corner of the house. Pausing beside the old cistern with its burden of pots, she glanced quickly about her. Nothing moved except gray-black tree shapes shifting with an occasional breeze. Nor could she hear a sound beyond water noises and the muted shrilling of crickets and peeper frogs from the woods.

The unearthly beauty of the moonlight and the fervid life that flowed through it tugged at her. She had no time for it, however; not when every patch of shadow might hide some unknown danger, when every step might bring her face-to-face with whoever had killed Sticks. Her heart was pounding. Her palms were sweaty in spite of the shuddering chill deep inside her. It was an enormous effort to make herself move, stepping softly along the shadowed walk. Two steps. Stop to listen. Two steps more.

At the rounded end of the front veranda, she stood on tiptoe to peer along its length. Nothing moved beneath the high ceiling. She stifled a moan of dismay. If no one was there, where had they gone? She whipped around in a convulsive movement, suddenly terrified they were behind her.

Nothing. She let out the breath she had been holding on a tremulous sigh.

Where in the name of heaven was Alec and what

was he doing? What was she doing, for that matter, hiding here, playing cat and mouse with some weirdo? If she had been thinking straight, she would have found her pistol, brought it with her, but it had never occurred to her. She clenched her fists, trying to hold the terror at bay. At the same time, she felt a bitter rage that she could no longer be safe and hidden in her own home.

Hidden. That word came to mind so easily. Could Alec be right, then? Was she really hiding out, afraid of life and living? It seemed possible, and yet she couldn't pinpoint the moment when she had decided never to leave Ivywild. Her reluctance to get in her car and face people had slid into deep seclusion so gradually that she hadn't recognized it.

Now she had been routed from her house, forced outside into the moonlit night. But she had no place to go. All that was left was to find Alec.

Tears threatened, but she blinked them away. She would not descend into maudlin self-pity. Neither would she be hounded and threatened without fighting back. She would reclaim her peace, she would do what she wanted with her house and land, her time, her money, and her life, and no one was going to stop her. No one.

Which was all very well, but she was still shaking with fear. She forced herself to move along the path again.

The fountain leaped and splattered among the glossy-leaved new roses. The spice of Bath's pinks mingled with rose fragrance, shifting like a vapor on the warm air. Turning at the front steps, Laurel moved around the brick basin of the fountain toward the front gate. She stopped with her hands on its pickets.

Above her, the Zéphrine Drouhin roses nodded pale heads whose dark rose color was bleached to lavender gray by the moon.

Then she heard it: the scrape of a footstep somewhere behind her, whispering on the path, coming around the corner of the house where she had just walked. Had whoever was there seen her? Did they know where she was?

Laurel didn't wait to find out. Pushing open the gate, she swung around it. Then she put her head down and ran.

She fled along the picket fence and down the drive that led to the garage, then swerved to sprint around behind it. The backyard was spread before her, a bright space shadowed by the trees and shrubs along the rear edge and by the great black wedge shape of the house. She had to cross it to reach the back steps. Once inside again, she could get her pistol. If she could scare off the prowler, then she could find Alec. With her gaze fastened on the geometric pattern of the moonlit steps and their black shadow, she made that last dash.

Something big and dark suddenly loomed before her. She cried out, tried to swerve, but slammed into a warm and rock-hard wall. Arms like steel ropes whipped around her, wrenching her to a halt. As she drew in air to scream, a firm hand was clamped over her mouth. Warm breath fanned her cheek, sifted through her hair, as Alec growled near her ear, "Gotcha. Finally."

She sagged against him, her teeth chattering. Her chest heaved as she tried to get air into her lungs. She trembled so uncontrollably that her voice came out in shaken gasps. "I thought...you were..."

"For God's sake, why?" He removed his hand from her mouth as he braced his legs and caught her close.

"I heard the front doorknob...rattle, and you were...gone."

"I was just checking to be sure it was still secure. I didn't mean to give you such a scare."

He had said something before about making a circuit of the house. Like a policeman on a beat, he would ensure everything was locked up tight at each security point. She had overreacted. Knowing that helped, but it didn't make the painful residue of terror go away. With a mute shake of her head, she burrowed into his strength, needing his solid presence and hard clasp to regain her equilibrium. Her cheek brushed his smooth heated skin where his heart beat in steady, endless cadence. He wore no shirt. That startling discovery penetrated, quieting her as nothing else could.

"I'm sorry," he whispered, smoothing her hair down her back over and over, rocking her as gently as he might a child. "I'm so sorry."

"I was so...afraid," she said against the firmness of his muscle-padded shoulder. "Afraid something had happened to you."

"Nothing did, nothing will," he assured her. As she slid an arm around his waist to hold tighter, he tucked her hair behind her ear, then touched her cheek. "Here, look at me. I said I'm fine."

She drew back a little to gaze into his face. His concern and remorse were there in its shadowed planes and angles. Also mirrored there was something that made her draw breath with a soft, winded sound.

He wanted her. His need was in his eyes, his voice,

his touch. It was controlled for the moment, but still perfectly visible.

She wanted him, too. She had wanted him from that first night when he had appeared among the tangle of her garden like some ancient warrior hacking his way through an enchanted thicket. She wanted him, now, here, with a sudden reckless courage that disregarded who and what he was, and what might come after.

The moonlight was warm around them, benign and without menace. The night sang of desire and warm fecundity. It brushed against them with weight and substance, inciting lust that was sweet and natural and without blame.

Beltane.

"Laurel?" he said, her name on his lips more a soft plea than a question.

She lifted her hand to trace his lips as she had longed to do for days without end. She fitted her thumb into the notch in his chin as if it were molded of warm clay. Daringly, she brushed her fingers down his throat and along his collarbone to the dragon that curled around his shoulder. She drew a deep breath of pleasure and completion as she took the feel of his smooth bronze skin inside her, storing the memory.

"Yes," she said, both plea and answer.

For the briefest of moments, she met his eyes. She saw them darken, becoming still pools. Then his lashes swept down. He bent his dark head and claimed her mouth.

He tasted of night freshness and need, sweet inducement and promise. He was the safety she required, yet also the danger she craved. He held her with reverence, with doubt and an edge of desperation. Then, with a low sound in his throat, his grasp changed, growing bolder. His kiss became a hungry seeking, a demand that she share his heat, accept his power.

She would, and did. Her skin prickled with awareness, her blood sang in her veins. The feel of him against her brought a fiery rush that banished her chill and left gladness in its place. Sighing, she opened to him, moved into him, needing more, giving everything.

The depth of her abandon was shocking. She had not known how much she longed to be touched. It disarmed her, obliterated her careful rationales. She wanted to feel her naked skin against him, needed his hands and mouth on her body. She ached to have him inside her, filling her emptiness with his hard heat.

Alec rocked as he felt her shift, pressing closer. The sweet taste of her sudden surrender went to his head like rich, potent wine. Dazed, he took what she offered and demanded more. He was ferocious in his need and in his fear that she could not mean it. With lips and tongue he sought to incite her to a frenzy matching his own.

He should not, he knew; he still had that much restraint. If he were half the man she deserved, he would draw back, wait until she was less emotional. He was taking advantage of her fear and loneliness, allowing his own rampant desire to overcome what he knew to be right. Recognizing it, he damned himself.

Ah, but she was so lovely, so perfect. Her curves were made to fit his hands. She responded to his slightest movement as if their minds were blended as closely as their bodies. He couldn't resist more than an instant and didn't try. He would take all she would allow—her softness, her grace and tender passion. He would use them to make a memory for them both. And if he could not hold her with it, he would hoard the recollection until he was shriveled and toothless and in need of its fire to warm his last breath.

He was defenseless, open to whatever she desired of him. She could use him, hurt him, even destroy him. It could be done, unknowingly, with a touch, a word, a frown. She could do it most easily by sending him away. She probably would; it was almost inevitable in time.

But until then, she would be his, whether she knew it or not, accepted it or denied it. He would have her to taste and absorb, to take into the last fastness of his soul. He would make her his so surely that, when he was gone, she would hunger for him as for food and drink, and never again be satisfied by any other man.

There was one thing more he could do for her.

Bending, he lifted her against his chest and strode toward the Italian garden. He shouldered under the portal and plunged into its shaded heart. There, beside the *Bocca della Verità*, he set her on her feet.

"I love you," he said, holding her gaze as he reached to place his hand in the Mouth of Truth. "You are my life. I will never love another woman as I love you, never want or need another person as I need and want you now. I will never hurt you, never desert you unless you ask me to go. These things I swear. Do you believe me?"

Did she? Laurel didn't know, nor could she find the words to explain how little it mattered. Not here, not now while the moon drenched them in its lambent light and the night breeze caressed their hot skin. Regardless, he required an answer, and she couldn't bear to let him think that she had none for him.

Reaching out, she trailed her fingers over the hard planes and ridged muscles of his chest, flattened her palms against him and rubbed in smooth circles for the pleasure of the friction. In soft tones, she said, "I believe you love me now, in this place, for this moment in time. I don't ask for more."

The sound he made was relieved, yet despairing. Hard on it, he grasped her hands and pulled her close. Then he took her mouth again as if thirsty for her sweet, moist breath.

Alec wrapped his arms around her, feeling the tight points of her breasts pressing into him, the flat surface of her abdomen against the hot length of him, the resilient brush of her thighs that felt firm and smooth even through his jeans. He wanted her naked and under him, clinging, begging. And he would have her. Now.

He swept his hand down her back and grasped the smooth curve of her hip through the silky fabric of her caftan and gown. Then, slowly, he began to gather the folds, dragging them upward as he plunged his tongue into the nectar of her mouth. He couldn't help himself, couldn't stop. She felt so good that his insides twisted with an agony of burgeoning pleasure. With movements abrupt when he wanted to be tender, hasty when he meant to be slow, he lifted the handfuls of silk he held and, releasing her mouth, stripped away the billowing folds.

Then he stopped, stunned by the alabaster perfection of her shape and her utter unconsciousness of it;

by the mystery in her eyes and the openness of her hands and by the fine, silvery curls at the opening of her thighs that were only a shade darker than the hair that swayed, shimmering, around her.

He must be crazy, driven mad by moonlight and abstinence while he worked for this woman. It was insane, but he could not move, could not reach out to take her. It was sheer respect that held him back, because in his heart he knew he had no right.

Laurel, uncomfortable under his devouring look, stepped closer. Lowering her lashes, she put her hands on his belt and slipped the buckle free, released the brass button, unzipped his jeans. She let her fingers glide across the flat, hard surface of his belly, enjoying the sensation, before she slid them under the waistband of his briefs and pushed them to his hips.

He was so strong, so powerfully made that she felt a quiver deep inside that might have been fear, but could have been anticipation. Warm and daring, she touched him, caressing, measuring him with middle finger, palm and wrist. He accepted it; accepted, as well, her hands on the hard curves of his backside, as she kneaded them, drawing him firmly against her. He breathed a soft imprecation then and, released from his trance, drew her down with him to the flagstones still warm with the stored heat of the day.

They moved together, absorbing the essence of each other with lips and tongues, finding the sites of greatest flavor and most fervid delight. She caught the lobe of his ear in her mouth and tasted the silver lightning of his earring, felt its fire. He cupped her breasts and wet them with his tongue, making the nipples tight and pink, gleaming in the moonlight. She clutched his taut, firm skin and laved it with her tongue, savoring its salt. He licked and tickled his way from her neck to her knees and back again, pausing for side excursions and deeper explorations. Their gasps and small cries, their moans and breathless instructions drifted on the breeze. Their shadows twisted and arched, then blended, always blended.

When they came together it was in hot wonder and sudden, sliding glory. For an instant, Laurel stared into Alec's face, overwhelmed by the wild, demanding look in his black eyes. He spread the fingers of one hand to cover and cup her breast, and the size and dark contrast of his hand on her pale flesh was startling, entrancing. She drew a whistling breath as he flicked the nipple, shivering with the exquisite torture, arching into it. Slowly, deliberately, he shifted one hand to the place where they were joined, abetting her pleasure, watching for it with sensual heat in his face. She should have been frightened or repulsed at his control; instead she was inflamed. She reached to touch his hand, to press closer against him. Her lips formed a silent plea.

Suddenly his air of detachment was gone. With a harsh sound in the back of his throat, he plunged deep. Feverish and desperate in his need, he caught her to him with hard strength, let her feel his power. She took it and answered with her own, clinging to him, wrapping her arms and legs around him.

Madness. Beltane, night of natural lust and the carnal call of fecund nature. It pounded over them, through them, echoing in their blood in ancient ritual and rhythmic magic that beaded their skin with moisture, throbbed through their hearts and swept, ringing, through their minds. It was old and also new, the love they made, both a spiritual binding and a glorious physical rut. Beyond thought or care, they moved and thrust and used each other. She felt his hot, silk-covered hardness pushing, filling her hollow loneliness. He sank into the liquid depth and satin grasp of her and understood it was the only home he would ever know, the only one he would ever need. Taking, giving, they tried with straining bodies and aching minds to become one; two parts of a whole. And came close, closer.

He caught her hands, pressing her palms to his own, meshing his fingers with hers as he raised her arms above her head. He let her feel his weight, rasping her belly and breasts with the soft friction of his body hair and his heat. Then he took her mouth, filling it as he filled her body, desperate for the total contact as he felt the first shuddering contractions of her fulfillment.

She lifted against him with a soft cry as she felt the internal shifting of her soul, contracting around him with convulsive need. He answered it with a final fierce effort.

The world grew dim, receding into ancient splendor, while above them the moon shone down, gilding their moist bodies, offering release from madness, granting the beneficence of peace. Around them the summer night sang on, seeking life, defying death; and they were a part of it.

12

"**Y**ou have some kind of gorgeous curves," Alec said, "for an old lady...."

They were in the shower with the water beating down on them. Facing each other, they stood with foreheads touching while Alec skimmed his soap-slick hands over her, pretending to be making sure she had no grit left from the Italian garden flagstones. The major portion of the water was pouring down his bent neck and shoulders. It splattered everywhere, forcing Laurel to keep her eyes closed. That was no great hardship since she could concentrate on the sensations caused by his carefully marauding hands.

Her voice not quite even, she asked, "What would you know about a woman's curves? You're such a young squirt, you can't have been around long enough to learn anything much."

"I'm doing my best to make up for lost time."

"This is your best, huh?"

He slid his hands to her backside and pulled her against him so she could feel the wet, heated hardness of his lower body. His voice thick, he answered, "Not quite."

"I thought so," she murmured, sliding her hips back and forth against him. "Do me a favor?" As she spoke, she shifted backward to brace her shoulders against the shower wall, then drew him between her spread feet.

"Anything, so long as we don't have to stop what we're doing."

"Never." She wiped water from her eyelids and gave him a smile laden with the euphoria that bubbled in her veins. "Only—would you make your dragon move for me?"

He shivered even as a laugh shook him. "Which one?"

"You've got more than one?" Her delight sounded in her voice.

"One's hot and one's not." He moved closer, reaching to fit their bodies together in a single powerful glide. "Can you tell?"

"Oh, yes... I can... Now..." The words were something less than completely coherent as she took him deep inside. "You can...move them both, then."

"Like this?"

"Something like...that," she agreed with another catch in her words at his surging response.

"God, Laurel," he whispered as goose bumps broke out along his arms.

She breathed in labored gasps. "What...about the other one?"

"Watch," he said. Bracing a hand on either side of her shoulders, he flexed his pectorals as he did slow and steady standing push-ups, back and forth, over her, against her.

"Yes," she whispered. "Oh, yes."

It was incredibly fascinating, the way the dragon tattooed on his chest and around his shoulder undulated with his movements. The other, lower movements were even more enthralling.

Never in her whole life had Laurel felt such free and natural sensuality. It flowed through her in unimpeded wonder. It was Alec who had released it, for he allowed no modesty, left nothing hidden or denied. Prudery was totally foreign to him; he had no use for it and would permit her none. And it was what she needed—this easy, humorous acceptance of what was true and natural between a man and a woman. She had longed for it all her life.

He was what she had needed, also, and always would.

Still, she would not ask for forever. She would be grateful for this moment and not look beyond it. She didn't care what he wanted of her, not really. Whatever it was, she would give it. She owed him something for all he had done, for the changes he had made in her. If he was using her, she had no right to complain, because she was also using him. It was possible her need for his youth, his strength, and the reflection in his eyes of herself as attractive and desirable was greater than anything he might ever take from her.

"Stay with me, Laurel," he said, his gaze meeting hers, its darkness indicating he was aware of her moment of distraction.

"Yes," she said, her eyes clearing as she looked into his. "I'm here."

A smile curved his mouth, giving him a look of ineffable sweetness. Then, bending his head, he laved the beaded nipple of her breast with his warm, wet tongue.

Lifting herself toward him, giving herself, she threaded her fingers through the black silk of his hair, whispering, "I'll always be with you."

Later she lay beside him in her bed with her hips

against his pelvis and his arm around her waist so he could clasp her breast in his cupped hand. Eyes open as she stared into the dark, she wondered what would become of them. There was no way to know, of course.

She lowered her sights, then, to the more immediate question of what she was going to say to him over the breakfast table. Which might be silly, she realized, but was the kind of mundane thing people seldom considered when they thought of wild, passionate affairs.

She needn't have worried; Alec didn't stay that long. As the first hint of dawn appeared behind the curtain, he roused, stretched and leaned over her to press a kiss to her temple. He was still for an instant, then he lifted the sheet to slide from the bed.

She could take the coward's way out and pretend to be asleep. He deserved better, she thought, and so did she.

"You don't have to leave," she said quietly as she opened her eyes.

He paused. "I wouldn't, except..."

"What?"

"I should check on Gregory."

That wasn't what he had meant to say, she was sure, or at least it wasn't all of it. "You're worried about my reputation, I suppose?"

"You're a nice woman, a respectable woman," he answered in quiet tones. "It matters."

She levered herself up on one elbow. "People have had us in bed for weeks. What you do or don't do isn't going to matter. Anyway, I don't mind—not if you don't."

He stretched out beside her again and reached to

cup her face in his hand. "The kind of rep I have could only be improved by being caught spending the night with the widow Bancroft. But I don't want to hurt you."

She thought of saying it was too late to worry about that, but couldn't see how the observation would be helpful. Lowering her lashes an instant, she asked, "Are you sure you aren't afraid of what people like Grannie Callie will say?"

A teasing note came into his voice. "You're asking if I mind that people will say I've been making love to the sexiest older woman in north Louisiana?"

"No," she said bravely. "Rather that I'm making love to you."

"There's a difference?" He tilted his head, the look on his face in the dimness far too understanding.

She gave a small nod. "A little matter of who made the first move."

Humor sounded stronger in his voice. "Far as I remember, that would be me. But you can put one on me anytime. Please?"

She smiled a little as she touched his chest, smoothing her fingers over the last scabs from his encounter with the pine tree. "You know what I mean."

"Maybe, but I thought I cured you of that kind of thinking last night."

"You tried your best." A trace of reminiscence was in her voice.

"I'll have to try harder," he said, the words rich with meaning. And promise.

He would be back. He didn't intend what had happened to be a one-time thing. She hadn't wanted—hadn't been able—to take that for granted. She sighed a little. Then, realizing he was waiting for her reply—

an indication that he had his own doubts—she gave him a direct look and an abrupt, "See that you do!"

His features smoothed, though his smile lingered. He reached to brush his thumb over her mouth. "I'll stay, if that's what you want. Only tell me what you prefer."

"I want you to do whatever you feel is right for you," she said quietly.

"What I feel would be right for me?" His voice deepened. "That would be to crawl back under the covers and make love to you for a year or two, until you can't think, much less move."

"Sounds good," she replied, with a slight twist of her lips.

"Hold the thought." He turned more serious. "But whatever takes place at night, come daylight I think I should turn into your hired hand and Grannie Callie's grandson again, at least until we find out what's going on around here. Somebody has a real problem. I don't know what it is exactly, or how I fit into it, but we need to play it safe for your sake. Okay?"

She nodded since it made sense. Regardless, as he kissed her hard and fast and rolled from the bed, she already missed him. Hopeless, she was hopeless.

The sun came up and Maisie appeared. Laurel showered, dressed, and ate breakfast alone. A short time later, she heard Alec ride up on his bike as if it hadn't been a mere two hours since he'd left. She dawdled inside the house, trying to keep to a natural routine, though she longed to rush outside and see if he looked the same, if he acted the same toward her as he had the night before.

She also worried about her own behavior. He might

want to be treated as her hired hand, but it was going to be awkward giving orders to the man who had shared her bed. She didn't think it would work.

There was no need for worry. Without discussion or instruction, Alec set to work painting the picket fence. It was an obvious job, one they had discussed a few days before. Since it was exactly what Laurel most wanted to get done, however, it was as if he had read her mind. It gave her pleasure to think that he might have, anyway.

The two of them behaved themselves fairly well during the morning, mainly because Laurel spent much of the day in the pottery shed. However, they did run into a small problem at lunch.

The day was so hot that Maisie set the meal out on the kitchen table. The three of them finished their chicken-salad sandwiches with iced tea, then Maisie got up to get the dessert of fresh huckleberries topped with whipped cream. Since the seeds of the huckleberries got stuck under the plate of her dental bridge, Maisie passed on them. Instead, she puttered around the sink, putting the dishes in the dishwasher and wiping countertops.

Alec, with a quick glance at Maisie who had her back to them, said to Laurel, "You've got cream on your mouth."

She licked her bottom lip. "Did I get it?"

"Nope," he said, his gaze intent. Half rising, he leaned close for a quick kiss, flicking away the rich sweetness with his tongue.

It was then that Maisie swung toward the table with a wet cloth in her hand, as if intending to wipe it. She lifted a brow as Alec dropped back into his seat.

"Just cleaning up around here," he said, his expression bland.

"I can see that." Maisie set her fist holding the cloth on her hip. "You want to watch that kind of thing."

"Why? You got any objection?"

"You get wet paint where it don't belong, and you'll be in big trouble."

"Where?" Alec asked, glancing down at his hands, then at Laurel's face and shoulder where he had touched her.

"Did I say you had already? I was just telling you to be careful."

Alec gave her a look of understanding as he said a mock-polite, "Yes, ma'am."

Maisie nodded, but as she turned back to the sink she was grinning. Alec, meeting Laurel's gaze, gave a wry shake of his head.

He was not quite so well behaved the following day. But then there was no denying that he was provoked.

Laurel heard a car drive up from where she was working in the pottery shed. It didn't stop in front of the house, but swung around to the side, stopping just behind Laurel's car in the open garage. Knowing that almost certainly meant the arrival of family, Laurel emerged from the shed in time to see her sister-in-law getting out of her car.

Zelda, Howard's sister, was the only one of his family who had ever been particularly warm or friendly toward Laurel. They had gone to school together, though Zelda had been a couple of grades ahead. Laurel had seen very little of her in the last two or three years, but it was a natural growing-apart rather than the result of any ill will.

Zelda had not changed at all. Her hair was still beige-blond, thanks to a liberal hand with the chemicals in her beauty shop, and cut in a twenties bob that did nothing for her square face. Her flowing rayon dress was a bit tight for her plump figure and its skirt was unbuttoned two buttons too high. Her dark burgundy lipstick and silvery blue eye shadow were an unlikely combination. Still, she radiated cheerful camaraderie as she gave Laurel a hearty wave. In the next instant, she caught sight of Alec. Her mouth fell open.

Laurel could hardly blame Zelda, for Alec was something to see. His hair shone in the morning sun with the iridescence of a grackle's plumage. He had pulled off his shirt, and the sun-gilded muscles of his upper body shifted under his skin as he held a gallon bucket of paint in one hand and leaned to catch a run on the fence picket he was painting. The white splotch of paint that decorated his abdomen from where he had gotten too close to his job made a strong and eye-catching contrast to his dark brown skin.

Zelda slammed her car door and moved around the hood toward the side gate. "Whoo-ee, Laurel, honey!" she called in lascivious appreciation. "Now that's what I call a fine boy toy!"

Laurel was familiar with Zelda's sassy, downright brassy attitude and compulsion to flirt with anything that manufactured testosterone. Alec wasn't. Laurel saw him stiffen, could follow the path of the dark red color as it spread under the copper-bronze of his skin. Her tone a little dry, she said, "Meet Alec Stanton,

Zelda. But you might want to be careful, since he wields a mean paintbrush.''

"Yes, and I bet that's not all," Laurel's sister-in-law answered with a chuckle and no regard whatsoever for the undercurrents around her. "Hi there, Alec. You get through here, you can come right on over to my house, you hear?"

He gave her a curt nod to acknowledge the introduction, but from the look on his face he was less than thrilled. It seemed a good idea to get Zelda away from him before she said something he might be inclined to answer with his own brand of frankness.

"I don't think he'll be free anytime soon," Laurel supplied with a quick, secretive smile for him as he glanced her way. "Come inside, Zelda, and we'll see if Maisie has coffee made."

Watching the two of them with avid interest, Zelda said, "Can't say I blame you for not wanting to loan him out. I'd keep him chained to the bed if it was me, I mean honestly! But I'll skip the coffee. Mom was telling me you've been redoing the front yard, and I'm dying to see."

"It's mostly what Alec has done. He's worked so hard, really done wonders."

"I'll just bet!"

Laurel gave the other woman a straight, unsmiling look as she felt her own irritation rising. "Let me show you the wall fountain and water mirrors around back."

"Oh, I want to see it all, honey. Nothing less than the grand tour will do for me." Ignoring Laurel, who had turned toward the rear of the house, she swept up to the gate in the fence and reached to push it open.

Alec looked up sharply. "Be careful of the—"

It was too late. Zelda snatched her hand away from the gate, but it was coated with white paint.

"Yuck," she said with a look of disgust. Then a lascivious smile curled her lips and she shot Alec a bright glance. "Of course, some things are worth winding up with sticky fingers, right? You wouldn't happen to have a handkerchief I could borrow, would you, honey?" Her gaze dropped below his waist for a leisurely appraisal, coming to rest on the cleanup rag that hung from the back pocket of his faded jeans.

Face impassive, Alec pulled out the cloth and stepped closer to pass it over the fence. Zelda batted her lashes and held her hand out for him to wipe. He paused, studying her.

White-hot anger flashed through Laurel. Stepping forward, she snatched the paint-stained cloth from his hand. "I'll take care of it. Thank you, Alec."

The look he gave her as he heard the dismissal in her voice was unfathomable. Swinging away, he returned to his painting.

"Spoilsport," Zelda said with sardonic amusement as she accepted the cloth Laurel pushed at her and began to clean her stubby fingers.

Laurel didn't answer. Taking the cloth again when the other woman finished with it, she used it to open the gate, then handed it back to Alec. Ushering Zelda into the front garden, she led her firmly toward the fountain.

"Interesting," Howard's sister commented with barely a glance for the careful construction. "Nice," she said about the new roses when Laurel pointed them out. "Well, I'll be," she remarked when she was led around to the far side of the house to see the lily pool and the flower-filled pots sitting on the old cistern. But her eyes lit up as they reached the Italian garden in the corner of the backyard.

"Wowzer," she said in awed tones. "This is where you hold the orgies, right?"

Laurel turned her head sharply to stare at the other woman, uncertain she had heard correctly. "The what?"

"Orgies, honey. You know. Moonlight and wine and that sweet young thing from around in front, all naked and ready?"

"Good Lord, Zelda," she replied, trying to sound as if she thought it was a bad joke. "Where did you get such an idea?"

"It just naturally springs to mind, sugar pie. I think it might have even if folks weren't whispering about it right and left. Of course, they're saying you and your Alec are worshiping idols out here, too, plus I don't know what other kinds of weird stuff."

Laurel couldn't breathe for long seconds. Finally, she said in shaken tones, "That's ridiculous!"

"Is it?" Zelda gazed around at the columns and flagstones edged with mats of herbs, then allowed her gaze to linger on the *Bocca della Verità* that hung on the back wall. "Most folks have a birdbath and a few petunias in the backyard. This is just plain decadent."

"Surely you don't believe such nonsense?" Laurel couldn't keep the distress from her voice. There was an idea growing in her mind that tied her stomach in knots and made her brain feel as if it were clamped in a vise.

Zelda sighed, her eyes mirroring concern. "Doesn't make much difference what I believe, honey. It's what people are saying that counts. I just thought you ought to know. Didn't figure anybody else would tell you."

"Yes, well, I—I'm glad you did."

"I don't know what gets into them sometimes. I mean, it seems like they get off on making up junk."

Laurel gave a slow shake of her head. "This is different somehow, or at least it seems so to me. Talk is fairly natural. It's what people do when they get together, it sets community standards. But the things that are being said and done are just plain vicious. Have you heard about the poison-pen letter?"

"Heard about it, but that's all. Somebody mentioned it at the shop, though nobody seems to have seen one of the things."

"Doesn't it strike you as a little..."

"Nutso," Zelda supplied as Laurel paused.

"Maybe. Or at least as if there's something personal behind it."

Her sister-in-law frowned. "You think somebody has it in for you?"

"It looks that way."

"Lord, I don't know. But you'll have to admit what you're doing is enough to stir folks up."

"What do you mean?" The words were blunt since Laurel was ready to admit no such thing.

"Well, Hillsboro is a pretty uptight place—conservative, you know. It would be bad enough you taking up with a younger man, but him being from the West Coast makes it ten times worse. Everybody knows how they are out there, into all sorts of way-out cults and off-the-wall sex mess."

"For crying out loud, Zelda! Everybody in the state of California isn't like that."

"Maybe, but you'll never convince folks in Hillsboro. Besides, it's not as if your Alec is a regular Redneck Joe, now is he?''

He wasn't, of course, for which Laurel was profoundly grateful. Still, she was only beginning to realize how unusual he was. In clipped tones, she said, ''What has that got to do with anything?''

''Don't get mad at me, honey. I mean, I see the appeal, really I do. Matter of fact, he reminds me of my dad, in a way—all the brooding good looks and macho charisma that females, young and old, adore and drool over. Guess maybe that's why I go for him. But I'm just trying to show you how it looks.''

''I can't help how it looks, Zelda. It's my life.''

''I know, I know. And you've got a perfect right to screw it up any way you want.'' As Laurel's mouth tightened, Zelda added hurriedly, ''Joking, just joking!''

Laurel did not smile. After a moment, she asked, ''Did Mother Bancroft ask you to come talk to me?''

The other woman put a hand on her ample hip. ''You've got to be kidding. You know Mom and I don't get along, haven't since she caught me in the back seat of Sheriff Tanning's car—with the fuzz on top, if you know what I mean.''

Laurel had a vague memory of the family stir over the incident. It had been a two-week sensation a few years back, some seven or eight months after Howard died. ''I'd have thought that was ancient history.''

''To most people, yeah, but you know Mom.''

Laurel nodded in grim agreement. ''She's been to see me. She seemed to think I need advice, but I can take care of myself.''

''Can you, Laurel?'' Zelda gave a small shake of her blond head. ''I don't mean to butt in where I don't belong, but you're not exactly the most sophisticated woman I know.''

Laurel knew Zelda considered herself an experienced woman of the world because she had slept around since high school. More than that, she had run away from home as a teenager, taking off for New York. She had spent a couple of years nibbling on the Big Apple before Mother Bancroft had found her and brought her home again.

''I don't know what that has to do with anything,'' Laurel said with some asperity.

''Don't you? You got married when you were just a kid, and since Howard died you've been out here by yourself. It would be real easy for some guy to bowl you over, take advantage of you.''

''I'm not a fool, Zelda!''

''I'm not saying your Alec is doing that. How could I, since I don't know the first thing about him? The point is, neither do you.''

Zelda looked past Laurel's shoulder as she spoke. Following her gaze, Laurel saw that Alec had finished on the other side of the garden, or else he wanted to remain near in case she needed him. He had moved his painting operation around to the pergola and bench not far away. It was obvious from the set look of his features that he had overheard.

Meeting his gaze squarely, Laurel said to Zelda, ''I know all I need to know.''

The other woman lifted a well-rounded shoulder in an eloquent shrug. ''Then there's nothing more I can say, is there? Except be careful.'' She gave Alec a sly look. ''Oh, yes, and next time you and your boy toy have an orgy, be real sure and invite me!''

''Right,'' Laurel agreed with dry sarcasm.

Alec spoke at the same time, his tone as jaundiced as the look he gave Howard's sister. "Make certain you bring your own grapes."

As his meaning sank in, Zelda's eyes widened and purple-red color mottled the skin beneath her makeup. Laurel choked on a laugh, turning it into a cough. Alec, imperturbable, turned back to his painting.

Zelda drew an audible breath. Then she gave an uncertain snicker. "Well, of all the nerve. Remind me not to get on your Alec's bad side, will you?"

Laurel bit her lip to keep from laughing as she turned toward the garage. "You still haven't seen the other fountain. It's this way."

"I'll take a quick peek," her sister-in-law said with a furtive backward glance at Alec. "Then I've got to be getting back to the shop. I've got a curl to do in half an hour."

They moved off, circling around the side of the house past the Bacchus fountain. Zelda pretended to be impressed, but barely paused in front of it before moving on to her car, as if she was anxious to leave. When they reached her Lincoln, she said, "Come see me, Laurel, honey, and I'll give you a trim, on the house. That's if you can tear yourself away from your—from Ivywild."

Laurel thanked her for the offer, adding the usual meaningless phrases of hospitality. Then, when Zelda had driven away, she turned back to where Alec was working.

He put down his brush and pulled out his cleaning rag to wipe his hands as he watched her come toward him. The scowl on his face brought a rise of trepidation inside her.

"Is that what you think?" he demanded as she

came close enough to hear him. "That I'm trying to take advantage of you?"

"Zelda said it. I didn't."

He crammed his cloth back into his pocket. "I'm not. I wouldn't. Not ever."

"I know that," she said quietly. And she did, at least as long as she could look into his eyes and see the sincerity in them like gold at the bottom of a deep-running stream.

His gaze changed, warming as he studied her face. Slow humor rose to tilt his mouth. "Of course, you can take advantage of me all you like. Matter of fact, you can peel me any time you're in the mood for— grapes."

She broke up; she couldn't help it. Shaking with laughter, she fell into his arms and pressed her forehead against his sun-warmed chest. "Oh, Alec," she cried, "did you see her face?"

Alec had indeed, and he didn't like it one damned bit. Gazing at nothing over Laurel's head, he felt his amusement fade, to be replaced by fierce protectiveness. God, what was going on? He couldn't believe the things that woman had unloaded on Laurel. If half of them were true, he and Laurel had big trouble.

They had also been spied on, or so it sounded to him. Somebody had seen the two of them in the Italian garden. It was the only way the rumors of an orgy could have originated.

The very idea made him want to strangle someone with his bare hands. He hoped to heaven Laurel hadn't made the connection, but knew it was too much to ask. She was too smart to let anything like that slip past her. Which didn't mean that she would say anything about it, of course. She wasn't the kind of woman to let every thought that passed through her head come out her mouth. Sometimes he wished she would. He would feel better if he knew for sure what was on her mind.

As if tuning in to his mood, Laurel grew quiet in his arms. She stirred, then drew back, bracing against his hold. Her face stark, she said, "There was somebody outside here the night before last when we—when you slept on the porch. I heard something behind me. That's why I was running when I nearly knocked you down. I thought then it was you I had heard, only you had turned and come back around the other way to meet me."

"No," he replied in grim denial. "I circled to the back after checking the front door. You came from behind me, and I turned around to catch you."

She nodded unhappily. "Whoever was out there saw us."

It didn't help Alec's feelings to know he had been right. He drew a shallow breath and let it out. "I'm sorry."

"For what? It isn't your fault there's a Peeping Tom sneaking around."

"It was my fault we weren't tucked up in bed like nice normal people. It was just that...you were so unbelievably beautiful in the moonlight and I wanted you, wanted to see the moon in your eyes when I made love to you. And I wanted no reminders, no comparisons with whatever you had with your husband."

"I know," she said, her gaze open and steady on his. "It was perfect. That's why it's so terrible that somebody is trying to turn it into something ugly."

"They can't do that unless we let them. We're the only ones who control how we think about it."

"Yes," she agreed, but the word was hardly more than a whisper.

"Anyway," he went on, "you were on private property, minding your own business. Whoever was out there is the one who should be feeling ashamed."

She gave him a small smile for his effort, although she didn't look convinced. After a moment, she said, almost to herself, "Why? Why would anyone try? I haven't done anything to them."

His grasp tightened. "Weirdos don't need a reason. Besides, it doesn't have to be you they're after."

"Meaning?"

"You were fine until I came along, now weren't you?" The words were tight.

She hesitated only a moment before she answered, "No. No, I wasn't."

"That's not what I meant and you know it," he said unsteadily. "And don't look at me like that unless you want to add to the gossip."

She gave him a small, tempted smile that immediately dimmed again. "I hate to think of Marcia and Evan hearing what's being said."

"If they've got any sense, much less loyalty to their mother, they won't believe a word of it."

"Even the part that's true?" Her gaze slid away.

He felt tightness gather around his chest. "That's the part that gets to you, isn't it? What those two will think."

"I'm their mother."

She looked embarrassed and unhappy, and it was his doing. Aching inside, yet stubborn, he said, "You're human."

"I should have had more—"

"What?" he interrupted. "Dignity? Self-respect? Or only more common sense than to get involved with me?"

"Oh, Alec," she said in soft rebuke.

He knew he should shut up, let it go, but he couldn't. "You wish you had, don't you? You wish I'd never come along, or that I'd go away so you could fall back into your safe rut."

"I don't think any of those things, but I wonder if it wouldn't be a good idea to be a little more discreet, at least until the talk dies down."

"Discreet," he repeated. "As in leave you alone."

"I didn't say that!"

"Only because you can't bring yourself to use the words. You're too much of a lady to hurt my feelings with a direct order to get out of your bed, so you're looking for a way to make me do it myself." He was saying too much, driven to it by watching everything he had gained go down the tubes. He couldn't help it. Sometimes he got these self-destructive urges and nothing less than a total flameout would do.

She was pale and there were tears rising to rim her eyes. "I didn't mean to hurt you."

"Well, you're damned well doing it."

"But since you brought it up," she continued as if he hadn't spoken, "then you might sleep somewhere else."

"Fine."

"By that, I don't mean…"

"Don't worry, I'm not going to get in a lather and go off somewhere to sulk. I may lay low for a day or two because you ask it, but you'll never be rid of me permanently. I don't care if the whole world watches over our shoulders and jabbers itself hoarse. I don't even care if your kids stand around bug-eyed with shock. You've got me, lady. Whether you want me or not, I'm yours."

There was something else she didn't understand, though she would, eventually. The fact was, he had her, too. She was his, and he wasn't going to let her go.

_____ **13** _____

Laurel worked late in the pottery shed. Maisie came to tell her she was leaving for the day and to ask about an errand she was supposed to run in town before she came to work in the morning. Not long after she left, Laurel heard Alec's bike as it roared off. She sat listening to the echoes for long moments, staring at nothing. When the sound died away at last, she closed her eyes tight in sudden desolation and clenched her hand around her carving tool. Then she took a deep, sharp breath, opened her eyes, and began once more to carve the clay in front of her.

The plaque she was working on was different from the others. For one thing, it was female. For another, the swirling design around the face was a floral motif instead of one using vines and foliage. The biggest change, however, was that the expression was not tranquil.

The woman in the clay was trying to get out. Her eyes were desperate, as if she were smothering. With her mouth open in a scream, she was fighting her entrapment. She was fighting, but she was losing.

There had been a certain technical facility about the first plaques, but this one came much closer to the kind of emotional expression Laurel had wanted to explore. It was also disturbing. She knew why, since she had the detachment to recognize her own features in the trapped woman. Still, she had not consciously chosen to use herself as a model, had not meant the figure to portray anything personal. It had come, she thought, from the turmoil inside her.

At the same time, however, there was a soft vulnerability to the face of the woman. Laurel wasn't sure what had brought that about, couldn't associate it with herself. Regardless, that softness somehow made the imprisonment harder to bear. It also made the figure more upsetting.

She lost track of time. Feeling neither hunger nor fatigue, she worked on, cutting fear and love into the clay face, buffing away the raw edges to make the image come alive. The light grew dim, and she turned on the big overhead fluorescent lights. The night deepened, growing cooler, and a breeze through the open door carried the scent of honeysuckle and roses. Still, she didn't look up—not until she heard the roar of the Harley again.

Alec had come back. She hadn't thought he would.

Anger that he had ignored her request rose inside her, but behind it, almost washing it away, was a sweet surge of anticipation. She wasn't going to run out to meet him, however, or change her schedule to suit his pleasure.

She bent over her work again, but her concentration was gone. She kept listening for his step, waiting for him to come to her. She couldn't imagine that he wouldn't; he almost always did. Yet what was taking him so long?

She heard the scuff of his approach. His shadow, cast by moonlight, fell across the doorway.

It wasn't Alec. The knowledge rang in her mind

the instant she realized he would never make that kind of scuffling entrance. Her heart jumped against the wall of her chest. She came off her stool in a fluid slide. Eyes wide, she faced the door with her carving tool held like a weapon in her hand.

The man slouched into the blue-white glare of the fluorescent lights. A crooked smile crossed his face and he ducked his head in greeting. "Evening."

"Gregory." She closed her eyes and eased back onto her stool as the strength left her legs.

"I didn't mean to scare you."

"No, no, it's all right." She managed a wan smile. "How are you doing?"

He grimaced. "I'm still here, which is something, I guess. But you were probably expecting Alec."

"Not exactly, except I thought I heard him ride up."

"The bike, yeah. I sort of borrowed it. Alec went to bed early, guess he was beat. Anyway, it didn't look like he'd be having a use for it, so…"

She didn't know quite what to say to Alec's brother. She barely knew him, and the extreme nature of his illness hung about him like a pall. Conversation with him was a little like crossing a minefield where any careless word could cause unexpected reactions. More than that, he seemed to be one of those people who had no idea how to go about polite give-and-take. Asking after people seemed like the safest bet until she could figure out what he wanted.

"So how is Miss Callie?"

"All right, I suppose. Works too hard, but seems to like it."

She suspected that most people worked too hard in Gregory's opinion. "Could I get you something to drink? Coffee and maybe some of the pound cake Maisie made today?''

Interest brightened his eyes. ''I don't suppose you've got Scotch and soda?''

''Bourbon and water,'' she offered, even as she wondered if she should. It was unlikely that he needed to mix alcohol with whatever he was taking for pain.

''That'll work,'' he said.

She studied him a moment, but decided he must surely know what he wanted and needed. Turning off the lights in the shed and closing the door, she walked with him toward the porch steps. She was glad of the company, really. The house loomed so dark and still it seemed that anything or anyone could be inside, especially since she had left the back door unlocked.

Gregory was as nervous as she was, or so it appeared. Glancing around, he said, ''It's sure spooky out here. I don't know how you stand it. You couldn't pay me enough to stay in this old house alone.''

''You get used to anything,'' she replied easily, leading the way into the screened porch and across it to the French doors that gave onto the hall, turning on lights as she went.

''Don't you ever think about getting away, living somewhere else?''

''Like where?'' In the kitchen, she took down a glass and filled it with ice from the side-by-side refrigerator. Rooting in the cabinets, she brought out the bottle of bourbon. It had been twelve years old when it was bought, and had been around long enough to celebrate its eighteenth birthday.

''Anywhere,'' he answered. ''Florida? California? Arizona? Sell this old pile and take off. There's nothing to keep you here.''

"Except my children."

"They're grown, aren't they? On their own?" he returned as he took the drink she offered.

"I suppose. But then, what would I do in Florida or California?"

"The same thing you're doing here."

She smiled as she poured a glass of water for herself and sat down across from him at the table. "Then why bother?"

He had the grace to laugh. A silence fell as he drank deep, then sighed and set the glass back on the table. Staring at it, he seemed to visibly relax. After a moment, he said, "I'm worried about old Alec."

"Is something wrong?"

"Yeah." He shot her a look from under his brows. "You."

She leaned back in her chair, folding her arms across her waist. "I don't know what you mean."

He shrugged a bony shoulder. "Well, it's like this. My brother's a nice guy, but he gets strange sometimes, goes all noble like some kind of superhero, thinks he has to take care of the world."

"I wouldn't call that strange."

"Even when what he's doing is bad for him?"

"Against his best interests, you mean," she said evenly. "Such as getting involved with a woman several years older?"

His smile was thin. "I knew you'd get it without a lot of fancy talk."

"Yes, but I don't know why you think it's so bad for him." She tightened her clasp around her ribs, not quite looking at the man across the table.

"Because he's been there already, and it turned out bad. I tried to give you a warning earlier, but I guess it didn't stick. He just doesn't need another woman falling for him, then offing herself when the going gets rough. It would send him over the edge this time. I know it would.''

"Offing? Are you trying to say his wife killed herself?''

He snorted. "That's the general idea.''

"But someone said he was arrested for murder.''

"Oh, did they? Shows how much they know. Actually, the cops had some idea Alec might have given her a hand, so to speak, but the D.A.'s office couldn't make a case. They'd never have gone to trial if her grown kids hadn't pushed it.''

"I see. Inconsiderate of them.'' She closed her lips firmly over the words.

"Certainly was, when Alec had been taking care of the old lady day and night for months.''

The old lady.

Was that how Gregory saw her? Laurel wondered. As another old lady Alec had been taking care of day and night?

Gregory was still talking. "I just don't want to see him go through something like that again. I'm not sure he can take it, wondering what he did wrong, tearing himself apart over what he could have done to stop it. He looks tough, and I guess he is as long as you're talking physical stuff, but he takes things to heart. If anything happened to you, I think he'd go off the deep end. Way off.''

Was Gregory right? She wished she knew. "That may be,'' she said carefully, "but I don't know what you expect me to do about it.''

"Cut him free. Do it now, while you can. Send Alec away for his own good. It's the only way he can ever get himself untangled, because he feels responsible for you now, and he'll never turn his back on what he considers his responsibilities."

Out of her pain, she said suggestively, "Unlike some people?"

"You got it." Gregory's laugh was short. "I know he's worth three of me, always has been. I also know it's time he quit trying to rescue everybody else and thought about himself."

"Are you quite sure," she asked softly, "that it's him you're worried about? Are you sure you aren't afraid that he'll use his time taking care of other people instead of being there for you?"

He sat back, letting his hands flop into his lap. His gaze wide on her face, he said, "You look soft, but you know how to fight dirty."

"Only in retaliation," she said grimly.

"Yeah, well, me, too. Think what you like, I don't give a damn. Alec is my brother, and I'm looking after him this time. He's never had a fair shake, you know? So he's got to the point he doesn't expect one anymore, just takes what he can get. But he deserves better. I don't want him getting in too deep with you—not if he's going to lose in the end."

She watched him for a long moment after he stopped speaking. Then she sighed. "All right, I'm sorry. I'm sure you're concerned; but then so am I. The last thing I want to do is hurt Alec in any way. The two of us discussed this situation and agreed that it would be best if we didn't...that is, if we remain on a businesslike, employer-employee basis for the time being. Short of firing him—which won't work because I've already tried it—I don't know what else to do."

"You fired him?"

She gave a short nod. "He kept coming back, anyway."

"And you think he's going to stay away now on your say-so?" Gregory asked with a laugh.

"He isn't here now," she pointed out with some emphasis.

"He was tired, and no wonder. Besides, he's not stupid. He'll give you time to cool off, time to miss him."

Was Alec that calculating? She didn't like to think so, yet how could she say? For all the hours they had spent together, she knew little more about him than she did Gregory.

"Then I don't know what you expect me to do," she said.

"Don't give him hope you don't mean to deliver on, because it will kill him when you take it away. Protect him from himself. Get rid of him."

"And if he won't go?"

"You're a smart woman, you can find a way."

She might, but did she want to? That was the question.

At least it was one she didn't need to find an answer to just now. "I'll think about it."

"Fair enough."

Gregory downed the rest of his bourbon and water, then got to his feet. She made no effort to detain him, but saw him to the front door. On the veranda steps, he paused and turned back.

"You won't tell Alec I came by, will you?"

"Is there some reason I shouldn't?" she asked, though more to put him on the spot than because she intended to entertain Alec with the news.

"He won't like it if he thinks I've been arranging things behind his back. He's funny that way—thinks he can interfere all he wants, but it makes him hot under the collar if anybody meddles in his business."

"Most of us are like that, I imagine," she answered.

Gregory hesitated, as if he meant to force a more definite answer from her, then his lips firmed. With a curt, "Good night," he took himself down the steps and out to the bike on the drive. A moment later, it peeled away, wobbling on its rear tire before it sped off into the night.

Laurel stood staring after it for some time, her gaze on the spot where the bright red pattern of its rear lights had disappeared into the darkness. Finally, she turned and went back into the house.

It was hours later that she sat straight up in bed. Her breath was caught in her throat. Her pulse hammered wildly in her veins. For an instant, her heartbeat was so loud in her ears that she couldn't hear. Then it came again—the noise that had cut through her dreams.

It sounded like breaking glass only duller. A rattling clatter followed on it like something falling, shattering into more pieces as it struck the ground. Torn from deep, almost-drugged sleep, Laurel couldn't force her brain to make sense of what she was hearing.

Then she knew. Her sculpted garden pieces. Someone was smashing them.

She flung back the covers and slid from the bed. Shaking as if from a chill, she moved to the bedroom window. She twitched the curtain aside a fraction and looked out.

Nothing.

The moon had set, the backyard was dark and still. Not a flicker of movement could be seen.

The noise had stopped, also, as abruptly as it had begun. Perhaps whoever was out there had heard her footsteps in the house or seen her at the window. What were they doing now?

Swinging around, she moved out of the bedroom and down the hall to the front door with its small-paned sidelights. It seemed brighter in the front garden, perhaps because the trees did not press so close. Still, she could see no sign of any intruder.

The view from the dining room was no better, nor that through the small panes of the back French doors. She put her hand on the handle of the French doors. Then she stopped, removed it again.

There was nothing she could do now to save her pieces; of that she was fairly certain. There was no reason, then, to go running out into the dark, and every reason to stay inside where she was comparatively safe. Still, the thought of somebody sneaking into her yard and destroying her property made her feel hot all over. All her work, all her pride of accomplishment, crushed in a few seconds. It went against the grain to stand by and do nothing when what she wanted was to tear out after them and demand to know what gave them the right. She wanted to strike back, fairly itched to knock somebody into next Sunday.

What kept her from it was common sense. Whoever was out there had a weapon of some kind in their hands. More than that, there was a good chance the same person had killed Sticks. The taste for spying, vandalism and poisoning they had shown so far didn't make them a good bet for perfect sanity. They could be waiting for her to open the door.

She wasn't going to stand by and do nothing, though. She was tired of being gossiped about and warned and terrorized.

First, she would call Dan Tanning and file a report with the sheriff's office. That would be a start. Then she could fight fire with fire by asking Maisie to call people and talk about the things that were going on and about who might be behind them. Yes, and better than that, she could get in her car and drive into town to Zelda's shop....

Get in her car. Leave Ivywild and drive into town. Just like that. Where had the idea come from?

Could she do that when just days ago the thought had seemed so impossible? Were her reasons strong enough to sustain her through such an ordeal? Was it possible when her heart was thumping so hard it shook her nightgown and the very idea made her feel sick and weak?

But what other choice was there? She couldn't just abandon herself to whatever this crazy person had in store. She couldn't hide away forever while someone crept closer and closer....

No. She wouldn't think like that. She wouldn't.

She could call Alec. If she picked up the phone, he would be here in a few short minutes. He would take care of everything while she sat back and watched and applauded.

Yes, but she didn't want that; didn't want to involve him any more than he was already, or to feel that she owed him anything else. It was time, finally, that she fought her own battles.

As she hovered there, she heard the sound of a car engine starting, then moving off into the night. Her tormentor was gone. He had struck fast, and left. Again.

She was almost certain he was no longer a threat, but she couldn't be positive short of venturing out. She had to do it, was driven by her need to see how much damage had been done. It took nearly an hour of watching and listening before she gained the courage.

The damage was total. Her *Bocca della Verità* lay in far-flung pieces, as if smashed by a sledgehammer, and the Bacchus fountain was a ruin. The water mirrors had been overturned and cracked, the flowerpots from the top of the old cistern dumped into the lily pool. The destruction was wanton and messy, as if whoever had caused it had enjoyed it.

She should call the police, she really should. But on second thought, the damage wasn't that great in terms of money, and the thought of the explanations she would have to give Dan Tanning and his deputies paralyzed her with indecision and embarrassment.

She couldn't face it. Still, something had to be done. Somehow, she had to find out who was behind this campaign of terror and stop them.

Suppose, just suppose, it was Alec himself? He had denied being the prowler the night they'd made love, but what if it was a lie? What if it had been a ruse to make her more dependent on him? As for destroying the plaques and other garden pieces she had made, he was the one person who knew exactly where they were and what they meant to her. And he had been mad enough when he left to smash things bigger and more valuable by far. She didn't like thinking he might have taken such a petty revenge. Yet how did she know what he was capable of doing?

It might also have been Gregory, since he hadn't exactly been pleased with her, either. Or it could have been Mother Bancroft. Come to think of it, Zelda hadn't been happy when Laurel had seen her last. Was everybody in Hillsboro out to get her?

Of course, there was nothing that said whoever had been out there tonight felt the least enmity toward her. It could be a case of cold and calculated revenge, which was infinitely worse. And maybe she should stop thinking about it before she frightened herself out of her wits.

Impossible.

As she lay awake, staring into the dark and feeling the great emptiness of the big bedroom around her, Laurel's mind spun in endless circles. Again and again, she went over the different people who might have something against her. Over and over, she thought of Alec and the way he had looked that afternoon and the things he had said.

Even when she drifted off to sleep, she heard the sound of breaking terra-cotta in her dreams. She was forced by some unseen presence to walk, step by slow and bloody step, over the shattered pieces. And at the end of the walk was her car with the door standing open, waiting for her. Only once she was inside, she had no control and knew it would take her where she didn't want to go. Knew, too, that she was never going to be able to find her way back to Ivywild.

14

Laurel's hands began to shake while she was putting on her makeup. She tried not to think about what she was planning to do this morning, but it didn't help. By the time she had walked from the house to the garage, her knees were wobbly and she felt light-headed. It was all she could do to open the door and slide into the driver's seat. Then she couldn't make herself turn the key.

Agoraphobia. That was the name for her problem. Not long ago, she would have denied that she had it. She would also have sworn she had no interest in leaving her house and that was the only reason she stayed. Alec had proved otherwise. Now she had to admit her fear of leaving Ivywild.

She would beat it this morning, she was certain, since she suspected her case was fairly mild. She had given herself plenty of time. It was less than fifteen minutes to Zelda's beauty shop, and she had at least an hour. All she had to do was turn the key and back the car out of the garage. She had done that before with Alec beside her. Surely she could do it again.

It took a good forty minutes and two trips back inside the house—one to check that she had turned off the oven, one to be sure she had unplugged the iron. Excuses, she knew, but she was unable to prevent herself from acting on them. It was anger that forced her back out of the house and into the car each time. That, and her dread of what might happen if she didn't do something to prevent it.

Finally she had the engine running and the Buick at the end of the drive, facing the road. Her hands and knees still trembled, but she had grown so used to it that she could ignore it. Terror that she had forgotten the driving rules and regulations beat in her mind, but she forced that down, as well. She wiped the damp palms of her hands on her skirt, took a death grip on the steering wheel, then eased her foot from the brake and stepped on the accelerator.

So far, so good. She was out on the road. As the minutes and miles passed, her hands grew steadier. Fear and dread gave way to satisfaction, then quickly became a cautious euphoria.

She had done it! She was driving, keeping the car between the ditches, getting used to the feel of being responsible for the vehicle again. Thank goodness she had a little time before she had to get out on the main highway. Thank God she had already gone this way with Alec on his bike, while he had been in control.

He had helped her more than she'd realized. Did he know? Had he recognized her problem all along? He must have; but, to his credit, he had not made her feel less competent, less of a person, because of it.

He was an unusual man. She was only beginning to recognize how unusual.

When she parked in front of the beauty shop at last, Laurel put her head on the steering wheel and closed her eyes. She felt drained, as if she had run a marathon. However, the ordeal wasn't over yet. Not only did she have to drive back home, but she had to get through the next hour with Zelda.

Her sister-in-law greeted her with a raucous yell from where she stood twisting an older woman's thin white hair onto permanent-wave rollers. "Laurel, honey, come in here! Have a seat, throw the magazines off that chair right there. This is just like old times, you coming in for a trim!"

There was nothing fancy about Zelda's shop. Set up in a small house trailer, its vinyl flooring and shampoo and comb-out equipment had seen better days. Bottles and spray cans lined the burgundy cabinets beneath the mirrors, while a broom stood guard over a pile of hair in assorted shades near the back door. Still, the place had an air of prosperity, with its array of new products and posters—possibly because it was just cluttered enough to make the women of Hillsboro feel at home.

Laurel spoke to the woman in rollers, whom she recognized as a retired schoolteacher—long retired, actually. Miss Dacey must be eighty-five or ninety if she was a day, Laurel knew, since the elderly woman had taught her mother.

"Haven't see you in a while, my dear," the elderly woman said.

Laurel, clearing the seat Zelda had indicated and sinking onto it, murmured something about getting out more.

"About time, too," Zelda said in her forthright way. "I was just telling Miss Dacey that it's not healthy, you staying cooped up out there at Ivywild. I blame myself for it in a way, I really do. I should have visited more, maybe talked you into going shopping or to a movie. But don't you worry, it's going to be different from now on.''

"It's nice of you to be concerned, but I'm sure you have other things to worry about," Laurel said with careful politeness.

"Yes, well, I do," Zelda said candidly, as she reached for a roller from the tray beside her. "Family and all that. Plus I have to work, of course, which you don't and never have."

"Ivywild keeps me busy, and my pottery," Laurel said, retaining her smile even in the face of her sister-in-law's derogatory tone. Then, seizing on the glimmer of an opening for what she had come to say, she went on. "I'll certainly be busy in the pottery shed this week. Can you believe somebody came to the house last night and smashed the Green Man plaques I spent so much time making?"

"You don't mean it," Zelda replied, pausing with a curl half-wound. "Of all the nerve!"

"They tried to break the columns Alec and I had cast, too, but the stoneware was too strong. I hope they dislocated their shoulder whacking at them."

"Ouch," Zelda said with a lifted brow and a one-sided grin. "Bloodthirsty, aren't you?"

"I'd like to take a pistol and put a hole through them! And I may, next time anybody shows up in the middle of the night who has no business being there."

Howard's sister tilted her head. "That include you-know-who?"

"If you mean Alec Stanton, he has nothing to do with it," she answered, the words tart.

"Uh-oh," Zelda said, rolling the last bit of hair on her customer's head, then reaching for the bottle of solution that sat ready. "Sounds like he must have lost his rabbit's foot where you're concerned."

"You could say that," Laurel murmured, looking away from the other woman. Not only was it true, but it seemed just as well that the information should become common knowledge.

The sharp smell of chemical solution filled the warm, moist air. A short silence fell while Zelda busied herself a few minutes making sure every curl on the older woman's head was well soaked.

Miss Dacey peeked at Laurel from where she sat with her neck bent forward. In querulous tones, she said, "You wouldn't be talking about Callie Stanton's grandson, would you?"

Zelda rolled her eyes, but Laurel summoned a smile. "You know him?"

"I know Callie, have for years, but can't say I'm acquainted with young Alec. I've seen him around, though, and he seems a nice young man."

"Why, Miss Dacey, don't tell me you like all that long hair?" Zelda said in teasing tones.

"And just why not?" the older woman demanded with raised eyebrows. "I've nothing to say against it, long as it's clean. Lord knows, young people always have to be different. Reminds me of the time when women started cutting their hair. You'd have thought they were Jezebels, every one, to hear people talk. They weren't, of course, any more than this young man is the heathen people are claiming. Besides, he looks like half the men on my television to me."

"Very true, Miss Dacey," Laurel said, smiling. "You're a woman after my own heart."

The white-haired woman colored with pleasure. "Pshaw. Just common sense."

"A lot of people can't see it, though," Zelda added with a shake of her head as she finished with the solution, then helped Miss Dacey from the chair and piloted her toward a hair dryer. "Just yesterday I heard somebody saying he ought to be run out of town."

"A mean, cruel thing, that," the older woman remarked as she shuffled across the room. "When I was a child, there was a stranger they dipped in hot tar, rolled in feathers, and rode out of town on a fence rail. They said he almost died."

"That was ages ago," Laurel said. "Surely they wouldn't do such a thing now."

"Hard to say what people will do when they get stirred up." The white-haired woman sat back and was quiet as Zelda flipped on the dryer, drowning out all other sound.

Laurel looked at Zelda in weary disbelief. "Where is it coming from, all this hatred and spite? I don't understand."

"Who knows how things get started?" Zelda said, lifting a plump shoulder. "But I guess if your Alec isn't hanging around anymore, that means you'll have to give up on doing anything else to Ivywild."

"Oh, he's still working," Laurel replied absently.

"I thought you said he was out of the picture."

"I only meant that there's nothing between us, not really." Her smile was wan. "How anybody could think there might be when I'm so much older, I can't imagine."

"I did wonder about that myself," Zelda commented frankly, then burst out laughing at the look on Laurel's face. "Just kidding, just kidding. Now, come sit in this chair and tell me what you want done to your hair.''

Laurel did as instructed—not that it mattered. Zelda shampooed her hair, trimmed the ends, and blow-dried it, but instead of brushing it into the simple style Laurel preferred, her sister-in-law reached for mousse and a teasing comb. When Laurel left she had one of Zelda's "big hair" specials that gave her the over-blown appearance of a cheap call girl. The need for a stiff hairbrush and a few minutes in front of a mirror to repair the damage was so strong that she was half-way home before she realized driving wasn't bothering her at all.

Alec stood in the pottery shed, staring at the latest plaque Laurel had made. His throat ached as he touched the straining female face that was almost concealed by flowers, trapped and smothering among them. The urge to crush the fired clay was nearly overpowering, as if that would free the figure caught inside.

It was Laurel, of course. He hadn't known she felt her imprisonment so much—he'd thought she preferred it. Wrong. She was fighting it as well as she could, but the weapons she had were not particularly strong.

He would help her if she would let him. Why wouldn't she? Was it just that she didn't quite trust him? Or was he, in some way he didn't quite understand, a part of what was holding her captive?

She was gone when he'd arrived this morning. A note had been left for Maisie saying where she was, but none for him. He had immediately started worrying about her having an accident, or maybe getting somewhere and freezing up, being unable to drive herself home. That was before he had seen the pieces of broken terra-cotta littering the ground.

She had been alone at Ivywild while it was happening. She must have been terrified. But she hadn't called him, hadn't stayed to tell him. She had driven off to the beauty salon as if her appointment was more important.

He wished she had been here, wished she had met him at the door yelling and shouting about how he had deserted her so that it was his fault the pieces of pottery she had been so proud of had been destroyed. Maybe he could have wallowed in his guilt, then gotten over it. Maybe he'd even have been angry enough to forget he had failed her.

She had sent him away. That was why.

No matter how many million times he told himself that, however, it made no difference. He never should have gone. He had known then it was wrong; known he should follow his instinct and stick close. Instead, he had let pride force him into walking away, and this was what had happened.

Regardless, he had learned something important from it. He had learned how much Laurel needed him, and how little she was able to admit it.

Alec had come into the shed looking for whatever she had been working on lately, hoping she had completed something he could hang in place of what had been destroyed. This new plaque wasn't it. The female figure was too private, too harrowing, to be displayed so casually.

He put it down, then stood with his hands at his waist as he looked around for something else. His gaze raked across a box on a high shelf. It had been pushed back, almost out of sight, but he was taller than Laurel, and could see and reach farther.

He was stunned when he opened the box and saw his own face staring up at him. No wonder she had hidden it. God, she was good. Too good. All the dewy-eyed sensitivity he tried so hard to hide stared at him from the plaque. Overlying it was his crass lust for her body and stupid male certainty that it was a prize to be won rather than a gift she might give freely.

"What are you doing?"

He swung sharply to face Laurel. Her arrival was a surprise, but even more startling was that he had been so fascinated with what he had found that he hadn't heard her car drive up. Voice even, he answered, "Looking."

"At what?" She came forward into the shed, away from the doorway where she had been little more than a silhouette against the bright sunlight outside.

He blinked, his gaze focusing on her head. "What have you done to your hair?"

She put up a hand to rake her fingers through the high waves and sausage curls, flattening one side even as she tossed the mass of it over her shoulder. "Never mind my hair. I want to know why you're in here."

He was silent a moment longer, distracted by the image of Laurel as both angel and wanton, torn by the need to have her look as he was used to seeing her and the urge to take her to bed and explore this different female. Finally, he said, "I came in here looking for another plaque to put up, but there doesn't seem to be one."

"No. Now, if you'll—"

"If you wanted to hang the one with my face, I wouldn't mind. I might even be flattered."

"That was not the idea," she said flatly. "Believe me."

"Just what was?" As her face tightened, he added hastily, "I'm not playing dumb—at least I hope not. I'd really like to know."

"Nothing," she said. "I was just...playing with the clay. The equivalent of doodling, I guess."

"I'd love to see what happens when you get serious."

Her gaze went to the female plaque on the side bench. "I doubt it. The results could be too much like a gargoyle, something to scare away the demons. Or people."

He shook his head. "Don't sell yourself short. You have a gift."

"I have a knack," she corrected him. "But it doesn't make any difference, so long as I enjoy it. Now, if you have nothing to do, I'm sure I can find something."

"Actually," he said, grinning as he moved toward her, "I had a few ideas. But I'm willing to listen to suggestions."

"Stop!"

She put out her hand as if she thought that would keep him away. He kept walking until her fingers were resting on the wall of his chest. "Stop where?" The words were tinged with irony. "Don't you think it's a little late to draw the line here when we've been much closer in other places?"

"I thought we agreed to be—"

"Discreet, yes, in public. But not in private, not

always." He looked thoughtful. "At least, I don't remember that part of the bargain."

"You know very well that's what I meant."

Her hand was trembling where she touched his chest. He could feel the shivers of her distress all the way to his toes. It affected him in many ways, not all of them admirable. With a wry smile, he said, "I know a way to make it all right."

"I'll just bet you do," she retorted.

His smile widened. "Oh, Laurel, you'll be the death of me. What do you think I meant?"

"I have no idea," she said, her lashes flickering, "but I expect it's something..."

"Sexy," he supplied as she paused.

"Lecherous, to say the least," she answered, raising her chin in defiance.

He caught her fingers that rested against him and lifted the tips to his mouth for a quick kiss. Still holding on, he said, "Well, I don't think so, but I suppose it all depends on why you get married."

Her fingers clenched involuntarily on his as her eyes snapped wide with shock. "Married!"

"It's a holy state ordained by God and consecrated—"

"I know what it is! I'm only surprised that you would mention the word." She tried to drag her hand free, but he wouldn't permit it.

"I'm not just mentioning it," he said deliberately. "I'm asking you to marry me."

She became perfectly still. "You aren't serious."

"As a preacher," he assured her. "I can't think of a better way to stop the talk, can you? Besides that, think of the advantages. Since I'm a decade younger, we have the same life expectancy. You won't ever have to be a widow again. I adore mature females who prefer golden oldies and know their own minds—and just look at you, perfect in every way."

"Alec—"

"Then there's that question you raised of sexual compatibility—"

"I didn't!"

He gave her a look from under his lashes. "No? I thought you did. You're a woman who requires a lot of loving, and guess what? I just happen to be the right age to provide it. And then some."

She stared at him as if waiting to be sure he was finished before she tried again to reason with him. He wasn't done yet, but it was only polite to let her have her say.

"You've got it all figured out, haven't you?" she said finally, lips tight.

"It didn't take a genius, especially after I realized exactly how I feel about you."

"You love me, I think you said."

The words held no joy. She didn't believe a one of them. In grim acknowledgment, he answered, "Yes, I do."

"You've loved me from the first moment you saw me."

His agreement was even, watchful.

"You will always love me, even when my hair is gray and I haven't a tooth in my head."

"I don't care if you're bald—or have enough hair for three women," he said with a glance at her hairstyle.

"Touching. But are you sure things are supposed to last that long?" she demanded, her voice turning strident. "Or should I plan on committing suicide when you get tired of having me around? And if I don't find the idea too attractive, will you be there to help me?''

He felt the blood drain out of his head, felt his breath stop as if he had been kicked in the chest. His brain reeled, then steadied, but the sickness rising inside him grew stronger.

"Who told you that?" he asked softly.

"What does it matter? I know."

"You don't know anything."

"She died, didn't she?"

"Yes, she did."

"By her own hand?"

"She was sick. Already dying, anyway."

"And you were arrested for her murder."

He looked away from her, putting a hand to his head, which had begun to throb. "It's a long story. But I didn't kill my wife."

"You weren't found guilty, you mean."

"Don't put words in my mouth! What happened in California has nothing to do with us. This is different. You're different in every way from Mrs. Chadwick. You're so young in so many ways that I actually feel years older—not that this has anything to do with age, yours or mine. It's about two people who can laugh and talk and enjoy the same things. A man and a woman who actually like each other but, most of all, can come together and make magic."

"Is that it?" she asked, the words only a breath of sound. "Or is it about money and being safe?"

"Laurel," he began, taking a step forward in spite of her restraint as he searched for the patience and endurance to try again.

"No." She backed away from him. "Just—no. I

don't want to get married. I don't want to marry you or any other man. Not now, not ever."

He moved after her. "Is it really me," he demanded, "or is it you? Maybe the whole idea just scares you to death."

"Maybe it's everything. I don't know," she replied. "But the answer is still the same."

She swung away from him, heading toward the house. To her departing back, he said, "What happened? What did your Howard do to turn you off marriage for life? Yes, and here's another question while we're on the subject—Was it enough to make you kill him?"

She heard him, he knew she did. But she didn't answer.

Alec stood where she left him, staring at nothing. After a moment, he turned to glance at the two plaques Laurel had done, his face and her own, leering male and trapped female. A short laugh left him. Picking them up, he took them to the Italian garden and hung them side by side where the *Bocca della Verità* had been. It seemed appropriate.

Afterward, he took an ax and attacked the woods that grew close to the back of the house. Clearing the undergrowth would leave less cover for whoever was sneaking around. Most of all, it provided the exertion he needed to keep him from doing something violent that would get him in trouble.

That was where he was, in the woods again with an ax in his hands, when the police car drove up. He stood perfectly still as he watched the man in uniform get out and make his way through the front garden, then mount the steps to the house.

* * *

Laurel looked up from paying her bills when the hard, steady chop of the ax stopped. She was already on her feet, moving toward the front of the house, when she heard Maisie open the door. By the time she reached the hall, the housekeeper and the sheriff were standing just inside while Dan Tanning, his hat in his hand, answered the usual queries from Maisie about the state of law enforcement in Hillsboro. He turned with a smile on his broad features as Laurel moved forward to greet him.

"Hope you don't mind me dropping by," he said in his slow, deep voice. "I heard about the problems you've been having out here and thought I'd check into it."

"You're always welcome, you know that," she said easily. "But I think you must have been talking to Zelda."

He ducked his head, flushing a little. "She lowers my ears for me now and then—as my dad used to call getting a haircut. I was by there this morning not long after you left. She's worried about you."

"I appreciate you coming by, but doubt there's anything you can do. I never caught sight of whoever was out there."

"Maybe I could just check out the damage, anyway." He waved his hat in a vague gesture that encompassed the outside of the house.

"There's not much left to see," she said doubtfully as she indicated they would go out the front door, then moved ahead of him onto the veranda.

"It's all cleaned up?" He gave her a narrow look from under his thick brows.

She nodded. "First thing this morning."

"And who did that?"

"Alec, when he got here."

A grunting sound that could have meant anything came from his chest. "I'll just look around, anyway, if you don't mind. Might be something that jumps out at me."

She led him from the house. As she walked, she was aware of his solid bulk behind her, as well as his close scrutiny. He was a straightforward man, she thought, with nothing particularly complicated about him. Whatever he said, he would mean—no more and no less. It was a relief, in its way.

A few inane remarks about the weather occupied them as they walked toward the back. Then they were at the Italian garden. Laurel felt her nerves tighten as she stepped through the portal and saw the male and female plaques hanging there, side by side.

Alec, of course. No doubt he was making a point. Unlike the sheriff, he was not a simple man.

Taking a deep breath, she explained about the pieces of terra-cotta that had been broken. The sheriff nodded his understanding. His gaze remained an instant on the two new plaques, but if he saw any resemblance in them to real people, he made no comment. Instead, he said, "You didn't find anything lying around that might have been used to cause the damage?"

"You mean a stick or something?"

"Length of firewood, baseball bat, hammer, crowbar, anything."

She shook her head.

"Too bad. Could have given us an idea whether it was just kids or somebody that meant business. We might even have been able to scare up a fingerprint or two from it.''

''I can ask Alec, but I'm sure he'd have mentioned it if he had come across anything.''

The look he gave her was intent, but he made no answer. Turning, she left the Italian garden and walked to the side of the garage where the Bacchus fountain had been. There was nothing of interest there now. Alec had shut off the water, leaving the basin sitting empty and forlorn beneath the raw pipe of the spout.

Dan whistled as he stared at the scars in the wood of the garage wall where blows had been struck to break the mask. ''I don't like this, Laurel. It's got a bad feel to it. I know it's none of my business, but I really wish you weren't out here alone at night.''

''I've been alone since last year when Evan went off to school. Now is no different.''

''I think it is, and I'm not just talking after Zelda, either. I went by to see Miss Callie, too, and she's up in arms about the whole thing. Then Howard's mother bent my ear about it a few days back. Maybe you should see about getting somebody out to spend the nights.''

''Who? Mother Bancroft? Zelda?'' She kept her voice light with an effort. ''I don't think so.''

''What about Evan? He could drive back and forth to summer school for a couple of weeks, maybe. Or could be your daughter and son-in-law could stay around.''

Evan was a possibility. As for Marcia and Jimmy, her daughter might be all right, but not with her husband in tow. ''I'll think about it.''

''Good.'' He paused. ''Meantime, I'll put one of

the girls in the office on the computer, see what they got in California about—certain people."

"You mean Alec?"

"And the brother."

"I don't think that's necessary."

"Maybe, maybe not. If they're clean, it's no big deal. If not—well, it's best to know."

There was nothing she could do to stop him. "You may find a problem or two, but it isn't anything I don't know about already."

"We'll see," he answered noncommittally. "But you're not to worry too much. I'll do my best to swing by here more often on rounds, or else send one of my deputies."

"You don't have to do that."

"I know I don't," he said, his tone low, "but I always was crazy about you, Laurel, you know that. I thought once, there, a year or so after Howard died, that we might get together, then..." He left the sentence unfinished as he looked away from her.

He was thinking, she supposed, of his bad luck in being caught with Zelda. Laurel might not have remembered if her sister-in-law hadn't mentioned the incident lately. Not that it had made any real difference, as far as she was concerned. She liked Dan well enough, could see his good qualities, but there was no chemistry between them. At least there wasn't from her point of view. Standing beside him did absolutely nothing for her heart rate. Unlike standing near Alec.

"I value the thought," she said quietly, "but I guess some things just don't work out."

He cut his eyes in her direction, then away again. Off in the woods behind the house, they could hear the sharp crack of an ax against wood once more. With his gaze fixed on the spot the sound was coming from, Dan spoke again. "So now you've got Miss Callie's grandson hanging around. I guess you're old enough to know what you're doing."

"I like to think so."

"You'll be careful?"

"Yes, I'll do that."

"Good." He reached up to rake a hand through his hair, then replaced his hat and pulled the brim low. "Guess I'd better be getting along. You think about what I said, now."

She agreed, then walked with him back along the wall of the garage and through the rose garden to where his black and white was parked on the front drive. He gave her a brief smile and a salute, then got in and drove away. It was a long time before she turned and went back into the house.

15

When Laurel walked out of the bathroom, Alec was lying on the bed in the darkened bedroom. He was propped up on her pillows with his hands behind his head, wearing only a pair of jeans. His smile was meltingly intimate.

She stopped, hovering with her hand clenched on the coarse-toothed hairbrush caught in the long, tangled skein of her wet hair that hung over her shoulder. Her heart began to do wild somersaults in her chest. Her mouth was suddenly dry. The first thing that flashed through her head was to wonder if the white cotton of her gown was as transparent as she suspected. As if it mattered.

Her voice blank, she asked, "How did you get in here?"

"I could pick old locks like yours before I could walk. It's a wonder somebody hasn't made off with everything you own. Or you." The look in his eyes as he surveyed her in her worn nightgown had heat around the edges.

"I suppose you have a reason?" She dragged the brush through the ends of her hair, which she held in her free hand, working at the tangles to avoid looking at him.

"A couple of them. Number one, you need somebody on guard duty—whether you believe it or not—and I'm available. Number two…''

She glanced up as he paused. ''Number two?''

His smile was deliberate, his voice husky. ''I was hoping maybe you had missed your boy toy. I thought you might want to take him out and play with him.''

The color that mounted into her face matched the images flaring in her mind. She hoped he couldn't see that telltale flush with the light behind her. ''After the things we said this afternoon? You can't be serious.''

''No?''

''Of course not!''

''Too bad.'' The shake of his head was mournful, yet the shadow of something like pain lay in the darkness of his eyes.

''Oh, come on!'' she said, lowering her brush and flinging the jumbled mass of her damp hair behind her. ''Surely you don't expect to be taken so lightly.''

He thought about it while his lips took on a judicious twist. ''Depends.''

''On what?''

''Who's doing the taking?'' he suggested with a lifted brow.

She closed her eyes. He was teasing again. Or was he? It was distinctly possible he was primed to go either way, depending on her reaction. She should have been angry, suspicious, but instead she felt the slow rise of relief.

The name she called him was not exactly a compliment, but neither was there any force behind it.

''I know, but you should see your face,'' he answered in grim agreement.

''It's not really funny.'' Her voice was querulous.

He shrugged a little, his gaze frank. ''I've met

women like your sister-in-law before. They confuse being rude and crude with being sophisticated. The only way she can bother me is if what she says turns you against me. On the other hand, I seem more than able to do that myself every time I open my big mouth.''

The somber tone of his voice and self-deprecating assessment were disarming. That they were meant to be, she didn't doubt for a minute; still, she couldn't deny the result. Without quite looking at him, she replied, "We both said things we didn't mean. The situation is so bizarre that I guess it's not surprising."

"Self-defense mechanism. For both of us."

It was a reasonable excuse if she wanted to accept it. In her agitation, she tilted her head and attacked the wet tangle of her hair again, muttering under her breath as the brush immediately became embedded in the thick swath.

"Hey, hold on," Alec exclaimed, coming off the bed in an effortless glide of firm muscles. "Keep on like that and you won't have any hair left." He moved toward her, took the brush from her hand. "Let me."

She resisted for a moment, but he was determined. Circling her wrist with his strong fingers, he led her back to the bed. He dropped down to sit on the edge, then made room for her between his spread knees. As he pulled her between his legs with her back to him, he drew her hair between her shoulder blades. Working with care, he released the brush from the long strands, then began to remove their snarls with deft efficiency.

His concentration was total. Combined with the feel of his hands on her hair, it was amazingly intimate. The effort it took not to lean against him, into him, amazed her.

She ought not to be doing this. She should have stood her ground and ordered him out of her house; should never have stopped to bandy words with him. She should have refused to come close at any price. Certainly, she should never have let him put his hands on her, even in so benign a task as brushing her hair.

She didn't have an ounce of common sense. Or the tiniest bit of willpower.

Clearing her throat after a moment, she said, "You're very good at this."

"I should be, don't you think?" he replied, tossing his own long ponytail over his shoulder with a quick gesture. "Of course, I started out on my little sister, trying to get her ready for school."

The image he evoked, of a teenage boy determined to make his sister look presentable, trying to take the place of mother and father to her, made her heart ache. She didn't want to be affected, knew he had no use for her compassion, but she still couldn't help it.

Before she could recover, he said, "I hear you're threatening to shoot people again."

She tried to look at him over her shoulder, but he was holding her hair and she couldn't turn her head. Subsiding, she asked, "Who said so?"

"Some older woman phoned Gran, said she heard it at the beauty shop. Gran asked me about it when I went home after work this evening."

"I was upset."

"So now, whoever comes around will be armed."

She gave an exasperated sigh. "What was I supposed to do? Turn the other cheek? Let them ruin everything you and I worked so hard to accomplish?"

"You don't have to do anything, not when you have me." His hands were steady, gentle, on her hair.

"Since I didn't know I would have you or anyone else, it seemed best to handle it myself."

"You'll always have me. Whether you marry me or not."

She jerked around to look at him, ignoring the pull on her hair. "Don't say that!"

"Why not, if it's true? I didn't mean to push you or ask more than you can give. It won't happen again."

She hated the resigned tone of his voice, hated that she had put it there even as she wondered what was behind it, what he was after. She began to shake her head. "Alec, I don't think…"

"Then don't try," he said, the words firm. "This isn't a big deal, I promise. You need me right now and I need you. We don't have to think about tomorrow or 'forever.' Only this moment, right now, matters. Is that so hard?"

It wasn't hard at all, that was the trouble. "Oh, Alec, you deserve more than just to be needed."

His lashes flickered and the definite molding of his lips firmed. "Let me worry about that." His gaze dropped to the silken tresses he still held captive in one hand. In lighter tones, he added, "That first night, when I saw you come out of the house, I thought your hair was like moonbeams. I like it much better like this, silky smooth, instead of fluffy the way it was this morning."

"Thank you. I think."

Her voice was subdued as she answered. He was changing the subject, and who could blame him? She didn't want to talk about everything that was between

them, either. Didn't want to think about all the doubts
and fears and problems. She couldn't—not while her
upper arm was pressed against the firm wall of his
chest and she could feel his taut thighs on either side
of her hips. His body heat surrounded her like a caress. His warm, clean scent mounted to her head like
a breathable aphrodisiac. She wanted him with a deep,
slow ache that nothing could assuage except his
touch, his strength against her.

What was it about him that muddled her thoughts
and destroyed her will to resist? She had heard about
men and women who risked everything for the sake
of a lover, but had never expected to understand quite
so thoroughly the urgency that moved them. At this
moment, she didn't care what happened next or what
happened to her. It was enough that Alec was here
with her. And she really felt she might die if he did
not kiss her.

Perhaps something of her longing was in her face,
for his movements stilled. He met her gaze, his own
dark and strained, yet tumultuous. He tossed the hairbrush aside and pulled her to him.

To Alec, it felt as if he had won. Lovely, lovely
prize. He would be generous in his victory, if he could
manage it when she drove him so crazy.

He kissed the delectable corner of her mouth,
which was as tender and moist as a child's. He
brushed the warm satin of her cheek with his nose,
felt it against his eyelids, his cheekbone. Moving to
her ear, he dipped his tongue inside, tasting her, then
caught her earlobe between his teeth. At the same
time, he smoothed his hands over her rib cage, moving upward to gather the cushioned softness of her

breast in his hand, capturing the nipple that tightened at once to a succulent bud. Perfect, she was so perfect, and so responsive to his least touch. The soft sound she made struck a chord inside him that resonated in his heart. With his lips he captured that sweet moan, held it inside him.

God, but he hurt with the pressure of wanting her. It wasn't just about sex, but about what was in his head, his heart, his lungs, every cell in his body. The need to feel her naked against him was so strong that he reached for the hem of her gown and pulled it up to her waist. He only released her lips long enough to skim the nightgown over her head. Then he took them again as he dragged her higher in his arms. He turned her completely to face him as, holding her against him, he lay back on the bed. Spreading his hands, he gripped her backside, pressing her feminine heat to him while her hair spilled forward, tickling, teasing, driving him mad with its fragrance and damp, silky softness along his face, neck, shoulders.

He loved it, loved her body, loved kissing her, thrusting his tongue into the moist velvet heat of her. He loved the sugar-sweet, minty toothpaste flavor of her mouth. Loved her. And he had to have her now, before he exploded.

In a swirl of hair and limbs, he heaved her over onto her back. Struggling, cursing in whispers, he unzipped his jeans and shucked them down, then kicked free of them. He put a knee between her legs, then followed it with hot, heavy, ready male. He slid into her, gasping, winded by the shock of pleasure. Her warm depths were encompassing; they held him, pulsed around him. He plunged deeper, his hands grasping her to him as he probed satin eternity.

She was his and he wanted her to know it, to feel it deep inside where only he could reach. He wanted her to join him, ride with him, take him as he took her. He used his strength to make her feel his need. When she opened to him, moved to accommodate him, he answered that movement with surging power, then fell into a hard, swift cadence.

Her breathing was ragged. He felt her shuddering effort as she matched his pace. It fueled his need, increasing it until his muscles moved with the heavy, powerful rhythm of oiled pistons. Harder and harder.

The low sounds he made were choked nonsense, a measure of his need to make himself a part of her. He wanted that with a desperate urgency that was a part of the dilating, fracturing wonder inside him. It spread, engulfing him, consuming him as he drove into her heat and moisture again and again. Never in his life had it been this fine, this complete. Never had he wanted so badly to take someone with him into the dark, red-hot heart of his most stark desire.

Possessed and possessing, he heard her soft cries, felt the quaking shivers of her pleasure. And abruptly he lost it, giving her everything he had while the muscles and tendons of his body clenched, freezing him into absolute stillness. Chest heaving, mind a burning blank, he held that deep, absolute penetration.

The frenzy passed. Slowly, inevitably, he subsided until he could feel her heartbeat against him. He lay there, supporting the majority of his weight on his elbows but absorbing her as if he could siphon love through his skin.

Long moments slipped by filled with nothing except the slowing pant of their breathing. At last, she stirred, lifted a hand to trail her fingertips through his sweat-moist hair. With a shiver of laughter and something more in her voice, she said, "Amazing."

His lips twitched. A light, airy joy washed over him. Shifting, he slid from her and turned onto his side. He dipped his head to lick the nipple of her breast, which was still tight and hard. His voice lazy, deep and as Southern as he could make it, he said, "Lady-my-honey, you ain't seen nothing yet."

Her abdomen quaked with her silent laugh, ending abruptly with a taut quiver of internal reaction to his suggestion. He felt his own lips twitch with pleasure for the effect he had on her. She was so responsive that she startled him sometimes, sent a tingle of pure excitement through him at others. He would like to stay in bed with her for aeons, exploring all the ways he knew to bring her pleasure.

Not that he was so experienced himself. He didn't much care for quick and casual sex. Like snacking on sticky candy when what he needed was a home-cooked meal, it didn't satisfy the hunger deep inside. Besides, it was downright stupid. AIDS was the major monster waiting in the dark, but there were others that could put a definite kink in your love life.

Which reminded him. He rubbed his lips back and forth over the warm ivory of the side of her breast for a moment while he gathered his thoughts. "Laurel?"

"What?" The aimless skimming of her hand along the ridges of his back ceased.

"You aren't using any protection, are you?"

There was a long pause before she answered, then the words were stifled. "It never occurred to me."

"Or to me, I'm sorry to say." His chest rose with the depth of the breath he took.

"It—could be a problem. I'm not quite old enough to be...immune to the consequences."

"I know. Would it bother you? I mean...I'm just curious, but would you hate having a baby now that your other kids are grown?"

Her gaze was somber as she stared into a dim corner of the room. "I don't think so. Not if I could be sure it would be healthy."

"I know what you mean," he said, then let his smile show. "But can you imagine the talk? Not that there wouldn't be plenty if you showed up at the drugstore checkout with a handful of prevention. I'll take care of it."

"You don't have to. I can handle it."

For an instant he thought she meant she might want his child. That possibility, followed by the realization that she couldn't have intended to say such a thing, struck him like a one-two punch to the heart. "I want to do it," he said, voice constricted. "It's my responsibility."

"Whatever you prefer." Her face was shadowed, her lashes almost resting on her cheeks.

"What I prefer—" he began as he flashed her a stern look. Then he stopped with his breath caught in his lungs. Her face was bathed in a mottled red light that flickered orange and yellow, dancing in shapes with the writhing triangularity of flame.

Fire!

He swung his head toward the window behind him. The drapes were not quite closed. The leaping light of the blaze shone through that narrow opening and around the outer edges. He cursed roughly, then wrenched himself up and out of the bed in a single fluid movement while reaching for his crumpled jeans. "Stay here. Call the fire department," he ordered over his shoulder as, dragging up his jeans and buttoning them as he went, he slid from the room.

Laurel made the call, but she had no intention of staying in the house. It was her shed burning high into the night sky with her pottery and her kiln and all the fine, unfinished treasures inside. All the pots, the tools, the knives, the brushes, the kaolin and the promise. Dragging on her gown, she sprinted from the house.

She halted on the back porch as she felt the heat that came toward her in rolling waves, smelled the hot, throat-catching, eye-burning breath of destruction. She stared at the red maw of fire visible through the shed's row of side windows, the powerful shooting flames clawing for the sky, the hot cinders swirling, then falling again like red shooting stars. Then she saw Alec kneeling, connecting a water hose to an outside water hydrant with hard, fast twists of his wrist.

She darted across the porch and down the steps, flying over the grass that already felt parched and warm under her feet. Clamping a hand on Alec's shoulder, she dragged him around toward her.

"Let it go!" she shouted above the muffled rumble and snap of the flames. "It's too late."

His gaze was sober, his face set. There was gray-black ash lying across his bare shoulders like a coating of feathers. "We have to wet down the house, try to save it."

He was right, of course, she knew that even as she said, "The fire department will be here in fifteen minutes."

Sardonic and unmoved, he only snorted. "If there's anything you want to save, you had better get it out."

Swinging away, he wrenched the faucet handle to the On position and dragged the hose toward the garage to play the stream of water over the back wall and roof. He had already backed the car out and parked it on the lawn, out of the way of the fire trucks when they came.

Laurel turned to stare at Ivywild with its walls a glowing pink from the reflected light of the fire. Dozens of antique pieces were in the house, from a 150-year-old Victorian rosewood settee to a 250-piece set of old Paris china complete with syllabub cups and knife rests. Picking and choosing from among the many treasures was so difficult she couldn't even think about it.

Availability of water was much better than it had once been, since Alec had put in several auxiliary hydrants while he was laying pipe for the fountain. There was one with a hose attached near what had been the Bacchus fountain. Laurel ran to turn it on, pulling the heavy coils of the hose near Alec where she could throw a stream of water on the house wall and its high roof.

As they worked, she called to him, "How did it start? Can you tell? Was it an electrical short, maybe in the kiln?"

"I don't think so." He lifted his head, drawing in a short, hard sniff. "Smell that?"

She copied his action, then coughed from the burn of smoke and the acrid, familiar fumes of something else in her lungs. Her eyes widened as she stared at him through billows of smoke. "Gasoline!"

"Exactly. Somebody sloshed it around—probably

from the can in the garage—then set it off and ran like a rabbit. And they did it while I was here, inside. Some guard I turned out to be." The look he gave her was virulent with self-blame.

"You couldn't guess anybody would do something like this."

"I should have kept better watch instead of—" He stopped, closing his lips firmly on the words.

Her gaze on the water she was directing to the roof, she said, "It's hard to guard against this kind of craziness."

"What if they had fired the house? What if you had been here alone, asleep?" His voice was savage.

"But I wasn't," she said, frowning. "They must have known that, since there was still a light on in the house. Which means..."

"Which means it wasn't something planned in advance, but a fast, crude job meant to get your attention. They didn't set out to kill you—this time."

The air was thick and hot, hard to breathe, and the crackling blaze behind them roared louder. "Why me?" she shouted hoarsely. "They could have known you were here."

He shook his head as he moved closer to help her soak the end wall of the house. "I thought at first that somebody might have followed me here from California. Not anymore."

"You mean your wife's grown children?"

"Or somebody connected to them." Precise and imperturbable, he sprayed the water on the building while the glow of the flames projected red lights in his hair and gilded his sweat-slick arms and shoulders with copper-gold. "It doesn't compute. I'm no threat to anyone out there now. Besides, I'm not the one who molds clay into life or who once had a big dumb dog with a strain of wolf for a guardian. Somebody knows your weaknesses, Laurel, and they're using them. Somebody can guess what you love most. Think about it, because they may not stop here. Think about what else you love that they might be able to destroy.''

She didn't want to, couldn't stand it, yet couldn't help herself. What did she love? Her children, of course. Ivywild. Oh, and one thing more. One person.

She loved the man working at her side to save what she valued. She loved Alec.

The truth of it shifted in her heart and mind with the feel of an earthquake. Bright, unbearable, shattering knowledge. How had it happened? She didn't want it, didn't need it, had given up all expectation of ever being seized with this kind of sentimental nonsense. Premenopausal foolishness, that was what it was; changing hormones not unlike the wildly unstable highs and lows that brought on the infatuations of puberty.

''Would you hate having a baby...?''

She would not accept this love. If she ignored it, maybe it would go away. Surely she could weather it without revealing her silly, mooning pleasure in looking at him, talking with him, touching him. Her cataclysmic desire to be held close in his arms. The deep, sharp ache of wondering what a child conceived in their combined images would look like, and how it would feel in her arms.

She had tried so hard to be rational and distant. It hadn't worked. Instead, she had succumbed with hardly a word of protest, and meant to do it again, given half a chance. Yet she wondered in despair if a man who wanted a woman, for whatever reason, would go to the trouble of killing her guardian dog, smashing the fruits of her creativity and burning down the only place where she could take refuge from him. If he would arrange it so that he was all that she had left.

He was, now. And she loved him; she really did.

She wondered if old Mrs. Chadwick had felt the same.

16

To Whom It May Concern:

Laurel Bancroft is a wicked woman. She has been caught fornicating in the sight of God and man. It is disgusting but true. She prances around naked, bowing down before her garden full of idols. Satan has entered this garden as the serpent into Eden. In his name, she and her lover do vulgar and unspeakable things. They mutilate animals and sacrifice them. Ask her what happened to her dog. If she is not stopped it will be a man, woman or child killed next time. Some of her evil has been cleansed by fire, but it is not enough. She should be treated like a witch unfit to live....

Laurel crumpled the letter in a convulsive movement. There was more, much more, but she couldn't stand to read it.

She had found the thing in her mailbox at the end of the drive when she went to mail a couple of bills.

The envelope was plain white, regular size, like a thousand others. The address was typed. There had been nothing to warn her before she opened it.

Her hands were shaking, her teeth clenched. That anybody would dare write such terrible things about her, that they could twist what she had shared with Alec into something so sordid, left her ill with rage and grief.

How many other people had received letters like this today? Would they throw the vicious words away as the product of a sick mind, or would they whisper and nod and tell each other they had suspected it all along? Would they stare at each other with secret delight, saying, "Well, where there's smoke there's fire. You know she's been odd for years, staying by herself out there at Ivywild like a recluse, as if ashamed of something…"?

She could just hear them. It drove her crazy. She had a wild need to do something, anything, to stop this smear campaign.

Who was doing this? Who? Actually, she could think of only one person who might care what she did in any way, shape or form, and that was Mother Bancroft. The older woman seemed unbalanced in her belief that Laurel should stay imprisoned at Ivywild for what she had done to Howard, but Sadie Bancroft had never suggested she thought Laurel anything other than a garden-variety husband killer. There had been no hint of any of the lurid imaginings laid out in the letter. Certainly, she had never offered physical harm.

That was, of course, before Alec had arrived on the scene.

Still, a poison-pen letter was no great leap from the

peculiar write-in campaigns her mother-in-law joined. If she had sent it, then it would be wrong to let it go unanswered in light of its weird slant and implied threat.

Alec was still working in the woods behind the house, as he had been for the past three days since the fire. Starting early and staying late, he seemed determined to remove any cover for whoever might be sneaking around. She should take the letter to him, since he was mentioned in it. He deserved to know what was being said, needed to be kept abreast of the latest developments.

She couldn't quite bring herself to do it. The letter was not only ugly and hurtful, but it was embarrassing. She shouldn't feel that way with Alec, but she did; she just couldn't help it. If she had been able to trust him, to believe in how he claimed to feel about her, it might not have mattered. But she couldn't, didn't.

She would talk to Mother Bancroft by herself. It might even be better that way. Her mother-in-law would have no excuse to make accusing remarks if she had no audience.

Walking into her bedroom, Laurel flung the letter on the old-fashioned dressing table and picked up her hairbrush. A few quick strokes and her hair was smooth. She clipped it back with a heavy barrette, then slicked on a little lip-gloss. Moments later, she was out of the house with her car keys in her hand.

The house Mother Bancroft had built for herself after Laurel and Howard married was as different from Ivywild as possible. A low ranch-style bungalow with beige brick and trim, it was compact, economical and totally featureless. It was set back on a small lot in the only subdivision Hillsboro boasted, with not a shrub or flower or vine of any kind to soften its rectangular lines or relieve the tedium of its flat green lawn. It always seemed to Laurel that it was not only a house without personality, but one that was proud of it.

There was a car in the drive, the red Honda Laurel's daughter drove. As Laurel pulled in behind it, Marcia came from the house with her head down while she pawed through her shoulder bag. She glanced up as Laurel opened her car door and got out. A startled look appeared on the younger woman's face and she came slowly to meet Laurel.

"Good grief, Mother," she said without preamble. "When did you start driving again?"

"Hello to you, too," Laurel replied with warmth shaded by irony as she put her arm around her daughter's stiff shoulders for a quick hug. The mockery was for herself as much as for Marcia. She had been so upset by the letter and the prospect of tackling Mother Bancroft about it that she had hardly noticed she was driving at all, hadn't even thought about her fears.

"It just seems too weird seeing you away from the house," Marcia said, returning the hug awkwardly.

"I'm trying to get out more. Are you in a hurry to leave? Shall I move the car out of your way, or do you have time to come back inside and visit for a while?"

A look of acute discomfort crossed her daughter's pale face. "Actually, I was going to the grocery store for Meemaw. I'll be back in a little while."

"You're running an errand for your grandmother? She isn't sick, is she?"

"No, no. I just— Well, I moved in with her a few days ago."

Laurel stared at the color creeping to her daughter's hairline, as Marcia looked everywhere rather than meet her mother's eyes. "Why?" Laurel asked. "What is it? Has Jimmy lost his job?"

"It's not that at all. If you must know, I've left him."

"You've left him," Laurel repeated slowly. "And you went to your grandmother instead of coming home to me."

"Don't make a big deal out of it, Mother. You've been busy with your garden and this Alec person. I didn't want to get in your way."

"You could never do that," Laurel said in distress.

Marcia shrugged, an uneasy movement. "Well, it would only add fat to the fire, anyway. Jimmy has been just insane about all the talk going around, ranting and raving about you and your young stud. When I told him I was leaving because I couldn't take any more, he called me all kinds of names, said I was just like you. I tried to tell him I might not have looked at another man if he had been a little less fanatic, but that made him twice as bad."

"Another man?" Laurel said in dawning incredulity.

Anger flashed in her daughter's eyes. "Don't sound so shocked. You're not the only one with a life, you know. Anyway, Jimmy slapped me. I don't have to put up with that, so I left. Besides, it might have hurt the baby."

"I'm not shocked, only— What baby? Are you pregnant, Marcia?"

Her daughter gave a defiant nod. "I am, as it happens."

"And you haven't told me? Good Lord, don't you think I might be a little interested?"

"Don't come unglued. I just found out myself four or five days ago." Her words were defensive, but also carried a sarcastic edge.

Four or five days ago. Before the fire, before the plaques were broken. Not that it mattered. Or did it?

"I can't believe Jimmy would endanger his own child," Laurel said, "or that you two are separating at such a time, for that matter."

"It isn't his."

Laurel stared at her daughter for an instant with her mouth agape; she couldn't help it. "Then whose is it?"

"Just somebody I used to know, okay? I mean, you know how Jimmy is, so wrapped up in his job and all the stuff he does at the church. He's always been so jealous, accusing me of this and that, saying things that make it sound as if I was some kind of sex fiend because I like it, instead of a normal woman with normal needs. I decided that I might as well have the sin since I was going to catch hell for it, anyway."

Love and guilt, compassion and grief shifted inside Laurel. This composed young woman had once been her little girl who had run to her with her cuts and scrapes and bruises, crying for comfort. All that had been lost when Howard died.

"Oh, Marcia, I'm so sorry," she said quietly. "Sorry you were having such problems and I didn't know."

"It doesn't matter. I didn't want anybody knowing.

The last thing I needed was somebody else telling me what to do.''

The words were a reminder. "You mean the way you talked to me about Alec. How could you sit there and say them when you've been doing the same thing—or worse, since you're still a married woman?''

Marcia compressed her lips and ducked her head, digging around in her purse once more until she brought out her car keys. Without looking up, she said, "It's not the same at all. At least I chose somebody my own age. I wonder what your Alec will think when you tell him you're going to be a grandmother.''

Laurel couldn't imagine, though her concern for the moment was with her daughter's problem. "I know that we haven't been close, honey, but I'd like to help you if you'll let me. You're welcome to stay with me if you like, for as long as you like. There's plenty of room at Ivywild, and I would enjoy having you.''

Her daughter jiggled her keys, sliding her gaze away. "Thanks a lot, but there's too much oddball stuff going on out there. I just don't think it's a good idea.''

"Because of the baby. I see." Laurel's tone was stiff to hide the hurt caused by the dismissal of her offer.

Distress flickered over Marcia's thin features. "That, among other reasons.''

"Your grandmother.''

"She wouldn't like it.''

"I see," Laurel replied in flat acceptance. "Well, the offer is always open.''

"Thanks, I'll keep that in mind." Marcia's voice

sounded thicker, and her gaze was a little less belligerent as she turned away.

Laurel almost let her go, then in an abrupt change of tone, she said, "Wait. You didn't get a letter this morning, did you?"

"A letter? I don't think so. Not here, anyway," her daughter answered as she opened her car door. "What kind of letter?"

She was lying, and not too well, Laurel thought. Or maybe she was telling the truth in a strict sense, if Mother Bancroft had gotten the letter. Marcia obviously didn't want to talk about it, however, or she wouldn't be pretending ignorance.

"It's nothing, really," Laurel answered dismissively as she swung back to her car, getting ready to move it out of Marcia's way. "Just a bunch of gibberish from somebody with a warped mind." She hesitated. "If you won't come and stay, maybe you'll visit more often?"

"Sure," Marcia said, but she didn't smile or look at Laurel, and she immediately cranked her car and put it in gear.

It didn't sound promising.

As Laurel pulled back into the driveway after letting her daughter leave, she saw the draperies twitch at the bungalow's living-room window. A grim smile curved her mouth. Her mother-in-law was watching, probably had been all along. She would be dying to know what she and Marcia had been saying to each other.

It was no surprise, then, when the first words out of Sadie Bancroft's mouth were, "I suppose your daughter told you she's pregnant?"

"Oh, did you see us outside?" Laurel spoke in

artless surprise as she stepped into the minuscule entrance of the house. "You should have joined us."

The other woman stared at her, her mouth pinched and nostrils flaring as if she smelled something unpleasant. Her hair was uncombed, her face puffy, and her eyes ringed by dark circles. Her shapeless housecoat had once sported a pattern of pink and blue tropical flowers but had been washed so many times the color was barely recognizable. Her cloth slippers were ragged and had been cut across the instep for comfort. She looked ill, or as if she had not slept in days. "I was busy in the kitchen," she offered finally.

"Cooking something special, I imagine, since you have Marcia with you now. Don't let me keep you from it."

Laurel wandered toward the kitchen area as she spoke. Everything in the house was so drab, from the vinyl on the floors to the light fixtures in the ceilings. It was also aggressively clean. Her mother-in-law's house had always been that way; Laurel had almost forgotten.

"We'll sit here in the living room," Mother Bancroft said, her voice grimly commanding.

"Actually, I won't be here that long," Laurel said, turning to face the other woman. "I've come about—"

"Marcia and Jimmy, I just knew it. I expect the gossip is all over town."

"You'd have a better idea about that than I do, I would imagine. But no, this isn't about Marcia."

The older woman's eyes narrowed. "Don't you care about what's happening with your daughter?"

"Of course I care!" Laurel snapped as her patience gave out. "She's my own flesh and blood!"

"That," Mother Bancroft said, "is perfectly obvious."

"Are you trying to blame me for her separation?" Laurel returned at once. "If so, then let me remind you that my daughter has seen much more of you than she has of me since Howard died. You're the one who pushed her into getting married, who decided that Jimmy was such a wonderful young man—upright, moral and Christian, the perfect husband. To me he was priggish, self-righteous and overbearing, but nobody bothered to listen to my opinion. So don't try to push your errors of judgment off on me, Mother Bancroft, because it won't work. If I've failed my daughter, it wasn't by influencing her, but by not fighting to keep her from you and your narrow-minded ways!"

"Of all the nerve! You can stand there and say such a thing when everybody knows you're living in sin with a man young enough to be your daughter's boyfriend?"

"Sin has nothing to do with it, since we are both free to do as we please. More than that, Alec is at least ten years older than Marcia, though I'm sure that wouldn't bother you at all if he was interested in her instead of me."

"You don't consider fornication sinful?" her mother-in-law demanded.

Laurel had only disdain for such a blatant attempt to take the moral high ground. "Frankly, I'm not sure there is such a thing. But it's an interesting word, don't you think? Maybe that's why you used it in the poison-pen letters you've been passing around!"

Mother Bancroft lifted a hand to her chest as she

stared at her with blaring eyes. "You think I would make up such filth?"

The older woman looked truly horrified at the thought. Her face was pale and a rim of moisture had appeared along the red edges of her lower eyelids. Laurel refused to be impressed. "Why not? You're the person who has talked about me behind my back for years, the one who has done everything possible to be sure that I felt the full weight of guilt for causing Howard's death. Now you see me escaping the fate you think I deserve. I'm getting out and doing things, finding some tiny bit of happiness with another man, and it kills your soul. So you're doing everything in your power to stop it."

"I wouldn't, I'm not! I got one of those horrible letters, too, this very morning."

The corner of Laurel's mouth curled. "If you got one, it's because you sent it to yourself."

Her mother-in-law stared at her, then a malicious look came into her eyes. "I didn't do it, but that doesn't make any difference, does it? You want it to be me. You'd like that because then you wouldn't have to be so scared."

"What I am is mad!"

"Maybe, but you're afraid, too," the older woman said vindictively. "You ought to be, too, because there's somebody besides me who thinks you should be punished. So you've got a bigger problem than Marcia, and this one is your own fault."

"That's crazy!" Laurel felt the hair rise on the back of her neck even as she spoke.

"Is it? You'd better start doing what's right, better stop sleeping with that young man in that disgusting way, or—"

"Disgusting?" Laurel repeated in indignation. "Frankly, I find that idea a little strange coming from a woman who once slept with men of all ages for reasons that weren't quite so nice."

Mother Bancroft turned as white as a sheet of paper. Gasping, she staggered away from Laurel and stumbled into the living room where she fell into a chair. A low moan came from deep in her throat as she rocked back and forth, holding her heart.

Alarm touched Laurel as she followed after her. "Are you all right? Should I call a doctor?"

"Stay away…from me!" The other woman held out a hand as if to ward her off.

"I have to do something if you're really ill."

"No! I don't need…anything. Especially from you. No." Mother Bancroft drew a rasping breath. "Just go away."

"I'm sorry, but I'm not sure I should do that," Laurel replied stiffly. It was impossible to say whether the older woman's distress was genuine or an act to prevent further argument.

"I don't want you here, don't need you, don't care if I never see you again," her mother-in-law said in rapid agitation. "Get out of my house."

That sounded more normal. She also seemed to be regaining her color, Laurel thought. To stay now would only upset her again. "Shall I call someone for you? Zelda, maybe?"

"I can do it myself," the other woman snapped.

Perhaps she could. Laurel turned from her and moved toward the front door. She paused with her hand on the knob and looked back. Howard's mother was staring after her with tight, bloodless lips and impotent malevolence in her eyes. Laurel left the house, closing the door quietly behind her.

Once back in her car, she sat motionless behind the steering wheel with her gaze fixed on the featureless bungalow, which was as tired and barren as the woman who lived in it. Her anger and triumph streamed through her veins like acid and bile, but there was no pleasure in them. She felt pity for the woman inside the house. She also felt pity for herself. Coming here to confront an adversary, she had only faced a phantom from her own mind. And now that it was vanquished, what was she going to do?

She had been so certain it was her mother-in-law behind the attacks. She could see her poisoning Sticks, not only because she despised dogs, but because poor Sticks had frightened her and made her lose her dignity. As for smashing the plaques and writing the poisonous letters, they had seemed the kind of underhanded acts she might think of to repay Laurel for defying her.

Firing the pottery shed was not quite the same thing, of course. It took considerable effort to imagine the older woman parking her car away from the house and trekking through the woods in the dark. It was even harder to think of her finding the gas can, spreading the flammable liquid, throwing the match, stepping nimbly out of the way.

Still, if it hadn't been her, then who was it?

There had been a certain comfort in being so sure of the identity of her tormentor. They were old enemies, she and Mother Bancroft; they knew each other, knew what to expect. Their warfare was petty, bloodless and had limits. The only damage was to pride, property and feelings. If someone else was involved, then all that had changed.

Who else disliked her so much?

It had to be a vendetta. She wanted it to be that instead of an attempt by Alec to isolate her and make her dependent. In spite of her momentary concern last night, she didn't really believe it was possible. Surely he wasn't that cunning and heartless and diabolically clever.

Marcia's husband, Jimmy, had slapped her around, and he might well be fanatical enough to feel that Laurel's supposed sins required punishment. More than that, he had enough macho swagger to think he could get away with whatever he might choose to do. Laurel had never cared for him, and he knew it. Still, she had always been polite. There had been no open animosity because there had been little contact. He didn't really know enough about her, surely, to destroy the things she loved.

Perhaps Gregory, then? He was clever and had a mind that preferred tangents. He both loved and hated his brother and had made it plain that he considered Laurel wrong for Alec, a danger to him in ways beyond the physical. Gregory might consider it a handy diversion from his dicing with death to separate them.

Did he have the strength? Alec had said his brother was better. But what did that mean? Did it mean anything?

Then there was Zelda. Gossip was her passion. Knowing the details of people's lives helped fill the emptiness of her own, and embellishing the details with a bit of lurid hyperbole was the creative license of her art. She had been annoyed with Alec, certainly, and not too thrilled with the changes at Ivywild. Still, she had no reason to be vengeful, and she was hardly one to rant about sin and Satan. More than that, she had always been friendly enough, in her fashion. Yes, and Sticks had been killed well before her recent visit.

Who else was there?

Maisie? It would be ridiculous to suspect her. And Grannie Callie was far too cheerful and busy with her own life, plus her concern for Gregory, to have time to interfere.

Marcia and Evan? Laurel refused categorically to suspect her own children. It was just impossible.

Dan Tanning had taken an unusual interest in her of late, and he might have some cause for believing he could get away with anything in Hillsboro. Regardless, what earthly reason could he have for trying to hurt her? The mild attraction that had existed between them for a short while gave him no cause to be jealous of Alec.

In all truth, it was hard to accept that anybody could, or would, try to harm her. Normal people didn't do things like that. Didn't that make whoever was behind this a nutcase by definition? Then what was the use of trying to uncover reasons and rationales since there might be none at all?

Laurel started her car and backed out of the drive. As she pulled away, she saw the curtains at the bungalow window jerk, then fall back into place.

17

Alec watched Laurel drive into the garage. A moment later, she emerged from its interior dimness and stood with her hand held to her brow, shielding her eyes as she looked toward the woods. He knew she didn't see him, couldn't penetrate the thicket where he had taken his stand.

She was pale and not quite composed. Wherever she had gone, whatever she had been doing, it had not been a comforting trip, he would judge, or a successful one.

Her shoulders sagged a little as she turned away. It wasn't from despair or fatigue or even defeat, he was sure, but because she wanted him and he wasn't there. He didn't intend to move, but his footsteps took him out of the dim, green shade and into the sun. She turned back and saw him.

He halted, fenced in by his own disappointment and appalled recognition. She had been afraid she would see him; had been relieved when she did not. The truth was there in her eyes.

He wouldn't allow it to matter. He knew she needed him, whether she admitted it or not, and that was enough. At least she didn't back away as he came closer. Her body was taut as he drew her into his arms, but then she sighed and yielded. Wrapping her arms around his waist, she put her head on his chest and shut her eyes.

Molten sunlight poured over them, healing, relaxing in its heat. A breeze drifted through the trees with a disconsolate sound. In the garden beyond the picket fence, bees made a drowsy hum. His arms full of warm woman, breathing the scents of her perfume and tree sap from the saplings he had been clearing, he felt marginal contentment. Then the drifting breeze brought the acrid stench of wet, fire-blackened wood and still-warm ashes.

Against the silk of her hair, he said, "I found the letter."

She didn't move, but he felt her sudden tension. Her voice was not quite steady as she repeated, "Letter?"

"You left it on your vanity table. Weren't you going to tell me?"

"I—don't know." The words were low and uneven.

He could think of several reasons why she might consider keeping it to herself. Embarrassment. Concern for his feelings. Fear of what he might do. There was one more.

"What have I done to make you not trust me?" he asked.

"Nothing," she replied as she lifted her head and released him to draw back a little, resting her hands on his chest as she looked up at him. "I just—had this idea I could take care of it myself. My mother-in-law was my choice for the person most likely to have written it. Apparently I was wrong."

It was plausible. It might even be true. Still, he didn't think that was all. "I failed you once," he said, "possibly even twice, and you thought I would again."

"Or I might have thought you wouldn't't," she said in low and musical tones. "She isn't a young woman, my mother-in-law, and I don't think she is particularly intelligent."

"But you are."

"Am I? I nearly killed her myself because I was too angry, and because I forgot how much it might matter if she couldn't tell me anything."

He wasn't sure she meant what he thought, but he had to ask even if she could feel the dread of her answer in his heartbeat under her fingers. "Such as who else might be familiar enough with Ivywild to find their way about in the dark? Besides me, of course?"

"Of course," she said. "And I still haven't found the answer."

She hadn't hesitated, had even managed a smile as she spoke, but the truth was there, anyway, hidden in the smoky blue depths of her eyes behind veilings of artifice and apprehension. She was trembling a little; he could feel the faint, fine shivering in her thighs against him. The warmth of her, the stalwart courage and delicate vulnerability, made him want to take her inside and teach her never to fear him again, or else to fear him completely. And he wasn't sure which impulse was strongest.

To keep his voice light and shaded only by whimsy was harder than anything else he had done or tried to do at Ivywild. "Are you sure you haven't? Possibly it has occurred to you that I might be the snake in your Eden?"

The effort it took to control her surprise showed

plainly in Laurel's face. Yet she was far stronger than he had expected, for she lifted a wary brow. "I've never much believed in that snake."

"You think Adam and Eve reached for that apple themselves?"

"Doesn't it make more sense? The forbidden is irresistible enough without any prodding from the devil."

"Poor Adam," he said in low tones. "I think the temptation Eve had for him had little to do with apples."

She gave him an oblique glance. "Do you, now?"

"I always figured he lost his paradise because he let Eve take the blame. He'd have been a lot better off if he had stood flat-footed and asked why in the name of Heaven the two of them had been made, if not for love and loving."

"Right in front of God and everybody?" she asked in husky mockery. "Adam might have been killed by the wrath of his benevolent God, and then where would he and Eve have been?"

"Together in paradise," he said. "If she had stood by him."

He watched her closely, wondering if she would take his point, and what she would do with it if she did. A pulse was beating in her temple. The breeze fluttered a soft tendril of silver-gold hair against her cheek. The sun burnished them, brought out a sheen of perspiration that made their skin cling where they touched. However, the trickle of sweat that ran down his back under his T-shirt was from pure fear. He was fighting for something important, and he was losing.

"They were together, anyway," she said.

"Were they?" The query was soft. "Or have they

always been apart because Eve could find no reason to trust Adam, ever again?"

Her gaze flickered from one of his pupils to the other, as if she were searching for something in his eyes that was not there. "I suppose Adam's guilt stood between them. Past crimes, they say, cast long shadows."

He drew a sharp breath. Before he could speak, the screen door slammed. Maisie came stomping out on the front veranda and looked around. Catching sight of them, she called, "Lunch, you two!"

"Coming," Alec replied, his voice floating on a tide of gratitude for the intervention. Also silent hosannas that some women, at least, were not complicated. Or enticingly lovely. Or so lethal in their infinite kindness.

It was midafternoon when Laurel's son appeared. Evan was alone this time. He looked around as he got out of his car, his attitude a little cocky, possibly from his nervousness. The kid saw him out there in the woods, Alec knew, since he was in plain sight, but Evan pretended not to notice. To be ignored felt like a slight, though Alec acknowledged it might also have been from sheer social ineptness. A wave would have done, or even a nod—Alec wasn't proud. He was protective, though, and being overlooked irritated him just enough that he didn't mind showing it. Moving without haste, he started toward the house.

He met Laurel and Evan at the ruin of the pottery shed. As she introduced them, Alec extended his hand. He thought the boy was going to refuse the courtesy, but Evan caught the quick look flung his way by his mother and accepted the handshake.

His grip was firm. For a moment, it seemed Evan

might make a contest of it. Then something he saw in Alec's eyes must have dissuaded him, for he spoke a polite greeting and stepped back.

Laurel, her voice strained, said, "Evan had one of the letters, too."

"It was sent through the mail?" Alec asked. He thought Laurel's copy had been hand-delivered to her rural mailbox, which was a federal offense in itself. Still, one with a postmark would be a much more damning piece of evidence.

Evan shook his head. "Just showed up in my box on campus. But that's not the only reason I came."

The words carried a trace of belligerence, as if part of a running argument that had begun as soon as he saw his mother. Laurel added to the impression as she said, "I'd have called you about the fire if I thought there was something you could do about it. There wasn't, there isn't."

"I guess it would have been all the same if the whole place had burned down. I'd probably never have heard about that, either."

Laurel gave him a stern look. "If you had called me about the letter instead of going to your aunt Zelda, I'd have been happy to tell you."

Her son looked uncomfortable. "I didn't know whether you knew about it. I figured it would be just as well if you never did."

"So you talked to your aunt who can be depended on to spread the story for miles around?"

"Aunt Zelda's not that bad. Besides, she knew about it already because she had one, too—not that it makes any difference. Didn't you give a thought to how I might feel, knowing you've got all this trouble out here? You're my mother!"

Evan shot Alec a defiant glance as he said the last words. Alec gave him a grim smile. Laurel eyed them both before she said, "I know, and I appreciate your concern, really I do. I just happen to think that school is more important for you now."

"I can deal with more than one thing at a time, Mom."

The exasperation in the boy's voice came from his need to be allowed to help. Alec understood it very well, and thought better of Evan Bancroft for it.

Laurel sighed. "There's nothing to deal with, Evan. Nothing anybody can do until we find out who is behind it."

"I could stay with you, watch out for you. I don't know exactly what's happening, but you should have somebody on your side, somebody to show people you're not alone out here."

Alec waited with his breath caught in his chest for what she would say. Would she acknowledge him and what they had become to each other, or would she accept Evan's offer? And if she permitted her son to move back into the house with her, where would that leave him?

The light breeze blew over the smoldering pile of charcoal in front of them. Alec could feel the sweep of the dead fire's remaining heat, smell its smoke. It felt a little like standing outside the gates of hell, waiting to learn his fate.

Laurel, her gaze on the woods where the growth had been removed from beneath the trees for several yards back, said, "I don't need anybody."

"Don't be ridiculous, Mom," Evan countered. "What if whoever set this fire decides to torch the house next? That big pile of dried-out wood will go up faster than a Christmas rocket. They may not stop there, either. What if they come in the house? They could get in any window without half trying, and the damn place is so big there's no way you could hear them until it was too late.''

She gave him a hard look that was completely at odds with the pale fragility of her face. ''What do you think you could do about it, then? Do you sleep any lighter than I do? Are you any better at using a gun?''

''At least there would be two of us to keep a look-out!'' Evan's gaze flicked to Alec for an instant of stabbing challenge.

Three, not two, Alec thought, but then Laurel's son knew that very well. If Laurel was trying to save the boy's feelings, it was wasted effort. Then she said it— the words he had been waiting to hear.

''Alec stays with me at night, Evan. I already have someone to watch over me and help listen for problems.''

The boy set his hands on his hips. ''Is that so? A fine lot of good he's been to you, from what I can tell.''

Alec winced a little at the words, but they had no power to dent the exultation rising inside him. ''You're right, Evan,'' he said in quiet assurance, ''or you were. Now I have a better idea what to expect.''

Laurel stared at him, her gaze bleak. He met it without evasion. She had admitted their affair. She had made him an official part of her life in front of her son, one of the few people who meant anything to her. Regardless, she wouldn't smile, didn't look happy about it. Tight anguish entered his chest along with the kind of hovering stillness that told him he had gone from minor to major danger.

"Get rid of him," Evan said to his mother. "You don't need him, and he's an embarrassment to you."

"Evan! You have no right to say such a thing. And you know better than to do it in front of someone."

"The truth is the truth," her son retorted, his face turning so red it was almost purple. "I can do a better job of looking out for you. Anyway, when he's gone there might not be anything to guard against."

The wariness inside Alec tightened a notch. "If I thought that was true for a minute," he said, "I wouldn't be here."

"You can bet on it, then," Evan shot at him.

"No!" Laurel cried in sharp intervention. "There's no need for anything more to be said about this, no reason for any changes. Besides, the fire may be the end of it."

She was afraid he and Evan would get into a fight, Alec saw, and she might well be right. He was keeping a rein on his temper out of regard for the fact that Evan had some right to be concerned, but his patience was not too reliable.

"You don't really think that," Evan replied in barely concealed anger.

The oval of Laurel's face was tight. "It's better than watching for a bogeyman in every shadow."

"Right," her son said hotly. "And makes about as much sense as having one in bed with you!"

Alec moved forward, but Laurel put a restraining hand on his arm. She lifted her chin, her face like marble and her eyes the fathomless blue of glacier ice. "Let me make this perfectly plain, Evan, then I don't want to hear any more about it. Your place is at school where you can concentrate on your studies and make the best possible grades for the summer quarter. I don't want you here where I would have to worry every minute that you might be attacked next. I have Alec. He's all I need.''

She was using him as a shield, Alec saw with sudden insight. That was all her public recognition meant. To admit their intimacy was better in her mind than the possibility of having to worry about, or even lose, someone she loved. But did that mean she thought he was more capable of taking care of himself than Evan, so ran no risk? Or was it proof that he was expendable?

He's all I need.

A few minutes ago, those words would have been a wonder. Now his only thought was, yes, but how? And why?

Evan tried every argument he could lay tongue to, proving in the process that he had his mother's intelligence and a fair degree of her notions of sacrifice. At the end of it, he and Alec had a better understanding, if no better rapport. However, Laurel did not budge an inch.

When Evan drove away, finally, Laurel stood watching until his car was out of sight. Her eyes were shadowed, her expression heavy with acceptance. At the same time, there was also a touching air of peace about her.

She turned to Alec as he stood by her side. ''It's getting late,'' she said quietly. ''I don't see much point in trying to get anything more done today. You might as well go and check on Gregory, if that's what you need to do.''

He gave a stiff nod. "I've been leaving him to Gran a little too much lately."

"You don't have to come back," she added, her gaze resting on his face. "Not unless it's what you want."

"It's what I want." He watched her, watched the way the afternoon shadows slid across her features and made shifting patterns of light and dark on her skirt and blouse. The way her eyes did not quite meet his. Inside him, there hovered a puerile need to hear her say she did not want him to return. He required that evidence of her caring and concern, even as he knew he would instantly reject any attempt to protect him.

She didn't extend it. Instead, she gave him a slow smile. Her gaze, dark with secrets, came to rest on his. Her voice as clear as a chiming bell, she said, "Hurry back, then."

Laurel stood and watched Alec zoom away on his bike. It occurred to her that she was always watching him go. One day, she knew, he would leave and not come back. She would be left alone in the big empty barn of a house. But not yet. Not yet.

Behind her, Maisie emerged from the house with her big purse hanging from the crook of her arm and her folded apron in her hand. It was time for her to go home, too. She clumped down the steps and stopped beside Laurel.

"You going to be all right here by yourself?" she asked abruptly.

Laurel nodded with a reassuring smile. Knowing Maisie was well aware that Alec had spent the last few nights with her, she added, "It won't be for long."

"I could stay awhile. My old man's working late this week and I won't have to get his supper for a while yet."

"I guess if anybody came around who was up to no good you'd hit him over the head with your purse," Laurel said with an affectionate smile.

"That would sure fix him, considering all the stuff that's in it." Maisie sobered almost at once. "I worry about you, honey. This business started out spiteful and mean, the kind of thing that happens when people get to feuding and fussing, but it's fast getting out of hand."

"Yes, I know," Laurel said, running her fingers through the hair at her temple. "It's so insane, since I don't know what the feud is all about."

"You're sure? You still can't think of anything that was said or done that might have set somebody off?"

Laurel gave a slow shake of her head. "Unless it has something to do with Alec, I have no idea."

Maisie was quiet for a moment. "If he's really the root of it, might not be such a good idea, him being here day and night."

"Tell him that," Laurel returned dryly.

"I see what you mean." Maisie pursed her lips. "I could maybe have a talk with Callie. Alec listens to her when he don't pay any mind to anybody else."

Maisie could be right, Laurel thought. "I'm not sure it would make any difference at this point. Besides..."

"Besides which, you like having him around?"

Laurel's smile was wry. "Am I that transparent?"

"You're different, I'll put it that way." There was

caring and sympathy in the older woman's gaze. "Well, all right, I'll go. But you be careful, you hear? Both of you. Be sure and lock the door when you go back inside."

"I'll do that."

Maisie nodded, then swung around and started toward her car. "See you in the morning."

Laurel did not turn immediately toward the house. A few deadheads on the new roses caught her attention, and she walked down the path to reach for them and snap them off. She was aware of Maisie getting into her car, which was parked on the grass off the edge of the drive, then grinding the starter. It was only after the third try with no results that Laurel looked up.

Maisie got out of the ancient, boatlike Cadillac and set a fist on her padded hip. Laurel moved in her direction. As she passed through the side gate, she called, "Problems?"

"Dang thing's gone and died on me. Guess I'll have to call the old man, though he won't be home till all hours."

"I could drive you," Laurel said, "but then you wouldn't have a way to come to work in the morning. I doubt the repair shop will send anybody out this evening."

"Oh, that old man of mine can fix the piece of junk a lot faster and cheaper, anyway."

"Tell you what, take my car, then," Laurel suggested. "It needs driving, and you can bring it back in the morning."

"You sure? You might need it."

Laurel laughed, a dry sound. "Oh, I'm not going anywhere."

There were more protests to overcome but, in the end, Maisie agreed. Laurel fetched the keys from inside, and the older woman drove off in the Buick. Laurel was left alone.

Alone.

The insect songs from the encroaching woods seemed loud in the stillness. The slanting rays of the sun no longer felt as warm. The warbling of the garden fountain had a melancholy note like the dreariness of rain on a winter afternoon.

Moving with quickening steps, Laurel went back along the path and into the house. She closed the big front door and locked it carefully behind her.

It was perhaps an hour later when the phone rang. She was chopping tomatoes on the cutting board for a light dinner of broiled chicken and salad. She didn't want to answer since nothing in the past few days gave her any reason to expect pleasant news. Still, it might be Alec or Evan, or even Marcia, checking on her. They would be concerned if she didn't pick up.

"Laurel? Dan Tanning, here."

"Dan, how are you?" she asked politely as she cradled the phone between her ear and shoulder and went back to her chore.

"Fine, though this isn't a social call. I don't want to upset you, but there's been an accident."

Laurel put down her knife, took a firmer grip on the phone. "It isn't Evan or..."

"No, no. It's Maisie. She ran off the road a few miles from town. She's hurt pretty bad—broken leg, internal injuries. Her doctor's called the medevac helicopter to take her to Shreveport."

"Oh, Dan, is she going to be all right?"

"Can't say, but she's having a fit. Swears she won't go until she talks to you."

"I'd be halfway to the hospital already, but I don't have my car."

"I know. God, Laurel, I nearly lost it when I saw that old Buick of yours wrapped around a tree. But not to worry. One of my deputies is on his way to pick you up. He'll be there in five minutes."

18

"**Y**ou can't go in right now," Dan said as he met Laurel outside the emergency room of the hospital. "The doctor is with Maisie, trying to explain things to her and her husband. Step in here and let me get you a cup of coffee."

"How bad is she?" Laurel kept her voice low as she allowed herself to be led into a waiting room.

Dan's eyes were shadowed, as if he had seen too many tragedies. "They've got her stabilized, she's conscious, and that's about the best you can say. She's not a young woman, you know."

"She was going to retire next year, with her husband." Laurel pressed her lips together, breathing deep, swallowing against the tight ache of tears. "I keep thinking it's my fault, that I should have driven her home."

"Then there'd maybe be two of you here."

He swung abruptly toward the coffee machine in one corner, returning a few minutes later with two foam cups. The brew was bitter, but the heat helped take away some of the shivery chill inside her.

"What happened?" she asked. "Your deputy said something about a steering problem?"

"Hose for the power-steering fluid came loose, squirted the sticky stuff all over the windshield.

Maisie couldn't see, and of course the steering went from easy to hard, just like that. Might have been all right if she'd had quicker reflexes or been on a straight stretch, but there's nothing but curves between here and where you live. She panicked, lost control, wrapped the Buick around a tree.''

Laurel gave the sheriff a taut look. ''The car hasn't been driven much in some time.''

''Maisie said Alec Stanton checked it out last week.''

''I suppose he could have missed something,'' Laurel answered in quick response to the insinuating tone of Dan's voice.

He stared into his own cup of coffee. It bent under the pressure of his fingers before he spoke. ''I heard from California.''

''And?'' The beat of her heart took on a sickening throb as she waited for his answer.

''He killed her, all right.''

There was no need to ask who he meant. It felt like disloyalty to Alec, but still she had to ask. ''How? What happened?''

''Painkillers. A massive overdose showed up on the autopsy. She was dying, but not fast enough, so he helped her along. They had been married seven months.''

Laurel's lips were cold, her brain colder. ''Why isn't he in prison, then?''

''Not enough evidence to convict. The medicine had been prescribed for her. Apparently he hoarded the pills over several weeks or even months.'' Dan shrugged a uniformed shoulder. ''Stanton's lawyer claimed she tucked them back herself, that she committed suicide.''

Ignoring the shading of sarcasm in his comment, she asked, "There was a trial?"

"Not for murder, but there was a big circus of a civil trial. The wife's heirs weren't too happy at being done out of the estate, as you can imagine—especially by the gardener, a kid their mama had taken in out of the goodness of her heart. They charged him with wrongful death and asked for an outlandish sum in damages. Didn't manage to make that charge stick, either, but by the time the thing was over, nobody won. Lawyers wound up with most of the money."

"But that doesn't prove Alec was guilty!"

"Lord, Laurel!" Dan replied in exasperation. "Just think about it. A man marries a wealthy widow twenty-odd years older than he is, then she dies under suspicious circumstances. What do you think happened?"

"If she was so sick, why wouldn't he have just waited?"

"Too impatient, I guess. How the hell do I know? But, if I were you, I sure wouldn't accept any marriage proposals from him."

Marriage proposals. She stiffened her spine as a shiver ran down it. "I'm not wealthy—far from it."

"Compared to what? Or rather, who? Ivywild is worth a bundle, and if you've spent even a fraction of what Howard had in the bank or what you got from the whopping-big insurance policy he was carrying, I'll be amazed."

"I didn't realize my finances were common knowledge." Her voice was brittle with distaste.

"Everybody's finances are common knowledge in Hillsboro," he said wearily. "I bet you can guess within a couple of hundred what I make a year."

She could. She looked away from him.

"Right. For a con man with next to nothing, you make a nice target. Think about it—that's all I ask. Just think about it." He drained his cup and tossed it into a wastepaper basket, then strode toward the door. "I'll go check, see if Maisie is ready for you."

Oh, Alec. Laurel's chest hurt when she thought of what he must have gone through in California. At the same time, she couldn't be easy in her mind. The things Dan had said were so damning. So logical. At least she didn't have to think about it just now. A low, thumping rumble in the distance signaled the approach of the medical-evacuation helicopter. If she was going to talk to Maisie, it had better be soon.

Abandoning her cold coffee on a table, Laurel stepped into the hall. Dan was coming to meet her. He waved her on. "This way, on the double."

The stretcher where Maisie lay was stationed near the hospital's back door, which opened onto the helicopter pad. Tubes and monitor cords draped the gurney like Christmas tinsel, and a team consisting of her doctor, two nurses and two aides stood by. Maisie's husband, a big, gangling man with a black rim of grease under his fingernails, was leaning against the wall, his arms crossed over his chest and his head down.

The doctor stepped forward to intercept Laurel. "Keep it short, Mrs. Bancroft, and make it as easy for her as possible. Try to stay calm. The last thing she needs is any more excitement."

Laurel nodded her understanding, but she was distracted. Maisie had opened her eyes and was reaching out to her, muttering her name. The doctor moved aside. Laurel's knees wobbled as she walked to the edge of the stretcher and took Maisie's cold fingers in a careful grasp. Dread loomed suddenly in her mind, clouding her ability to think. She was afraid of what Maisie might say.

"Oh, Laurel, honey, I'm so glad you got here," Maisie said, her eyes huge, the pupils expanded with the drugs already circulating in her bloodstream. "I was afraid you wouldn't. Not before—"

"Never mind," Laurel broke in, keeping her voice soft and steady with an effort. "I'm here now. Was there something you needed to tell me? Is that why you asked for me?"

The white head dipped in a slight nod. "It was you, not me. It was you supposed to be in the car. I've been thinking, studying about Sticks and Alec and the letters, about everything. You got to be careful."

"I know, and I will be." The words were automatic, meaning next to nothing. Outside, the sound of the helicopter was rising to a roar. Its triangulated shadow hovered on the concrete landing pad, while the tall pines nearby whipped in the mechanical wind.

Maisie pulled Laurel closer, though she was trembling so hard the stretcher shimmied on its wheels. In a rapid undertone, she said, "It's on account of that other killing. I heard a few whispers, but paid no mind. I should have listened."

The doctor squeaked forward on his rubber-soled shoes. "That's enough, Mrs. Bancroft. It's time to go."

Laurel glanced at him and began to ease aside. The team of nurses moved forward, releasing the stretcher's brakes, gathering IV lines and monitoring equipment. Maisie's husband stepped to the glass doors to shove them open.

Still, Maisie would not release Laurel's hand. She held on with desperate strength even as the stretcher began to roll. "You talk to Callie," she said, her eyes pleading. "She used to be a nurse, knows more about what went on than she's ever told. But she'll talk to you if you tell her I said ask. You do it now. You hear?"

Murmuring assurances, squeezing her hand a final time, Laurel stepped back. She thought Maisie appeared quieter, more comfortable in her mind as she was wheeled out the doors. Then her pale, rounded figure under the green sheet was lost from view as the hospital personnel closed ranks around her. Assured and efficient, they bundled her into the helicopter. The rotor blades whined into a higher tempo, then began to whip the moist, warm air as if beating a meringue. Seconds later, Maisie was gone.

Turning carefully, holding the pain of Maisie's suspicions inside her like a mother carrying a spoonful of bitter medicine to the mouth of a child, she faced the hall. She stopped.

Alec was there, standing tall and strong and wind-ruffled, with his motorcycle helmet in his hand. His eyes were as hot and hungry as the dragon's that lay hidden on his shoulder. Derision and anger showed in every magnificent, taut line of his body. He had heard what Maisie had said. Or perhaps Dan, standing not far away with his hand braced near the gun on his belt, had said something that had made the situation clear. It would not have taken a great deal—not for Alec.

"I was on my way out to the house when I saw them dragging your Buick out of the ditch," Alec said, his eyes black yet sightless as they rested on her face. "The door was caved in on the driver's side, the seat soaked in blood. I thought," he added softly, "that you must have been in it."

She drew a swift breath. "Oh, Alec, I'm sorry. But you know about Maisie?"

"I do now."

"When Dan called, I thought only about her. It never occurred to me that you…"

"Let it go," he said abruptly as the lines at the corners of his eyes lost some of their depth. "Where are you headed from here?"

"I hadn't thought." She rubbed at the ache beginning behind her temples. "Home, I guess."

Dan stepped forward, moving between them. In a heavy assumption of authority, he said to Laurel, "I'll take you."

"I have my bike," Alec countered.

He didn't plead or demand or make any promises of comfort or even safety. He didn't hold out his hand as Dan was doing. All he did was wait with his shoulders stiff and legs set in a wide stance. Regardless, Laurel could feel the strength of his will surrounding her like a steel cord, closing tight, and she wasn't sure she wanted to be free.

"The bike is fine," she said, not looking at Dan. "I think it would be good to blow the cobwebs out of my brain."

"You sure, Laurel?" Dan put both hands on his wide belt—a mistake since it showed the sweat stains under his arms.

Laurel gave him a faint smile. "Apparently. I prefer to do my own checking, you see."

"Then don't blame me for what happens."

"I wouldn't think of it," she said, covering the short distance between her and Alec, taking his arm.

The two men exchanged a long look, combative on one side, impassive on the other. Then Alec took her hand from his arm and meshed his fingers with hers, holding them firmly as he turned and moved with her down the hall.

The ride back to Ivywild didn't take long. Laurel had only begun to subdue her pain and regret by the time they arrived, and had done nothing about her disorganized thought processes. He held the bike for her to dismount, then swung off and followed her to the veranda. When she unlocked the door, he caught her arm before she could step inside.

"Let me," he said, and went ahead with caution and efficiency, gliding through the darkened rooms on either side of the hall. Returning down its long length after a few seconds, he flipped on the light. "Looks to be all clear."

She went straight to the kitchen. She started to make coffee, but remembered that Alec didn't like it and took down the bourbon bottle instead. She needed the courage, not to mention the sedative effect for her strung-out nerves.

He came to stand in the doorway, watching her. "Don't," he said, the word compressed. "Not for me. I prefer you to remember that I was willing and in full command of my tongue when I made my confession."

She set the whiskey bottle on the countertop with great care. Crossing her arms over her chest to hold herself together, she said, "I'm not sure I want to hear it."

"I think you're going to have to. Paying for my

own mistakes is one thing, but being set up as a scapegoat is something else again.''

"Who do you think is setting you up?" She turned to face him with her back pressed against the cabinet.

"Good question. We might figure it out between us, but first there's some garbage we need to get out of the way."

"About your wife." The words came out barely above a whisper.

"About my wife," he repeated. "It's a long story. You want the full version, or the condensed one?"

He was watching her, his gaze annihilatingly straight. She was the one who looked away first. "Whatever you want to tell me."

"I'm not sure how much of it you've heard from Gregory. You know we moved to the Chadwick place after Mom died, and Mrs. Chadwick took an interest in us, right?" At her quick nod, he continued. "She was especially taken with Mita, my little sister. I think she enjoyed buying clothes for her, sending her to school. Mita was a bright, sweet kid—still is."

The look of pride that came and went across his face touched Laurel more than the most fervent declaration of affection. "Mita is some sort of doctor now, isn't she?"

"A pediatrician. She remembered too well all the times she was sick as a kid and there was next to no one there to help her. Until Mrs. Chadwick, that is."

"That's what you called the woman you married— Mrs. Chadwick?" Laurel wasn't sure whether her question came from curiosity or the need to delay what she didn't want to hear.

"She was my boss lady and benefactor a lot longer than she was my wife."

"I see."

"I doubt it," he corrected, his voice tight. "It wasn't the way you think, the way everybody seemed to think. I didn't worm my way into her bed, didn't flatter her or make up to her or any of the ridiculous ideas people have of a younger man who marries an older woman. I was in and out of the house all the time. We used to talk over tea—she served it every afternoon with silver, china, linen napkins, the whole bit. We were friends. Then one day she called me over to where she was sitting on the patio. She had been to the doctor, she said, and had only a few months to live. A year, max. She didn't want to leave what she had to her children, who never came around and wouldn't care if she dropped off the face of the earth so long as it didn't disturb their busy schedules. But she was afraid they would create problems, tie everything up in court for years, if she willed it to me and Mita. If I married her, it would make everything more binding, plus she could start to transfer assets immediately. Besides that, she needed someone to look after things, look after her, when the time came that she was no longer able to do it for herself."

"So you agreed."

He put a hand on the back of his neck, gripping tightly. "It was just a legal arrangement. We never shared a bedroom, never slept together. For one thing, she was so sick it was impossible. And for another, she was more like a mother than my own had ever been, so it was entirely too...Oedipal."

Laurel made a soft sound at the sudden insight. He watched her for a moment, then his voice hardened as he went on. "I don't mean to say I would have refused to carry through if she had insisted—I owed her too much for that. But she wasn't the kind of woman who would have been satisfied with gratitude, no matter how fervently expressed, and I was too young at the time to have the courtesy to pretend anything more."

She wondered, briefly, if he had aged to that point now. However, asking didn't seem polite or sensible. She prompted instead, "And then?"

"Then one night, when the marriage was maybe six months old and the pain too much for her to bear any longer, the time came for repayment of her generosity. She asked me to kill her."

"Kill her?" Laurel repeated the words because she wasn't sure, with the compression of his voice, that she had heard them correctly. The answer, however, was in the sallow copper-bronze shade of his skin. She added in a near whisper, "What did you do?"

He sighed and turned to put his backbone against the doorjamb, tilting his head against it, as well. "I wanted to do it, I really did. Can you understand that? I wanted to end her unbearable pain, end my own night-and-day vigil—end the whole, wearing travesty. It would have been so easy. I had been studying martial arts with Mr. Wu for years by then, knew every trick he could teach me, plus a few I picked up in back alleys. A little pressure in the right place, and it would have been over. She would never have felt a thing. There would have been no sign." He paused. "I couldn't. I just—couldn't."

The air left her lungs in a telling rush. She was so weak with relief that she might have fallen except for the cabinet behind her. Her voice no more than a whisper, she said, "Thank God."

He turned his head toward her, and his features

were perfectly still. "What faith," he said shortly. "If I'm that good at acting the natural-born killer, maybe I should take up television wrestling."

"Maybe you should tell me how your wife really died." If she had thought before that he could kill, given the right reason, she now believed him every bit as innocent as he claimed. Which either made her willfully pigheaded or was fine proof that love really was blind.

"Mrs. Chadwick was a determined woman." His mouth turned down at one corner. "You remind me of her in that, sometimes. When she knew I couldn't, or wouldn't, help her out of this world, she began to palm the painkillers I was giving her and hide them in a drawer beside her bed. On the evening she finally had a big enough hoard, she called a beautician to the house to give her a shampoo, manicure and full makeup. Then she took a long perfumed bath and put on a pink satin gown. She sat down and wrote her notes of goodbye—one for me and one for her children. Then she swallowed all the pills she had saved and lay down on the bed with her nightgown arranged in perfect folds and her hands together on her chest like some medieval queen on a tomb. When I went to check on her, she was—" He stopped and turned his face away while his jaw tensed until the muscle stood out like a rock in his cheek.

"You loved her," she said softly.

He pushed his fingers into the tops of his jeans pockets and swallowed visibly. "Not like you mean."

"I didn't mean it that way at all," she assured him. "I just…think there was something more between you than you've said."

"She was kind, always," he replied with a glance

that dared her to find his reasoning unusual. "She taught me how to speak fairly correct English, how to eat with the right fork, how to appreciate fine things and recognize value when I see it. She let me and Mita stay with her when we had nowhere else to go. She kept us safe so we could be together, dressed us, sent us to school, taught us self-respect and made us respectable in a way we had never been before. I looked up to her exactly as a dumb peasant back in the old days might have looked up to some fine lady who was good to him. I'm not ashamed to admit it, and I don't regret anything. Except, maybe, that I couldn't do the one thing she ever really needed from me."

"If she was everything you say, then she was probably proud that you couldn't," Laurel said. "Anyway, she seems to have managed it herself without too much trouble."

"I knew what she was doing," he admitted in a voice like glass breaking under a steel roller. "I found her hoard of pills in that drawer weeks before she died. I found them and I left them there. I refilled her prescriptions as often as I dared, and gave her medication closer together than was prescribed so she could take one now and then—not hurt more than she could bear."

"You couldn't have known she would really do it."

The look he flashed in her direction was edged with old grief. "I knew," he repeated with emphasis. "I could have stopped her, but I didn't. If that makes me guilty of her death, then all right, I'm guilty. But I don't regret it for a minute."

So now she had the full story. She waited for some

feeling of condemnation. There was none. She was hardly in a position to cast stones, of course, since she had her own guilt to manage as best she could. Yet she felt no revulsion at all. It was easy to second-guess the moral calls made by other people, but no one could say with certainty whether they were right or wrong until they had stood in the exact same place in a world that changed its orbit a little every day.

"Tell me about the legal business," she asked abruptly.

His head came around. Voice husky with amazement, he said, "You believe me."

"Yes."

"Just like that."

"It was the truth, wasn't it?" The heat of a flush rose under her skin as she spoke.

"Every word, but I expected— I thought it would take more to convince you."

She shielded her eyes with her lashes, afraid of what he might see there if he looked too closely. "I want to hear the rest of it, anyway."

His gaze moved over the pale oval of her face, lingered on her hands, which still had a tendency to tremble, then came to rest on the countertop behind her and the scattered remains of the salad she had been making when the call came about Maisie. "You haven't had dinner, have you?" he said. "Eat something while we talk, and I'll tell you."

"I don't think I can, but I could make you a sandwich."

"I've already eaten. Force yourself."

"I can't, really." When his face did not lose its implacable cast, she swung from him in irritation.

"Oh, all right. But I want details while I'm at it. All of them."

She listened carefully while she finished the salad she had started earlier, then sat down to pick at it. It was a sorry tale of avarice and trumped-up indignation. When Mrs. Chadwick's grown children could not force the D.A.'s office to bring a murder charge against Alec, they had done their best to see to it that Alec did not enjoy what he had gained by their mother's death. The court proceedings had been lengthy and virulent. The popular press had had a field day with the scandalous details of the rich older woman and her young lover, with all the emphasis on "Lady Chadwick's Lover" that might have been expected, given the circumstances. The final decision had been in Alec's favor—the will had been upheld—but, as Dan had said, it was the lawyers who had benefited. Alec had been forced to sell the estate to pay the fees. What was left had been used to put Mita and himself through four years of college and, later, to help take care of Gregory.

Hearing the pain in his voice as he spoke, Laurel knew he had hated the notoriety, the loss of the respectability he had spoken of with such intensity. She thought it possible that his unconventional appearance and attitude were a reaction to all the slurs and suspicions that had come his way, a variation of the adage about dogs and bad names. She hated to think of the humiliation he had endured, with no one to stand by him, no one to take his side.

At least she had no need to go to Miss Callie for the details as Maisie had suggested. She knew everything she required.

"You mentioned that the Chadwick heirs might

have something to do with what has been going on here," she said. "Was there some particular reason?"

Distaste curled the corner of his mouth. "They preferred sneak attacks. Causing problems that could be blamed on me, doing me out of the job I valued would be right down their alley. To make my life miserable was a specialty with them for so long, I guess I've gotten used to looking for them in everything."

"It makes sense, but Hillsboro is a long way from California."

His nod of acquiescence was brief. "I was so wrapped up in my own past problems, so afraid that you would be hurt because of me, that it took me a while to see you were the main target."

She put down the forkful of lettuce and tomato she had been carrying to her mouth. Her face stiff, she said, "Now you may be hurt because of me, instead."

"That isn't important." His gaze was intent in spite of the offhand inflection of the words.

"Maybe not to you," she stated slowly, her eyes dark blue with consideration. "For me, it changes everything."

19

Alec sat in the swing on the dark veranda, keeping it moving with one foot, ignoring the squeak of its rusty chain, while he thought about what Laurel had said. It was one thing, or so it seemed, if he was hurt because of his own decisions, but something else again if he came to grief for her sake. The hint of concern in that bit of convoluted logic sent some odd, almost-forgotten feeling tripping along his veins. He thought it just might be hope.

She was still inside. She was supposed to be taking a bath, though he had heard her on the phone a short while ago. He had checked all the windows and doors, then made his rounds of the yard and the cleared area surrounding the house. He had stood awhile among the trees, watching and listening, but he had found nothing out of the ordinary. So far as he could tell, no unwelcome company was anywhere around.

He quartered the night with an alert gaze once more, even as he increased the pace of the swing with a firmer push of his heel. He was doing his best to be vigilant, but it wasn't easy with Laurel rising like a vision in his mind. He would never forget the way she had listened to what he had to say—with no sign of horror, no shocked comment, no withdrawal. She had understood.

He hadn't been prepared for it; couldn't get over it. He had expected to use every argument at his command to persuade her to see his side. It wouldn't have surprised him to have been shown the door.

If he hadn't known how special she was before, he knew it now. She had her own griefs as reference points, of course, but she was still amazing in her tolerance. He had pulled no punches, and she hadn't flinched from what he'd said, or from him. Instead, she had accepted his word.

It was possible that a part of it was because she cared, although he didn't dare take that for granted; she had never said it, after all. Still, it showed her trust, and the gratitude he felt for that gift rose inside him like a shout of triumph. It made him feel that nothing she could ask of him would be too much, no sacrifice too great. She deserved whatever he had in him to give.

And he loved her with every ounce of his being, every last faltering beat of his heart. Without her, he had no purpose or reason for living. She was his peace, his light, the still waters of his soul. She was sun and moon to him; sweet dreams, the pleasures of a soft breeze, and the fragrance of old-fashioned roses. He would protect her with his last breath, or die trying.

Yes, or die loving her, because he wanted her with a virulent need that sapped his strength and fired his brain with images that would not go away. He wanted to lie down with her somewhere and not get up until they were both sated—say, in fifty years or so. He wanted to see and taste, caress and hold, every part of her; to know her so intimately that he could tell her from a thousand others at a single touch in the dark.

He thought of going inside and dragging her from the bathtub, all slick and wet, to make love to her on the cool tiles of the floor. Or maybe helping her dry herself, taking the drops of water from her back and belly one by one with lips and tongue. Or catching her before she put on her nightgown, draping her long hair around her, using it to bind her to him while he...

The screen door creaked as it opened. Her shadow, thrown across the veranda floor by the hall light behind her, shifted and moved as she stepped outside. She walked toward him with her nightgown, caftan and cape of long hair swinging with her gentle, gliding steps. She looked so guileless yet stunningly seductive that his tongue clung to the top of his mouth and he felt the back of his neck grow hot and stiff.

"What are you doing out here?" she asked as he held the swing still while she settled beside him and tucked her bare feet up under her gown and robe.

"Thinking." It was the most he could manage.

"About what?"

"Just...things," he said softly. He couldn't begin to unravel his complicated impulses toward her and was afraid that any attempt might set off a more primitive response than she was prepared to accept. He set the swing moving again in a steady back-and-forth tempo.

"Such as why people act the way they do, the feelings and past events that move them?"

Humor colored his voice as he answered, "In a way. You, too?"

"You could say that." She went on with barely a

hesitation. "I called just now to check on Maisie. She
came through the flight well and is holding her own."

"That's great. Gran will be glad to hear it." He
had called his grandmother earlier, not wanting her to
get the story first from some garbled account on the
grapevine.

The hair falling over Laurel's shoulder shimmered
in the dim light with the movement of the swing and
the deep breath she took. "I hate that it was Maisie in
my car," she said in constricted tones. "She could
have died."

"Or you could have."

She made a quiet sound of assent. "I think maybe that's why I feel so...alive. Does that sound
strange?"

He turned his head to watch her, his every sense
springing into full alert at the timbre of her voice.
"Sounds natural to me. Mother Nature has a way of
making sure we appreciate what we have, of seeing
to it that, in spite of everything, living strikes us now
and then as a fair bargain."

"It's a little heartless, don't you think?"

"Why? It doesn't mean you don't care. What's the
alternative, anyway? Beating yourself up over whatever happened while moaning mea culpa? I don't see
how that's supposed to help."

"I know, but I shouldn't feel so..."

She stopped. In the silence, the moonlight shadows
shifted over the front garden and the fountain played
in musical counterpoint to the whisper of the night
breeze. The scent of honeysuckle and roses drifted to
him along with the sweet, warm, mind-blowing fragrance of clean female.

He traced a path with his gaze from the white oval

of her face down the graceful curve of her neck to her breasts. Even through the double layer of clothing she wore, he could see that the tips of her breasts were as tight with promise as new rosebuds.

"What is it you feel, Laurel?" he asked, his voice deep, steady. "What is it you want? Tell me. Or show me. I won't think any less of you for it, I promise. And I won't fail you. There is nothing you can ask that I won't give with absolute pleasure."

Laurel stared at him with incredulity for the understanding in his voice. The seduction of it brought heat and heaviness to her lower pelvis. "Shall I, really?"

"Please," he said, the single word as rough as the bark of the pine saplings he had cut around her house.

She swallowed against the tightness in her throat as she reached to touch his face, trailing her fingertips along the hard planes and over the strong angle of his jaw. Skimming down his neck, she flattened her palm over the spot where she knew his dragon tattoo lay sandwiched between his heart and his soft cotton shirt. Then, clutching the cloth for balance on the dipping, gliding swing, she rose to her knees and eased one thigh across his lap to straddle him.

"What," she asked softly as she settled into place, "do you think of this?"

"I'll tell you, when I catch my breath," he said. Kicking the swing into a higher pace, he put his hands on the curves of her hips, holding her firmly in the cradle of his thighs.

"It's all right?" Her words were a little anxious.

"No," he answered on a near groan. "I'd say it's more like fantastic."

A sound between a laugh and a sigh left her, then she slid her free hand behind his head, tangling her fingers in his hair. She found the thong that held it confined and slipped it free before dropping it to the floor. Then she wrapped the coarse black silk securely around her hand.

"I'll cut it tomorrow if you don't like it," he offered.

"I'll do it," she said, "but only a little. I love having a..."

"Handle," he supplied, his lips curving in an irrepressible smile.

"Exactly." She used the leverage of it to raise herself, fitting herself over his long length more precisely.

He drew a harsh breath. His voice not quite steady, he said, "I feel it's only fair to warn you that, as fantastic as this may be, it could lead to things that will have our letter writer firing off a fresh batch of hate mail."

"I don't care," she replied, then ruined it by immediately adding, "Do you think he's out there?"

"Or she? Not really—at least I saw nothing just now."

"We're only swinging," she said, tilting her head slightly, holding his shadowed gaze as she rose and fell with a gentle movement against him.

"Yes, and giving the word something more than even a sixties definition."

"You're sure you don't mind?"

"Only if I lose it—my mind, that is—which I may if we stop. Not to mention my temper and my grip."

"We can't have that," she said in soft sympathy, leaning to press her warm, pliant lips to his.

She tasted of sweet woman and wanton glory. Her tongue slid sinuously along the quilted inner lining of his mouth, retreating before he could capture it with delicate suction. He was forced to follow, invading for the retrieval, the seizure, the thorough ravishment. At the same time, he slid a hand between them, creating greater contact, greater friction against her moist softness. Her low moan was his reward.

She didn't have on panties—that was his next discovery as he burrowed with his fingers under the silk of her gown and caftan draped over him. His brain nearly exploded, but he didn't let that throw him off stride. Instead, he took advantage, combing her curls with gentle precision, finding and concentrating on the fragile flesh that would provide the most pleasure to them both, eventually. And all the while, he diligently pumped the swing, easing lower on his backbone as each push of his long legs sent them swooping higher.

Laurel freed her mouth as she drew a swift breath of surprise and delight. Releasing his shirt and his hair, she smoothed both hands over the surface of his chest. Then, as if in desperate need of the feel of bare skin against her, she sought the buttons of his shirt. She dragged them from their holes one by one, her fingers now nimble, now clumsy, depending on his manipulations under the hem of her gown.

"You're so good at this you must have done it before," she said somewhat breathlessly.

"Never. But I learn fast. With the right incentive."

She laughed and leaned to nibble on his taut pap.

"Witch," he muttered.

"Devil," she gasped, as he rewarded her with a deeper incursion of a single finger, a higher swing.

After a second, she asked, "Do you think maybe our letter writer was right, and we're depraved after all?"

"If this is depravity," he said, "I never want to be normal."

"Yes," she agreed and put her hands on the waist of his jeans, jerking the copper button from its hole.

He helped her, lowering the zipper, peeling down the cloth that clung to the muscles of his legs, pushing it lower to prevent the zipper's metal teeth from chafing her smooth inner thighs. She sank onto him, sighing as she took him deep. He filled her, held her while he moved with a slow, erotic twist of his hips, which tested her hot, silken inner walls and satisfied something possessive deep, deep inside him. She sighed, keeling forward to brace her forehead against his, closing her eyes. He was still while he savored sensations too rich for easy recognition.

Then they took flight. Soaring and dropping, they glided in wide, breath-catching swoops accompanied by the protesting squeak of the swing. They went up and down and up again, light as air, joined inescapably, and as delirious with it as birds that mate on the wing.

They were free, untethered by pettiness or grief, doubt or fear, or even responsibility. They were alive and glorified by it. They knew its magic worth, accepted it with full, pounding hearts and strong minds.

"Look at me," Alec said, his tone low yet harsh.

Laurel heard him, heard the deep need in his words. It was hard to do as he asked—an exposure of self far beyond mere nakedness—yet she opened her eyes by degrees. His gaze took hers, held it, invited her into the dark depths of his own. Who he was, what he was and how he felt were there for her to read, without evasion or hindrance. Finally knowing, accepting, she released all interior restriction and allowed him access to her innermost self. He took it, took her, and held her fast while the night coalesced, chiming in accord, around them.

Afterward, he rose and, still holding her to him, still joined with her, walked into the house. They fell into the bed, laughing, to begin all over. When the transcendent instant came again, they were, for that moment, almost sated, almost happy, almost safe. Almost.

Laurel came awake slowly. The light in the room was dim and watery. It was raining beyond the windows, a steady downpour illuminated by brief flickers of lightning and shaken by occasional thunder. It was a soothing yet amorously exciting sound, one connected with some dim dream of the night and early-morning hours. She let it sink into her while a slow smile curved her mouth. No, not entirely a dream.

Turning her head on the pillow, she sought the man who had slept beside her. He was watching her, his gaze proprietary yet thoughtful as he lay on his stomach with his chin propped on his stacked fists.

"Again?" he drawled, the bored disbelieving tone in direct contrast to the warmth in his eyes.

"Whatever. If you promise I don't have to move a muscle."

"Does that mean I get to have my way with you exactly as I please?"

"Exactly," she said and sighed in an attempt at demure and maidenly acquiescence.

"What happens if you move, after all?"

She jerked up a suspicious brow. "After all of what?"

"Whatever," he mocked her. "Do I get to 'move not a muscle,' then?"

"If you can," she replied, giving him a slow and completely wicked smile.

"A challenge," he said. "Your first mistake." He moved in for the attack.

Long minutes later, as she lay spread-eagled under him, held to the bed by the manacles of his hands and the hot, fierce hardness of him, he gave her a triumphant grin and declared, "I win."

"You took unfair advantage of my defenseless state," she said, trying not to laugh.

"Yes, and will again, every chance I get. But I've thought of a different prize I want."

"Anything. I am yours to command."

"I wish." The words were derisive. "What I had in mind was an abduction."

She wasn't sure he was joking. His expression had changed, the laughter dying out of his eyes. Warily, she asked, "What kind?"

"Temporary. Unfortunately. I'm thinking of taking you with me to California." He moved gently inside her, creating breathtakingly pleasurable friction.

"California—" she said, ending with a catch in her voice.

"Where you will be safe."

He wasn't joking at all, she could see, but was deadly serious. She closed her eyes tight while a shiver rippled over her. Then she opened them again. "Am I supposed to agree," she asked, "because I'm too weak to refuse? Or do you intend to force me to go with you?"

His face changed, the planes and angles hardening to tempered copper. Abruptly he released her and ripped free. Slinging himself away from her, he rolled to sit on the side of the bed with his hands gripping the mattress edge and his head bent forward. The dark, curling tail of his hair shone between his shoulder blades. Goose bumps sprang out over the surface of his skin. A shudder gripped him, then he was still.

"Alec?" She sat up, ignoring the throbbing emptiness inside her as she reached out to him.

"Don't!"

"I didn't mean it."

"Yes, you did," he said in instant repudiation.

"I only thought that you..." She trailed off, unable to put her suspicion into words.

"You thought I meant to use sex to make you agree to what I wanted. I would never do that. Never! I suppose it's my fault for playing at dominance, but I thought you knew it was a game. I thought you understood."

"I do. Now."

"No, you don't. You don't know how thin the line is between pretending and reality, how easy it would be to step across it when the stakes are high enough. No, or how deep the fear goes that I will. Before I can manage to overcome it, you have to trust me—maybe even more than I trust myself. I thought you did, but you can't. You don't, and you never will."

"That isn't true," she said against the press of unbearable regret. "Anyway, you can't expect me to read your mind. I'm only a woman."

"A woman, my woman who I need to protect. But I can't—not with things the way they are. I need to take you somewhere away from the danger, somewhere where I can watch over both you and Gregory without being torn apart between you. Let me do it. Please?''

The desperate sound of his voice made her heart ache, but the emphasis he placed on his brother's name set off a chime of alarm in her mind. Was it possible he thought Gregory was behind the things that had happened? Was that why he was so determined to keep watch over her? And was his concern, just possibly, for his brother's protection rather than for hers?

"You are free to go. I'm not holding you," she said quietly.

He turned his head slowly to stare at her. "Oh, but you are," he replied. "I just had no idea your grasp was so hard."

20

Laurel was frying bacon when the storm began to pick up again. By the time she lifted the savory strips of meat from the electric skillet and put them to drain on paper towel, the world was dim and watery-green and rain was falling in a hard, drumming downpour. She kept glancing at the clock, thinking Maisie should be arriving at any minute. She wasn't, of course, and might never work again, which was why Laurel was trying to get back into the swing of doing for herself.

Alec was in the shower—she could hear the water running. Whether he would stay to eat breakfast she didn't know; she wasn't even hungry herself. Still, she needed to pretend that something was normal just now, even if it was only a meal.

She was breaking eggs into the skillet when the phone rang.

"Mother? Can you talk?"

It was Marcia. The nervous, edgy sound of her voice, combined with her question, gave Laurel a sick feeling in the pit of her stomach. "Yes, what is it?"

"Oh, good. I was afraid he might be there—Alec, I mean."

"What difference would that make?" She couldn't keep the sharpness from her tone.

"Because it's about him, of course," Marcia said,

the words just as biting. "Or at least, it's about the two of you."

"I don't think I want to go into this again," Laurel began.

"No, and I can't say I blame you," came the surprising answer. "This is different, though. I hate being the one to tell you, but I don't want you to have to hear it from someone else. Brother Stevens preached against you at prayer meeting last night."

"He what?" She reached to turn off the heat control on the electric skillet. This was going to take a while.

"I know how you must feel, and I'm so sorry because I expect it's my fault, in a way. Because of Jimmy, you know. He's been wanting me to go see Brother Stevens for marriage counseling, but I refused. I mean, why sit through it when I know exactly what the man's going to say, right? Marriage is a holy ordinance and I must pray to God to show me the way to righteousness, then beg my husband to give me another chance. But I won't beg, Mother, and I don't want another chance! I can't stand it anymore. I can't stand it anymore!"

"Oh, honey," Laurel said in distress, "I never knew you were so unhappy." She should have known, Laurel thought; might have if she had come out of her self-imposed isolation long enough to look around her. Typical mother-guilt, but she couldn't help it.

"Never mind, I didn't mean to get off on that. About the sermon? I wasn't there, but I'm told Brother Stevens started out about Maisie, praying for her recovery, then went into this spiel about how Alec had been working on your car, getting it to running again, so he must be to blame for the accident. Only Brother Stevens hinted it wasn't an accident that the car went off the road, and that it was only by the grace of God that you weren't in it.''

It was all true, as far as it went. Just how far did it go?

"Mother? Are you still there?"

"Yes, yes, I'm here."

"Oh, I thought you might have hung up. Anyway, Brother Stevens said that you were supposed to be a sacrifice, but it didn't happen that way. He said that you're under an evil spell cast by Alec, that the two of you have been practicing Satanic rites, killing animals, and all that weird mess that was in those horrible letters. Oh, Mother, and he said that if anything happened to you, it would be the Lord's will, that you should never have become involved with a man so much younger, and with a past so steeped in iniquity. His words, not mine. He said that the wrath of God would smite you both for your sins, that whatever happened would be a judgment upon you.''

It was like hearing a death sentence. The words had been proclaimed in public and backed by the power of the church. Laurel's scalp prickled and her breath came in short gasps, yet her reaction had nothing to do with a fear of God. It came, rather, from her sudden, clear understanding of the purpose behind this latest crisis.

Whoever was behind what was happening had chosen the way it would end. She and Alec had been found guilty in the eyes of the community.

Alec was right.

He was to be the scapegoat.

Alec was slated to be the real sacrifice in the garden

they had built. Slowly but surely, the blame for what had happened in California was being attached to him here in Hillsboro. Surely and steadily, the responsibility for everything that had gone wrong at Ivywild was being shifted to his shoulders. Finally, when everything was done, he was to take the burden of guilt—and the punishment—for whatever might be going to happen to her.

"Mother?" Marcia's voice came, anxious and concerned, in her ear. "Did you understand me?"

"Yes," she answered. "Yes, I think I did."

"I don't believe all that stuff, and you're not to think I do for even a minute. I've known for a long time that you didn't kill Daddy on purpose, since I got old enough to see what you were like, think for myself. I certainly knew by the time I—well, by the time I was unfaithful to Jimmy. Oh, and then he went so crazy, cursing me, saying such mean, ugly things. He reminded me of Meemaw and how she used to be about you. I don't deserve to be treated like that, and I thought... Oh, Mom, I don't think you did, either!"

"Thank you, Marcia," Laurel said, her voice strained as her throat nearly closed with the press of tears. "That means a lot to me."

"Evan hasn't thought it was right for a long time, but he was never as close to Meemaw."

"I...appreciate you telling me." Laurel was happy, yet sad at the same time. She should have reached out to her children long ago. It had taken Alec to show her how to stand up for herself, how to let go of the past and think of the future, think of other people.

"So," Marcia went on, her voice uncertain, "what will you do?"

"I don't know. I'll have to think about it."

"You can't just stay there and let things happen to you. You've got to fight this thing, got to make a move, somehow, even if it's the wrong one."

"I'm sure you're right." But if she made the wrong move, who else would be hurt? Marcia? Evan? Alec? Where would it all end?

"We'll help you if you'll let us, Evan and I," her daughter said, the words strained, as if she wasn't sure her offer would be welcome. "You just have to tell us what to do."

Laurel filled her lungs with air, grasping for a thought that had lain dormant, like a slug in winter, in the back of her mind for days. Exhaling again in slow control, she replied, "It might be best if I did nothing, after all. Everything was quiet and simple as long as I was here by myself. Maybe it will be that way again if I just—"

"Stay there at Ivywild without anyone? Oh, Mother, no!"

It sounded so strange, that plea coming from Marcia who had never wanted her to change anything. "You can't fight gossip and innuendo, honey," Laurel said, her voice steady, "and you can't stop people from talking. I don't know who is so against my relationship with Alec that they would go to such extremes to end it, but I only have two choices the way I see it—I can stay or I can go."

"Go? You mean somewhere else? With Alec?"

"I take it you don't like that idea?" Her words were more caustic than she had intended. The last few days had worn her nerves away to the raw ends.

"It's not that, exactly."

"What?"

"Brother Stevens hinted that Alec's brother has AIDS, that the cancer he's dying from is the kind that takes over in the last stages, when the immune system can't fight any longer. You know it's contagious, especially in—in intimate situations. I don't mean to sound unkind or stupidly alarmist, but, really, Mother."

"What are you suggesting?" Laurel said in terse accents.

"A fling is one thing, particularly when you didn't know about his brother. But to even consider a long-term commitment is, well, almost suicidal!"

Laurel was quiet for a long moment while her mind raced. Then her thoughts settled, solidified. She knew exactly what she had to do. As well as how it must be done. And when. She also knew it required far more courage than she had ever needed to overcome her fear of leaving Ivywild.

"Mother?"

"Yes, love, I'm here," she said softly. "I'll always be…here."

Laurel threw the food she had been cooking into the trash after she hung up the phone, then she opened the windows to air out the smell. The sound and scent of the rain swept inside on the warm, moist air. Clamminess coated her skin, and she shivered. Sick, she felt so sick and cold and desolate. At the same time, she was gripped by a dark, icy composure that left her mental processes detached and implacably certain. It made what she was about to do seem right and inevitable, as if there could have been no other way from the very beginning.

She turned from the window above the sink as Alec

walked into the kitchen. She clenched her hands together in front of her until they felt numb.

His hair was towel-wet and pulled back from the strong, angular beauty of his face. Steady determination shone from the darkness of his eyes. He wore no shirt in the warmth of the rainy summer morning. The dragon that clung to his shoulder could be seen in its entirety, including its tail looped around his shoulder. Coiled and dangerous, it seemed to have a glint of laughter in its eyes.

She wanted to remember Alec like this. Always.

For a single instant, she allowed herself to feel the ache in her lower body that remained from the love they had shared, and to feel, as well, the deeper ache in her heart. Then she closed it off, wiping all feeling from her features like clearing marks from a chalkboard. Lifting her lashes, she looked him in the eyes.

Alec paused, his every sense tingling with the near-painful alertness of imminent danger. He searched Laurel's pale face, her stiff stance. Treading warily, he moved closer and watched as she shifted away to put the table between them.

"Since it's raining," she said in tones that scraped like a knife on a glass cutting-board, "there's nothing to be done here at Ivywild, and you probably need to spend some time with Gregory. I think it will be best if you go home for today. In fact, I think it would be even better if you don't come back."

"You're firing me again." The words were as tight and hard as the fist he held at his side.

"That's about the size of it. If you'll tell me how many hours you have this week, I'll send a check to—"

"To hell with the check! If this is because of what happened in bed just now, it's like using an Uzi to kill a mosquito."

"What happened in bed only convinced me of something I should have known all along," she said, relentlessly reasonable. "This isn't going to work. Even if it wasn't for the age thing, we're just too different."

Alec saw his own face reflected in the chrome side of the toaster on the countertop. It was the dull, copper-gray color of an old penny. "The age thing," he said, "as you call it, doesn't matter a damn bit. Nor do our differences. The truth is, I scare you."

She opened her mouth as if to deny it, then changed her mind. "Cause enough to call it off, don't you think? Love and fear don't go together."

"Who says? You scare me spitless, woman, and I still keep coming back, keep trying to reach you."

"Proving what?" She lifted her chin so quickly her hair gleamed like frost on drapings of corn silk. "Bravery or stupidity? There's nothing for you here. How much plainer can I say it? I'm not rich enough or fool enough to be useful to you beyond a few quick rolls in the hay. We had that. Now it's over."

Light-headed with the sudden ebb of blood from his head, Alec said, "Not for me."

She turned her shoulder to him, gripping the back of a chair and holding so hard her fingertips turned white around the neat, shapely nails. "Maybe you think I'm ungrateful? I'm not. I know what you've done, or tried to do. You released me from my prison and gave me back my true self so I'm a whole person again. The thing is, I have other uses for this new woman than tagging along at your heels, begging for attention.''

"Right," he replied between his teeth. "Only it's me you don't want tagging along like a kid. You don't want me dragging at your skirt tail, pitching tantrums, so you're weaning me in a single morning. Don't you think that's a little cruel?"

"It could be," she said, turning back to him, her eyes as cold as a Nordic sea, "but you tend to bite when aroused, and I have my health to consider."

"If you mean I'm a mad dog—"

"I mean your brother has AIDS, and any exchange of bodily fluids has suddenly lost its appeal."

"God, Laurel!" His chest hurt, as if from a strike straight to the heart.

"I'm sorry. You seemed determined to know the worst."

She didn't look sorry, or particularly conscious of what she had just done to him. He couldn't breathe, could hardly think for the agony in his mind. Speaking in carefully measured cadences against it, he said, "Sweet, gentle, caring, lovely lady, beautiful in spirit. That's how I thought of you from the first. I was wrong, and that's my mistake. Yours is in thinking I would ever touch you, knowing I might cause your death."

"Is that supposed to convince me? I can't say it does, but then I've already admitted to a failure of trust."

"But not to one of common decency. I am not HIV positive. Gregory is, yes, though his illness is no plague to be retreated from in horror and disgust. It's a human tragedy, just like any other disease that afflicts us poor mortals. It's betrayed promise and vanished hope that will be repeated again and again until it's stopped. Or until we are all ghosts dancing on borrowed time.''

"Poetic," she said with tight disdain, "but I was speaking of you."

"So was I. If you can turn away from me because of Gregory, then you are not the woman I thought I loved. So you can shut yourself away again, here in your old house with your old ideas, if that's what you want. But in the end, you'll be no better off than my brother. You will still be caught in a prison of your own making, enduring your own brand of living death.''

Now their pain was shared, he thought, for the look in her eyes was blank, unseeing. The knowledge gave him no satisfaction, no end to his own grief. He needed violence for that, or the comfort only she could give. Afraid he might seek either one—or both—he swung away and blundered out of the room, out of the house.

He was halfway back to Gran's house, riding hard and fast, before he realized he wore only a pair of jeans. They were soaking wet, and the rain hitting his face streamed backward into his hair. But the moisture in his eyes had nothing to do with the weather. Nothing at all.

Laurel waited until she heard the roar of the bike fade away down the drive. Then she let free the high, keening cry that strained, knife-edged, in her throat. It sliced through the humid air of the high-ceilinged room, vibrating off the dangling light fixture over the kitchen table and making the crystal in the china closet sing. Before its echoes died away, her knees gave way and she fell back against the wall behind her and slid down to crouch on the floor. Huddling there, she dissolved in acid tears.

She would have been quiet and controlled about it if there had been anyone to see or hear, but there was no one. So she assaulted the old walls with her racking sobs, letting her anguish fill all the cool, empty rooms. She cried until her eyes were swollen and her nose red and her cheeks chapped from scrubbing away the dripping tears. Cried until her throat was raw and her head throbbed and her chest felt as if a tight band were holding her ribs in place.

She struggled to her feet and made her way to the bathroom where she blew her nose, then wet a washcloth and bathed her face. In the midst of telling herself she couldn't cry any longer she saw her swollen face and was wrenched by the memory of the pain in Alec's eyes. The endless, molten grief of loss swam before her vision and washed down her face again.

It was hours later, sometime in the night, when she stopped, finally. She slept, curled into a ball in the middle of the bed that smelled of love and Alec. In the morning, she awoke headachy and sore and not quite herself. She felt as if she had become the ghost Alec had called her—a pale and wan wraith drifting from room to room, from bed to table to bathroom and back again.

She lost track of time, hardly knew whether it was day or night, light outside or dark. Sometimes she thought about calling for news of Maisie or to talk to Marcia or Evan or even Zelda. The effort seemed too much. Everything was too much.

Yet inside she was crying aloud at the loss of everything that mattered. Sticks, gone. Her pottery, gone. Maisie, gone. Alec, Alec, Alec. Gone.

Just as painful was the amputation of promise, the death of hope. Who had said that or something similar? Alec, of course, about Gregory. It was also true of her, just as he had shouted at her. And like a prisoner who had almost escaped, being closed back into her confinement was twice as hard to bear. She felt as if she were smothering, shut away from air and light by all the sneers, lies and gossip, the narrow, borrowed opinions, all the malice concocted by little, little minds.

She forgot to get her mail. Never thought of mowing. Left the fountain and reflecting pools filled with blown leaves and debris from the rainstorm. Failed to clip the deadheads from the roses so they almost stopped blooming. Let dust and pollen lie in drifts on the veranda. Allowed the milk in the refrigerator to sour and the bread to turn moldy. Nothing mattered.

She was dying slowly, being buried alive under the memories. Alec sitting bareheaded and at peace on top of the old cistern. Alec placing Sticks carefully in his grave. Alec falling, boneless, from the pine tree. Alec sitting on his bike, showing her the fountain, teaching her she could not have killed by design, teaching her to love. Loving her.

But he wasn't at Ivywild. He was gone, so he was safe.

It was some tiny consolation.

Still, she was alone. No one to see her. No one to hear her. No one to care. She felt as if she had become invisible. She must be a ghost, then, and ghosts could not love. But they could hurt. They could die from the pain of remembering love. And remembering how they had coldly, deliberately killed it.

21

Gregory was fading fast. Like a light plane running into trouble at a high altitude, his angle of descent had been a long, fairly even glide. Now, near the end, it suddenly accelerated to become a steep rush toward a crash landing.

It hurt Alec to watch him. Hearing him was even more painful, for Gregory was not going quietly. And who could blame him?

He refused to go into the hospital, preferring to wait for the end in the bed where he had slept during the long, special summers he remembered as a boy. Alec sent for Mita, who flew in at once. Calm, quiet and superefficient, his little sister relieved Grannie Callie of much of the heavy work by providing Gregory with clean sheets and special meals. Mita's medical training also proved invaluable for keeping the invalid free of pain. Still, she spent only short periods of time in the sickroom. Gregory preferred that Alec take care of his personal needs and rested better when it was he who watched over him, heard him curse, dried his tears. So Alec sat and watched and listened and tried not to think of anything else, anyone else. He would not think of Laurel, but only of the brother who was leaving him.

Gregory's sudden decline made a good excuse for

why he was no longer going to Ivywild. Gran seemed to accept it, but Gregory did not. His questions were straight and to the point. Alec gave him no more information than necessary, but still his brother read what he wanted into that small amount, and his comments on the deceit and fickleness of women were bitter.

Alec found them hard to take. He would hear no slur against Laurel, allow no ugly epithets attached to her in his presence. Gregory's partisanship sprang from concern, he knew, but Alec still got up and walked out when it started and didn't come back for hours. Gregory learned to moderate his language or forfeit his brother's company.

They held long discussions, the two of them, in the middle of the night when neither could sleep. They talked of the dysfunctional past they shared, and of the strange drug and liberation years of the sixties and seventies that had caught and held their mother in their snare like some hapless insect in amber. They came to grips with the result of those years—her aimless drifting from man to man in search of a perfect love that could not be found. They spoke, too, of Gregory's drug use with HIV-infected needles, and of the nature of AIDS that caused it to be regarded with all the superstition of some medieval scourge.

The last seemed to help Gregory. It did Alec no good whatsoever.

Yet, in those midnight hours when his defenses were down, his mind wandered to Laurel and the things she had said. Try as he might, he could not make his knowledge of her mesh with her callous dismissal of him. He could not believe she was that shallow or her affection so fleeting. Or perhaps it was only that he didn't want to believe it.

One hot night in early July, he sat reading an old Zane Grey Western he had taken from Gran's bookshelf, leaning back in the chair next to Gregory's bed. His brother's frail form hardly lifted the sheet. His painfully thin face lay in shadow, since the only light in the room was the small floor lamp beside the chair. The low hum of the window air conditioner drowned out the night noises. It made the air in the room more frigid than Alec liked, but he endured it because Gregory, fighting the fever that was slowly baking him, required the coolness.

He turned a page. The sound, faint as it was, caused a change in Gregory's breathing. His brother turned his head on his pillow and lay staring at him for long moments. His eyes burned deep in their sockets, his lips were bloodless. His hands on the sheets were austerely elegant in their skeletal shaping.

"Did you need something?" Alec asked quietly.

Gregory began to shake his head, then stopped. "Yes, maybe I do. I need to tell you I was wrong."

"About what?" Alec lowered his book to his knee, putting his hand flat on the page to hold his place.

"Your Laurel. She was stronger than I suspected."

Alertness spread through Alec, though he moved not a single muscle or tendon, allowed nothing to show on his face. "I can't say I'm surprised, but in what way?"

"She took all the stuff I told her about you and didn't let it matter. Where most would have backpedaled like crazy, she kept asking for details, for reasons. The talk didn't faze her. She made her own judgment, and it was a fair one. I was impressed. I was also jealous.''

"Jealous?"

"Nobody ever looked at me as she looked at you. Nobody ever saw me as clearly. Nobody ever carved my face from memory the way she did yours. And I knew—know—that nobody ever will.''

"It didn't mean anything." The words were flat. Alec stretched his hand out over the double pages of the open book and pressed down until the ends of his fingers had no more feeling.

"I thought that at first. I thought she was one of those women who like to try something different, sort of like taking a strange dessert from a cart because it looks exotic. I didn't want her sampling you just because she was older and might feel like a younger man made for a lighter choice—one that wouldn't count.''

"Thank you very much," Alec said with a notable lack of appreciation.

Gregory smoothed the sheet. "Yes, well, most relationships like that don't last, you know. I mean, what's there to talk about once you get out of bed? And people assume men aren't looking for anything permanent, so women feel free to indulge. But that wasn't good enough for you.''

"It didn't occur to you that I might handle the problem myself?"

Gregory gave a hoarse laugh. "Not really. You've worked so hard for so long that you haven't had much time for women of a certain sort. On top of that, you don't take things lightly—never did, never could. You're serious, you deal in forever. I knew your Laurel could hurt you without intending it, maybe without even knowing it.''

Alec leaned his dark head against the high chairback, staring at the faded wallpaper on the far side of the bed. ''I'll give you credit for that much, at least.''

''Yeah, but as I said, I was wrong. Whatever the two of you had, it was special. I could see that every time you mentioned her name, every time you thought of her. Now I think something must have come between the two of you, something to do with the stuff going on at Ivywild. I don't know what it is exactly, and I can see you're not going to tell me, but it would be a shame if it turned out to be permanent.''

''You don't know,'' Alec said, the words barely above a whisper.

Gregory was silent, his eyes fixed on Alec's face. Then a harsh laugh shook his painfully thin frame. ''You think I had something to do with all that mess? Flattering, but that much hostility takes a lot of energy, and I don't have it. Or the imagination. Besides which, it would be awfully hard for me to build up my snot-nosed kid brother as the devil incarnate.''

''I would ask you to swear it, scout's honor, but neither of us was ever a Boy Scout.'' Alec's gaze was direct.

''True, and yet what reason do I have to lie?'' Gregory watched him with the lamplight shining a sickly yellow on the perspiration that sheeted his face.

Alec wanted to believe him. It was only a small step from there to accepting what he said. He sighed and ran a tired hand over his eyes, then back through his hair. In implied apology, he said, ''It was only a vague idea. But I wish I had some clue about who went to so much trouble to make sure Laurel and I didn't stay together.''

"Find out why," Gregory said. "Then it should be easy enough to make out who."

"That's the trouble—there's no reason that makes sense. It's all just spite and venom."

"Nobody has anything to gain?"

"Not that I can tell. It isn't as if me being around was going to affect anybody's inheritance, as it did with Mrs. Chadwick. Laurel is young and healthy. She should live fifty years or more, even outlive me."

"Then somebody must have something to lose."

"Like what? We've ruled out money."

"Power. Prestige. Social position. Secrets, maybe. That's the kind of thing people kill for in this part of the country."

"I hadn't thought about it like that," Alec said in slow consideration.

"Because you've been hung up on all the weird stuff. There's nothing to that part. You know it, I know it. Whoever put it out there knows it. So that leaves the practical angle."

It was easy to see the intelligence in the ravaged face, easier still to regret, in impotent rage, its useless loss. There was also affection buried deep in the hollow eyes, along with a lingering shred of doubt. "I should have talked to you sooner," Alec said. "You seem to have noticed a lot that I missed."

"It was as much my fault as yours that you didn't," Gregory answered. "I was too wrapped up in myself to be of any use."

"While my thoughts were on other things entirely," Alec agreed with irony.

"It's about time. Lovely things they were, too. If

they hadn't been, I would have had no reason to envy you.''

"You wanted Laurel." The words were simple, without heat because there was no need for it now, nor would there ever be.

"Who wouldn't?" Gregory said and tried to smile, though it was a poor effort.

Alec put his book aside, then reached to take his brother's hand. "Then we're more alike than anyone would have thought."

The contrast between their hands, one pale and emaciated, the other strong and brown, was so marked that any comparison could only be a mockery. Still, Gregory returned the gentle pressure of Alec's clasp. "Yes," he said, his lips curving in a tremulous smile. "I think we may be."

The minutes blipped past on the digital face of the clock on the table. Alec thought Gregory slept. He was mistaken, for after a while his brother stirred. Voice hesitant, he said, "I don't think I made any difference, do you? I mean, by talking to Laurel? I didn't have anything to do with whatever is wrong between you?"

Alec met his brother's gaze, his own steadfast and as firm as his handclasp. His voice was even, though perhaps a little husky, as he said, "No, not a thing. Don't let it worry you anymore."

Gregory closed his eyes as if he could no longer hold them open. "I'm glad."

After a time, Gregory's breathing grew a little deeper, and he seemed to sleep. The lines of pain and illness eased from his face, and he looked younger than he had in some time. Later, in the hour just before dawn, he sighed in his sleep, and finally let go

of Alec's hand, which he still held. His breathing
stopped, leaving the room quiet, so quiet, and far, far
too cool.

Alec rose and stood there for long seconds, his
hand lying on his brother's face. Then he lifted it,
turned away. Crossing the room with quiet, steady
treads, he switched off the air conditioner.

People came to the funeral chapel for the service
who had not shown their faces in Grannie Callie's
house while Gregory was alive. Not that the numbers
were great, even then. Most were Gran's friends. The
older they were, the more comfortable with death—
or so it seemed to Alec—and the greater their respect
for its rituals. Whether it was a matter of obsolete
childhood training or of simple familiarity was impossible to say.

Alec sat on one side of his grandmother in the front
pew reserved for family mourners, with Mita on the
other. One or two distant cousins occupied the pew
behind them. The other attendees sat well back, leaving them in isolation.

They also talked. The sound of whispers and low
comments reverberated against the walls in waves like
ocean surf. Alec could sense the stares boring into the
back of his head, feel the concentration of fixed gazes
like a weight on his shoulders. A miasma of morbid
curiosity hung in the air. Alec refused to let it matter.
With an arm around the narrow shoulders of his
grandmother, he focused fiercely on the silver-gray
metal of Gregory's closed casket with its blanket of
red and white roses. All he wanted was for the for-
malities to begin so that they could be over at last.

It was the rising tone of the whispers, like a disturbance in a beehive, that alerted him. He glanced around, following the line of sight made by turning heads.

A soft curse feathered across his lips. He closed his eyes briefly, then opened them again. She was still there.

It was Laurel. Laurel—thin, pale, regal in black, and incredibly, gloriously beautiful with her hair coiled like a shining crown on top of her head. She paused for a moment in the doorway, taking in the situation. Her face seemed to turn whiter, if such a thing were possible. Then, looking neither right nor left, she walked down the aisle of the chapel to the front pew where he sat.

She hesitated, her gaze dark blue with trepidation. She was shaking, the fine tremors running over her in endless sequence. His heart twisted in his chest as he realized the effort it had taken for her to be here, to walk to where he sat. He reached out his hand.

She stepped toward him, stumbling a little but recovering with grace. Her fingers were icy as she grasped his and held on tight. Then she seated herself beside him and stared straight ahead.

God, but he was an idiot.

Alec could no longer remember the things she had said or how he had felt. All he could think about was taking her in his arms and warming her, wiping away the stricken look in her eyes, making her smile.

What was she doing here? Why in holy hell would she stay hidden for weeks, then show herself on the one day and in the one place that was sure to start tongues clacking even louder than before?

He could think of only one reason. It was for him, only for him. She had come because she didn't want him to face everyone virtually alone. She still had some concern for him, even if nothing else. But thinking wasn't knowing, and he didn't dare trust his instincts.

Nor did he dare look at her, smile at her, touch her beyond holding her cold hand. He should let that go, too, and would as soon as he could force himself. The last thing she needed was more talk about her.

Now, when he would have liked a longer time with Laurel beside him, the ceremony began without further delay and rushed along toward its end. The prayers, the eulogy, the words from the preacher sped by. The empty ceremony of the mourners filing past the sealed casket went forward and was quickly done. Then they were all outside, standing in that awkward moment while the casket was loaded into the hearse. His grandmother was crying, and he comforted her for a moment. Then, taking his sister's arm, he turned with Mita to introduce her to Laurel.

She wasn't there. She was gone, had slipped away as silently as she had come. The stabbing ache inside him was a warning of how much it mattered. It was also an incentive—one he vowed with grim purpose to act on as soon as he was able.

He was held up by family obligations and decorum until nightfall. Even then, he had to escape while the others were clearing the kitchen or taking their baths. Still, he felt more himself as he discarded his suit and tie for his jeans and straddled his bike. The rush of the soft night air helped clear his head, leaving him single-minded and purposeful for the first time in days.

The long hours sitting with Gregory had given him time to think and to remember. He didn't have all the answers, but he thought he had some idea of the right questions to ask. It was time to find out.

Laurel heard the bike long before it pulled up outside the front gate. She wasn't really surprised Alec had come, but hadn't expected him so soon. She had thought tomorrow afternoon, perhaps, since she knew too well the thousands of details that had to be settled after a death in the family. Then there was his sister here from the West Coast who would want to spend time with him. No, Laurel had not expected him tonight. Yet, she was ready.

With nothing else to do during the long afternoon, she had straightened the house, dusted furniture that had not seen a dust cloth in some time, vacuumed and mopped in a frenzy of effort. Then she had taken a bath and put on a jumpsuit with full, skirtlike legs in pale yellow printed with aqua and burgundy. She had even swept the veranda before flipping off the ceiling light above the front door and sitting down in the swing to enjoy the scents and sounds of the front garden. She had also figured out what she was going to say—how she was going to explain showing up for the funeral after having told Alec she never wanted to see him again.

She met him at the foot of the steps, not so far from where she had seen him the first night he'd come to Ivywild. In the light slanting from inside the house, he looked much the same as then. He was just as broad and strong, just as starkly handsome, just as intent behind his indolence. Yet, deeper lines had been carved around his eyes and mouth, and there was a grim set to his shoulders that had not been there before. He looked like a man who had discovered what he wanted and who intended to get it one way or the other. A shiver ran over her, then died away to stillness.

He wasted no time on preliminaries. Coming to a stop in front of her with his hands braced on his hip-bones, he asked, "Why?"

"Duty," she replied on a choked half laugh. She had understood him well enough to know exactly what he would say. "Why else do people go to funerals except for duty and pure dumb fellow feeling?"

"I thought there might be something else."

"Well, yes," she agreed. "Maybe because I owed you something for what you tried to do for me, even if the experiment turned out less than successful."

"Oh, I succeeded," he said. "You just undid it again with your own two hands."

The T-shirt he had on, faded black with silver lettering advertising a long-defunct rock band, covered his dragon completely. That was a pity. But the soft, dark material was so shrink-wrapped to the hard musculature of his chest that it made her fingertips tingle with the need to touch. Turning away from him a little desperately, she said, "Would you like to come inside? I could get you something to drink."

He remained where he was. "What I would like are answers."

"I don't have any for you!" she retorted, swinging back in sudden anger so that the wide legs of her jumpsuit flared around her. "I'm sorry if you thought that my showing up today meant something special. It didn't. Call it an impulse. Call it a gesture for Miss Callie. Call it pity, if you prefer, but don't make it into something it's not."

"You're the one who made something of it, Laurel," he said in compressed certainty.

"No."

"First you shut yourself up in this place like a nun, not seeing a soul. When you leave it, finally, you march into the Hillsboro funeral chapel and sit down beside me as if you belong there. You did that in spite of all the things you said. You did it regardless of what I might think. You did it even though you were literally shaking with fear of the consequences. So I ask you again—why?"

"For me," she said, lifting her chin. "I did it for me."

His thick brows meshed above his nose. "I think you'll have to explain that."

Indecision and despair chased themselves across her face, then vanished. "Maybe you did a fair job of making sure I was alive, after all, because I found out I couldn't stand being shut up again. I hated having nothing to do except mope. I despised letting all your work go to waste. And I purely hated the feeling that I had been defeated without ever beginning to fight."

Some of the tension eased from his face. As she stopped, closing her lips in a tight line, he said, "So you decided not to stand for it."

"You could put it that way. After Zelda called to tell me about Gregory, the walls began to close in on me. I felt that whoever had put me back where I was before was standing somewhere watching and laughing up their sleeve, gloating because of everything they had taken from me. It made me mad."

His smile began at one corner of his mouth and spread across it before rising to his eyes in a shimmer of pure pleasure. He shook his head. "And I thought I would have to do that."

A trace of her annoyance remained as she guessed at his meaning. "Make me mad?"

"Furious. At me. Or whoever. At the world. Whatever it took to wake you up. If that failed, I was ready for more drastic measures."

"Such as?"

He stepped toward her with sure, heated purpose. It was then that a shadow edged forward, coming toward them along the path that led from the back past the cistern and lily pool and around the curved end of the house. Alec saw it first and caught Laurel's arm to drag her behind him. There was no time for more. The shadow became a square figure in a stylish dress and resolved itself into Zelda, with a sly smile on her lips, which were painted the red-black color of rum raisins. She moved forward with less care, her high heels clacking on the sidewalk.

"Lord, but what are you two up to out here in the dark?" she asked brightly. "Something scandalous, I hope."

"Good grief, Zelda," Laurel said, easing from behind Alec. "Where did you come from?"

"My usual parking place, down the road a piece. I've gotten good at making my way in the dark, if I do say so myself. But I'm getting sick and tired of it, so I'm going to quit."

Disgust edged Laurel's tone as she spoke. "You mean you're the one who has been spying on us?"

"Among other things." Zelda chuckled as she lifted her right fist. The pistol she held in her plump grasp caught the light with a deadly gleam. "But, as I said, I'm dead tired. So now I'm going to get rid of you, darling Laurel. Oh, yes, and your boy toy. I really think poor Alec is going to be so tormented by the death of his dear brother and your fickle behavior that he shoots you. Then he'll turn the gun on himself. A terrible tragedy, but what a fitting end for such a doomed romance. I just love it. Don't you?"

22

"That's crazy." Laurel's reaction was quiet, for all its biting emphasis.

"Oh, I don't think so," Zelda answered with amusement. "I'd say it's brilliant, actually, the way I set things up. You're the one who's nuts for showing up at the funeral after you had been warned so many times. But I knew you would, I just knew it. You really can't be trusted since darling Alec came to town."

Alec stirred beside Laurel, his gaze black and dangerous as it drilled into the other woman. Terrified by what he might do, Laurel put her hand on his arm. If Zelda thought she was so brilliant, maybe she could be persuaded to expound on it. That might give them time to think, time to do something to disarm her.

"I could be trusted before?" Laurel said. "I don't understand what you mean."

Zelda's smile was pitying. "Oh, honey. Before, you were Howard's sweet little wife and he kept you in line. He watched you like a hawk—you couldn't sneeze without him knowing it. I admit you gave us a problem when you began talking about redoing the old place, starting with the garden, but he was going to nip that in the bud. Then you killed him. But it was all right, because you were such a guilt-ridden little martyr it was fairly easy to control you. All we had to do was keep you shut up with that damned vicious dog for company."

"We?"

"Oh, Howard and Mama and me to start, then just me and Mama, of course."

"Of course," Laurel echoed, trying to make sense of what she was hearing. Another question formed in her mind, but Zelda continued blithely on.

"Mama was really upset when Dan Tanning came sniffing around you, breathing heavy. I mean, the sheriff, of all people! Horrors!" Her smile turned complacent. "I fixed him, though. Jeez, what a dickhead, thinking I really wanted to climb into the back of his patrol car with him. Bumbling idiot. But he was so embarrassed at being found out, so put off by all the things Mama said, that he didn't show his face at Ivywild again. Useful thing, talk, sometimes, when it's about somebody else."

"I can see that."

The other woman's face swelled with sudden anger. "Then you had to start again about that damned garden!"

The muscle in Alec's arm turned rock hard at the change in Zelda's tone. Hastily, Laurel said, "I don't understand what's so wrong with that."

"No, you wouldn't, and that's the whole point, you stupid little fool. Why the hell else would I go to so much trouble? God, you nearly gave me a heart attack the day I came here and saw what you had done before I could get close enough to check on things. You might have already found—" She stopped abruptly, clamping her lips shut as she drew a deep, hissing breath through her nose.

"Sticks." It was Alec who spoke the dog's name, the single word shaded with contempt. "You killed Sticks because he was keeping you from prowling around."

"Good riddance, too. The beast hated me and Mama."

Alec gave a short laugh. "I always knew he was a smart dog."

"You were worse than he was." Zelda turned on Alec with her lips protruding and her solid bulk planted squarely on two well-shod feet. "You nearly caught me a couple of times, and might have if I hadn't grown up playing hide-and-seek in the woods around Ivywild. But I'm faster than I look."

"You'd have to be. And smarter," Alec added in dry wonder.

He was trying to enrage Zelda, Laurel thought, to draw her attention away from her. He was succeeding. The other woman turned her pistol on him as she narrowed her eyes.

Quickly, Laurel asked, "Just what was it I wasn't supposed to find? I think I have a right to know what's so important around here that I have to die for it."

"You have no rights," Zelda said in wrathful contradiction as she spun back toward her. "You never did. I told Mama it was a mistake to sell the house to you and Howard, told her you'd outlive him, or else your dumb kids would go poking their noses where they didn't belong one day when he wasn't around. But would she listen? Oh, no! She couldn't stand it. She had to turn over the responsibility before her nerves and heart failed her under the strain. Jesus

H. Christ! When it was all that stupid cow's fault in the first place."

"Genetics," Alec said, "are pretty reliable. A stupid cow usually gives birth to a stupid—"

"The cistern!" Laurel interrupted, overriding the deliberate insult Alec was intent on making to draw the gun's barrel back in his direction. "That's the place Howard used to go ballistic about when the kids played in the yard, or when I wanted to plant anything around it. Too dangerous, he always said. The sides might cave in. But you didn't like the idea of having the weeds and briers cut from around it, either."

"Yeah, like maybe that's where the body's buried?" Alec suggested, his tone goading.

Zelda drew a whistling breath. "How did you—" She stopped and her face twisted as she glared at him. "Smart-ass. You weren't even guessing, were you? Just popping off. Well, I'll tell you, anyway, since you're not exactly going to spread the news. That's where the body's buried, all right. The body of my dear departed daddy."

Zelda's father. Sadie Bancroft's husband who was supposed to have walked out on her decades ago, when Howard was a teenager. Even as Laurel absorbed the idea and its implications, Alec tucked his thumbs into his jeans pockets and shook his head.

"Unbelievable," he said, patronizingly sarcastic. "Who put him there? You?"

"We all did. Mama and Howard and me." A shadow moved over her face.

"But—why? What happened?" Laurel asked.

"He was going to leave her on account of her being gone down to Leesville one time too often. But no man walked out on her, she told him, and to prove it, she picked up the pistol and—'' Zelda shuddered and stopped abruptly. "It was awful."

"It must have been, because you loved him, didn't you?" Laurel kept the words quiet, tentative.

Zelda's mouth twisted and her eyes glittered with unshed tears. "I was his girl, his little princess. He took me everywhere with him—fishing, hunting, everywhere. He taught me to shoot a gun, drive a boat, fix a car. When I was up for basketball queen, he spent a hundred dollars buying votes at a penny apiece." Her voice dropped to a whisper. "He was my daddy."

"You saw your mother shoot him?" Alec asked, tilting his head.

"I saw her point the pistol at his back, yell at him, but he just kept walking. I grabbed her, wrestled her for the pistol. The thing went off and Daddy fell. Mama said—she said she wasn't really going to shoot. She said she didn't pull the trigger, didn't mean to, wouldn't have done anything except scare him if I hadn't..."

"She blamed you." Laurel spoke the words with stunned compassion.

"I did it. I think I did, at least I sort of remember.... But I didn't mean it. Never, ever. I didn't want my daddy to die." The words were almost a plea for belief.

"It was an accident. Surely the police would have understood. There was no need to put him—"

"No!" Panic flared in Zelda's pale eyes. "Mama said they wouldn't believe us. Anyway, everyone would know. They would say mean and spiteful things behind our backs."

"Everything would have come out, wouldn't it?"

Laurel said. "How your mother had been picking up soldiers and taking money for sex. How their marriage had been on the rocks for years. Maybe how she poured hot grease in his ear once?"

"Shut up! Shut up!" Zelda screamed as she took a quick step toward Laurel.

Alec tried to block her line of sight, but Laurel moved around him. "People know, anyway," she said. "The old women always know. Maisie told me something about it, and she wanted me to go and ask Grannie Callie about the rest, only I misunderstood her."

Zelda gave an ugly laugh. "Oh, I know people have always whispered behind our backs. They've always talked about how I slept with half the football team before I was sixteen, and the rest of them after I got married. Not half of it was true. But Maisie was the worst to talk. She never liked me or my family, always took your side against us. I'm glad—glad that old bitch was in your car when it went off the road. Glad it happened that way even if you were the one meant to hit the ditch."

"Maisie didn't mean anything. The talk had nothing to do with liking or disliking you personally," Laurel said. "People are just interested in other people, what happens to them and why. I doubt she had any idea what you did to your dad."

"I didn't do anything. I loved him, I really did, but I didn't want to go to jail. Mama said I would, and so would she because I was a minor. The only thing to do was drag him out and—" Zelda trailed off, her eyes wide with remembered horror, before she drew breath and began again. "Oh, God, his legs and arms flopped every which way. And he hit his head when he fell in—I heard it. I used to dream that he wasn't dead, that he was lying there bleeding, or else he was trying to claw his way out like some horror monster.''

''What you're planning for us won't be any better,'' Alec warned. ''It will come back to you, even if you get away with it. Besides, it's not likely to help matters if people like Grannie Callie begin to put two and two together.'' He took a long step forward. ''Why don't you give me the weapon?''

He had allowed Laurel to put distance between them, and now he was adding even more. Maybe he thought he could talk Zelda into abandoning her plan and maybe not; Laurel didn't know. But if it didn't work, then he meant to draw Zelda's fire while making a play to overcome her.

Laurel wanted to live; she knew that now. She longed to break free of the past holding her to Ivywild and explore the wide, wide world and whatever life had to offer. But not without Alec. Never without Alec.

She had to do something, and do it now, or he was going to die. She couldn't allow that, for if she couldn't live, then she wanted desperately for him to live for her.

She moved forward in slow determination. If she drew Zelda's fire herself, then Alec would have his chance, a split second of time to launch whatever he had in mind.

Her voice even, strong yet pensive, she used it as a weapon. ''You don't really remember killing your dad, do you, Zelda? Not like I remember killing Howard. That was an accident, too. It wouldn't have happened if he hadn't been so panicked by the thought that I was on my way to buy roses to plant around the cistern, hadn't been so determined to stop me. But I'm still haunted by the sound of my car hitting him, still feel as if it was my flesh and bones that struck him instead of chrome and steel. His death will always lie on my conscience, even if it's no longer on my heart. Just like ours will be on yours.''

"This is different," Zelda said, attempting a sneer. "I'm different now."

"Are you? But you're haunted by the death of your dad, aren't you? And not just because you may have fired the shot that killed him. Why? Did you have the chance to help him that night? Could it be you might have done something that would have let him live?"

The last words had come to her on the spur of the moment as she saw Alec's black gaze fixed on her. She prayed that he would understand them.

Zelda gave a bark of near-hysterical laughter. "Don't be silly! He was dead when he went in the cistern. Dead, you hear me? And don't think I'm moron enough to fall for what you're both doing. God, what a pair of idiots—so determined to take the bullet for each other." Her voice turned ugly. "I've got enough for both of you, believe me."

"What you don't have," Alec said, speaking to Zelda although his eyes held Laurel's in heated captivity, "is the grace to understand the impulse to save the person you love. You have no heart or vision, lack the intelligence that makes these things of value. No one has ever said to you that you are his lodestar and his hearth, the air he breathes and the spirit that is living's only joy. No one has ever said that the long years have no meaning without you, that time will cease to exist unless you are there. No one has ever told you he loves you more than the least small breath of transient life, and will only love you more in death.''

"Are you through?" Zelda asked with exaggerated contempt.

He was. Laurel could see it in his eyes. Heart pounding, breath coming in gasps, tears rising to blur her vision, she searched for some way to stop what was coming, to stop him. There was nothing. Nothing. And so only one thing was left.

"I love you," she whispered. "I love you, too."

He heard, for the sweet joy of it blazed in his eyes. But even then he was turning, whirling in hard, controlled strength. Muscles contracting, gliding in the swift attack taught by an old Chinese gardener, too fast to follow, too powerful to stop. The bend at the waist, the lashing kick at full extension.

A heartbeat too late.

The pistol Zelda held blasted, spurting a streak of flame in the gathering night. In the same fraction of a second, Alec's hard, booted foot caught her midsection, driving her backward, jarring the weapon free. Its dark metal shone as it arched high, then clattered to the walk. Zelda screamed as she plunged into the tangled thorns of an old brier rose. The piercing sound almost covered the flat thud of a bullet striking flesh.

A cry tore from Laurel's throat. She lunged to catch Alec as he staggered, then collapsed. Her knees buckled under his weight. She let herself drop to the ground as she used her thighs to cushion his fall.

He clutched his upper chest, his hand gleaming red in the dim light. "The weapon," he said in hoarse warning. "Get the weapon."

Laurel lowered him to the walk. Glancing around

in a wild search, she spotted the pistol. She lunged for it as Zelda began to kick and moan, struggling to release herself from the grasp of the old rose.

As Laurel came up with the pistol in her hand, the other woman gave a strangled moan that became a harsh sob. She fell back, scratched and bloodied, amid the thorns.

Laurel scarcely noticed. Scrambling back to Alec, she set the weapon beside him for safety while she took his hand away from the wound. It was a welter of wet, red-black cloth and blood-splattered silver lettering, though his face was calm as he gazed up at her. His eyes were clear. Deep in their darkness shone the bright joy of one who has sought and found his personal grail and can now let go of striving, forget lesser quests.

For his dragon, when she pulled the soft T-shirt away, had a great, gaping hole in its side. It would need, desperately, whatever arts and magic of regeneration it could bring to save itself and the man who wore it.

Alec moistened his lips. "I didn't...fail?"

Tears sprang, hot and fresh, to rim Laurel's lower lashes. "No. Never."

"Good." His mouth twisted in brief satisfaction.

A single tear slid down her cheek to fall like a droplet of silver onto his chest. He did not see it. His eyes were closed, folded in their sockets, and, in the light of the moon just rising, his lips no longer smiled.

The nurse was young and attractive, with a cynical tilt to her mouth and an expansive notion of her power. As she stepped into the waiting room, she scanned those seated there, saying with crisp impatience, "Alec Stanton family?"

Miss Callie rose, shoving herself up unsteadily with her hands on the chair arms. "I'm his grandmother."

"You can go in now."

"Is he...?" The elderly voice faltered.

"The acting physician will explain when he has time."

As Mita rose to put her arm around her grandmother, Laurel moved quickly from the window where she had been standing to support her on the other side. Together, the three of them turned toward the door.

The nurse stepped in front of Laurel. "Are you related?"

"No." It was the most Laurel could force through her set teeth.

"Then you will have to remain here."

Grannie Callie paused. Laurel did the same while she took a deep breath, then let it out slowly. "I don't believe so."

"I must insist," the woman in uniform said.

Laurel had been harassed and threatened and mocked in the past weeks. She had seen her pet and her property destroyed. Tonight she had faced down a killer and watched the man she loved be shot. She was in no mood for more impediments. Face hot but eyes cold, she replied, "Insist and be damned."

Marcia, gaining her feet, jerked her head at her brother in the chair beside her. The two of them sprang toward the nurse, each of them putting a detaining hand on one of her arms. "Alec Stanton saved my mother's life this evening," Marcia said in a hurried undertone, "and she tried her best to save his. I

wouldn't get in the way if I were you. It really might
not be safe.''

Laurel gave her daughter a brief, grateful smile.
Marcia nodded in return. Then Laurel put a gentle
arm around Miss Callie's waist and nodded to Mita.
They stepped past the nurse and into the hallway.

He lay on the bed looking stalwart and mahogany-
dark against the white sheets, in spite of the paleness
of his face. He was alive—the equipment that surrounded him, beeping and humming, said so. But his
eyes were sealed shut and his breathing so shallow
that it scarcely stirred the hospital gown that covered
him. Beneath it, the bandage on his shoulder was
bulky and laced with tubes that ran down the strongly
turned perfection of his arm and disappeared over the
bed's far edge.

Miss Callie sighed, a tremulous sound. ''Thank
God, oh, thank God. I could not have borne it if…if
it had turned out like Gregory.''

''No,'' Laurel said in soft agreement. Her gaze met
Mita's dark eyes, so like Alec's, before she turned
back toward the bed.

A lengthy silence fell as they watched him. Alec
slept on, oblivious under whatever anesthetic they had
given him while they repaired his chest.

After a time, Miss Callie stepped closer and
touched his hand in a gentle, soothing gesture. Shoulders drooping with tiredness, she turned toward the
door. As Laurel hesitated she lifted a hand. ''No, no,
I just need to sit down a moment. Mita can come with
me. You stay, so someone will be here in case—that
is, when he wakes up.''

The door closed soundlessly behind the two
women. Laurel turned back at once to the bed. This

time she stepped right up to it and took Alec's hand in hers, wrapping her cool fingers around their lax strength. It was there, that strength, whether he was conscious or not. In some curious fashion, he still dominated the room, making it appear small and barely able to hold him.

How long she stood there, she had no idea. Sounds penetrated from the outside—the voices of visitors leaving, the rattle of a wheelchair, announcements on the public-address system. Once she heard an ambulance. Later on, she recognized the noise and activity of the nurses changing shifts. She didn't move, but stood rubbing her thumb gently over the bones and veins of Alec's hand.

One moment he was comatose. The next he was watching her with cogent thought in the rich chocolate darkness of his eyes and a frown between his brows.

She'd had a great deal of time to consider what she would do if and when this moment came. Smiling slightly, she said, "Hello. Will you marry me?"

His gaze was abruptly opaque. He directed a slight nod at his shoulder as he said in husky consideration, "That bad, is it?"

She should have known it wouldn't be so easy. Stifling a sigh, she said, "There are other reasons for marriage besides deathbed grandstanding—which you don't need. Or pity."

A dark brow lifted. "Gratitude, then."

"As Marcia so nicely put it just a little while ago, if you saved my life, I also saved yours. Where does the gratitude come in?"

"Your children are here?" The words were steady, if not particularly loud.

She nodded. "Supporting their mother as children should."

"And they don't...mind?"

"If they do, they aren't saying so since they know it will do no good." As his gaze held hers, unwavering, she gave a small laugh. "Actually, I don't think they dare. It seems we have become a formidable pair in the eyes of Hillsboro. Our reputations will no doubt grow with the telling, come daylight."

Brief amusement came and went across his face, which was so pale under its layer of bronze. "It was you."

"Not alone. Which is the way I want it from now on."

"You don't need me."

"You're mistaken." She said the words with deliberate emphasis. Then she went on quickly, in part to save him from the effort, but also because she was afraid she would lose her courage otherwise. "You asked me to marry you, and I refused you. I'm sorry if I hurt you, but there were reasons that I thought were important at the time. Now they are gone. But if your pride demands that I beg, well, then, where would you like me to start?"

"It doesn't!" His revulsion at the idea showed in the curl of his upper lip.

"Then you've changed your mind."

"No, but..."

"But I seem suddenly older and more decrepit than you thought, and you've decided you would rather find some young thing to share your swing?"

"God, no! You don't fight fair."

Brightly, she said, "Who said this was a fair fight? But what was it that got to you? The swing, I think?

I could as easily have mentioned sharing your shower. Or your moonlit garden."

"Laurel."

The sound of her name on his lips, the look in his eyes, were enough to stop her cold. And freeze-dry her heart. Against the pain, she cried, "What more do you want? I told you I love you."

"Under duress. Like a final meal for the condemned, or a last request." He waited.

"Oh, is that what you think?" she asked, breathing again in a sudden rush. Then she frowned. "Of course, I could take it that all the stuff you said was last-chance business, too."

A slow smile curved his mouth and he turned his head from side to side. "You aren't going to give me the satisfaction of hearing you say it by yourself, are you?"

"Again? Well, yes, in between."

He sighed. "Between what?"

"Swinging and showering, maybe. But I'm really not being fair. Suppose I told you that marriage to me means becoming a grandfather overnight?"

"What? Oh, Marcia, I guess. Bribes will get you nowhere."

Her voice a little strained, she asked, "You really don't mind?"

"I like babies, but I've never been a grandfather, never really had one for a role model. You'll have to show me how to go about it."

"I've never been a grandmother, either," she informed him in pretended annoyance.

"Then we'll learn together. Maybe bribes will work, after all."

"I've got more," she said, her eyes bright with something besides laughter.

"Do you, now?" He paused. "Well, are you going to tell me or not?"

She swallowed and nodded. "I need a gardener. It will be a long time before Maisie comes back to work, if ever, so I'll be too busy in the house to manage the outside."

"For how long?"

"The position is open-ended. I also need a model for my sculpting, since I'll be going back to it as soon as I can have another shed built. Which reminds me…"

"You need a carpenter."

"Are you any good at that?" Her gaze was hopeful, but not quite focused.

"I," he replied, "am a master with a hammer. And a few other things."

"Good. Because I don't really like staying by myself at night, so I'll need a night watchman. Yes, and as long as you're there, you can make yourself useful warming my cold feet…and other things."

"You're going to drive me crazy," he said with conviction.

She turned her head a little, not quite certain he was joking. "Why would you say that?"

"Because there are so many things I'd like to do to you right now, and I can't move."

"Oh." Her smile was only a little fractured by tears. "That was something else. I don't think I can live without finding out exactly what your poor dragon is going to look like when he comes out from under the cover."

"Come here," he said, his eyes sparkling like jet, "and maybe I'll give you an advance peek."

She looked over her shoulder. "I don't know. There was a nurse earlier who didn't even want me coming in here, much less climbing into bed with you."

His grasp on her hand tightened. "I'll take care of her. Come here."

"Well, but you haven't said you'll marry me."

"And I'm not saying it—not until I hear a lot more about what's in store for me."

She put one knee on the bed, then took it down. "You haven't even said you'll be my gardener."

"Didn't I? We can discuss that, too. Along with job incentives. And bonuses. Also the hours that I can give you after I find myself a position as an engineer somewhere within reasonable driving distance."

"You're a hard man, Alec Stanton," she said, sighing in defeat as she climbed up beside him.

He opened his good arm and used it to lock her against his side as she eased down to face him. "Indeed, I am," he murmured against her cheek. "What are you going to do about it?"

"Not much just now, but I suppose we can talk about that, too."

"Talking," he countered, "is what got me into this fix in the first place."

"I thought it was gardening," she said, closing her eyes as she absorbed the hard, healthy strength and sure power of him.

"It's all the same," he replied with some distraction as he tried to figure out how to touch her without hurting himself. "Both are never-ending affairs."

"Like loving," she suggested, solving his problem by moving closer.

He sighed in satisfaction and lightly brushed her lips. As he moved in for a deeper kiss, he whispered, "Exactly like loving."

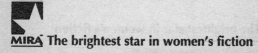

New York Times bestselling author

LINDA HOWARD

Was this the man she'd married…or a total stranger?

When Jay Granger is escorted by the FBI to the bedside
of her injured ex-husband, she is unprepared for her
own reaction—something is different about him.
Although he doesn't remember anything, his effect on
her is intense…sensual…uncontrollable. And each day
as he grows stronger, he gains back more of his life.
Including Jay.

Linda Howard delivers a suspenseful and emotional
story of love and deception…

WHITE LIES

Available in May 1997 at your favorite retail outlet.

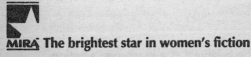

MIRA The brightest star in women's fiction

RISING TIDES

the compelling sequel to *Iron Lace*

Aurore Gerritsen, matriarch of one of
Louisiana's most prominent families, has died.
And the future of her family is at stake.

Nine people—some family, others strangers, all
heirs to Aurore's fortune—have gathered for
four days for the reading of her will. As a lifetime
of family secrets are revealed one by one, those
present learn things that will irrevocably drive
some of them apart and bring others together.

bestselling author

EMILIE RICHARDS

Available in May 1997 at your favorite retail outlet.

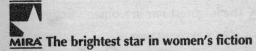